Sister Lumberjack

Sister Lumberjack

Candace Simar

North Star Press
www.northstarpress.com
Since 1969

First Edition

North Star Press of St. Cloud Inc.
www.NorthStarPress.com

Paperback ISBN: 978-1-68201-150-8
Ebook ISBN: 978-1-68201-151-5

simar@tds.net

www.CandaceSimar.com

To the Benedictine Sisters,
thank you for changing the world.

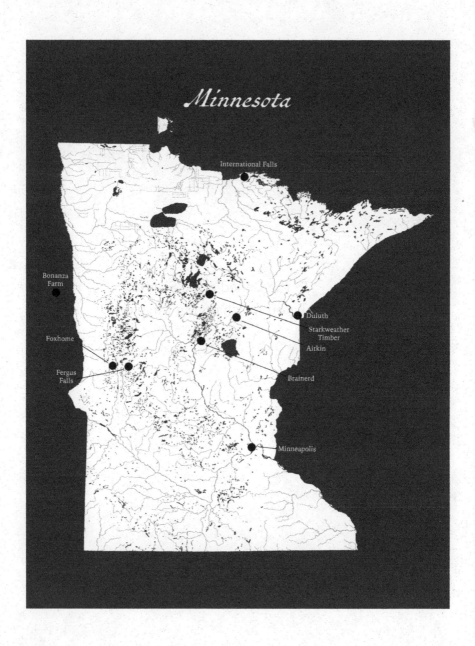

Minnesota

International Falls

Bonanza
Farm

Duluth

Starkweather
Timber

Foxhome

Aitkin

Fergus
Falls

Brainerd

Minneapolis

1893

Chapter 1
Solveig

Solveig Rognaldson reached for Rasmuss's red-flannel shirt hanging on a peg by the cook stove, and buried her face in its warm folds. The tattered old thing still carried his scent. She slipped her arms into the sleeves.

"Damn you, Rasmuss," she whispered as she stepped outside the cabin for evening chores. "How could you leave me?"

The prairie stretched flat and treeless, except for the basswood growing beside the house. In the summer months, she often sat under its spreading boughs, looking up through its foliage. Today it stood naked against the tinted sky. The leaves around the trunk lay cracked and brittle, like the ending of her life.

The wind, her constant friend, slapped her face and whirled apron strings around her body. The sun dipped like a bloody egg in a sea of blazing pinks and orange, a backdrop behind the outbuildings. Ragged fields stood empty. The horses raised their heads and whinnied, hoping for the lump of sugar she sometimes carried in her apron pocket.

She passed the wheelbarrow lying upside down half-way between the barn and manure pile. Her son, Halvor, so addled by his new wife, would forget his head if it were not attached.

Solveig had left Norway to find her way, and landed near Foxhome, Minnesota. She, so tall and gawky, with teeth too big for her mouth, never expected to find someone to love her. Together she and Rasmuss made a life. They survived the Massacre, struggled for every inch of ground, out-lived the grasshoppers and somehow made it through the dry years.

His death last winter ruined everything.

They counted on Rasmuss's wages at the logging camp to pay the mortgage. Solveig scrimped every penny. The banker apologized, but the note must be paid in the spring or everything they had worked for would be gone.

A wedge of geese flapped giant wings in a ragged vee, the birds taking the lead by turns. A goose veered back from the point in deference to another who flew forward to take over. Their mournful calls mirrored her loneliness.

They would squeak by if Halvor worked at the logging camp this winter, and if he earned a little more than last year, and if the team hired out at the same rate or higher than last year. Nip and tuck. A lot of maybes.

Their future balanced on the blade of a knife.

Heartache brought a stumble to her steps as she walked across the yard. This farm was her life. The fields around the out-buildings, the rich soil, and the land as flat as a dinner plate. Hardly a stone to pick, Rasmuss had always bragged. No stumps to grub on the Breckenridge Flats.

Her life ended with Rasmuss's death, or at least began its ending.

A broody hen clucked in the weeds. Solveig groped under the hen, and retrieved a brown egg from beneath the bundle of feathers. It pecked her hand in return.

"Shame on you." Solveig shooed it back toward the coop, and headed toward the barn, still carrying the egg. The wind pushed behind her, at least out of her face.

Solveig was about to cross the threshold into the barn, when she heard muffled voices. Halvor and Britta were arguing. Solveig had not known the newlyweds to disagree.

Britta grew up as the pampered, youngest daughter of a Fergus Falls minister. She hid her face when Tildie birthed her calf, wept when Halvor shot a raccoon eating the baby chicks, and turned her nose at the wild goose Halvor brought home for Sunday dinner. Nothing suited her.

Solveig thought to make a noise, clear her throat, or call out to Queenie, the cat. Anything to let them know of her presence. She knew better than eavesdrop, but hesitated a moment too long. Solveig stood frozen at the door, out of sight behind the calf pen, still clutching the egg in her hand.

"We have to leave tomorrow," Britta said. "Papa said they'll only hold the job at the hardware store until then."

Solveig drew in a quick breath. She could not be hearing correctly. A long silence, and the sounds of kissing. A murmur of voices that Solveig could not understand.

"Ma expects me to go to the logging camp on Friday," Halvor said.

"I'd die in this lonesome place without you." More kissing. "Don't go."

Solveig waited for Halvor to set his wife straight. Someday he would inherit the farm. It was his duty to keep it afloat. He had promised Rasmuss on his death bed.

"I must," Halvor said. "There'll be hell to pay if I don't."

"You are a married man now. It is time to get out from under her rule."

He had made a mistake in marrying Britta. A farmer and a town girl were as mismatched as hitching a plow horse with a high stepper.

Britta yammered about the Singing Society, whist club, and square dancing. She went on about their life in the parsonage with her parents, and how Solveig could move into Widow Gunderson's boarding house once the bank foreclosed.

The hackles rose on Solveig's back. She was not ready for a rocking chair yet.

"It's better in town," Britta said. "Not like this stodgy, old place." More sounds of kissing. "I hate this farm—stinky and dirty. Look at my hands from working outside. My complexion is ruined."

"All right, all right," Halvor said with a reluctant chuckle. "I'll tell her tonight. Maybe we can salvage something before the bank forecloses." Squeals from Britta and more kissing. "Ma won't like me taking the lead on this. She's always worn the pants in the family."

Solveig gasped. She pressed the egg so hard that her fingers broke through the shell. This could not be happening. She wiped the sticky yolk on her apron and tossed the broken shell to Queenie, who had left her kittens to rub around her skirts. The cat lapped drips of egg from the tops of her worn shoes.

A blaze of white-hot anger seared through Solveig's brain. Foolish child. Didn't Halvor realize that all their years of work and struggle had been so that he could inherit the farm someday? They had a wooden house with glass windowpanes and a team of good horses. Their fields were under cultivation. All this was to be handed to him on a platter. Ungrateful pup.

"Your father left it to you," Britta said. "She's not even your real mother."

She was Halvor's mother, whether she had given birth to him. Damn her.

Solveig scooped Queenie in one hand, and stumbled toward the garden patch farthest from their voices. Her heart pounded and her breath came in ragged gulps. Anger brought white blotches of rage before her eyes. Solveig took breaths to calm herself. The cat clawed to get away.

Once she reached the garden, Solveig faced into the wind. "This can't be happening," she screamed. "I hate her!" Her constant companion, the prairie wind, caught her words and carried them away. The cat scratched her hand. "Go then. You are no better than they are." Solveig dropped to her knees in the dirt. The cat streaked back to her kittens.

Something happened when a woman lost her man. A loss of place in the family and community. A loss of respect. The farm belonged to her. Halvor had no business to make decisions without her consent.

Halvor had been a skinny, snot-nosed boy when they found him, just learning to toddle around the room. His mother had died in childbed along with a new baby. His frantic father, half-starved and exhausted with grief, begged her and Rasmuss to take Halvor. The man had a house full of children, a farm to manage during the Sioux Massacre, and feared Halvor would not survive without a mother.

Her young husband, so tenderhearted, gave in to her pleading to take the boy. It didn't mean that she had worn the pants in the family. It did not mean that she had demanded her way.

The garden stood empty except for a stray rutabaga, a single row of cabbages, and a patch of kale. She slapped at a sticky fly, then dropped to her knees in the dirt. She probed the damp soil around a patch of knapweed, felt the grit of soil pushing under her nails, and smelled the loamy earth. She hooked the tap root, and yanked it out of the ground.

If only there had been children of their own. A daughter to work beside her in the kitchen. A son to take over the farm and appreciate what they had built over a lifetime of hard work. Children of her blood might love her more.

Solveig crawled to the rutabaga, and jerked it from the ground. The young couple walked together toward the house on the other side of the cowyard. Halvor carried the milk bucket, and glanced over his shoulder toward Solveig in the garden. It would have been sensible for Britta to gather the eggs while she was in the barn, but that girl was useless in anything practical. She knew how to tally a whist score, but had no sense when it came to everyday work.

Solveig pushed to her feet and shook dirt from her apron, then gathered a cabbage for tomorrow's stew. Clouds clustered in the northwest. Weather moving in.

She scooped up the pile of weeds to throw to the hogs, and walked quickly toward the barn, avoiding Halvor as long as possible. Solveig grasped the rough frame of the barn door. The homey odors of cow manure and dried hay. She patted the dried mud around the wood, mud that Rasmuss had placed with his own hands. His handprint showed. She placed her hand inside the print, feeling his presence.

She always felt closer to Rasmuss in the barn, knowing all the hours he had spent there with the cattle and horses, shelling corn, or winnowing grain. This year the corn filled the crib. Rasmuss would have been pleased with their harvest, even though it was far from a bumper crop.

Solveig looked toward the house. She knew her son. Halvor would not back down. He wanted to leave? Then he would leave. But he would not get a penny from her.

He would not take the horse and wagon. By God, she would leave him out in the cold. She'd leave the place to the church rather than to a son who deserted his widowed mother.

An orange kit mewed and clawed for his mama's teat. Queenie purred and stretched even though her kittens were past weaning age. "We're in the same place," Solveig whispered to the cat. "Young ones ready to head out on their own."

Solveig felt for eggs in the nesting boxes along the wall, not bothering to light the lamp. A rat leapt from a nest, and the cat tore away from her kittens in pursuit, setting up a chorus of anxious mewing.

Solveig wiped an egg with the corner of her apron. It was twice the size of the others. A double-yolker. "That's how to do it," she cooed. Gumbri could be depended on to carry her weight.

As all adults must learn to do.

It belonged to her. All of it. This land, the barn, the house, the tilled fields, the hayfield, the rock pile, the team, the animals, and the farming implements they had managed to accumulate. And the mortgage. She was the landowner. It was up to her.

Solveig squared her shoulders and set her jaw. She would do it herself. Logging camps needed cooks. They needed kitchen helpers. A cook earned as much as a foreman, according to the handbills. She was pushing sixty, but she had her health. She knew how to run a kitchen. She was a good cook. She could do it if she tried. She had no choice.

Halvor and Britta packed their trunk when Solveig entered the house. She hung Rasmuss's shirt on the peg and ground beans for a pot of coffee. The dampness of evening had settled, and a fire in the stove took the chill out of the house. Britta went outside.

"Ma." Halvor's voice squeaked. "We need to talk."

Solveig clamped her lips. She would not make it easy for him to abandon his promises to his dying father.

"I found a job at the hardware store," he said. "We'll live in the parsonage with Britta's folks." He did not look her in the eye. He made lengthy explanation for their leaving.

"You've made up your mind," Solveig said. "You're making a mistake."

Working for someone else never paid off in the end. They had taught him that much. He would end up with nothing. The coffee was slow to boil. She stoked the stove and slammed the lid, then pulled a clean cup and saucer from the shelf.

Britta's fault. A pretty girl always led a man around by the nose.

"Move to town with us," he said. "Widow Gunderson has a rooming house."

"Over my dead body," Solveig said. His stab of betrayal stoked a fire in her chest hotter than the stove. She splashed water on spoons in the dishpan. Anything to keep her hands busy. "They'll carry me out feet first."

"Face reality." He looked toward the door as if hoping Britta would come and stand with him. "You can't run the farm alone."

"I'll manage." They had given him everything, sacrificed, and slaved for him. Thank God, Rasmuss was not alive to witness his actions.

"You will lose it in the spring anyway. Be sensible," Halvor said.

"It's my business, not yours."

"We're leaving tomorrow."

"Be on your way, then."

"Ma..."

"You'll not take my team," she said. "Or anything from this farm." They could walk the twelve miles to Fergus Falls, for all she cared.

"You know we can't pay the note, even if I slave at the logging camp all winter. Maybe get killed doing it."

His jaw set as rigid as her own. He did not ask her opinion. Her name was on the deed, not his.

"Do as you will," Solveig said in a strangled whisper. "But if you go, don't come back. Leave now, and that is the end of it. You'll be cut off." The anger drained her strength.

She walked over and slipped into Rasmuss's old shirt. "Chilly tonight." She folded Rasmuss's flannel arms across her chest. She sat in her favorite chair and picked up her knitting, stabbing the needles into the yarn with each stitch. The smell of boiling coffee filled the room. She was not hungry. She would not cook supper. She was done being their servant.

Britta crept back inside, looking from one to the other like a scared rabbit. Halvor invited his wife to walk with him over to the neighbors. Likely they would ride into Fergus Falls with them. They had done it before.

They did not say goodbye. Neither did Solveig.

Solveig sat alone, her blood churning in her ears. Another death. Another grief too hard to bear. To be left high and dry with the mortgage coming due. She had failed as a mother. She had failed to teach him fidelity. One wiggle of his pretty wife's finger, and all sense left him.

Solveig could not stand the empty house any longer. She jerked on her shawl and stomped outside. The wind met her. She hurried to the barn as it whirled her skirts and snatched her breath. The animals lowed in their pens. The hens roosted on top of the feed trough. She stooped to right an overturned bucket.

The bitch. Solveig grabbed a pitchfork and tossed straw into the calf pen.

Halvor changed when he met Britta. The hussy. Solveig pushed her way out of the barn and barred the door against wolves. Then she shrieked into the face of the wind.

"I hate her."

Her friend carried her words away. Though diminished, her anger remained. Her life was ruined. Gunnar Jacobson would come in two days. He and Halvor always traveled together to the logging camps. Gunnar would be surprised, but she knew that he would take her with him if she asked. She was his godmother, after all, and his mother had been her dearest friend. Solveig would be packed and ready to leave when he arrived. She would rent out the team to a logging camp by herself. She would find kitchen work. She would save every penny. She did not need Halvor or his Jezebel wife. To hell with them.

Tomorrow she would sell the shoats, cow and calf, haystack and hens to Helmer Olson, who had offered before to buy them. She would bake flatbread for the journey. And cookies. She would hard-boil all the eggs. She would make do somehow.

Rasmuss would not like her working out, but he wasn't there to complain. Halvor might raise a fuss.

She would not tell him. She would leave a note on the kitchen table, if by some chance he returned to the farmhouse. She would do what she wanted. This was America, after all. She was white, free, and over twenty-one.

She started up the ladder to the loft where she had slept since Halvor's marriage. Then she changed her mind, and turned to the double bed that she and Rasmuss had shared for so many years. She threw Britta's quilt on the kitchen floor. She climbed into her own bed. It felt good to be back where she belonged, even if her heart ached.

She pretended to sleep when Halvor and Britta came home. They lit the lamp and whispered together when they saw their bed occupied. Then they climbed the ladder to the loft.

Solveig's mind raced. She would bring along her best hens to the logging camp. Maybe foolish, and extra fuss, but a few eggs meant better baking and a start for a new flock in the spring. There was always a way to make things work out. It just took patience and perseverance.

Finally, when she heard Halvor's snores from the loft, Solveig lit the lamp and packed her sturdy travel trunk once used on her trip across the ocean. Her name blazoned across the side: *Solveig Olasdatter*. How young she had been, naïve and optimistic about the future.

Everyone talked of opportunity in America—even for plain girls if they were unafraid of hard work. Solveig indentured herself to an Episcopal priest in return for passage and five years of labor. At Bishop Whipple's she had met Evan Jacobson. He knew Rasmuss from his stagecoach route. The years fell into place as if by plan. Everything worked out for the best.

As it would now.

Solveig packed aprons and everyday dresses in the bottom of her trunk along with handkerchiefs, petticoats, and nightgowns. She packed mittens and rubber overshoes, her warmest shawls, sweaters and underwear. She tucked bars of homemade soap into the toes of her everyday shoes. She added socks, sheets, and blankets. She fetched a butcher knife from the kitchen and a set of candles. She took the box of matches. Then she packed her chamber pot wrapped in a braided rug. A woman her age needed her comforts. When she finished, she returned to bed.

As she drifted off to sleep, another worry intruded into her mind. Even if she paid the note in the spring, she could not put in a crop. She had no money for a hired man. Maybe someone would work in exchange for shares of the harvest.

There must be a man looking for work. She would hire neither a slacker nor a Catholic. Why, an unscrupulous hired man could rob a landowner blind—or kill her in her bed. Someone who did not frequent poolrooms or saloons. Finally, she slept.

Chapter 2
Nels

On a North Dakota bonanza farm, Nels Jensen collected his wages from the foreman. Thirst turned his thanks into a whisper. It had been a parched summer. His hands trembled as he fastened the money in overalls that hung on him like a scarecrow. He had worked his behind off, caring for the horses, pitching bundles, loading, and driving the wagons of grain from the fields to the granary. A never-ending ribbon of train cars carried the wheat from a thousand acres to the Minneapolis rolling mills.

"Nels, you did a hellofa job." The foreman grasped his hand in a firm handshake. "You may be skinny as a bean pole and ugly as the business end of a mule, but you never shirked."

The other men called goodbye as they left for winter work, mostly logging camps in Minnesota. If only Nels could stay where he was. An easy job, wintering at the corporate farm. A lot easier than slaving in a logging camp in weather cold enough to freeze his eyeballs.

"I'd keep you on if I could afford it," the foreman said with a shrug. "To hell with bankers and politicians. We will all be on the bum unless this panic turns around. By next year we'll know which way the wind blows for the rolling mills."

It was rotten luck all around. The owner was some big shot back East who couldn't be bothered with seeing to things himself. The relentless wind rattled the rafters. He glanced through the rippling window glass. Horses stood in a line, facing into the prairie wind.

Nels had mostly cared for the horses and tended the water cart. He mucked barns and spread manure for next spring's planting.

Someday he would be the landowner instead of a hired man. He would turn furrows of black dirt and raise wheat and corn. With a little patience, he would build a small dairy herd and raise a flock of hens. His folks would join him from Denmark. Heck, he would find a wife and raise a family.

Bad luck had slowed him down, but that had changed. His wild days were behind him. It was time to settle down and make a real start in America. It was long overdue.

"Going to the woods?" the foreman said.

Nels nodded. "Hoping to work with horses this year, maybe as a skidder."

"Don't let the snow snakes get you," the foreman said with a grin.

Nels could tell that the foreman liked him. Hell, he said as much. No small compliment from that knuckle-headed German.

"Come into town with us," Hiram Dover, a manure-spreading friend, poked his head into the doorway. "Let off a little steam before we head to the woods."

Nels shook his head. "My train leaves at noon."

He had learned his lesson once and for all, and a bitter lesson it was. Most of the men working the bonanza farms had bottle fever, and the lumberjacks, too. Or rather, bottle fever had them by their short hairs. Last fall he had blown his summer wages in a glorious drunken brawl that lasted a week. Sadly, he had repeated the process after logging season last spring.

He vowed never again to give into that awful thirst that crept upon him like a stalking lion. This year he would bank his pay and ride the cars to Brainerd. He would arrive early enough to get a job as a skidder, working with horses while earning higher pay. Horses would make winter bearable. He had started at the bottom as a road monkey and swamper. It was high time he lived off the cream.

Nels's parents had scraped together his passage to America. In return, Nels promised to send for them once he became established. He had been in America for five years and had yet to save a single dollar.

Even now, Nels could not send for them. He had made mistakes, but now his feet were back on the narrow road.

"Come on Nels," Hiram coaxed. "Just one for the road."

Nels touched the pocket holding his money, making sure the button fastened. A black safe sat in the corner of the office, a fancy contraption with a combination lock. He considered asking the foreman to keep his money in the company safe. Others did it, and it would be no skin off the foreman's ass since Nels would return in the spring.

But asking the foreman to hold his money would be admitting to a problem. Maybe the foreman would change his mind about trusting him if he knew of Nels's penchant for liquor. Besides, the bank paid interest. Nels needed every cent.

He would open a bank account in town.

"Nels, you red-haired son of a biscuit," Hiram said. "Are you too good for your old pals these days?"

The train didn't leave until noon. Surely one beer would not hurt. A nickel, that is all. "Let me swing by the depot and buy my ticket first." Nels gathered his turkey, a knapsack holding his possessions. Working in the north woods required the warmest of jackets, socks, and boots. The bag bulged heavy, but he dared not lighten his load. Winter clothes were expensive to replace.

He would also stop at the bank. "I'll meet you at the Devil Dog afterwards."

Nels headed to the barns to say good bye to the horses. He rubbed their soft noses and fed them sugar lumps from his pocket. They alone seemed to understand him. They whinnied their farewells as he pulled up his collar and headed out of the barn and down the path toward town.

When he got to the bank, he found a sign propped in the window. *Closed for a death in the family.* Damn bankers, blood suckers feasting on the sweat of the common man. Feet up in the shade, no doubt, while the rest of the world slaved for their bread.

He debated about heading back to the farm and the company safe. He did not want to carry cash, much less keep it in the bunkhouse over winter. A bad experience the prior year had taught him the folly of doing that. He looked around to make sure he wasn't being watched, and then sat down on the boardwalk and removed his boot. He tucked most of his money into his sock, leaving only a dollar and his train ticket in his shirt pocket.

Nels eyed the sun. It would be hard to go to the farm and be back in time for the train. He would find another bank, maybe in Brainerd, on his way to the logging camp. He did not want to miss his train.

He headed for the saloon with a throat as dry as grain dust. The sound of hooves clomping on the streets reminded him of Copenhagen. His father would be amazed that they had harvested twelve acres of wheat in a single day using modern machinery. Nels vowed to write a letter home and tell them about the bonanza farm. He would have time on the train.

He climbed the rickety step into the Devil Dog. A wave of stale beer and cigar smoke slapped his face. A tinny piano pounded in the corner and a tired woman dressed in red sang a sad song. Her dress barely covered her chest, revealing a jowly neck draped in creped skin. She was old enough to be his mother. Even so, the men swarmed around her, plying her with drinks and reaching out with grasping hands.

Sickening. He turned to leave.

A drunken man draped himself over the bar, called for whiskey, and pulled a handful of silver change from his pocket. He scattered the sparkling coins across the counter with a tinkling clatter. "Drinks on me!"

Only a fool turned down a free drink. Nels deserved it after all his hard work. He vowed one beer and a speedy exit. He had an hour before the train left.

"How about a shot of squirrel whiskey?" the barkeep said once Nels's glass emptied. The barkeep wore a dirty white shirt with faded green suspenders. His long mustache twirled into short curls on either side of his face like a leering grin. "On the house."

"Never heard of squirrel whiskey." Nels's throat muscles worked and he licked chapped lips.

"No?" the barkeep said. His biceps stretched the fabric of his shirt. "You're in for a treat." He chuckled a dry laugh and reached for a bottle under the bar. "Squirrel whiskey won't make you fly, but you'll jump around a little."

Nels hesitated. A free drink of whiskey was better than free beer. Hiram played poker in the corner and it looked like he intended to stay all day. There was plenty of time to get to the depot by noon.

The liquor hit him like a sledge hammer.

Nels woke up feeling like someone had taken a mallet to his brain. His tongue glued to his teeth and his mouth tasted like dog shit. He was propped against the outside wall of the train depot, but he had no idea how he got there. He shivered in the early morning air. His socks and boots lay beside him. The contents of his turkey littered the ground.

His heart lurched. His pocket held only his ticket. He searched his other pockets. Just pennies. His boots and socks were empty. His entire summer earnings had vanished like the dew drying off his bare feet.

He gathered his wits. The squirrel whiskey. He had heard of knock-out drops.

A railroad worker chalked train schedules on a black slate hanging on the outside wall of the depot.

"What day is it?" Nels said.

"Tuesday," he said. "You in some kind of trouble?"

Damn that dirty barkeep! He would get his money back if it was the last thing he did.

He pulled on his socks and boots, checking again lest any money remained hidden. He repacked his turkey, stuffing his winter gear as fast as he could. He could not wait to get his hands on that dirty thief.

"What's wrong?" the railroad man said.

"Robbed at the Devil Dog." Nels stood to leave. "Took all my wages."

"Which one got you? Maybelle, the card sharp, or the squirrel whiskey?" he said with a wry laugh. "They prey on greenhorns."

"I'll kill him." Nels was not a greenhorn.

"Might think twice. Last week a man lost an eye."

Nels stopped. He had seen it before, heck, lived through it. An unscrupulous person ruined another's life. Back in Denmark, it had been the noblemen grabbing the best land, getting positions in church and state.

"Constable comes by on Thursday," the man said. "Wait and make a complaint."

It would not end with the complaint. Nels would have to stick around to testify. Hard to prove he hadn't drunk it all away as he had done many times before. Besides, it would boil down to the word of an immigrant against a Yankee. Delays would ruin the advantage of his train ticket. He would end up back as a swamper, freezing his tail off for a pittance.

Nels swallowed the hard truth. He would find no justice in spite of all the hoopla about liberty. He must leave as planned. When he returned to the bonanza farm in the spring, he would deal with the bartender. He had beat the money out of his sorry hide.

"What's his name, the barkeep?" Nels said.

"Myron or Merlin or some such. Englishman with the surname of Pinchpenny," the railroad man said. "Used to bare-knuckle with the circus. Not a man to mess with."

Pinchpenny. He would pinch his pennies, all right. Nels had never fought in the ring, but he was strong from hard work. Next spring, he would teach Pinchpenny not to mess with a man with Viking blood flowing in his veins.

"I missed my train," Nels said. His words tumbled thick and his mind turned slow and groggy. He pushed his ticket into the man's face. "Still any good?"

"Yep." The man pointed to the clock on the building. "Next train leaves in a quarter hour. At least leave a written statement for the constable. Like I said, there is a lot of complaints against the Devil Dog."

"Do you have a sheet of paper?"

Chapter 3
Sister Magdalena

In Duluth, Minnesota, Sister Magdalena worked suds up to her elbows, scrubbing dirty linens at Saint Mary's Hospital. The clock showed a quarter past ten. She finished the linens and started a barrel of dirty clothes from the orphanage across town.

Since childhood, she had imagined herself with heroic virtues that would be esteemed by others. It seemed the laundry room provided an unlikely path to sainthood.

The morning would never end. Her days in the vegetable gardens flew by like magic. Now that it was autumn, she was stuck in the laundry room of the hospital. She hated the stinky work, but the Rule of Saint Benedict urged her to do everything for the love of Christ. She usually managed to be cheerful.

Sister Magdalena took note of the names inked on the inside of the small shirts, dresses, and short pants. She prayed for each child as she scrubbed spots and stains: Susan Stepanek, Maggie Glum, Billy Jones, Jimmy Morgan and many others. After noon prayers, she would hang the wet clothes outside to dry. The wind off Lake Superior whipped a frenzy of swirling leaves outside the little window overlooking the Duluth harbor. The clothes would dry in no time. She glanced at the clock.

Sister Hildegard knocked on the door frame. "I need your help. I wrenched my back lifting a sack of flour." She hunched over and held her lower back with both hands. Her face scrunched with pain. Her veil hung to the floor like a white curtain. Even in her agony, Sister Hildegard looked as neat as a nun should look.

She was one of the older members of the Duluth Convent, twice the age of Sister Magdalena's twenty-five years.

"I'm not finished with my work." Sister Magdalena wiped her hands and straightened her cincture and coif.

Sister Hildegard groaned. "Laundry will wait. Hungry patients will not."

Sister Magdalena suspected others overestimated her ability to do things because of her strength and size. They called on her to heft packages, kill rats, or butcher hogs. It was true that Sister Magdalena could carry a barrel of salt, split stove wood, or reach the tallest cupboard without a step stool, but she was hopeless in the kitchen.

"I can't," Sister Magdalena said. The Rule of Benedict clearly stated to help someone in need. "I don't know how to cook."

Her mother had tried her best, but finally gave up. Sister Magdalena milked cows, separated cream, and pulled calves, but could not as much as boil an egg without disastrous results. Her brothers teased that she burned water.

"Nothing to cook." Sister Hildegard dismissed her with a wave of the hand. "Soup is on the stove. Biscuits in the oven for noon. Finish kneading the bread dough for supper."

Sister Hildegard did not wait for an answer, but left, still clutching her lower back. "Keep the stove fired," she called from the door. "A cold oven sours the bread."

Red leaves showed on the maples outside the window, brilliant against the blue sky and white clouds. Sister Magdalena trudged downstairs to the basement kitchen as if entering a dungeon. A horse and wagon clattered on Third Street. From upstairs came muffled footsteps and murmuring voices.

The basement kitchen connected to the wards by an open staircase in the corner. Practical, but it made for a lot of going up and down stairs to haul water and wood, deliver meals, and bring in supplies. Sister Magdalena's bulk made the steps cumbersome, and she bent low to avoid banging her head.

The kitchen stank of fish soup and cabbage. The dough piled in a heap on the table.

Sister Magdalena sniffed again. Something burning. She ran to the stove, almost tripping over the gray tabby cat that kept rats at bay, and cracked open the oven door. Black showed around the edges, but the biscuits looked salvageable. She whisked them out of the oven, burning her fingers in her haste.

Novice Agatha rushed down the steps in a dramatic flurry of gray habit and veil. The young girl had not made her first profession or earned the title of sister. The Rule of Benedict said to treat everyone with respect for the love of Christ. Saint Benedict had never dealt with Agatha.

Sister Magdalena had kept her temper when Agatha spilled the wash water, dropped clean sheets in the dirt, and almost smoked them out of the laundry by poking too much wood into the copper boiler. Sister Magdalena swallowed the sharp words forming on her tongue when Agatha pulled carrots out of the garden along with the weeds. Maybe the girl knew something about cooking.

Agatha hurried to the stove with her red, pimply face. "Sister Hildegard says you need help." The stove lid screeched as she stuffed wood into the box. Acrid smoke overpowered the smells of cabbage and fish.

"Mind the draft," Sister Magdalena said. Didn't that girl know anything? "Finish kneading and I'll serve the soup." At least she would get out of working the dough.

Sister Magdalena filled the serving pail with soup and another with biscuits as Agatha tackled the dough. Sister Magdalena stacked tin cups and spoons on top of the biscuits.

The bell sounded for noon prayers. Footsteps clattered overhead as the nursing sisters hurried to the chapel. She and Agatha should do the same.

"What will we do?" Agatha looked up in alarm, flour turning her face pasty white. "We haven't served the noon meal."

Sister Magdalena eyed the spilled flour, the dirty utensils scattered across the table, and the cook stove that puffed black smoke with every downdraft.

God surely understood their predicament. Mother Superior would not.

Agatha tossed her veil over her shoulder, leaving floury prints across her apron.

"Hurry, we'll do it together." Sister Magdalena gathered the buckets, one in each hand, when a great belch of black smoke came from the stovepipe along with a loud whoosh.

The stovepipe glowed red in the elbow. A chimney fire.

The whole hospital might burn down. Sister Magdalena dropped the buckets to the floor and reached for the salt box. Agatha pushed past with the water bucket and made ready to douse the stove.

Water warped hot iron. How long the sisters had scrimped and saved to purchase the beautiful, new stove. There was no money to replace it.

"Stop! Close the dampers instead." Sister Magdalena sprinkled salt in the fire box. Time slowed. She watched Agatha put the bucket down as if in a dream. Agatha leaned to close the dampers and bumped the stove lid with her elbow.

The novice's veil dipped into the firebox.

Sister Magdalena tried to speak, but before a word formed on her lips, a finger of flame climbed Agatha's veil toward her face.

Agatha shrieked, stepped back, and slapped at the fire. She tripped over the bucket of soup and sat in a sea of cabbage, potatoes, and carrots. The burning cloth reeked.

Flames licked closer to Agatha's face. The novice shrieked in terror and slapped the fire with her hands, making it worse.

Sister Magdalena had to do something. She grabbed the water bucket and dumped it over the girl's head. Agatha sputtered and coughed. The cat yowled and streaked behind the wood box.

"Are you hurt?" Sister Magdalena searched for burns on the young girl's neck and cheeks. Red, but no blisters. Nothing serious. The stovepipe no longer whooshed. The elbow pipe returned to normal. The fire was out, and the stove spared. Disaster was averted.

"No, Sister," Agatha said, choking and gasping. "Only drowned." Water dripped from her face. Her charred veil drooped to one side. Great sobs shook her shoulders.

She looked like a wet dog.

Sister Magdalena chuckled, and handed Agatha a dish towel. The novice mopped her face and arms.

"What will Mother Superior say?" Agatha said. "We missed noon prayers, ruined dinner and made a terrible mess of Sister Hildegard's kitchen."

"You're not hurt." Sister Magdalena muffled a chuckle. "That's all that matters." Sister Magdalena dropped to her knees and sopped soup with an old rag, trying to suppress a giggle. Her knees dampened with fishy broth. Bits of carrot smeared orange across the front of her apron. She looked no better than Agatha with her smudged hands and filthy cassock.

Sister Magdalena's giggles turned into chortles. A stray dumpling rolled under the stove. The cat raced as if after a mouse. Hilarious. Sister Magdalena laughed until tears rolled down her cheeks, leaving her gasping for air.

Her father once expressed concern for the convent if they ever put his daughter in charge of the kitchen. How he would cringe if he saw her swimming in soup with the novice on fire. Sister Magdalena howled and wiped her face, unable to control her laughter.

"What's all the commotion?" Sister Lucy clomped down the stairs into the kitchen. She was a foot shorter than Sister Magdalena's six feet, and wore her usual pickle-faced pout. "Where's Sister Hildegard?"

Sister Magdalena struggled to answer, but no words came. She pointed to Agatha's burnt veil, then to a dumpling under the table, and a potato rolling under the stove. Prim Sister Lucy and disheveled Novice Agatha were as opposite as could be. Lucy looked a perfect example of order, and Agatha was completely undone. Sister Magdalena's own behavior was inexcusable. The Rule of Benedict warned against frivolity.

"I don't see what's so amusing," Sister Lucy said with a loud sniff.

Mother Superior came down the stairs, her skirts swirling with each step. "Explain yourselves." Mother Superior waited for a reply. She was almost as wide as she was tall.

Sister Magdalena quit laughing. Agatha covered her face with her singed veil. Sister Magdalena wiped her eyes, and squared her shoulders. She faced Mother Superior.

"Our apologies, Mother. Sister Hildegard hurt her back, and we tried to serve dinner to the patients. We ran into a few problems." Sister Magdalena was out of breath from laughing. "We'll clean it up."

"Be quick about it," Mother Superior said. Sister Magdalena detected a glint of merriment in her dark eyes. The older woman pursed her lips and clasped her hands before her, almost as if in prayer. "The Rule of Benedict states that nothing comes before the Work of God. Absence at prayers will not be tolerated, and I will expect a kneeling pardon in the refectory tonight." She turned to go, then turned back for one more admonition. "Sister Magdalena, come to my office after you finish here."

She turned on her heel and climbed the kitchen stairs, holding her habit high enough to reveal black stockings and button shoes. She climbed upward without bumping her head.

"Hurry up with the food," Sister Lucy said. "The patients are hungry." She followed Mother Superior, as bristly as a banty hen.

"I'm sorry," Agatha wailed. "I'll never be a nun. It's too hard." She wrung water out of the hem of her habit.

"Give it time." Sister Magdalena stifled a grin.

"But a kneeling pardon?" Agatha said. "I'll die of embarrassment."

"That's nothing." Sister Magdalena waved her hand. "The road to eternal life is paved with obstacles." Somewhere upstairs rang a small bell. Heavy footsteps sounded on the floor.

Where else could a poor girl have access to books, education and art? Sister Magdalena shuddered to think of her life if she had married the widow-man, Harvey Schmitz. She would be slaving for him and his eight children plus cooking three meals a day. Thank God she was blessed with the gift of a vocation. She adhered to The Rule of Benedict and did all for the love of Christ. It was a good life.

Agatha would find her way, too, if she didn't give up.

Sister Magdalena wiped her eyes and gathered her wits. Her thoughts scrambled as to what to serve in place of soup. There were biscuits. She might use the apple jelly set aside for Christmas.

"Go back to the convent and change," Sister Magdalena said. "I will serve the meal. Come back and we'll clean up the kitchen together."

Sister Magdalena lumbered up the stairway after Agatha, bending low and careful not to spill the bucket of tea in one hand or the pail of biscuits in the other. She refused to think of her distaste for hospitals. She would serve the patients as Christ. It was her duty. She would do it with all the energy and enthusiasm she could muster.

She swallowed a giggle. She would sketch a picture of Agatha with her veil on fire in her next letter home, like a modern-day Pentecost. She imagined her brothers laughing as she entered the ward and sniffed the hideous odors of urine and antiseptic. The room rustled with restless men, groans, and coughing.

The loggers came to Saint Mary's Hospital with broken bones, gashes from slipped axes, accidents with horses or falling timbers. Sometimes they came to die. Many were alone in a strange country, without family to turn to for help. The young men reminded her of her brothers back in Wisconsin, with their prideful ways and zest for living. They thought themselves invincible.

Sister Magdalena ladled tea into tin cups. "Oh, the delicious soup made for your dinner," she said in a boisterous tone. "But do you see any soup, my brothers?" She handed each patient a biscuit with a dab of jelly. "An unfortunate accident robbed your stomachs."

Groans sounded from the far corner.

"What kind of accident?" one of the patients asked. His head swathed in bandages, and below the white layers of cloth peeked two black eyes and an unsightly gash alongside his nose.

Sister Magdalena bantered to hide her disgust. The more hideous the wounds, the worse the coughing, the fouler the stench, the more she teased—something she had learned from her brothers.

"The worst accident," Sister Magdalena said. "The kind that makes a grown man cry."

"Worse than having a widowmaker fall on your head?" The man had been logging south of Duluth when a sudden wind dislodged a tree hung up in the branches of another tree. Yesterday when she had delivered clean linens to the ward, she overheard him talking about his accident. He had a younger brother attending seminary.

"It's bad enough," Sister Magdalena said. "Even though no blood was shed."

She teased the story. Each man guessed what accident robbed their bellies.

"I'll bet an Injun came begging at the door, and you gave it away," a man called out.

"No Indians today," Sister Magdalena said while doling cups of tea and overbaked biscuits.

"A bum, then," another man said.

"No bums," Sister Magdalena said.

She headed toward the groaning patient in the far corner. She avoided him as long as she could, steeling herself to be courageous in his suffering. She did not know how the nursing sisters, like Sister Lucy, stood it day in and day out. Perhaps the reason Sister Lucy always wore a sour expression.

"And you, my brother," Sister Magdalena said. "What kind of accident do you think has befallen our soup?"

The man grabbed her arm and pulled her closer. He smelled like the outhouse. Blackened teeth filled the open maw of his mouth. "Kill me, Sister," he pleaded in a thick Irish accent. "For the love of Jesus and His Sacred Heart, kill me now."

Sister Magdalena drew back. She crossed herself and touched the Saint Benedict medal around her neck.

"I'm dead already." He dropped back on his pillow. "Doctor says I won't last a month. Lung fever. Another thirty dollars down a rat hole if I live. That's enough to get my wife through the winter."

Sister Magdalena's hand trembled as she placed it onto his shoulder. "Hope in God, my brother."

"Don't speak to me of God." He knocked the cup out of her hand. It skittered across the floor, forming puddles of tea. "He's turned His back on me. It's me and Gertie, alone in this country, and a baby on the way."

The room grew quiet.

Sister Magdalena wiped up the spill and gathered the cup.

"Promise me, Sister." He grabbed her arm and pulled her toward him. He spoke directly into her face. His breath roiled her stomach. "Take care of her when I'm gone. Gertie Murphy in the shacks by the waterfront."

Sister Magdalena stumbled out of the ward.

"Promise me, Sister!" he called after her. "Gertie will end up on the street."

The man's request to be killed, so obscene, was almost understandable in context of his situation. The hospital charged a bare minimum, but many were unable to pay even that paltry sum. And his desperate wife left behind.

No patient should feel guilty for receiving care. Logging, farming, and mining all carried dangers. Falling trees, slipped axes, buckled saws, runaway teams, cave-ins, sickness, or goring bulls. It happened all the time. But life was even harder on immigrants who faced life without the support of family. They had no one to turn to in times of emergencies. In Sister Magdalena's experience, the ups and downs of life were mainly of the down-version, and to be expected.

Sister Magdalena must visit the woman. She would see for herself what Gertie Murphy was up against, if Mother Superior would grant permission. Sister Magdalena had already missed prayers, made a mess in Sister Hildegard's kitchen, and almost drowned Agatha. Mother Superior had no reason to grant a favor. She sighed. Obedience, never easy, felt even more burdensome this day when everything had gone wrong.

Agatha returned to the kitchen wearing a clean dress and veil. She kept her eyes down and made no mention of the fiery incident. Neither did Sister Magdalena. They finished cleaning the kitchen.

Sister Magdalena stepped outside into the fresh air. Smoke rose from every chimney and seagulls collected grain dribbling from a leaky sack in a passing dray. She waved to the driver, breathed deeply, and headed for the convent down the street from the hospital.

A cold wind blew off the lake on the eastern end of the city and tangled Sister Magdalena's soiled veil, mirroring the turmoil in her mind. Dry leaves crunched under her feet. Sister Magdalena raised her face to the sun, as if to soak in its final rays before the next season. Winters were bad this far north.

Her emotions churned as she tapped on Mother Superior's door. "Kill me," lingered in her thoughts like a bad smell.

"Sister Magdalena," Mother Superior said. "Enter and be seated."

Sister Magdalena perched on a wooden chair before the table that served as Mother Superior's desk. A neat pile of correspondence filled the left corner. A pen and inkwell stood in the right corner. Behind Mother Superior hung a large crucifix. A statue of the Blessed Virgin gazed lovingly from a shelf. A rosary draped across her outstretched arms. Blue beads reflected the afternoon light from a small window.

"Please explain what happened today," Mother Superior said. She placed her two index fingers to her lips and listened as Sister Magdalena fumbled an explanation.

"You must attend the Work of God," Mother Superior said. "Without prayer, our work is fruitless."

"Yes, Mother." Sister Magdalena was without excuse.

"And the spilled soup, chimney fire, and near disaster?" Mother Superior said. "Are you satisfied with your morning's performance?"

Sister Magdalena shook her head. She covered a carrot stain on her cassock with her veil and hoped Mother Superior had not noticed.

Mother Superior squared her shoulders and took a deep breath. "Sister Lucy suggests you transfer to the nursing sisters. You are strong and healthy. You have a good rapport with the patients."

Sister Magdalena gaped in horror. Physical strength was one thing, but caring for the sick was something else. The mere thought of helping a patient use a bedpan made her squirm with anxiety. She almost fainted if someone cut a finger. Even Agatha's near-disaster with fire caused her to erupt into laughter, not pity. She would be a terrible nurse.

"Perhaps you worry about training," Mother Superior said. Kindness showed in her eyes, and she reached a hand toward Sister Magdalena. "The doctors prefer strong backs and obedience above education."

"It's not that." How could she put words to the dread she felt even hearing of the possibility? "I do not feel called to nursing."

"Your intellect is wasted in the laundry, I'm afraid." Mother Superior straightened her back and reached for the pen and ink. "I have requests for more teachers, workers for the orphanage. The new school in International Falls lacks leadership."

Sister Magdalena took a breath. Maybe this was her only opportunity. She fished for the words to explain her feelings. "If I could do anything," she blurted in a torrent, "I would work with the patients in a different way."

The words poured out. She told about the man who begged her to kill him to spare money for his wife. She spoke of the financial burden of patients who needed care they could not afford. "It is a need greater than their injuries and sicknesses." She thought again, then added in a humbler tone. "At least equal to their need for medical care."

The eyes of the Blessed Virgin gazed upon them as if pondering the words hanging in the air. Sister Magdalena had spoken her mind. Surely presumptuous. She would be banished to the nursing wards.

"The Rule of Benedict says to listen with the ears of the heart," Mother Superior said. "I will pray, and I ask that you be in prayer, as well." She pushed away from the table and stood to her feet. "Let us discern God's will." Mother Superior folded her hands. "You have many talents, and my job is to make sure you become the person you were created to be."

Sister Magdalena felt her jaw drop. Others were talented, but she was not blessed with spiritual gifts.

"I have need of someone to collect a donation," Mother Superior said. "No doubt, you could handle yourself if a thief were to accost you." She told Sister Magdalena that she must travel by rail car south to Minneapolis, switch cars and go on to Fergus Falls on the far western edge of Minnesota to meet the donor.

"A benefactor bequeathed a sum of money to us," Mother Superior said. "His widow is too old to travel and will entrust the gift only to one of our sisters."

"When do I leave?" Her heart quickened. A chance to travel by herself on the cars? An adventure.

"Tomorrow. Agatha will take over the laundry." Mother Superior frowned and the vertical lines deepened between her eyes. "This gift is a godsend. I am counting on you to keep your wits about you and represent the convent with decorum. No foolery." She looked into Sister Magdalena's eyes. "Don't let me down."

She, Sister Magdalena, a Benedictine nun, was entrusted with an important errand. The convent needed money for the orphanage, academy, and hospital. Immigrants from all over the world flocked into Duluth for work in the shipyards, logging camps, and mines. The needs were relentless.

The bell rang for Afternoon Prayer. They stood to their feet.

"Spend the rest of the afternoon in prayer," Mother Superior said. "There will be a community meeting to discuss expansion, when you return."

Her brother had cautioned that life in a convent would be boring. Sister Magdalena stifled a grin. There was nothing dull about serving God.

That night, Sister Magdalena knelt next to Agatha beside the refectory doorway as the others filed by in silence, some glancing with pitying eyes. Their Benedictine community consisted of only twenty-seven nuns, a handful of postulants and five novices. The other sisters stood behind their chairs waiting for the table grace.

Mother Superior nodded at the guilty pair. They humbly admitted their fault of missing Noon Prayers. Mother Superior nodded again, but did not smile or motion them to arise. The chairs scraped across the floor. Crockery clattered as the simple meal was served. No butter or sugar—all luxuries were omitted to provide funds for their many outreaches.

The only voice was that of the designated reader. Sister Lucy, assigned reader for the week, read aloud a chapter from *The Imitation of Christ* by Thomas a' Kempis. No time wasted in idle chatter, not even during the meal. Instead, the sisters feasted their minds on the great writers of the Church along with their bread and soup.

The Great Silence began with supper and lasted until after breakfast.

Sister Magdalena struggled to kneel upright, her back and knees aching. Except for Agatha's stupidity, she would be seated and enjoying supper.

Thomas a' Kempis was one of Sister Magdalena's heroes. She leaned into his words for strength. "Be not angry that you cannot make others as you wish them to be, since you cannot make yourself as you wish to be." Her conscience pricked. She smiled at the novice at her side.

Sister Lucy closed the book. The community stood to their feet and waited for the final blessing. Sister Magdalena and Novice Agatha remained on their knees as everyone filed out of the refectory.

Mother Superior walked over and knelt beside them for a long moment. Finally, Mother Superior rose to her feet. Only then did she indicate with a nod and a gesture that the two offenders could stand.

Novice Agatha's foot caught in her skirt and she tripped as she stumbled to her feet, causing enough commotion that

Mother Superior frowned. Agatha's face turned crimson, and Sister Magdalena reached a steadying hand.

Mother Superior handed a folded note to Sister Magdalena as they spooned cold soup in silence. Sister Magdalena waited until Mother Superior left the room. It was short and to the point: *When you return there will be a community meeting. Come prepared to share what God places on your heart.*

Sister Magdalena's stomach lurched. It was not as if God sent written instructions. The will of God was an intangible thing, a longing more than words. Not exactly true, since God spoke through Scripture, Sacred Writings, and the Traditions of the Church. Saint Benedict urged all to listen to each other, as God often spoke to His people through others, whether great or small, young or old.

She left the refectory and headed toward her cell on the second floor of the convent. Her room waited, clean and stark. Only a narrow cot, bedside stand with pitcher and wash bowl, and a straight-backed chair furnished the tiny room. A crucifix graced a whitewashed wall. Nothing else. Her few garments hung from pegs on the opposite wall. Sister Magdalena liked its simplicity. Entering her cell always brought peace. She knelt by her bed and prayed fervently for God's will.

After a long while, she climbed into bed. She could only ask. It was up to Him to speak.

Chapter 4
Solveig

Early Thursday morning, Solveig dreamed about Rasmuss. In the dream he took both her hands and sang as he had done so many times. *God give you strength wherever in the world you go.* Rasmuss could not carry a tune, but oh, how she loved to hear him sing. He made up the melody and used the words from Peer Gynt, a favorite Henrik Ibsen play Rasmuss had seen in his youth. He once used money saved for new shoes to purchase a written copy. It was something he took with him to the logging camps every winter.

How like Rasmuss to appear, even though in a dream. They faced problems together and drew strength from each other. Only a cruel God would take him from her as age nibbled away her abilities and Halvor deserted her.

All day she watched for Gunnar, the son of her dearest friends, Evan, and Inga Jacobson, her first friends in America. Gunnar worked the logging camps in the winter and bonanza farms in the summer, and left his wife alone to run the Pomme de Terre store in his absence. She was a saint to put up with his wanderings. Inga had filled many letters with her worries about Gunnar.

Solveig figured the young man showed ambition. These days a man had to keep the wolf from the door however he could. But, a mother always worried.

Gunnar showed up as the milky sun settled cold in the autumn sky. He had his mother's brown eyes. Inga's sudden death had been another sorrow added to a brutal year. Loss upon loss. No one had warned Solveig how graveyards would snatch those she loved and leave her alone.

"There's been a change of plans." Solveig wiped wet hands on her apron. She waved him to the table and reached for the coffee pot. She chose her words with care. The less said about her spat with Halvor, the better. She placed a dish of jam and a plate of bread on the table beside a bowl of potato chowder. The steam from the soup tangled with Gunnar's scruffy beard. "Halvor took a wife and moved to Fergus. I am going instead."

Gunnar let out a low whistle. "Halvor? That sly dog." He grinned. "Never thought he'd take the plunge into Holy Matrimony." He slathered butter on bread still warm from the oven. "And moved into town? Never pictured him a city slicker."

He downed the bread and took another slice, slurping soup. "Sure you know what you're getting into?"

He was too polite to tell her that it was a bad idea for her to work at a logging camp. She knew what he meant. A hen scratched in the leaves outside the window, its feathers fluttering in the wind. Solveig's feathers bristled, too

"They need cooks," she said.

Gunnar nodded. "Found that out my first year as a swamper." He reported cold soup, turned meat, sour bread, and weak coffee. "That belly robber almost starved us. Lived on prunes and hard-tack." He spoke around another bite. "Lumberjacks freeze all day and sleep rough. Good food is their only comfort."

Solveig nodded, but a sick feeling settled in her gut. An inner voice cautioned that she was stepping into deep water.

"Not taking the team, then, I suppose." Gunnar swiped at his mouth where a dab of strawberries dripped onto his beard. "Barn bosses work horses to death if you do not keep watch. Last year Rasmuss went nose to nose with a toploader putting too heavy a load on Buck and Young Bob."

Solveig refilled his bowl.

"Better to leave the horses home than risk ruining them altogether," Gunnar said. "Overfeeding kills horses. No more than six pints of oats a day, I always say. Fresh water. Treatment if calked or down with colic."

She clamped her lips together. She knew better than share her money troubles, but there was no way around it. A burst of wind slammed dried leaves against the window pane and howled around the eaves. Outside the empty egg basket blew across the yard and lodged against the wood pile. The sun had almost slipped beyond the western horizon. Solveig lit the lamp.

"I will bring the team myself." Solveig hoped she sounded more confident than she felt. The truth wiggled its way into the open. "My back is against the wall." Solveig admitted that she would lose the farm unless she earned enough to pay the note coming due on the homestead. "Would have been all right if Rasmuss..." Solveig took a breath to strengthen her voice. Even so, it came out in a near-whisper. "His death, you know."

Gunnar swirled the cup in his burly hand. "A rowdy place, a logging camp. Rough language. All kinds of shenanigans." He paused. "No place for a God-fearing woman."

Solveig snorted. "At my age? I can take care of myself." She turned to the sewing box in the corner and pulled a long hatpin from a pincushion. "My grandmother named it a woman's best friend. I'll keep it close."

"No guarantee a camp will need both a cook and a team." He twisted his lips into a thoughtful frown. "What would Halvor say if you're stuck alone someplace?"

Halvor did not care about her or the farm. She would do it or die trying. A cold anger settled hard on her chest.

"Your pa gave Rasmuss and me that basswood tree as a wedding present," Solveig pointed through the kitchen window into the twilight. The leaves fluttered around its trunk like a flock of brown birds pecking seeds. "We think of him every spring when it blooms."

The "we" unnerved her, the switch to "I" still unfamiliar. She poked another stick of wood into the cook stove, though Gunnar had rolled his shirtsleeves for the heat.

"As long as you understand the risks."

Solveig scraped the coffee pot across the iron stove top. She fiddled with the damper. She did not want to look Gunnar in the eye.

"I could watch over the team," Gunnar said. "A cook is stuck in the kitchen from before light until after dark. You would not know what was going on with the horses."

She drew a sharp breath of relief. He was a good boy, her godson.

"But I'm staying on as river pig in the spring." Gunnar chewed and swallowed hard. "I can take you out to the camps, but you'll have to find your own way home."

Solveig drew a sharp breath. River pigs herded the logs downriver to the sawmills. They worked during the spring thaw when the water ran high, after everyone else had gone home. Broken bones, crushed limbs, or drownings often occurred. Top pay, but they earned every cent. Foolish for Gunnar to take such a risk, but ambition drove a man.

"Many thanks." Solveig said. She had worked with Buck and Young Bob for years. She would drive them home herself.

He handed her a fistful of handbills from different logging camps. She fingered the list of positions. *Cook, cook's helper, kitchen boy. Top wages for those willing to work.*

"What's the difference between camps?" Solveig said.

"Bigger outfits pay the best. Otherwise, they are about the same. They all have the same bugs." Gunnar laughed. "One thing about a lumberjack. He never sleeps alone." He told of a young swamper who asked for a bunk without bedbugs. The foreman put him next to the lousiest jack in camp. "That learned him quick. Between the fleas and bugs, the men spend most of their free time scratching."

Solveig shuddered. No sense worrying about foolish comforts when cold cash was involved.

She had ventured into the world before. Back then she had nothing to lose. Her father said that even if she was not a beauty, she would never starve if she worked hard and kept her nose out of other people's business. She would follow his good advice now.

Solveig scrutinized the handbills. Maybe a logging company would not hire a woman, even a plain-faced widow like herself. It was her last hope.

Gunnar went to bed early. They must leave at dawn to catch the noon train in Fergus Falls. They would reach Brainerd the following morning.

Solveig added the small stack of her grandmother's neatly penned recipes into the trunk. Bestemor's handwriting crawled across the paper like bird tracks, perfectly formed and rounded. She was another loved one in the grave. Solveig clutched a recipe close to her chest and willed her grandmother's face to come into her mind. Nothing but shadows.

The morning broke cold and clear. No cow to be milked. No young stock to feed. No crowing rooster. Even the wind held its breath.

"Where will you leave the wagon over the winter?" Gunnar eyed her trunk. "We always rode bareback." He rubbed the edge of his prickly face with his thumb. "No way to tie a trunk on a horse." The scratching of his thumb on whiskers whispered through the room.

Panic rose in her throat. She had not considered how they would get to the depot in Fergus Falls. She had not planned where she might store the wagon over winter. She had no stomach for asking favors of Britta's family, the only people she knew in Fergus Falls. And she would rather not face Halvor's disapproval of her leaving.

"We've the old pony cart and Young Bob trained for it," Solveig said. "It's stashed behind the barn."

Rasmuss had built the foldable cart when they first married. How often they had driven across the prairie with Old Bob and a picnic lunch.

Old Bob ruined his wind pulling the stage to Fort Abercrombie in a mad dash ahead of marauding Sioux. Evan Jacobson, Gunnar's father, and that team of horses had saved their lives. She and Rasmuss rescued Old Bob in turn, buying the impaired horse from the army sutler for one dollar. Old Bob only ambled, but they loved him like a thoroughbred. Rasmuss wept at his death, and insisted they name the next horse after him. And the next.

Solveig grabbed her shawl and knitting bag. Gunnar left to find the pony cart. Solveig reached for the sourdough starter and stopped the bottle with a wad of cloth. She filled a basket with two loaves of bread, a dozen boiled eggs, and a crock of pickles. She packed matches and a few sticks of dried kitchen wood. She added her smallest kettle, a jug of milk, a tub of butter, a few potatoes, carrots, a pound of dried navy beans, an onion, a lard can filled with flour, and a slab of bacon. She crammed a cooking pot with cookies, tucked a bottle of water and a wedge of cheese into the basket, and covered it all with a clean cloth.

Enough to survive on the trail, even if she did not find work. She pushed the negative thought from her mind. There was always work.

Solveig counted four silver dollars and two quarters from the sugar bowl on the corner shelf. Carefully Solveig slipped the silver coins into a small cloth bag around her neck. She stuck the hat pin into her braids, and tied her kerchief.

Solveig gritted her teeth. She would not let her confidence follow Rasmuss to his grave.

She gathered her favorite rag rug and laid it across the contents of her trunk. How empty the floor looked without the rug woven from Halvor's baby dresses. Solveig added a chunk of hard soap, a pair of bee's wax candles, and the coffee beans and grinder. She closed the lid with a clunk and turned the key. Then she slipped the key into the pouch around her neck.

Solveig wore Rasmuss's old shirt and her heaviest sweater. She wrapped herself in her warmest shawl and mumbled good-bye to the kitchen, her clean bed without bugs, the embroidery basket, and her few books. She bit her lip and tasted blood.

On a last-minute whim, she grabbed Rasmuss's turkey holding his logging gear—warm cap with earflaps, heavy mackinaw, and sturdy boots. Perhaps she might sell them to someone at the camp. She added Ibsen's *Peer Gynt* on top, making it feel as if Rasmuss were going with her.

Solveig marched to the chicken coop with resolve, as Gunnar hitched the horse to the cart. The few remaining hens came running, expecting kitchen scraps. Instead, Solveig pulled a wooden crate from the rafters. She snatched Gumbri by one leg and stuffed her into the crate along with two black hens. Three eggs a day meant twenty-one eggs a week, if the shock of the move did not send them into molt. Eggs meant cakes. Eggs lightened shortbread and flapjacks. Why, years ago eggs brought a dollar apiece in the Black Hills gold fields. The *Fergus Falls Daily Journal* wrote about it. These hens were her gold mine. Eggs to be sold, meat in an emergency, and a new flock if she managed to pay off the bank note.

Solveig nailed the lid on the crate of clucking birds. It was Britta's fault. Plain and simple. Britta destroyed their family. Anger propelled Solveig through those final moments. She dragged the crate with one hand and hoisted a feed sack to her shoulder with the other. Gunnar raised an eyebrow, but loaded the cart while she ran into the house for one last chore.

She penciled a hasty note on the back of an old calendar page. She looked around the cabin, and hurried outside, careful to snug the door against the coming winter.

Once in the cart, Solveig arranged her skirts lest they flutter and spook Young Bob. The wind caressed her face. She tucked the sourdough bottle between her feet and covered with a horse blanket made from Old Bob's hide. She patted the robe, and fingered the cuff of Rasmuss's shirt beneath her shawl. Then she gathered the lines. Gunnar mounted Buck.

"Ready?" he said.

Queenie streaked across the yard and leapt into Solveig's lap.

Solveig rubbed the cat's ears and chin. "I almost forgot you." Mr. Olson had the kittens. She fingered the train tickets in her reticule. Reassured, Solveig flicked the lines. Young Bob pulled the tiny cart with ease. He had never failed to do what she asked. Solveig spoke a reassuring word to the hens at her feet. Gumbri blinked sharp eyes through the slats.

"Don't worry," Solveig said. "Everything will be fine."

The cart bounced over a rough patch in the trail. Solveig steadied Queenie in her lap. She did not look back.

On the edge of town loomed the new State Hospital for the Insane. Next to it stood the County Poor Farm where people without family ended up. Her old neighbor, Olga Everson, went to the Poor Farm after her man died. Solveig shuddered. She would die first.

Buggies crowded the streets. Smoke from hundreds of chimneys smudged the air. Farmers flocked to the bustling stores, stocking up for the long winter ahead.

She craned her neck for a glimpse of Halvor at the hardware store. An older man swept the boardwalk, but no sign of her son. Stopping to say goodbye would only cause an argument.

The note on the table would do if he cared enough to check on her. She turned her face and hardened her resolve. To hell with him. To hell with everyone.

When they finally arrived at the depot, Gunnar loaded Solveig's trunk and baggage into the train car. Overhead a cold sun peeked through gray clouds, and a brisk wind swirled her skirts. The steeple of the church poked into the sky.

Gunnar lugged the hens to the stock car. "I'll ride with the team and find you when we change trains in Brainerd."

Solveig bristled. She traveled across the Atlantic Ocean before he was born. On her own, she rode the train from New York to Bishop Whipple's house in Saint Paul.

"I'll manage," Solveig said with a huff. "It's not my first journey, you know."

She would not board until the team settled in the car, despite Gunnar's promise to handle them on his own. Buck's dark coat gleamed as he navigated the unfamiliar wooden ramp. Young Bob shied away, no doubt frightened by the hollow sound of hooves on plank. Gunnar pulled on the halter rope, but Young Bob reared back as a glint of sun transformed his eyes into blazing fire.

Solveig gasped. Everything depended on the horses. A single misstep, a broken leg or fall meant financial ruin. A logging camp only hired teams. She could not repay the note without their wages.

She stepped forward to help, but a young man leapt to the loading ramp and grabbed Young Bob's halter on the opposite side of Gunnar. Together, they calmed the horse. Young Bob returned to sanity and followed Gunnar into the car. The stranger shook Gunnar's hand and disappeared into the depot.

Solveig breathed again. Gunnar waved from the doorway. She swallowed hard at the cold reality of her situation. She, so proud and independent, could no longer manage the team on her own. The whistle blew again.

Solveig's skirts tangled around her legs, causing a stumble as she climbed the wobbly stool up to the passenger car. She clutched Queenie in one arm, and grabbed the porter's outstretched hand with the other. The porter wore a blue uniform with white cuffs and collar. His black face glistened with perspiration. She had not seen a Negro since the war. Back then, a man in Saint Paul owned a slave to tend his livery business.

Solveig's knees creaked, and she rubbed a pain in her lower back. Riding a small cart over bumpy trails suited a younger woman. She straightened her spine and held up her chin. She must appear more active and vigorous than she felt. Everything depended on it.

The car divided into seats at the front and a baggage area at the rear. At the front of the car, a wood stove belched dark smoke. Solveig breathed easier when she found a rear seat next to the baggage, as far away from the smothering heat as possible.

A man boarded the train carrying a brace of geese and a shotgun. Behind him came a drummer with his sample bag. They sat a few seats ahead of Solveig.

Solveig flagged the porter. Despite Gunnar's assurances, she had to hear for herself.

"Sir," Solveig said. Perhaps it was wrong to address him as she would a white man. "Can you please tell me that the stock car will arrive in Brainerd at the same time I arrive?"

"Yes, ma'am," the porter said. His voice stretched smooth with that lilt of the southern states. He studied her ticket with all seriousness. "Every car goes through to Brainerd. There you'll take the spur line going north to Gull River Timber."

A young man pushed into the car, jostling Solveig without apology. He wore stained overalls and heavy work boots. His face bristled with several days' growth of blond beard, accenting blood-shot eyes. He reeked of sweat and carried a bulging pack. Queenie yowled and scratched to get away. The young man stumbled into the rear seat across from Solveig, behind a young mother with a crying baby and fussy toddler. The whistle sounded warning.

He was the man who helped with the team.

"You'll need to confine your cat to the baggage area, ma'am," the porter said. "Can't be bothering the other passengers."

Surely it would not matter if she kept Queenie in her lap. The cat would yowl all the more if confined to a basket in the back. Solveig set her jaw. She paid good money for a ticket, and saw no need to be separated from her pet.

"I'll hold my cat." Solveig gestured toward the now-snoring young man sprawled across the aisle. "My cat is quieter than other passengers."

The porter looked at the cat, the crying baby, and snoring man. He nodded. "Yes, ma'am. Make sure you keep it on your lap."

A heavy-set woman wearing a wide-rimmed black bonnet tied with a bright orange scarf plunked into the seat beside Solveig. She was younger than Solveig by a decade. She clutched a wick-er basket and an ornate black velvet reticule. Orange ribbons tied around her neck. Her skirt boasted matching embroidery across the hemline. A silver *solia*, a Norwegian brooch, clasped the openings of her shawl. Her wide face flushed, and tiny dots of perspiration covered her upper lip. The woman pulled a lacy handkerchief from her reticule and mopped her face.

"*Uff da, fyda.*" She fanned her face with the hanky. "I almost missed the train." She mopped the back of her neck. "My husband got tied up at the bank, wouldn't you know, and forgot to pick me up. I'm visiting my sister. She's married to the Lutheran pastor in Brainerd." She fanned and mopped her face again. "Liv has a new baby, number nine, can you believe it? She needs my help."

"Pleased to meet you, Mrs…." Solveig dreaded listening to her prattle for a hundred miles. Solveig would no more wear bright orange than a bucket over her head. Surely, she could make an excuse for moving. A few seats stood vacant by the stove. The only open seat in the rear was beside the drunk man. She pitied the one stuck with him.

"Mrs. Roverbo," the woman said.

Solveig introduced herself and made small talk as more passengers entered the car.

"Brainerd is a wild place," Mrs. Roverbo whispered. "Terrible. Saloons on every street. Criminals and confidence men. Peculation and drunkenness prevalent." She shuddered. "Liv says it is not safe for a woman to walk alone on the streets. Is your husband meeting you?" Her piercing eyes searched Solveig's face, as if seeking impropriety.

Solveig shook her head. "I'm widowed."

A nun dressed in a black and white habit entered the car. She was tall and heavy set, a giant, really. Of course, she looked taller with her head gear and long folds of cloth. The sister headed to the open seat beside the man across the aisle.

"*Uff da,*" Mrs. Roverbo hissed and pulled her skirts aside. She spoke in a loud whisper. "Minnow eaters right here in Fergus."

The nun overheard Mrs. Roverbo's rude comment, but her eyes showed merriment. There was a steady calm about her person. Solveig knew better than to put up with the monkery so despised by Martin Luther.

The drunk man woke up and gaped at the nun. He pulled over and hugged the wall as the sister sat down beside him.

Mrs. Roverbo pulled her shawl tighter and flagged the conductor. "Can just anyone ride the cars?" She pointed her chin toward the nun.

"Yes, ma'am." His wide smile flashed white teeth. "Anyone with a ticket."

"Can you believe a man would force his daughter into such a life? No woman would wear such garb of her own free will." Mrs. Roverbo sniffed. "Slaves of the Pope."

The nun looked their way, and Solveig saw in her expression what she thought was amusement. Mrs. Roverbo's rudeness was laughable. The baby screeched. The young mother tried to both sooth him and keep the toddler busy. Solveig thought to lend the poor woman a hand, but the nun reached over and took the toddler. The sister dangled her rosary in front of the little one while the young mother nursed the baby.

The train lurched forward, chugging east toward logging country.

Lutherans were dead set against Catholics, but at her age, Solveig would not easily be persuaded into popery, even if the nun tried to proselytize. If she had a chance, Solveig would like to inquire about the kind of life she led. Women had few options, even in these modern times. Solveig suspected the nun had an interesting story.

"Did your sister have a boy or girl?" Solveig said. If only she could trade places with the drunken man. Funny that she, a Lutheran, preferred sitting with a nun rather than with a Lutheran minister's sister-in-law.

With that, Mrs. Roverbo pulled a letter from her reticule, and read the entire thing aloud. Solveig listened with one ear, worrying about the team. Bitterness tasted in her mouth. She deserved better than what she had been given in life. Rasmuss was gone. Halvor married that spoiled brat. Solveig wiped a smudge off the window, and peered out as the train moved east.

Trees lined the tracks on both sides. She had become a woman of the prairie, used to open vistas and solitude. Mrs. Roverbo's constant chatter irritated like her aching bunions before a change in weather.

Solveig's age settled hard on her bones. What if she could not save the farm despite her best efforts? What if she were forced into the Poor Farm? What if she must bow and scrape for charity after a lifetime of standing on her own? What if she never heard from Halvor again?

Her future loomed like a threat. All her life she had looked forward to betterment. Now she faced decline. She was too old for this. Too old to change.

The man across the aisle woke with a snort. Solveig shook her head. He should be ashamed of himself. She thought to thank him for his help with Young Bob.

She did not.

Chapter 5
Nels

Nels closed his eyes and rested his throbbing head against the cool window glass. Another hundred miles and he would arrive in Brainerd, in the heart of timber country. He thought to bum a ride north on a spur line to Gull River Timber. He carried no money for a ticket.

A nun plopped beside him. She was tall and stout and filled the wooden bench. Just his rotten luck. He pulled as far away as possible. She smelled of lye soap.

To spend the night with a penguin? What would the boys at camp say? Nels scanned the car for an empty seat to no avail. Even worse were the bawling brats ahead of him. Damn his bad luck. He should have walked.

The car rounded a curve and puffs of engine smoke spiraled into the sky. The toddler screamed. The nun spoke kindly to the woman and took the toddler into her lap. Nels pressed closer against the window. If he flattened himself just right, he glimpsed the mother's breast as she nursed the baby. She was not bad looking and her breasts bulged with milk.

The baby slept and the mother retrieved the child with a sincere thank you. The nun reached into her bag for bread and cheese. Nels's belly growled. She must have heard, for she handed part to him.

At first, he shook his head, but he had eaten nothing since breakfast the day before. He mumbled his thanks and gobbled it down. The nun offered a few crumbs to the little child ahead of them. The nun was about his age. Maybe twenty-five. Her face looked young.

"I'm Sister Magdalena," she said. "Heading back to Duluth."

Nels mumbled something about the logging camps.

"Our hospital cares for loggers," she said. "Dangerous work."

She was not so bad. Nels hunched against the window and feigned sleep. Out of the corner of his eye he saw her fingering beads. Nels was not much of a Lutheran, but his priest in Denmark had warned against praying a rosary. He squeezed his eyes tight.

Maybe she would pray that his luck would change and he could send for his parents. He was not any good at prayer himself.

Impossible. He dozed through the long afternoon. They halted in small villages along the way to refill the water tanks, and the journey turned into a halting and jerking misery. Men hiked alongside the tracks toting turkeys on their backs. Everyone headed to timber country. Far better to ride the cars, even though the hard seat made his hinder sore.

Evening slipped into darkness. The sister prayed many times. He needed prayer, but pride locked his mouth. The nun got out at a water stop and returned with a few apples. She offered one to Nels with a smile. How sweet it tasted. Afterwards, he slipped into a restless sleep, startled when the porter called out, "Brainerd!"

An older woman across the aisle gathered bundles and baskets from the rear of the car.

Nels stumbled past, not waiting to help her, as his mother would have insisted. He needed to be first in line to pick a plum job.

An engine with two cars huffed and smoked on the next track. He sneaked around the back of the caboose. No one was in sight. Yard apes were known to beat stowaways with truncheons. He scrambled up the side of the car and stretched flat on top.

His face felt as stubbly as the ragged straw in the wheat fields of North Dakota. He blew into his hand, smelling the stink. He used both hands to smooth his hair. His insides growled.

He would soon be eating at Gull River Timber. The jacks feasted at every meal. He remembered the haunches of beef and slabs of pies.

The train creaked forward and black smoke belched from the stack. He pulled up his collar and hugged the top of the car as he listened to the calls of flying geese and the locomotive whistle. The wind carried a whiff of balsam. Piles of logging debris littered the butchered hillsides. A person could walk for miles from stump to stump without touching the ground. Logging opened land for farming. He pitied the poor farmer dealing with all the stumps.

They arrived at Gull Lake. Nels climbed down and trotted toward the office at the edge of the water. Gull River Timber paid the best wages. Nels had worked for them the winter before as a swamper, clearing the brush around the trees so the fellers could get at them. He helped build corduroy roads over the swampy places by laying long poles horizontally side to side. Those roads jarred your teeth, but were better than slogging through mud. He even drove the ice wagon. He came with experience.

Last year the company logged the south and east area, and this year they would log the north and west. They used the same camp to spare the expense of rebuilding someplace else. Crews hired on through the summer to clear logging trails and ready for the coming season.

Better wages waited for those sharp enough to snag the best jobs. He was not a greenhorn anymore, and this was his year to improve himself. Trees crashed somewhere behind the buildings. He pushed open the screen door.

"Shut the door for the flies," the man at the desk said with a snarl. He wore a green tinted visor and square spectacles. His fingers carried indigo stains, and a blue patch on his lower lip revealed his habit of wetting a pen in his mouth. He looked maybe a decade older than Nels.

The clerk leapt to his feet, brandishing a fly swatter like a sword. His arm blurred in a flurry of swatting. "Now you've done it." He stood breathless from his massacre. "I almost had them cleaned out. What do you want?"

Horses brought flies. Nels restrained himself from explaining the futility of the man's exertions. No matter how many flies the pencil pusher killed, he would never get them all. Especially with a ragged window screen.

"I'm looking for work." The expensive train ticket paid off in the end.

"Your name again?" He snatched a fly in his bare hand, squished it and dropped it in the spittoon, leaving a smear of blood on his fingers. "We have a variety of jobs open."

When Nels gave his name, the man turned to a short list beside the inkwell. He looked up with suspicion. "I was mistaken. Everything is filled," he said with a cold look in his eye. He bent over his ledgers.

"Look again." He felt the blood drain from his face. "I worked here last year."

"Nothing for you here." The man smashed a fly crawling on the table. "Be on your way."

Nels jerked his jacket tighter around his shoulders. Pissant pencil-pusher. He swallowed a knot of anger. It was not fair. Last year ended in disaster, but Nels was neither a thief nor liar.

Nels held the door open as he hefted his turkey. Clouds of flies swarmed around the clerk who launched another killing spree.

"Shut the door," he yelled. "Damn you."

Nels slammed it as hard as he could. His cheeks burned. Midseason the previous year, the bull of the woods transferred him to the ice crew. Nels sprinkled water over the ice-roads to smooth them for the giant loads of logs. He worked all night and slept during the day. How could he prove his innocence when no one was around to vouch for him?

Nels suspected Jacob Pettibone stole money while Nels slept. Jacob, oily and slick, always lurked on the fringes. More rotten luck.

Nels stood on the steps and contemplated his next move. It was too risky to bum a ride back to Brainerd on the train. The railroad men already looked his way.

Horses skidded logs to the landing. It would not be work to spend the day with horses

"Get going," the pencil pusher yelled through the screen. "You're not welcome here."

Bile rose in the back of Nels's mouth. Sonofabitch Yankee. He left Denmark expecting pork fat fried in its own grease. Instead, he had no job, only a few pennies to his name and no idea what to do next. He was ruined.

He pulled handbills from his turkey, ones saved for toilet paper. He knew most of the camps, but not Starkweather Timber. Nels stuck his head through the door.

"Hey mister," Nels said, "Where's Starkweather Timber?"

"You again? Shut the door!" The flyswatter blurred in the clerk's hand.

"Where is it?"

"Up the Mississippi as far as the Skunk River and west to Stink Lake. It's a long haul."

"Know anything about it?"

"Git," the clerk said. "I've said all I'm going to say."

Nels wanted to wring that little weasel's neck. He would like to dynamite Gull River Timber Company to hell. He had to do something or he would explode.

He stalked around the side of the building, looked around to make sure no one could see him, and unbuttoned his trousers. He took aim and pissed on the wall, aiming as high as he could, spreading his mark like an old timber wolf.

The anger left with the pissing, leaving him both triumphant and overwhelmed. What could he do? His plans for a prosperous season fizzled away.

He fastened his trousers, and reached again for the Starkweather handbill. Hard telling if Starkweather was reputable or some haywire outfit that would rob him blind. One never knew with maverick operations.

There were other camps. He would try them before risking the unknown. Maybe there was still time before the farm hands arrived.

Damn Jacob Pettibone.

Nels took a breath and trotted to the shoreline where he hailed a mail boat just leaving the dock. The oarsman was an older man wearing a chambray shirt with sleeves rolled up to his elbows. A grimy fisherman's sweater knotted around his waist, and a corncob pipe clamped in the corner of his mouth.

"Where you going?" Nels said.

"Back to town." The mailman mumbled around the pipe stem. "Need a ride?"

"If it's not too much trouble." A boat ride would spare aching feet.

"Trouble is yours. You can row."

A steady wind chopped the waters, and white caps turned the lake into a checkerboard of blue and white. Seagulls swooped around them, dipping into the water with their bills. The mailman pulled on his sweater before dropping a line over the side of the boat. Then he leaned back for the ride.

"Where you heading?"

Nels felt the pull of water against muscle. He was a lot younger than the mailman and strong from working the harvest, and yet he grew almost too breathless to speak. He yanked off his jacket. "Know anything about Starkweather Timber?"

"Heard old Starkweather is a mean sonofabitch," the mailman said. "Wins timber stands in poker games—and has a reputation for cheating." He jerked his line and pulled a glistening fish into the boat. "Holy smokes, look at the size of this pike."

The fish struggled and slapped his tail against the floor of the boat, sending a spray of water onto Nels's face and bags of mail. Gulls shrieked. The mailman gloated.

"Why go so far north when places around here are hiring?" the mailman said. "Pay is better with the big boys. Waste of shanks mare to look elsewhere, if you ask me."

Nels bent into the oars and rowed. His muscles burned.

"Want me to spell you?" the mailman said. "Takes a lot of elbow grease to get across Gull Lake. I am used to it."

Nels shook his head. He had agreed to row the boat in return for a ride. He would stick to his word. "Does he pay up on time?"

"Starkweather? Haven't heard otherwise." The man wrestled the hook out of the fish's mouth. "Works his men like a sonofabitch." An eagle glided over the boat, and geese gathered on the water, making ready to head south. "There's talk of shenanigans with the ladies."

Nels did not care what the boss did if he paid his men. "I'm not scared of work."

"Good thing." The man cast his line again. "You'll find plenty of it in this life."

They discussed other timber companies in the area. The mailman had mail for them, and Nels tagged along, though his back ached and his arms felt on fire. Every place was hiring, but when Nels gave his name, the doors slammed in his face. Thick as thieves, those lumber barons. Nosy as old hens at a church social. He was blackballed.

He ended the day in a Brainerd saloon, lingering over a glass of ale. Nels had once prided himself on his common sense, but lately it had left him. How could he have let himself be swindled by Myron Pinchpenny?

He fingered the coins in his pocket. A logging camp provided room and board. Another job would leave nothing after paying for a rooming house. Besides, if the logging camps around Brainerd would not hire him, maybe the businessmen wouldn't either. Word traveled fast. Perhaps he could change his name.

"Another beer?" the barkeep said.

Nels recognized a Danish accent and introduced himself. Johann Carlson stood squatty and muscular with a wide face and brown eyes.

Nels would rather drink than eat. He nursed the glass of ale as long as he could. His stomach twisted. This should not be happening. He was a good worker.

He studied the Starkweather advert again. Might be he could catch a ride on a keelboat.

"Know of any barges going upriver?" The comfort of speaking his mother-tongue warmed him as much as the ale. "Thinking of trying Starkweather Timber."

"Supplies head to the big operations by steamboat these days." The man fetched a crock of pickled eggs and pushed it toward Nels. "But keelboats still supply the jobber camps."

Nels shook his head.

"On the house." The man winked.

Nels eyed the eggs. "I appreciate your kindness, sir." He swallowed hard. "I'll not deny that my stomach is scraping my backbone, but my folks taught me to work for my keep."

The barkeep broke into a huge grin. "My God, we have enough work in this place to keep you going all night." He pulled a stained apron from a nail on the wall behind the bar. "I can't give you a job, but I'll give you supper if you wash these dishes."

About midnight, Nels finished the last dirty glass. He sank into the corner of the saloon where the barkeeper allowed. Nels pulled his jacket closer around his shoulders.

"There's jobber camps scattered through the woods," the barkeep said. "Captain Ben said he is heading north day after tomorrow. You might trade labor for passage on the *Mud Hen* as far as Stink Lake."

"It is a long way up there. Who knows if Starkweather is still hiring?" Nels said.

"The undertaker down the street is looking for someone." He blew out the lamps and barred the door. "It would be a lot closer than Stink Lake."

Chapter 6
Sister Magdalena

How odd to be idle in the middle of the day. Sister Magdalena entered the chapel and tried to pray. The sun shone through the stained glass, refracting the light like a prism.

Her trip to Fergus Falls proved uneventful. She arrived on time, drank tea from primrose teacups, and ate dainty sandwiches cut in the shape of shamrocks. She pinned the bank draft from the benefactor securely inside her habit.

Sister Magdalena sneaked a peek at the bank draft while at the depot. Her eyes almost popped out of her head at the number of zeroes. The sisters could repair the orphanage roof, start the school in International Falls, and perhaps have enough to build another hospital.

Her seat partner on the train convinced Sister Magdalena even more of the needs of the lumberjacks. Nels Jensen's growling belly had kept her awake as they traveled. Poor sot. A nice enough man, but bogged into the mire of alcohol.

Mother Superior expected Sister Magdalena to hear what God might say about a future work assignment.

Open my mouth O Lord to bless thy holy name. Cleanse my heart also from all vain, perverse and distracting thoughts.

Her thoughts went back to the train ride and the mother with a toddler and a newborn. The naughty two-year-old was rambunctious, no doubt as Sister Magdalena had been at that age.

Sister Magdalena had been born Ida Widegrave, the only daughter in a farm family with eight older brothers. She grew

taller than the boys and could hit a baseball farther. Her class-
mates teased her about big feet and broad hands. "Lummox!" the
boys chanted when she tripped over the hearthstone or slipped
on the icy path.

Even so, none of them could outspell her during the Friday bees
or surpass her in her studies. Ida devoured every book she could find
and begged for more. She borrowed books from their parish priest
about the saints, martyrs, and great theologians of the Church. The
priest was the only person she knew with a personal library.

She took top marks in geography and Latin. She graduated
from eighth grade at the head of her class, but additional schooling was not possible for a poor farm girl. It didn't matter that she
was smart. The years passed, and her friends found husbands.

Men were not interested in a girl taller than they, or smart-
er. Of course, there were men, usually older widow-men, who
sought wives to help with farm work or care for their children.
Harvey Schmitz approached her father several times. Schmitz
had a house full of children and a hundred acres of land under
tillage. He could barely read and write. Marrying him meant a life
of servitude, of losing herself.

Her priest suggested religious life as an alternative. "A strong
and smart girl like you would be a help in missions."

Ida knew a few religious sisters. Those holy women devoted
themselves to prayer. They were educated, independent of husbands, but obedient to a prioress. Ida reasoned that if she had to be
under the authority of someone else, as her father said all women
must be, she would rather obey a woman than some old farmer.

"You'd go crazy in a cloistered convent," her brother said one
day when they were pitching hay into the haybarn. She had confided her dream of entering the convent. "You are a tomboy. They
will never let you in."

She socked his arm. They chased around the barn, throwing
hay down each other's necks, shrieking, and causing enough commotion that their father scolded from the milk house. Even so, she
knew he was right. She would not fit into a cloistered community.

The priest spoke of religious orders where nuns served in more tangible ways. Benedictines were building schools and hospitals across Minnesota. "It is a hard life. You could do it."

Her father, at first skeptical, agreed to pray about it. He looked older than his sixty years, still grieving the loss of his wife. Two of her brothers were married by this time, and their wives took over the household.

One day, her father called her into the kitchen. The smell of fried fish lingered in the air, and Ida propped opened a window to freshen the room. A spring breeze fluttered papers on the table. Papa placed his hand on his newspaper to hold it in place.

"The priest is right about your vocation." Papa's eyes showed the weight of his decision. "You have taken all the schooling there is around here, and Lord knows your potential. This is your chance, but I hate to see you go."

"Oh Papa." She burst into tears and hugged him tight around his neck. His beard pricked her cheeks, and he smelled of sweat and barn. She couldn't explain why she cried, whether it was joy, relief, or the sudden grief of knowing his permission meant leaving home once and for all. Nuns rarely returned home. Maybe for a parent's funeral.

"Papa," she said through her tears. "Thank you, Papa."

"Think, Daughter, think hard. Taking religious vows is serious business. No horsing around like you do with your brothers."

The sound of footsteps in the hallway jolted Sister Magdalena back to the present. She pulled her rosary from her pocket. The coral beads had been her father's wedding gift to her mother. When she left for Duluth, her father pressed the rosary into her hands.

"Your mother would want you to have this." Papa choked with emotion. "Remember that your conduct reflects on her—and all of us."

She accepted the beads, overwhelmed with the realization that she might never see her home or father again. The swing in the old oak tree swayed in the breeze, her favorite calf frolicked in the pasture, and her brothers left the hayfield to say goodbye.

She wanted to both stay and leave, but she had to choose. The future dangled like a dream before her eyes. She kissed them all and left Wisconsin to follow God.

She never regretted her decision. The letter last year arrived too late for her to attend her father's funeral.

Sister Magdalena pulled her thoughts back to the present. She bowed her head and meditated on the Sorrowful Mysteries. She paused where Simon the Cyrene was compelled to carry the Cross of Christ. She did not want to be forced to follow Christ.

She prayed for the passengers on the train. For Nels Jensen, the young mother so harried and worn, the older woman across the aisle, and the woman in flamboyant finery with her accusations. She prayed for the porter, trudging up and down the aisle. How tired he had looked. She should have helped him.

She began the novena for the benefactor who had donated money for their mission. Then she prayed for her brothers, sisters-in-law, nieces, and nephews.

She had learned her alphabet by reciting her brothers' names: Ambrose, Benjamin, Clarence, Dominic, Ethelbert, Francis, George, and Herbert. Her mother named the children alphabetically, and Ida came after eight sons. Her mother longed for a daughter, someone to help her with the housework. Instead, God sent Ida, tall and strong as her brothers, hopeless at cooking, and greedy for sweets and second helpings.

"Ida." Mama groaned. "I prayed for a daughter, and God sent a whirlwind."

Sister Magdalena fought impatience. She wanted this day of prayer to end. Obviously, God was not in a chatty mood.

At least not to her.

Ida encountered God at her First Communion. Kneeling at the altar, she received the Body, Blood, Soul, and Divinity of the Blessed Savior. She felt a sweetness beyond beauty, a bit of heaven, along with a stirring that stayed with her. She wanted to do something with her life, something bigger.

She told her mother.

"A calling, you say?" Mama said.

"I'm not sure," Ida said. Once the words left her mouth it was too late to take them back. She felt like a lightning bug caught on a pin.

Mama fetched the Holy Water and made the sign of the cross on top of Ida's head. Then she removed the Saint Benedict medal from around her neck. She kissed it and slipped it over Ida's head.

"Maybe God has a plan, maybe not," Mama had said. "My father gave this medal to me on my Confirmation Day. Lose it, and I will skin you alive."

Sister Magdalena sighed and fingered the Saint Benedict medal from that long-ago day. She was impatient with Novice Agatha, let alone a room filled with dull students. She could only imagine the headache of trying to keep the orphans quiet. Once again, she felt drawn to do something else, something to help the loggers and their families.

The community meeting loomed like a dark cloud. God promised to lead her, even if she could not hear His voice. It was enough to take one step at a time. Even when He was silent.

Chapter 7
Solveig

Solveig had watched the nun during the journey. Catholics were less enlightened than Lutherans, yet the sister demonstrated unusual piety. While Solveig stewed about Halvor and inwardly cursed the chatterbox beside her, the nun prayed and helped the young mother.

The nun nodded to Solveig as they left the cars in Brainerd. The young man who had helped with the horses shoved between them, interrupting any chance at conversation.

"Watch yourself," Mrs. Roverbo hissed at her back. "Why that young man might just as soon knock you on the head and steal your money as look at you." She clutched Solveig's arm and leaned closer. "You have to be more careful."

Knock her on the head, indeed. Solveig's muscles bulged after years of farm work. She was steady on her feet. If anyone tried to steal from her, she would make him regret it.

Her father always said to keep her nose out of other people's business. Solveig hurried to the stock car, anxious to get away from the busybody.

"Hurry!" Gunnar waved to her. "The train leaves for Gull River Timber right away."

Solveig needed a few minutes to clean up before meeting prospective employers, but the smaller train already belched black smoke and tooted its horn. Gunnar fetched her trunk and Solveig lugged crates and bundles into the stock car, the homey odors of horse and hay a welcome change from Mrs. Roverbo. Young Bob and Buck whinnied. She lowered Queenie into the straw.

Solveig's eyes adjusted to the gloom and she sat on a bench in the far corner. She unlatched the crate and loosed the hens. She held on as the locomotive lurched backwards.

Queenie yowled and leapt into her lap.

Gunnar yawned. "Now that you are here to keep watch, I'll stretch out for a snooze. We'll be there in an hour."

Solveig had not considered that Gunnar must remain awake to watch the team. Her cheeks warmed. Her son danced and played whist while Gunnar shouldered his responsibilities.

"Many thanks," she said. "I can never repay you."

"You can." He sprawled across the straw. "Let me hire out with your team. Better pay for me, and a closer watch over Young Bob and Buck. I would not trust a team of my own to a barn boss. Both of us get ahead."

Solveig wished Halvor was as sensible as her godson. She numbered her grievances against him as they chugged north to Gull Lake. Young Bob tossed his head and Buck rolled anxious eyes. Gunnar snored.

Solveig sprinkled grain for the hens. Queenie scurried after a mouse. Solveig squinted through a crack between the slats to peek outside.

Great corridors of pine trees lined the tracks. Their piney smell blended with engine stink. Then an open stretch. Solveig gasped. Ragged stumps, piles of slash, and branches littered the ground. A man skidded logs with a gray horse. The gray stepped between the stumps. A sharp stob alongside a hoof or a protruding branch could injure that horse. She patted Buck, reminding herself that Gunnar would care for the team.

First came the ax and then the plow. It was not pretty.

She rested her eyes, unable to sleep. She prayed the Lord's Prayer but stalled at *forgive us our trespasses as we forgive those who trespass against us.* She would never forgive Halvor and Britta. She could not.

After what seemed forever, the train slowed with squealing brakes.

"Gull Lake. We are finally here." Gunnar stood to his feet and brushed straw from his clothing. Young Bob whinnied and braced as the train stopped. "Wait with the horses while I find out where we go."

Gunnar opened the doors, jumped down, and hailed a railroad man nearby. Solveig tucked a stray lock of hair under her braids and smoothed her skirts. She shooed the hens into the crate. She held Queenie at the door of the car.

A man climbed off the top of the car and skulked behind a pile of freight before he beelined toward a building by the lake. Solveig hoped he found a job. She hoped they all would. *God, please. Let there be work.* She squeezed Queenie until the cat yowled.

"Sorry," Solveig said to the cat. "Guess I'm nervous." She secured Queenie in her basket with clammy hands and a tickling throat. "Be patient."

Why was Gunnar taking so long? The sun sparkled on the waves and a flock of geese settled on the choppy water.

The man from the train slammed out of the building, and banged the door. Things must not have gone well for him. He stalked around the side of the building and, in full view of the boxcar, pissed on the wall. It was an act of defiance, the voiceless protest of someone without a say. He buttoned his trousers and trotted toward a boat by the dock.

Pissing on Gull River Timber. She grinned. She wished she could piss like a man. She would piss on that banker who would not extend her note. She would piss on Britta. Maybe on Halvor, too. She laughed aloud as the pisser rowed away and Gunnar returned to the car.

"We'll leave the team and baggage until we speak to the clerk in the office," Gunnar said. "The cars head back to Brainerd in an hour."

Solveig eyed her trunk. Safer to keep it with her, but it was too heavy to drag along. Gunnar promised to tote it to her quarters once she secured a job.

An emotional wave, stronger than any whitecaps on the lake, shook her confidence. She wanted to talk to the railroad man herself. What if they misunderstood, and the train whisked away while they were in the office?

She acted like an old woman worried about the price of butter. She reined her anxieties. Gunnar knew what he was doing.

Solveig stretched a crick from her lower back. A brisk gale fluttered her bonnet strings. Her body relaxed. She was a prairie woman, more comfortable in open spaces. The waves dipped like grasses in the wind.

She followed Gunnar to the office. Crashing sounds came from beyond the wall of green. A horse whinnied, and a man called "timber."

Gunnar opened the door for Solveig to enter.

"Shut the door for the flies." A clerk shrieked and swatted in a swirl of arms and swatter. "Just get them cleaned out and someone lets another bunch in." He wore a red face, a frayed suit, and a partial cap with a green visor. "What do you want?"

This weasel held her future in his sweaty hands. No wonder the pisser left his mark.

She waited for Gunnar to answer. He asked about a job as skidder with his own team. They talked wages. If Halvor had been there to manage the team, their combined wages would have paid the note.

A black anger rose in her chest. That Jezebel had ruined her son.

"Your mother can return on the train," the clerk said. "I'll show you the stable." He swatted a fly on his desk with enough force to fell an ox.

"I'm not his mother." Solveig licked her teeth, always dry when she felt nervous. She took a breath and pulled back her shoulders. "I'm a cook looking for work."

The clerk pushed his visor back and looked her over. "Impossible," he said without hesitation. "We do not hire petticoats. None of the operations do." He reached over and swatted a fly on the wall, and another crawling on the window glass. "Women are trouble. You know what I mean." He straightened his visor and looked at her with a grimace. "Even old ones."

So, he named her old and troublesome. A sudden sob clutched Solveig's throat and she swallowed hard lest she further embarrass herself. She wanted to give him a *chiliwink* that would make the miserable creature's ears ring.

"I own the team," Solveig said, searching for a scrap of dignity in this terrible situation.

"Good for you," the clerk said. "We've hired your son and your team."

Solveig steamed. Had he no respect for his elders? Gunnar grasped her elbow and steered her outside. He nodded to the clerk as if in apology. It did not assuage her wounded pride.

The breeze caught Solveig's skirts and wrapped her in a calico cocoon. Overhead an eagle rounded, dove down, and plucked a fish from the water. She breathed in the balsam and lake, and willed calmness to return.

"Good news," Gunnar said with a grin. "I'll manage the team and hand over their wages to you in the spring." He pleaded. "We both come out ahead. Your team will be safe with me."

Gunnar had his mother's clear eyes and determined chin. He had made up his mind. She couldn't blame him, though she tasted the bitterness of the situation. Invisible, she was. A woman alone, inconsequential and unseen. Her cooking skills did not matter. She wore a dress and could not be hired.

"Return to Brainerd," Gunnar said. "Buy a ticket home. Halvor will give you a ride from Fergus Falls." He sympathized, but assured her it was for the best. "You see how men act. A logging camp is no place for a lady."

Grief pressed hard on her windpipe, and she took a ragged breath. Then another. Her godson did not ask if the team's wages would pay her note. They would not.

She expected Britta to carry her weight on the farm, though her daughter-in-law knew nothing about chores. Now it was Solveig's turn to stand alone.

Gunnar unloaded Young Bob and Buck, their shiny-black coats a tribute to the curry comb Solveig used on their backs. She thought to kiss them goodbye, but hesitated. Kissing horses was something Britta would do.

Anger sparked her resolve. To hell with Gull River Timber. The young man from the train had the right idea. Piss on them. Piss on them all.

She stalked to the train and perched on the hard seat inside. The hens stared with bright eyes from the crate. Gumbri cooed encouragement, a friendly sound in the dim light. A railroad worker latched the door. The car felt lonelier without Gunnar and the team. She settled back to determine her next step. She needed to figure something out by nightfall. She could not afford a hotel.

She could try other camps, but she did not have a way to get to them—or a means to carry her trunk. It cost money to hire a dray. She might seek employment in Brainerd instead of going to the camps. Hotels hired cooks and maids. A small wage, no doubt, not enough to pay the bank. She was too tired to sleep, too frazzled to think and almost beside herself with worry. She tallied the wages from the team, and subtracted that number from the note. Halvor would have satisfied the bank if he had not deserted her. But now, *vonlaus*, hopeless.

The train clattered. Her bunions predicted bad weather. Solveig squeezed Queenie until the cat yowled. A plan fell into place.

She would cache both trunk and hens with the stationmaster. He might accommodate her for a few eggs. She once worked as a servant. She knew how to farm, launder clothes, do basic sewing and raise a child. She was not about to give up yet. Not by a long shot.

Chapter 8
Nels

The next morning, Nels stopped at the undertaker's office. *Bean and Green Undertakers and Furniture* scrawled across a plate glass window on Laurel Street. A hand written sign stuck in the corner: *Help Wanted, Slackers need not Apply.*

Inside wooden caskets stacked in one corner and wooden chairs filled another. A coffin balanced on two saw horses near the front window. The deceased was a young man about his age and wore the same shirt. One side of his head looked misshapen. Cedar boughs lining the inside of the casket did not eliminate a fetid odor.

"May he rest in peace," said a wheezy voice at Nels's elbow. "Are you a friend or relative?"

Nels shook his head and stepped back, tripping over his own feet.

The man with the wheezy voice wore a white shirt under a black waistcoat. He reeked of chemicals and soap. He was older than Nels and his sparse hair slicked with oil.

"Strange the ways of the Lord." He rubbed his hands together in front of his chest. "Some live too long, and others, like this poor boy, are snatched in their prime." When he spoke, his Adam's apple bounced in his long neck.

"I don't know him," Nels said.

The man brightened at the information. He drew himself up to his full height, and clicked his heels together as if he were a military officer.

"You're here about another funeral. My name is Mr. Thaddeus Bean," the man said with a slight bow. "We service all Christian religions." He stepped closer and Nels stepped away, jostling the sawhorse. "We give a nice two-dollar funeral. Embalmment extra, of course. The trains convenient for those to be interned elsewhere."

"Not here about a funeral. I saw the sign in your window," Nels said. A train whistle blew loud and long. A lumber wagon rattled down the street. A shriek came from the sawmill on the nearby Mississippi River. "I'm looking for work."

"Even better." The undertaker relaxed his shoulders and removed his waistcoat. "We seek someone willing to give an honest day's work in return for excellent compensation."

Nels introduced himself and asked about the job.

"You will dig graves, set markers, fetch ice and unguents, drive the hearse, and tend the horses. I have an extra suit that might fit. You need to look professional to deal with the public."

Horses appealed to him and the duties seemed reasonable. The pay equaled what he had earned at the bonanza farm.

"Are you by any chance a vocalist?" Mr. Bean carried a hopeful gleam in his eyes. "A strong Irish tenor would be an advantage."

"No." Nels might not get the job after all. "I used to play the harmonica a little."

"Hmm. I have not been asked for harmonica music, but one never knows. A little music lightens the heavy hearts of the bereaved. Wouldn't you agree, sir?" Mr. Bean leaned over and sniffed the casket. "Hmm. You are turning." He pulled more balsam branches from the shelf and tucked them around the body. "I cannot wait to plant you, my rotting friend."

"What happened to him?" Nels's voice cracked. He tried not to breathe.

"This careless man was struck by a runaway team." Mr. Bean arranged a cedar bough in the corpse's hands like a nosegay. "Sadly, a cautionary tale to exercise attention when crossing streets." He turned to the corpse, almost as if Nels were not present. "You have no one to mourn you, dear friend, and your burial cannot be postponed. Nothing personal, but your smell grows offensive, and soon you will burst out of your skin." He chuckled a reedy laugh.

"Who is he?" Nels shuddered, Mr. Bean's conversation with the dead man unnerving.

"Likely some bloke heading to the woods," Mr. Bean said. "There's always a few who come to us without kith or kin." Mr. Bean's voice drifted away and he stared out the window, then snapped back to the business at hand. "He strong but unlucky. Perhaps a Swede?"

Nels shrugged. The man looked like a hundred other men he had known. Sturdy shoes worn thin in the soles. Canvas overalls and cheap flannel shirt. Curly blond hair framing his bruised face. Looked like the horses had run right over him. Maybe he had been drunk. The mournful sound of a whistling train sounded over the street sounds outside the shop. "How will you get word to his folks?"

Mr. Bean shrugged. "*Bean and Green* cannot be responsible for those who do not carry identification. This man had no letter of introduction, no laundry label, nothing." He sighed. "Luckily for us, he had enough cash on him to pay for his burial. But not enough for a marker. A pauper's grave, I am afraid."

Nels swallowed hard. Nels had no ties in America other than the jacks and field hands he worked with and his drinking pals on payday. He carried no identification. Of course, he gave such information at the logging camps, but Nels had never considered he might die of other causes.

"You will collect corpses at any hour. God calls day or night and we must oblige." Mr. Bean was all business now. "And prepare the graves."

Nels fumbled to think clearly. "I'll need a place to stay if I take the job."

Mr. Bean pointed to the corner where the coffins stacked high. "You can sleep in one of those if you'd like." His Adam's apple bobbed again. "Pull one into the storeroom if you're squeamish," he chortled. "Our customers will not bother." He pointed his chin toward the back door. "There's a Chinese laundry down the street and a boarding house for a reasonable fee." He looked Nels over from head to toe and leaned closer. "In return for these amenities, you would be expected to be available to assist as needed." His voice dropped to a whisper. "Embalming cannot be done alone."

Nels startled. He had handled dead animals and it could not be much different. He was not superstitious but his stomach clenched just the same. It was time he made something of himself. Five years in America and nothing to show for it.

Mr. Bean gave directions to the cemetery. "I will teach you the business, Mr. Jensen. Everyone dies. A young man like you could make a fine living in mortuary science."

"I'll need an advance," Nels said. Last year a man asked for an advance at the bonanza farm and received it, much to everyone's amazement.

"I'll pay today's wages after his burial," Mr. Bean said. They shook hands. Mr. Bean's clasp was soft and woman-like. Nels wiped his hand on the back of his trousers.

"I'll help you load the coffin," Mr. Bean said. "Mr. Green describes decay as the smell of money, but even so, the odor is most permeating in hot weather, and is only a portent of greater indignities. We must quickly transport him to his final resting place."

Mr. Bean showed him to a small log barn out back. Nels gulped fresh air. The team, one dappled and one bay, nickered a welcome. Nels made friends with the horses as he loaded the coffin into the hearse and headed toward the edge of town. He slowed the team to a walk, thinking of the mishap of the hearse's occupant. A sawmill screamed. A farm boy sold pumpkins by the side of the road from a wagon heaped with the orange vegetables. An Indian hiked across the railroad tracks with a deer slung across his back. He tried to imagine living in Brainerd and becoming an undertaker. He imagined his name emblazoned on the window of the showroom: *Bean, Green and Jensen Undertakers and Furniture.*

Nels urged the horses to the top of the hill. Fall leaves crunched under their hooves. A woman hung laundry by a shack near the cemetery gate, the towels flapping in the wind. A dog dug in the weeds. Nels shooed the animal away. He found the numbered plot and began to dig. It was harder than he had expected, and difficult to square the corners. By the time he dug six feet down, Nels felt the sides of the grave pressing in. He could have stumbled while drunk into the path of a dray. He shuddered and leapt out of the dark hole.

The coffin had lifted easier with Mr. Bean on the other end. Nels jerked on the wooden box. A rough edge snagged the satin lining of the hearse with a sickening rip. Nels yanked harder. The box landed on one end at his feet. The corpse shifted inside.

What had Mr. Bean been thinking to send him out alone? Only the dog watched his every move. Nels looped a rope on one end and pulled it toward the misshapen grave.

It did not move.

Nels grunted and pulled harder. It did not budge. One edge of the wooden box dug into the soil. He tried to dig away the soil around the offending side. The horses nickered.

Of course. He secured the rope to the horse's halter and urged the animal forward. The coffin landed on its side in the dark hole. "Whoa."

He had made a mess of it.

Nels thought to bury the coffin as it landed. No one would ever know. The dog whimpered as if chiding him to remember his responsibility.

"You're right," Nels said to the dog. The dog wagged its tail. "He deserves better."

Nels jumped into the grave to reposition the coffin.

Something liquid dripped onto his hands. Nels scrambled out of the grave and rubbed his hands with dirt. His stomach churned and he tried very hard to think about something else.

Level or not, the coffin would rest where it landed. He filled the grave with soil, shoveling as fast as he could, the sandy pebbles bouncing off the wooden box. The dog wandered away as if in disgust.

There should be more than a cattywampus casket in an uneven hole in the ground. Everyone deserved at least a prayer. He counted three church spires from on top of the hill. A clergyman should pray over this poor man. A memory of the giant nun praying flitted through his mind. She would pray if she were present. He knew she would.

His mind roiled. Anything could happen. No one was safe. He pulled off his cap and mumbled *The Lord's Prayer* in Danish, though it had been a long time since confirmation and he had forgotten some of the words. His mother would be horrified to know that he had not once attended church in America, not even at Christmas.

Nels returned to the shop preoccupied with his own immortality. Life was short. Death waited for everyone. Mr. Bean came out of the back room to meet him. Another dead man stretched out on the table. Flies buzzed around the body. Church bells sounded somewhere in the village. The saw mill screeched a war whoop that raised the hair on Nels's neck.

"Just in time," Mr. Bean waved him over and nodded toward the corpse. "We need your assistance."

Nels inched toward the table. He could do it. There was good money in undertaking.

"Here," Mr. Bean handed him cotton wadding soaked in an aromatic. "Stuff his mouth with this."

Afterwards, Nels scrubbed himself at the pump next to the barn. He soaped himself a second time and rinsed in the rusty, icy water. He changed into his spare clothing in the storeroom and washed his dirty clothes under the spout outside. They reeked of that strange chemical smell that lingered in the shop. He scrubbed them again, and draped the wet clothes over a fence by the barn.

He penciled his name inside his shoes. The pencil would wear off in time, and he made a mental notation to keep it as bold as possible. He added his parents name and address. At least if he died, someone might be kind enough to notify his parents. He would not rest in an unmarked grave.

Mr. Bean handed Nels three silver dollars. "You've earned it. One for today and two in advance payment for the rest of the week." He turned to leave. "Tomorrow you will dig this man's grave. His funeral will be at Temple Baptist Church at three o'clock."

The weight of the silver cheered him a little. It was enough to buy a meal at the boarding house, but his stomach roiled. Thirst occupied his mind but he pushed it down with all his strength. Things were different this time. He would save his money and make a start.

"By the way," Mr. Bean reached into his pocket and pulled out a leather thong with a blue stone hanging from it. "This was on the man you just buried, a lucky charm I would suspect. Perhaps it will bring you more luck than it did that poor fellow." He tossed the pendant toward Nels and left.

A most unusual stone. With an apology toward the poor stiff in the cemetery, Nels slipped it around his neck. It did not belong to Nels, but it belonged to no one.

He balanced an empty casket across two saw horses in the back room as far away from the corpse as possible. Nels was used to bunkhouses of snoring men. This place stank worse than the camps. He tied balsam needles into a handkerchief around his nose. It helped a little. He climbed into the coffin, throwing his bedroll over himself.

Nels turned to his side and the coffin shifted. Nels turned on his back again, afraid to topple his bed and damage the inventory. He lay as still as he could, reading the labels of the bottles stacked around him as daylight faded. *Formaldehyde. Myrrh. Attar of roses. Arsenic. Lye. Sandalwood.* One of them was the source of the cloying stench. He counted the funeral wreaths stacked on top of a wooden box. The horses nickered from the stable out back. Flies buzzed around the windows.

He remembered the corpse in the next room. The sides of the coffin closed around Nels. Not a breath of fresh air. A bat swooped in the shadows. A fierce thirst burned his throat. He had money to quench it—and eternity to rest in a coffin.

Nels scrambled out of the box, grabbed his turkey, and stumbled from the shop. He retrieved his clothes off the line and was almost out of the yard when he remembered the dollars in his pocket. He had worked one day. He returned to the shop and placed two dollars on the table, keeping the one he had earned.

He eyed the money. He had worked hard enough that first day to earn more than his daily wage, but his parents had not raised a thief. He was an honest man despite Jacob Pettibone's accusations. A drunk, maybe, but an honest drunk.

The stink of the place brought bile to his throat. What had he been thinking? Starkweather Timber would be better than *Bean and Green*. Anything would.

Chapter 9
Sister Magdalena

In Duluth, Sister Magdalena remained in Saint Mary's Chapel after Mass, empty except for a young aspirant kneeling in the back pew. The sweetness of beeswax candles lingered in the air. The golden monstrance held the Blessed Sacrament. A silver crucifix hung behind the altar. Sunlight through the stained-glass window set the Sacred Heart of Jesus on fire.

Sister Magdalena lowered her bulk to the creaking kneeler.

She recognized the altar cloth as one she had worked on as a novice. How they struggled with those French knots. The result was a work of art, though Sister Magdalena had offered little help. In one corner was a small flaw where Sister Magdalena's scissors slipped while trimming threads. But still, a work of art like each person God had created.

Sister Magdalena gazed at the crucifix. His Holy face. His hideous death. His gruesome passion. Difficult beyond difficult. She knelt for a long time, letting the silence envelope her. The aspirant rustled and coughed, then left the chapel, still coughing, her shoes clicking on the wooden floors, and the door closing behind her.

Alone at last. Sister Magdalena allowed her body to relax. She crossed herself. *Hail Mary, full of grace.* Praying the rosary was like traveling by train. She started in one place and ended up somewhere else. Each Mystery showed glimpses into the life of Christ. No one could ever plumb His depths, no matter how often one meditated upon Him. With each bead, Sister Magdalena prayed for the sick in the wards, their families and especially for the lumberjacks in the woods.

Only poor people took the risky job. Rich men, educated men, chose easier work. If she were a man, she might have been a lumberjack, too.

Sister Magdalena forced her thoughts back to the crucifix. *Could you not wait with me one hour?* Jesus suffered alone as did the patients in the wards. Mr. Murphy's request reverberated in her mind.

If each lumberjack contributed a small sum to a health care fund. She shook her head, determined to hear from God. *The Lord is with thee.*

A dedicated fund so all could receive medical care without expense. Ridiculous. The men would not part with their hard-earned wages.

Blessed art thou amongst women, and blessed is the fruit of thy womb, Jesus.

A dollar would be enough. Thirty thousand men worked the woods of Minnesota. The money would care for injured loggers. Any leftover funds would build more hospitals.

Mother Superior would laugh in her face at such a preposterous idea.

Holy Mary, Mother of God, pray for us sinners now, and in the hour of our death.

Sister Magdalena prayed for her brothers in Wisconsin, and for the repose of her father's soul. She prayed for the wife of the dying man on the ward. Her thoughts swirled back to the idea of each paying a little for the good of all.

No matter what she did, her mind kept going back to the idea.

She prayed for Saint Michael the Archangel to defend her from the devil's onslaught. She determined to go to confession and seek counsel from a priest. She heard nothing from God.

Sister Lucy knew how to discern the voice of the Lord. She knew what to do in any situation. Sister Magdalena was wasting her time.

Chapter 10
Solveig

The next morning Solveig awakened on the station bench in the Brainerd depot. Every bone in her body complained. The place reeked of cigar smoke, and the room was cold enough to show her breath. She rubbed her arms and stomped her feet, trying to warm up before heading to the back house. She had slept in her clothes the last two nights and longed for a bath and hot meal.

The sign read *No overnight loitering.* She scurried out of the station as the stationmaster cast a dirty look in her direction. He was a nice man, and she would not abuse his kindness. She must return home unless she found employment that day.

Heavy fog drooped over Brainerd like a shroud. Solveig dodged between a dray and a milk wagon to cross Front Street. She balanced on the boards stretched across the mud, barely able to see the opposite side of the street in the murk.

Everything stank of garbage and sewage. Solveig lifted her skirts away from the filth. A pig splashed in the mud. Roosters crowed. A cow urinated on the boardwalk, spattering her dress. Dogs barked and a yoke of oxen pulled a lumber wagon. It seemed the entire animal population of Brainerd traveled the morning streets and sidewalks.

Solveig had spent the previous day searching for work. The Headquarters Hotel was hiring, but she would have nothing left after food and lodging. The banker's wife wanted a housekeeper in exchange for room and board. The Methodist church needed a char woman, but the pay was a dollar a week. She tallied to the penny what she needed for the bank note. Perhaps the banker's wife would let her work for room and board with the understanding that Solveig be allowed to char for the Methodist church on Saturdays. Still only a dollar a week. Not enough. Not even close.

It was time to let go of her pride to save the farm. Halvor would be furious if she took a job in a tavern. Rasmuss would roll over in his grave. Her people back in Norway would be horrified. Respectable women did not enter such establishments, let alone work amidst rough men and fancy ladies.

The one bright spot, if she must endure such humiliation, would be Britta's reaction. Like pissing on her wall. Let Britta explain to her father's parish about her mother-in-law's new job—the job made necessary because of Halvor's abandonment.

Solveig passed a log school building, and slowed to listen to the children playing in the yard. Solveig had longed for a large family. Instead, she had health and strength to make her own way.

Jack's Saloon on Laurel Street posted a hand-written *Help Wanted* sign in the window. It looked in better repair than most places. Hopefully that translated to better pay.

She mustered her courage to inquire when a tousled man stumbled out of the saloon. He bumped against her, reeking of liquor, pushing her onto the muddy street.

It was the pisser from Gull River Timber, the man who had helped calm Young Bob.

"Look what you've done!" Solveig pointed to her muddy feet and soiled skirt. She struggled back onto the boardwalk. How could she find work when she was as filthy as the pigs rooting in the mud?

He lurched aside and retched into the weeds. "Don't feel so good." Then he retched again. He slouched onto the steps like a sack of oats, held his head in his hands and groaned.

A prim woman wearing a velvet bonnet and kid gloves held her skirts away as she passed by with a look of disgust, clutching her little boy's hand as if the child might become contaminated. She pressed a lacy handkerchief to her nose.

"Shame on you. What would your mother say?" Solveig whispered to the man.

"Nobody's business," he said.

Solveig's anger melted. He was in trouble. He had been turned down at the logging camp, just like her.

"You are right. It is none of my business, sir." She hesitated. "I have a son about your age. It is not easy to forget that I am a mother, Mr..."

"Call me Nels."

A burly bartender, wearing sleeve garters and a spattered apron, stepped out on the stoop and took a menacing posture.

"Move along," the barkeep said. "You're blocking foot traffic." He pushed up his sleeves. "Be on your way and be quick about it."

"I'm Solveig Rognaldson," Solveig said. "Let's go for breakfast."

"Spent my undertaker money," Nels said.

Undertaker? She must have misheard. "I'll pay." She needed information about other logging camps looking for cooks.

"Couldn't eat nothing," Nels said.

"It will settle your stomach," Solveig said. "I will not take no for an answer. You helped with my horse at the train, and I owe you."

"I like horses," Nels whispered.

The Headquarters Hotel stood as the tallest building in Brainerd. The bottom floor boasted a dining room, but Nels steered her to the Last Turn Saloon next door.

"Better grub for less money," Nels said. "The Headquarters steals you blind and robs your belly."

Solveig hesitated at the dingy doorway, stepping away from an overflowing spittoon on the top step. Inside, a slouchy man in a wrinkled shirt pointed to a dark corner table.

They were the only customers. The crockery and table looked clean enough. The flapjacks came with sorghum syrup and needed more lightening, but were reasonable at 4 cents, including coffee. A tough looking man pushed through the door and up to the bar. Rough language spewed from his mouth as he stuffed his face with pickled eggs and called for beer.

Nels did not look up from his plate, shoveling pancakes into his mouth without speaking.

"I'm in trouble," Solveig said. "I don't believe in sidestepping the truth." Nels looked up, bleary eyed with greasy hair hanging down over his forehead. "Gull River Timber hired my team, but they would not hire me. No women allowed."

"Dirty bastards." Nels mumbled an apology for his language. "Makes no sense. You're too old to cause trouble with the jacks." A flush rose above his whiskery cheeks. "No offense, ma'am." He chewed and swallowed another fork full of pancakes. "They wouldn't hire me neither."

Of course, she was too old to cause problems, but his words stung all the same. She supposed every woman longed to be young and pretty enough to turn heads. Not that she had ever known that experience.

"Did you work there last year?"

"I did." He wiped his mouth with the back of his sleeve. His eyes showed hopelessness, stirring Solveig's motherly concern. "I was set up, made to look like a thief. Framed."

"I saw you urinate on their building." Solveig grinned. "Good for you. Wish I could do the same."

He grinned back, a boyish grin with a blush rising on his stubbly cheeks. "No one will hire me except the undertaker." He shuddered. "I'd rather die than work with stiffs."

"Don't be silly," Solveig said. "There are other jobs."

"Not for me," Nels said. "I'm ruined in civilized country."

He shoved the Starkweather handbill across the table. Solveig squinted and stretched her arms out to read the fine print.

"This one maybe," Nels said. "No one in their right mind would go that far into the woods unless he had to." He told her what he knew about the operation and where it was located.

"You going by train?" Solveig said. "Steamboat?" The advertisement listed cooks, cookees, flunkeys, and stove tenders besides a long list of draymen, sawyers, filers, teamsters, barn boss, road monkeys, axmen and swampers. They needed everyone.

"No money," Nels said. "I might wangle a job working a barge in exchange for passage to Starkweather."

"They need cooks," Solveig said. A plan fell into place, clicking step by step in her mind. She would pay a few cents for Nels to haul her trunk to the barge. He might do it in exchange for the meal she had just purchased. She would use the emergency funds tucked inside her camisole to pay her passage. She had to try.

"No guarantees, Mrs. Rognaldson." Nels shook his head. "It might be a wild goose chase."

"Call me Solveig," she said. "I must risk it. I need the money."

"They're hiring at the hotel," he said.

"Doesn't pay enough." She hesitated, hating to share her business with a stranger. Finally, she took a breath and explained about the bank note coming due in the spring. "Without a better job, I'll lose everything I have."

"It's a long way up there," he said. "If they take me, I must accept the job whether or not they'll hire you. You would be stuck out in the middle of nowhere. How would you get home?"

He sat with his haggard face in his dirty shirt with vomit splashed across the front. He did not look like someone with good prospects for being hired.

"What if they won't hire you?"

"Don't know. Back to the undertakers," Nels said with a grimace. "Or tie a hang rope."

"Don't say such a thing. Think of your mother." Solveig reached across the table and touched his arm. "You can make a go of it, if you try."

The door opened and a pair of lumberjacks swaggered to the bar. Soon they were roaring with laughter at a crude joke told by one of the men.

"Let's go." Nels pushed back from the table. "It's no place for someone like you."

"I'm going with you to the barge," Solveig said. "Maybe they have room for one more." She might earn her passage by cooking for the crew. Or exchange eggs.

Solveig counted pennies to pay the bill. Nels mumbled his thanks as they stepped out into fresh air. Solveig hunched her shoulders. The lifting fog revealed ramshackle buildings and filthy boardwalks. The pig had moved to a garbage pit by the depot.

"Weather moving in." Nels pointed to a bank of dark clouds on the western edge of sky. "Hope you brought your flannels."

Chapter 11
Nels

Nels bent under the weight of Solveig's trunk. She was a nice old gal, but a tightwad, not willing to spend five cents on a dray. "What you got in here? Rocks?"

The fog left a lingering haze. Loads of firewood for sale lined the streets. Wood lay free for the taking at every logging site. If he had a horse and wagon, he might start a business, or head west and homestead.

"Complaining won't help." Solveig toted the crate and basket without complaint, though from time to time, she paused to ease a crick in her back. Nels's pride would not allow him to be shown up by an old woman. He gritted his teeth and bowed under the burden.

One of her chickens squawked, and Solveig paused to gather an egg from the bottom of the crate. She held it up with a grin. "Your supper, young man. Worth all your effort."

Nels snorted. She was plucky to bring hens to a logging camp. A cat would be welcomed in any kitchen. But hens? He would like to see the cook's face when she carried the crate into the cookshack. Maybe the barn boss would let them roost with the horses, if the barn boss was better tempered than old Stumpy at Gull River Timber. That old geezer would just as soon slit your throat as bid you good morning.

"I'll suck an egg anytime." Nels shifted the trunk to his other shoulder. God only knew what he would do if Starkweather did not pan out. Solveig might expect him to tote her trunk all the way back to her home in Foxhome. And if she got the job, she would be hard put to bring her gear home again in the spring. They neared the crossing where *The Mud Hen* moored within one hundred feet of a steamboat being loaded with freight.

A flock of swans flew southward, riding under a bank of gray clouds. A chain of pelicans settled on the water with splashing white wings. A whiff of wood smoke and sawdust skittered on the breeze along with the fishy smell of river.

The *Mud Hen* was planked, more than fifty feet in length, and about eight feet wide. The bartender had said that the *Mud Hen*, built in Pittsburgh, was the sturdiest craft on the Mississippi. Today the sail fluttered helplessly on a broken mast, like a surrender flag hitched to a pole. Not so sturdy. No wonder Captain Ben needed men to man the oars.

Nels followed Solveig down the steep bank to the Mississippi River.

"Careful of my trunk!" Solveig called back.

"What about my neck?" Nels said.

A man clambered up the bank toward them. He wore heavy boots and a red, plaid shirt. A broken nose twisted on his face. A straggly beard stretched over his neck. His smile showed a missing front tooth.

Nels's heart sank. It was Ten-Day Johnson, a swamper from last year's crew.

"Well look who the cat dragged in," Ten-Day said with a slap on Nels's back that almost pushed him down the bank. He grabbed a handle of the trunk. "As I live and breathe, it's Fingers Jensen." The weight of the trunk divided between them. "You owe me money."

Ten-Day was always sticking his nose where it did not belong. He got his name from his usual length of employment before his pesky curiosity led to fights. He had been fired from just about every outfit in Minnesota. Nels's hated nickname would stick like a bad smell if Ten-Day brought it along to Starkweather.

"I owe you nothing." Nels measured his words. "I did not take your money. Pettibone set me up."

"Course he did." Ten-Day hefted his side a little higher. "Careful now, it's slippery."

Together they lugged the trunk down the bank and rested it on the shore. Nels did not recognize any of the men loading wooden boxes on the rickety barge. Solveig was already talking to the captain.

"You brought your ma along?" Ten-Day said. "Didn't know you were still dragging on the tit."

"She's not my mother." Nels heard Solveig asking about lard. "She's looking to cook for Starkweather Timber."

Ten-Day's attitude grew more respectful. No jack in his right mind got crosswires with the cook.

"I'm heading to Starkweather, too," Ten-Day said. "Couldn't find work nowhere else."

Solveig and Captain Ben shook hands. The captain signaled for Nels and Ten-Day to load Solveig's trunk onto the barge. Nels approached Captain Ben and arranged to work for passage.

"Know anything about Starkweather?" Nels asked Ten-Day. He had an uneasy feeling that he might be walking into a mistake. Ridiculous. Work was work. He reached up and fingered the stone around his neck for luck. He would draw his pay in the spring and head back to the Red River Valley. It would all work out.

"Renegade outfit," Ten-Day said. "Heard he works the men half to death. But, the way I figure, it helps to be half-man and half-wild cat to survive any logging crew." They dropped Solveig's trunk on board. "Hoping for the best, expecting the worst."

"Looks like she'll be cooking this leg of the journey," Nels said.

She perched on her trunk, holding her cat, the crate of chickens at her feet. Her gray hair wound around her head in braids like a crown.

"Content as the Queen of Sheba," Ten-Day whispered.

A crow flew close overhead, a sure sign of bad luck.

"Good news," Captain Ben said. They settled at the oars, a dozen men with room for a dozen more, everyone griping about the weather and sore backs. "Mr. Starkweather arranged for a tow from the *Albert Gale*." The crew whistled and stomped. "We'll steam all the way to the Skunk without lifting a paddle."

"How did old Starkweather manage that?" a man wearing an eye patch said.

"Who is he?" Nels whispered to Ten-Day.

"They call him Squinty," Ten-Day said in a low voice. "Lost an eye working as a brush ape for Weyerhaeuser a few years back."

"Starkweather may have won a game of cards," Captain Ben said with a lopsided grin. "Just like he won the jobber camp. But you did not hear it from me."

More hooting and stomping. Nels relaxed. Maybe it would not be so bad after all. It was fifty miles upriver until the Skunk. They would get there in no time.

The *Albert Gale* built up steam and tooted its whistle.

"Captain." Solveig stood to her feet as the wind flurried her skirts around her legs. She licked her buck teeth.

Nels should have warned her, about what, he was not sure. He hoped she would not make a fool out of herself and jinx her chances with Starkweather.

"May I speak to the men?" Solveig said.

"Go ahead," Captain Ben said, though he frowned. No doubt, he wondered what this farm woman might say to the crew. Nels tried catching her eye. A captain was king of his vessel. No one else counted.

"An evening red and a morning gray will set the traveler on his way," Solveig said. "Old wives' tales prove true more often than not, and I'm an old wife, so I should know."

Laughter and guffaws. A deadhead drifted downriver, scratching the side of the keelboat. Squinty pushed the stray log away with his oar.

"Men, I'm cooking my passage to Skunk River," Solveig said. "There will be something special for supper if I get a cookfire before dark."

A wave of whispers rustled through the men like wind through the pines.

"What you making?" Squinty said.

Reputations were won or lost at such times. Nels had the feeling that Solveig stood on the cusp of either failure or defeat. The men would turn scornful if she disappointed.

"Thanks to my girls," Solveig pointed to her chickens, "I have eggs for a batch of doughnuts, but I'll need daylight and dry weather to fry them up."

"Doughnuts!" A surge of energy traveled man to man around the *Mud Hen*. Men worked for beans and salt pork, at best biscuits or johnnycake. They dared hope for nothing better. But doughnuts.

"You heard her." Captain Ben lost his frown and tipped his cap in Solveig's direction. "I haven't had bear sign in a coon's age, missus. Put your backs into it, boys. Sooner we get there, the sooner we eat."

The keelboat lurched forward to the center of the river and snugged up behind the *Albert Gale*. Its side-wheels churned, building speed as it inched upstream. A low whistle moaned. A lanky crewman tossed a rope from the stern, and Squinty secured it with flair.

Solveig sat with her back straight as a pole amidst sacks of potatoes and barrels of flour. She smiled as a mother might indulge a brood of children. Her cat bounded onto her lap. Solveig leaned over and pulled another egg from the crate.

"Look here, boys," Solveig said. "My girls at work."

Nels no longer noticed her buck teeth or lined face. She handled herself like a straw boss. Heck, she could probably run the whole outfit. She was strong, a person to hold to, someone you could count on. Just like his own mother.

But not someone to cross.

Chapter 12
Sister Magdalena

Mother Superior sent Sister Magdalena to accompany Sister Bertina to the new school in International Falls. Sister Bertina would stay as a teacher. They brought books and supplies. When Sister Magdalena returned from that arduous journey, she visited another donor in Minneapolis to collect a donation for the orphanage.

It was almost winter, and Sister Magdalena chafed under the burden of discernment. If God wanted an outreach to loggers and their families, He was being mighty quiet about specifics.

Sister Magdalena knelt in the hospital chapel until her knees hurt. The sun through the stained glass showed a smudge that one of the novices had missed. Sister Magdalena looked around to make sure no one was watching, lumbered to her feet, and polished the smudge with spit and a corner of her veil. She straightened the hymnals and rearranged the book shelf. She dribbled a few drops of Holy Water over the geranium and plucked dead leaves.

Voices murmured in the hallway, and footsteps clicked on wooden floors. A horse-drawn dray clomped by on the cobblestone street. Far away a ship in the harbor called like a bellowing heifer.

Sister Magdalena returned to her pew and sat until her backside fell asleep. It was hopeless. No doubt God spoke to Mother Superior much quicker than He was speaking to her. And why not? Mother Superior had been in religious life much longer than Sister Magdalena. Mother Superior acted calmly and with wisdom—unlike Sister Magdalena. Too many brothers, she reasoned. It was easier to learn virtues without bad examples.

A delicious fragrance drifted into the chapel. Sister Hildegard fried doughnuts on Thursdays. Today was Thursday. Sister Magdalena got up to visit the kitchen. Perhaps a misshapen doughnut needed eating.

She walked through the ward on her way to the kitchen. Nursing sisters bustled with patients, postulants scrubbed the floors, delivery boys toted bundles of laundry from the orphanage, and doctors scribbled orders.

She was almost to the kitchen stairs when someone called her name.

"Sean Murphy is asking for you," Sister Lucy said.

Oh no. At that moment, Sister Magdalena wanted only to eat doughnuts. Perhaps he would again ask her to kill him. She suppressed a shudder.

"He's still alive?" The delicious smell of frying grease made her stomach growl. "You're better with sick folk."

"He's asking for the tall sister." Sister Lucy chuckled. "Actually, he asked for the giant penguin. That must be you."

"Send for a priest. I wouldn't know what to say."

"He wants you," Sister Lucy said. "No one else will do."

Sister Magdalena hesitated. She was under Mother Superior's instructions to be in prayerful discernment, not visit sick men in the wards. However, she had not been instructed to scrounge for doughnuts in the hospital kitchen either. The Rule of Benedict clearly stated to give priority to the sick.

"It's your path to holiness," Sister Lucy said cheerfully.

Sister Magdalena could have wrung Sister Lucy's skinny neck.

Sister Magdalena dragged her feet to the stinky ward. Ragged breathing came from behind the moveable screen that shielded Mr. Murphy's bed from the others.

Sister Magdalena forced herself to walk behind the screen. He lay with closed eyes. Sister Magdalena crossed herself. "Mr. Murphy." Maybe he was asleep.

"Finally." His yellowed eyes snapped opened. "What took you so long?"

Sister Magdalena mumbled an excuse.

"That's the trouble with this place." He coughed and choked. "I ask for help, but by the time it comes, I've forgotten what I needed." More coughing.

He had forgotten. She turned to leave with a sigh of relief.

"No." An alarming gurgle sounded in his throat. "I remember now."

Sister Magdalena looked around for a nursing sister.

"Promise me." Mr. Murphy's voice was so low that Sister Magdalena bent closer to catch his words.

"Promise you what?" Sister Magdalena pulled a hard-backed chair closer to the bed and sat down. He smelled like turned meat. She wanted to run, not stay.

"That you'll care for my wife after I'm gone." His groping hands found her little finger and squeezed until it felt like it would break. "There's no one else."

Impossible. Sister Magdalena was in no position to care for anyone. She was under vows. She had no money or resources. Even her time was not her own. She started to pull away, but he grabbed her arm.

"My Gertie had never been outside her village." His eyes lit up with her name. "I promised her mam that no harm would come to her in America." He coughed until his face darkened to an alarming blue. "She's a good girl, my Gertie. Almost entered St. Bridget's Convent, but I talked her out of it." He closed his eyes. She stood to leave.

"Wait." His eyes opened. "I shouldn't have talked her out of a vocation. She'd be safe now if I hadn't." Another jag of coughing. "She is too beautiful. Men will ..."

More coughing. All words choked off. Sister Magdalena waited, horrified at his purple face, his bulging eyes, and the way veins etched like rivers on his nose.

"What can she do without money or family?" He gasped for breath. "And a baby coming."

"I'm not free to take on responsibilities. Sister Magdalena could not help this man. Her reason sounded like a feeble excuse. "I am under vows."

"You're strong," Mr. Murphy whispered. "You're the perfect one to take care of her."

Sister Magdalena sighed. "You don't understand."

"But you'll try?" He pulled her closer toward him. He would not last long. Even she could see that. "Promise me that you'll try, Sister."

Sister Magdalena nodded. "I'll try."

Sister Lucy came carrying a tray clanking with bottles and spoons. She looked as pickle-faced as ever. Sister Magdalena tucked her hands into her sleeves and stood to leave.

"Don't forget," Sean Murphy called after her. "You promised."

Sister Magdalena hurried out of the room. What could she do? Her days filled with work and prayer. She could not send Mrs. Murphy to her own family, even if she had money for a ticket, which she did not. Her brothers had families of their own.

Sister Lucy caught up to her, breathless from hurrying, and still holding the tray. "What were you thinking?"

"What did I do now?" It was a wonderment how trouble found her.

"Promising that dying man you'd care for his wife and child." Sister Lucy sniffed. "I heard you myself."

"You're the one who demanded I speak to him," Sister Magdalena said. "I promised I would try to help her. You know there is nothing to be done."

A bell sounded, and Sister Lucy scurried down the hall.

Sister Lucy was everything that Sister Magdalena was not: neat, organized, tidy, punctual, and dignified. Crabby, but never in trouble. Sister Magdalena sighed.

Chapter 13
Solveig

The *Mud Hen* glided up the Mississippi behind the *Albert Gale* as Solveig dangled her fingers in the water. The steamer zigzagged to avoid snags or sandbars. The Mississippi twisted through pine forests. Patches of red sumac, blue sky, and white swans reminded her of an American flag.

The side-wheel on the steamboat churned like a woman making butter. Solveig let the icy water flow over her fingers until they ached. She moved to the center of the barge and sat on her trunk.

It was cold and getting colder. Charcoal clouds hid the sun and the wind bit from the north. It felt like an early winter coming.

Solveig preferred a lazy autumn, slow days with sun, and warmth into November. She loved fall, the harvest tucked away, the woodshed full, and haystacks to feed the stock. *Koselig*, the Norwegian word for the coziness and contentment of home.

Winter already pressing in and she adrift without a place to lay her head. She needed a job and she needed it soon.

She pulled out her knitting and worked the heel of a new sock. Her worries intertwined with each stitch: Rasmuss's death; Halvor's decision to marry and leave the farm; her foolishness at signing the bank note in the first place; the fate of her beloved team in the hands of Gunner Jacobson at Gull River Timber; her future if she failed to pay the mortgage; and whether she could find a job at Starkweather Timber.

An hour passed and then two. The men dozed at their oars. Sometimes one told a bawdy joke, too low for her to hear.

Clouds thickened. Solveig calculated they must be nearing the town of Aitkin where they would moor for the night. She forced the yowling cat into the basket and latched the lid. Solveig found her mixing bowl and added ingredients for doughnuts. She covered the bowl with a dishtowel and wedged the bowl between two wooden crates where it would not spill. She peeled potatoes and onions for supper. Then she sliced bacon, cutting until her hands and wrists ached.

Aitkin looked to be a sleepy town. Shacks sprouted along the river bank. A church spire rose above the treetops. The *Albert Gale* looped ropes to a pier on the edge of the river. The *Mud Hen* chose a rickety dock away from the main pier to set its moorings. The *Albert Gale* bristled with activity, and a few men in city finery climbed off the steamboat with a great deal of boisterous laughter.

Solveig stumbled ashore with wobbly legs, still feeling the toss of the river beneath her. It had been thirty-one years since she had traveled to America on the *White Dove*. That voyage took a solid month. Back then she had braved the Atlantic with barely a qualm.

Solveig released the hens to scratch in the sandy shore. They would return to the crate with darkness. She was not as certain about the cat. She left Queenie yowling in her cage. Solveig tucked her hands beneath her shawl to warm them and turned her back to the wind.

"I'll need two cookfires," Solveig said to Squinty who was already building a fire along the shoreline. "One for the dough-nuts and the other for supper." She gathered scattered twigs and branches. "I don't want rain spoiling the doughnut making."

Squinty hurried to build another fire. Solveig put the lard on to heat for doughnuts using a beat-up old pan from the crate of cooking pots. Over the second fire she fried potatoes and bacon in a huge cast iron skillet. She mixed a batch of baking powder biscuits. While the biscuits baked in a Dutch oven, she began rolling and frying doughnuts.

The men devoured them as fast as they came out of the grease. They stuffed them in their mouths, blew on burnt fingers, and jostled for more. Solveig laughed to see them. They had little pleasure in this world. They were like hungry boys grasping for home.

A few sprinkles fell as they finished their meal. The men scattered to set up camp, and Solveig cleaned up after supper. She would sleep in the little wanigan built in the center of the *Mud Hen*. Tents popped up like mushrooms in the forest. They were almost finished when it began to sleet.

Solveig awoke in the middle of the night and peeked outside. Snowflakes fluttered to the ground. She pulled the chicken crates closer to her pallet, and welcomed Queenie to snuggle under her blankets.

If she could not find a job at Starkweather, she would beg a ride back to Brainerd with Captain Ben. She worried that he might leave Starkweather Timber before she knew about the job. She would not survive walking back through this wilderness.

She awoke the next morning to a world of white. Fog hung over the river, shrouding the trees and bushes with icy drapes. A skiff of ice formed on top of the water bucket. Solveig shivered ashore and built a fire with firewood squirreled in her wanigan. Even at home, she made a practice of laying aside dry wood before she went to bed.

"Any of them bear sign left?" Squinty said.

"Sorry," Solveig said with a laugh. Her mother-heart warmed to the young man's words. She had always yearned for a bunch of boys. This ragtag bunch had not been what she had in mind, but they would do. Her breath puffed clouds before her mouth. "If I'm hired on at Starkweather, I'll make another batch."

"Won't do me no good," Squinty said. "The captain won't linger at Stink Lake."

The water numbed her fingers as she dipped the coffee pot into the river. She stirred a batch of pancakes as the men made ready to leave. Captain Ben kept an anxious glance at the *Albert Gale*. The smell of coffee put a hurry in their actions. She fried pancakes as fast as she could. The men stuffed their faces and held out empty plates for more.

"Hand me a few more monkey blankets, will you?" Nels said.

Solveig chuckled at the lumberjack slang.

"Almost makes me risk the other eye to put my feet under your table," Squinty said. "Almost, but not quite." He went on to say that the *Mud Hen* was heading for warmer climes. "No siree, I've no intention of freezing to death at another Minnesota logging camp."

"Hurry up boys," Captain Ben said. "We don't want to miss our tow."

But they need not have worried. The *Albert Gale* was fog-bound. The men grumbled at the delay, but Captain Ben assured them of the need for caution.

"A snag could rip out the bottom," he said. "That's what sank the *Sea Wing*."

"I thought the *Sea Wing* went down in a twister," Nels said. "That's what I heard."

"Well," Captain Ben stroked his handlebar mustache. "The weather may have turned, but I happen to know it was a snag that took her down."

The talk shifted to the panic, the unreliability of newspapers, and the sorry state of shipping, now that the railroads were pushing them out of business. Solveig fetched another shawl from her trunk and huddled behind the wanigan, half listening to the men's conversation, and worrying about the mortgage. Ten-Day showed a ragged deck of cards, and the men played for bent nails and wooden matches.

The sun finally burned away the fog, but the *Mud Hen* had lost half the morning. It was early afternoon by the time they reached the mouth of the Skunk River that meandered northwest from the Mississippi River. The *Albert Gale* tied up to a stump as men unloaded its cargo.

"What are they doing?" Solveig asked Squinty as the barrels and sacks grew in a small mountain on the shore. "It's in the middle of nowhere."

"It's for Weyerhaeuser, ma'am." Squinty pointed to a railroad track and a small shack nestled in the trees. "Weyerhaeuser has a big operation on the north side of Stink Lake. You cannot imagine the number of board feet coming out of that camp."

"I thought Starkweather Timber was on Stink Lake," Solveig said.

"Starkweather is a jobber camp, barely two square miles on the south side of Stink Lake." Squinty spit over the side of the barge and wiped his mouth with the back of his hand. "The big companies won't mess with small acreage. Weyerhaeuser is the big cheese around here. Starkweather is a pimple on Weyerhaeuser's backside."

Solveig looked toward the north for a sign of Weyerhaeuser Timber. She suspected they already had a cook, but she might try there if Starkweather did not pan out.

Squinty barked for the men to start poling up the Skunk River. The Skunk wound back and forth like a young girl's uneven stitches. All cattails and swampland. They soon left the Mississippi behind. It had been thirty years since the Indian Massacre, but gory memories crowded as they poled through the gloomy tamarack swamp with its stumps and ghostly shadows. A perfect place for a sudden ambush. Of course, the Sioux were long gone from Minnesota, and the Chippewa were mostly civilized.

Scraggly tamaracks held yellow needles. A moose grazed nearby, strings of green weeds hanging from its mouth. It gave a warning snort. Queenie hid under Solveig's skirts and curled up on her shoes.

Then, just when Solveig thought they would never leave the swamp, they rounded a bend and white pines stood tall enough to block the sun. A graceful doe raised her head and startled as they passed. A bear waded along the shoreline, no doubt, looking for food before his long sleep. The hens gossiped in low murmurs. This time of year, the water was low, and the men pushed the loaded barge through winding curves and rush-clotted narrows. They stabbed their poles into the rocks or sand, leaned on it heavily, then walked along the plank to the stern of the boat where they yanked out the poles and repeated the process with grunting expletives. Captain Ben kept a steady pace.

The crew worked together like a perfectly trained team, like dancers, though Solveig had not seen more than a dance or two in her life, her people being pietist Lutherans who did not believe in such foolery.

"My broken back," Nels said. "Should have stuck with undertaking."

"More muscle and less jawing," Captain Ben said. "We're almost there."

"I've a treat when we reach Stink Lake," Solveig said loud enough for all the men to hear.

"More bear signs?" Squinty held a hopeful look in his good eye.

"Something from home," Solveig said.

"You heard her." Squinty marched forward pushing the *Mud Hen* up Skunk River. "Put your backs into it, boys."

Solveig gave the hens a few grains of corn while the men poled into the muddy bottom, then pushing backward as they marched in an organized line toward the front of the keel boat. She rummaged in her trunk and pulled out her knitting. As she knitted and purled the gray wool from last year's ewe, Solveig evaluated the working habits of the men. Ten-Day rested on his pole as much as he could. Squinty prodded him to keep up with the other men. Ten-Day was like a sticky fly, getting in people's faces and asking personal questions. He should work for a newspaper and get paid for his curiosity. He would never amount to much anywhere else.

Nels was no shirker. He would make a good farmer if only he could beat the bottle. Some men never found their way. She finished the sock as noontime turned to midafternoon. Finally, the river widened into Stink Lake.

"There it is," Captain Ben said. "Starkweather Timber ahead."

Three workmen stood at the mouth of the river holding axes and shovels. Captain Ben slowed for a short conversation. Solveig strained to hear what they were saying, but the wind blew their words away. Captain Ben was not happy.

"They are damming the river, boys. Hurry or we will be stuck here all winter," he said.

On the south side of the lake, log buildings squatted against the backdrop of pines that stretched to the sky. The men exchanged poles for oars and rowed toward the camp.

Canada geese floated alongside the barge, gawking with curious eyes. An eagle dove for fish, splashing with strong wings and coming up with a mouth full of flapping fins and tail.

"Why dam the river?" Ten-Day said.

He would be better off concentrating on his work than posing so many questions. Too curious for his own good, in Solveig's estimation.

"To get the water levels high enough for the spring float," Squinty said. "The Skunk flows through Stink Lake. The dam backs the water up. The logs pile on the ice, the ice melts, they tear down the dam and the logs go whooshing down the Skunk River toward the Mississippi. Then onto the saw mills in Brainerd."

"A real dam?" Solveig pictured how it might work. "Made out of what?"

"They'll drop trees across the mouth of the river and patch it with mud and branches."

A dark dread settled over her. She tallied the miles to Foxhome. Everything depended on this job. Lord help her if she failed. Surely, Halvor would not let his mother end up in the Poor Farm. Maybe he would.

She had to do something or lose her mind with worry. Solveig delved into her trunk. She handed out molasses cookies, careful to avoid jutting elbows and oars.

"At least we can sit down when we row," Nels said. Though it was far from warm, he had removed his sweater. His rolled-up sleeves showed a frayed and filthy underwear cuff. Ten-Day had Captain Ben by the ear asking more questions.

"Where do we go when we get there?" Solveig said to Squinty. Nervous perspiration trickled down her neck. That fly-swatter clerk at Gull River Timber had robbed her confidence.

Squinty pointed to buildings on the shoreline. Heavy forest surrounded the camp. Huge boulders clustered to one side and a rough dock jutted out into the water.

"See that building west of the dock?" Squinty said. "You can tell it is the cookshack by the smoke from the chimney this time of day. That long building to the east of the dock must be the bunkhouse." He pointed to a log cabin standing off by itself. "That must be the office."

"What are those other buildings?" Solveig said.

"One is the barn, the other a blacksmith forge. The bigshots have their own dwellings. The filers, surveyors, and top loaders," Squinty said. "Maybe the bull of the woods."

Her mind swirled with the terminology. She had much to learn.

"Where do we go?" Solveig's stomach turned with anxiety.

"Go straight to the office and ask for the pencil pusher. The *Mud Hen* is your only way back to civilization if Starkweather doesn't take you. Captain Ben will not dally with the dam going up. Don't get stranded." He straightened his eye patch as he paused for breath.

"I'll hurry," Solveig said.

"Old Starkweather is an ornery cuss on a good day. And he favors younger women and prettier ones at that." Squinty nodded an apology. "But you are no bean burner. He'd be a fool not to snap you up."

She thanked him. Every pot must stand on its own bottom. She tied a clean apron over her wrinkly dress and pushed a stray lock of hair into her braid.

The *Mud Hen* bumped against the dock. Squinty jumped out and secured it to a post. Everything smelled of pine. No stink about the lake that she noticed.

"Hear them harps?" Squinty threw back his head and closed his eyes. "Wind in the pines is the best music in the world."

Solveig paused in surprise. The wind, her friend on the prairie, had come with her. It swooshed through the tops of giant pines a hundred feet overhead.

The trees would be gone by spring and the harps would cease. The ideal setting of lake and pines would become the same as the ragged landscape by Brainerd. She pushed the image out of her mind. The land had to be cleared for cultivation. First the ax, then the plow.

A crew of men lay a corduroy road across a swampy area that led from the woods west of the cookshack to the lake, lining small logs snug against each other to make a solid road. The snow hadn't lasted, thank God, but patches of white clung in the shadows. A giant tree lay beside the bunk house, and an axman whittled away its limbs, the sound of his ax a fraction of a second after it gouged into the branches.

"Come, Solveig," Nels said.

He held out a hand. The dock trembled under her weight. Her legs wobbled after a day on the water, and she held tightly to Nels until she reached dry ground. Squinty promised to watch over her baggage. He was already tossing barrels and bundles onto the dock, eyeing the dam builders as he worked.

"They're closing us in," Captain Ben said. "Two bits for anyone willing to help unload."

Solveig, Nels, and Ten-Day made a beeline toward the office as soon as they were ashore. They need not have worried about being first in line. The others were eager to earn a little extra cash. Nels lacked ambition. If he were her son, she would tell him so.

"We'll sleep cold this winter," Ten-Day said with a groan as he pointed toward the rough looking building before them. "Can see into the bunkhouse through the cracks."

"We'll caulk if it gets too bad," Nels said. His voice carried a hopeful tone, and Solveig realized how young he was, about the same age as Halvor. "Like Gull River Timber last year," Nels said. "We can do it again."

The cookshack was a long narrow building with the door on one end and a curl of smoke on the opposite. Solveig wanted to stop for a look, but the *Mud Hen* would not wait. Her throat choked with dryness. This was her chance.

The barn was a log frame with a few boards tacked around to keep out the wolves. A haystack stood outside the main door. A team of oxen dragged logs toward the landing. Their lumbering slowness brought curses from the man goading them forward with a pointed stick.

"Good Lord, oxen in this day and age," Nels said. "It's a haywire outfit for sure."

"Will we meet Mr. Starkweather?" Solveig said.

"Hope the big shots don't show up until payday," Nels said. "That's all they're good for."

"Amen," Ten-Day said. "The push is the devil's spawn in any camp, but Lord deliver me from the brains of the outfit. I got sideways with one back in Pine County," he said with a crooked grin. "He ballyragged me until I socked him in the nose for firing a jack hurt on the job. He set his goons on me." He pointed to his flat nose. "Left their mark."

"My goodness," Solveig said. He must be exaggerating.

"For God's sake, keep your nose clean this time around," Nels said. "We're a million miles from nowhere."

The entered the gloomy commissary, lighted only by a pale shaft of light through a dirty windowpane and a kerosene lantern hanging from a wire strung over a small table. On the far side of the room was a set of bunkbeds. The store carried shelves of snuff, Tom's Tobacco, Peerless Tobacco, Spearhead Tobacco, towels, jackets, mackinaws, Castoria Laxative, leather mitts, rubber boots, Victor's Croup Salve, overalls, and Boar's Head Liniment. She almost tripped over a spittoon while reading the names on the boxes. She took a breath to slow her racing heart.

A hard-edged man sat at a table near the door. He was built like a bull. His muscles bulged against his shirt sleeves. He wore a red mackinaw and a scraggly beard. His jaw worked when he saw them.

"Good God," Nels whispered. "Jacob Pettibone." The color drained from Nels's face, and Solveig heard the air leave his lungs in a huff.

"I thought at least I'd be rid of the likes of you, coming north," Pettibone said with a sneer. "We don't cotton to thieves and shirkers at Starkweather Timber."

"Thought you'd still be lording it over the brush apes back at Gull River Timber," Nels said.

It must be a bad dream.

Pettibone lunged toward Nels, but was interrupted by an older man who breezed in through a side door with the air of a nobleman. The elegant gentleman sported a neat goatee and a swallow tails coat with a stovepipe hat. A gold watch chain draped across his chest. His shoes gleamed, and he wore immaculate white gloves. He was about Solveig's age or maybe a bit younger.

It was the brains of the outfit, Mr. Starkweather himself.

The clerk came out from behind the counter rubbing his hands together and half bowing. "Mr. Starkweather," he said. "The *Mud Hen* arrived. These men are here for work."

"Send them away," Jacob Pettibone said with a growl. "We don't need troublemakers at Starkweather."

"Now, now," Mr. Starkweather said. "Not so hasty. We need strong men with willing backs and experience."

He looked past Solveig as if she did not exist.

"Mr. Pettibone," Mr. Starkweather said. "Take inventory and secure the new supplies."

A dark flush rose on Pettibone's clenched jaw. Ten-Day grinned and poked Solveig in the ribs with his elbow.

"Mr. Elliot and I will finish here," Mr. Starkweather said.

Pettibone glared at Nels, then lumbered out the door, his hobnailed boots making little holes in the puncheon floor. Mr. Starkweather sat in Pettibone's vacant chair with the clerk beside him. The clerk was a short, thin man with a receding hairline. He carried a ledger clutched close to his chest and had the habit of pulling his skin away from his Adam's apple with his thumb and forefinger.

"Now then," Mr. Starkweather said. "This is Mr. Elliot."

Mr. Starkweather eyed them like a man buying a horse. His eyes flickered across Solveig. He raised an eyebrow but said nothing.

Ten-Day piped up. "Been a flunkey, a swamper, and road monkey. I've learned the ropes. Hoping to be a skidder or maybe a loader this year."

"Do we have need of a skidder or a loader, Mr. Elliot?" Mr. Starkweather said.

Mr. Elliot scanned the roster before him. "Yes, sir," he said in a high, squeaky voice. "A skidder."

"You can handle a team?"

"Yes sir." Ten-Day's grin showed missing teeth.

"No pugilism allowed," Mr. Starkweather said. "By the looks of your face, you've indulged in fisticuffs a time or two."

"No, sir." Ten-Day squirmed beneath Mr. Starkweather's gaze. "I mean, yes, sir."

"Which is it?" Starkweather said. "Will you cause trouble?"

"No, sir," Ten-Day said. "I learned my lesson and learned it good."

Solveig craned her neck to see if the *Mud Hen* still moored at the dock. They men talked around her. The curse of widowhood. A woman turned invisible without a husband. She was trapped like a mouse in the corner.

"I've been a swamper, an icer, and a road monkey," Nels said. "I would like to try my hand at skidding or teamstering, maybe cant hook work. I learned horses at a bonanza farm last summer. Have a job waiting for me again in the spring. I'm a hard worker. You won't regret it."

"You look like a drunk, sir." Mr. Starkweather stood to his feet and glanced at his watch. "I do not tolerate intoxication among my crew, especially in the upper bracket."

"Never drink on the job, sir," Nels said. He dropped his eyes like a little boy caught stealing sweets. "Only after payday."

"Explain the use of fid hooks." Mr. Starkweather waited like a schoolmarm as Nels squirmed for the right answer.

Solveig held her breath.

"As I thought. You don't know a thing about loading timber," Mr. Starkweather said. "Normally, I'd trust Pettibone's judgment, but we're in somewhat of a pickle." He snapped his watch closed. "We need a full crew. I will give you a chance. But only one." He turned to leave and then looked back. "I'll take you on as a swamper. Mr. Elliot, do the paperwork."

The door slammed. The air in the room left with him, and everyone, including Mr. Elliot, let out a breath. Nels's shoulders slumped.

Solveig had not spoken a word. Time was getting away. The *Mud Hen* would be leaving.

Mr. Elliot pointed a lead pencil at the men. "Axmen." He scribbled something in his ledger book with a flourish. He named their wages at thirty dollars a month. He pushed papers toward them for signatures.

"Jacob Pettibone will be mad as hops," Mr. Elliot said in a whisper. "Pettibone thinks he's God Almighty, he does, and has an in with Starkweather. If I were you, I would keep out of his way."

"Do you have a full crew?" Ten-Day said.

"Hell no," Elliot said with a snort. "We need one hundred twenty men and have barely fifty. We need more oxen, more horses, more scalers, filers, more everything. But it's early. More men coming this week." He turned his full attention to Solveig. "And you, ma'am?"

"I'm looking to cook," Solveig spoke up, making a special effort to stand taller and hold her stomach in. "I've a clean hand in the kitchen, and these men will vouch for my skills."

Mr. Elliot pulled the skin away from his neck with a frown. Accordion music sounded from the direction of the bunkhouse. "Mr. Arvid Lillo is our cook. We call him Irish." He inspected his tally sheet, running an ink-stained thumb down the list of names. "We've never thought to hire a woman, though we need cookees and flunkeys." He pushed away from the table. "I'll ask Mr. Starkweather."

Solveig opened her reticule and pulled out two doughnuts wrapped in a clean handkerchief, saved for the occasion. "Here is a taste of my work. One for you, and one for Mr. Starkweather."

Mr. Elliot took a bite and chewed. He closed his eyes with a "mmm." He swallowed and licked his lips. "Like my mother's." He went through the door where Mr. Starkweather had exited. Solveig glimpsed a four-poster bed.

"Which pays the best?" Solveig said in a whisper to Nels. "Cookees or flunkeys?"

"A cookee," Nels said. "Flunkeys are at the bottom of the heap along with road monkeys."

Mr. Elliot returned with a smile. "We'll take you on as a flunkey for twenty-four dollars a month."

"I'd rather be a cookee," Solveig said. "To help Mr. Lillo with the cooking."

Mr. Elliot frowned and calculated some figures on a scrap of paper.

Solveig knew from the handbill that a cook made forty dollars a month, one of the highest paid people at camp. Twenty-four dollars a month would not pay her mortgage.

"We could pay you twenty-six dollars a month as a cookee," he said.

Solveig could tell he was irritated by the way he pulled the skin away from his Adam's apple as she tallied the numbers. Earning twenty-six dollars a month meant no train fare back to Foxhome. Almost enough, but not quite.

"You couldn't go a little higher?" She had nothing to lose. There was not anyone else in line for the job.

"Timbermen are log rich and cash poor," Mr. Elliot said. "And there's the panic on Wall Street." He wrinkled his forehead and cocked his head to one side. "To tell the truth," he said in a whisper, looking over his shoulder lest he be overheard. "We're desperate. Mr. Lillo threatens to walk off the job unless we hire someone right away. I'll ask again." The sounds of voices through the doors. A long discussion.

Mr. Elliot came back wearing a puzzled expression on his face. "Your doughnuts made the difference. Mr. Starkweather is willing to raise your pay to twenty-eight dollars a month." He shook his head as if in wonderment.

Solveig stretched out her hand. "It's a deal, Mr. Elliot." It was enough.

She fished in her reticule for her last doughnut, the one saved for herself. "Thank you, Mr. Elliot. I appreciate your efforts on my behalf."

"But where to put you." He snagged the doughnut with his pointer finger and stood to his feet. He had half of it in his mouth when he spoke again. He pulled the skin away from his neck.

Mr. Elliot hurried off and Solveig agreed to meet him in the cookshack. She scribbled a note to Halvor telling of her whereabouts. Then she scribbled another to Gunnar asking him to send word about the team. Squinty tucked them in his pocket with a promise to post them as soon as they reached civilization.

Afterwards, she realized that she had forgotten to greet Britta. In fact, she had not mentioned Britta at all.

Squinty hoisted her trunk onto his back. Solveig picked up the crate and basket. Together they trudged to the cookshack over a rocky path. Squinty cursed when he tripped over a stob. He deposited the trunk inside the door and jogged back to the keelboat with a tip of his hat.

Solveig stood at the doorway, unsure what to do. The cook-shack reeked of boiled beans and stale grease. Two long tables stretched end to end down the length of the room. Metal plates and cups lay on one table, ready for supper. At the far end of the room stood a man stirring a huge cauldron on a gigantic cook stove. A long table stretched from side to side before the stove. On it lay mixing bowls, crocks, pans and sacks.

On the wall hung a hand painted sign in crude letters: *Come in, Sit down, Shut up, Eat, Get out.* Not the friendliest welcome she had known.

The cook stood skinny, unshaven, and wore a filthy apron. A cigar dangled out of the corner of his mouth. He argued with Mr. Elliot in loud tones gesticulating with the cigar to emphasize his point.

"You asked for help, and now you have it," Mr. Elliot said. "Quit bitching."

"Hell, ya, but a petticoat?" the cook said. "Women don't belong in logging camps."

"She's here or you'll explain to Mr. Starkweather why not," Mr. Elliot said. "She's hired, by God. That is the end of it."

"Where will she bunk?" Lillo said. "She can't have my room."

Solveig stood awkwardly by the door, not knowing if she should walk over to the men or wait until acknowledged. She pretended to examine a thread on her shawl, careful to keep her eyes down.

"You'll move in with the surveyor," Mr. Elliot said. "It's the best we can do."

"To hell, I will. Supplies walk away unless I'm here to keep an eye on things." The cook banged a spoon on the edge of the iron pot. The sound echoed like a warning. "You can't expect..." He reached for a stick of stove wood, and Solveig feared he might use it as a weapon. Instead, he stuffed it into the firebox.

Mr. Elliot flagged Solveig over toward them. "Solveig, this is Mr. Lillo, your new boss."

The cook looked her over with a snort. "Ever cook for a bunch of men?"

"Yes, sir." It was not the whole truth. Solveig cooked for a dozen men back in Norway. Never for so many. "Glad for the chance."

"Get to work, then, damn it. Supper in less than an hour."

He stomped into a side room with loud clattering and slamming.

Solveig looked around. She had no idea how Mr. Lillo managed his kitchen. She picked up a wooden spoon and gave the pot of beans a stir. "I don't mean to displace him," she said to the pencil pusher. This was not going well.

"None of your concern." Mr. Elliot's forehead furrowed. "Just do the job."

Pans of johnny cake baked in the oven alongside a haunch of beef. She poked a broom straw into the center of the cornbread. Not quite ready. She added wood to the stove. The beans needed salt. A pepper mill sat on the edge of the shelf. She ground a fine drift across the top of the pot, stirred, and tasted again. More salt. Much better.

Always there would be dirty dishes, and never enough hot water. She filled a metal dishpan from a bucket on the floor and put it on the side of the stove to heat. She filled the tea kettle from the water bucket. She used the remaining water to fill a blue speckled coffee pot. She placed the pot on the stove to boil.

Mr. Lillo came in stinking of liquor and shambled to the stove.

"I didn't know what to do."

"You're such a great cook." His eyes glazed and his speech slurred. "You figure it out."

"Damn mice." Mr. Lillo stomped a scurrying mouse. "Overrun this place." He grabbed the corner of the cupboard to keep from toppling over. "Where do we find a cat in this goddam country?"

Solveig smiled. Maybe things would settle into place.

Chapter 14
Nels

He staggered under the weight of his jinx. Nels grabbed his turkey and followed Ten-Day to the bunkhouse with spirits as low as the clouds hanging over Stink Lake. What were the odds of landing in the same camp? Pettibone would have his gizzard on a platter.

To hell with Jacob Pettibone and Starkweather Timber. Working with Mr. Bean at least kept him above ground.

He turned toward the lake, but the *Mud Hen* floated half-way across the open water. He calculated the long walk to Aitkin. He had no money to ferry across the Mississippi.

Weyerhaeuser's lay somewhere north, but he faced a long walk around the lake to find it. Maybe they carried the same black list. The timber barons gambled and took their ease, thick as thieves, while poor men slaved and made them rich. Damn them all.

Snow spat in the dreary sky. Starkweather Timber weighed like a prison sentence. No winter job at the bonanza farm. Rolled of his summer wages and blackballed from better camps. He buried a poor stiff, then stretched his arms on the keel boat. Then Pettibone. Of all the God-awful things to happen to a man.

Panic pulled him even lower. All his struggle for naught and trapped on Stink Lake until the logging season ended. Nels must hunch up and take whatever Pettibone and Starkweather Timber dished out.

"Hurry up," Ten-Day called. "What's taking you so long?"

Nels followed into the bunkhouse. The smell of fresh logs and woodsmoke lingered along with stinky socks. Milky light filtered through a window beside the door. Lighted lanterns hung down the center of the room and cast a feeble glow. A wood stove on the opposite end gave the only heat. Two barrels heated water on top of the wood stove.

Three-tiered bunks lined both sides of the bunkhouse. They were muzzle loaders, heads to the walls and feet to the center, jammed so close together that the jacks climbed over the end to climb into bed. Two jacks shared each bed, six men to a bunk. Straw replaced mattresses. It looked clean enough, but would soon stink like a barn and crawl with bedbugs.

A folded blanket lay at the foot of each empty bunk. Only one per man. God Almighty, it was a piss-poor outfit. A deacon's bench at the end of each bunk served as the only seating. Most of the beds stood empty, but a few draped with the possessions of those already at camp.

He headed toward the woodstove where Ten-Day warmed his hands.

"Bunk mates?" Ten-Day said. "I'd rather sleep with you than a stranger."

He pointed to a bunk nearest the barrel stove. Nels nodded and climbed to the top bunk. Good idea to find a spot near the fire. His head brushed the ceiling when he sat up. Cedar and pine boughs added to the bedding remedied bedbugs, and added extra cushion to the limp layer of straw.

"Do you snore?" Nels asked Ten-Day.

"Hell, yes." Ten-Day roared with laughter. "I fart like a horse, kick like a mule, and talk in my sleep. You're lucky to have me, darling."

He pressed his twisted nose toward Nels's face, puckering his lips, and pretending to kiss him. Nels pushed him aside. Good Lord, how would he stand being paired with this lunatic? Nels made a mental note to fetch a cedar pole to stretch down the center of the bunk. He would keep himself to himself.

"Get off that bunk." An old man perched on the deacon's bench on the other side of the stove. He balanced a bare foot on his opposite knee and pared toenails with a small knife. He wore a shapeless hat and pants. His face bristled with whiskers. Bags hung under both eyes and he looked as desolate as Nels felt.

Nels clambered down. No sign of clothes on the empty nails by the bunk. It looked unclaimed.

The man barely looked up from his toenails. "I say where a man sleeps and where he doesn't." His feet gnarled like a tree branch and his toenails grew thick as a horse's hooves. He swiped a thick finger between his toes, sniffed the toe jam, and wiped it on his pants.

"They call me Ten-Day. We did not mean to overstep. Is this bunk taken?" Ten-Day patted the top bunk. "You must be the bull cook. Did not see you sitting there, my mistake. We'd rather be near the fire if it's not too much bother."

"And every jack wants to be a toploader," the bull cook said. "Why should I give the best bunk to a couple of swampers?"

Ten-Day's face flushed and Nels butted in before Ten-Day made trouble. No jack in his right mind got sideways with the bull cook.

"Where do you want us to bunk?" Nels said. "We'll sleep wherever you say."

"Damn right you will." He glared at them. "You pups come in all piss and vinegar. Why, when I was younger, I could have combed your hair with my hobnail boots and eaten your liver for Christmas."

"Our mistake," Nels said. "We thought you were one of the jacks."

"Because I'm so pretty?" He returned to his toenails, grunted, and cursed his feet. The smell of him wafted stronger than the smoky stove.

"So where do you want us to bunk?" Nels said. Just his luck to be stuck by the door, waking up every time a jack went out to piss, the draft of the open door a misery during the coldest weather.

"Aw hell. Take the one you want and shut your mouth," the bull cook said.

They scrambled back to the bunk with their things, before he changed his mind. Nels looped his turkey on a peg on his side of the bunk.

"Sun up to sun down six days a week. Boil up on Sundays," the bull cook said. "Jump in the lake if you want a bath. Don't expect me to haul water." He sniffed and spat in a box of sand.

"Make your bed and keep the place clean or I'll throw your outfit in the fire. Clean out the washbasin after you wash up and hang up the towel after yourself. I keep a clean bunkhouse or my name ain't Pokey Kokott."

"You a Polack?" Ten-Day pressed closer to the old man.

Nels cringed.

"Careful, boy, or you'll face the wrong end of my fist," Pokey said.

Ten-Day would get them both fired.

"No drinking. No gambling except for match sticks. No brawling and no spitting under the stove." He pointed to a box of sand underneath the stove that prevented fires and to other boxes of sand scattered around the room for those who chewed tobacco. "I see you spitting under the stove, and I'll have your hide." So many of Pokey's teeth were gone that his tongue hung out the corner of his mouth as he pared the final toenail, barely within reach. "Lights out when I say they go out. No lying abed in the morning. Goes without saying there's no talking in the cookshack."

Nels nodded. Every camp was the same. The bosses paid men to work, not gab. Conversation over meals kept them from the cut and sometimes led to fights.

"Is it true that bull cooks build their voices by hollering down rain barrels?" Ten-Day said. "I want to be a bull cook someday. Better than being out in the cold."

"The hell, you say," Pokey snorted. "Up stoking fires three times a night and keeping the cookstoves hot enough to fill your bellies. Hauling wood and water until I'm dead in my tracks and yet must drive the wanigan out to the cut." He folded his knife and slipped it back into his shirt pocket. "Scrubbing floors and tending lamps. Up at night shoveling paths to the privy. You want my job? You can have it."

Nels tried to catch Ten-Day's attention to quiet him, but Ten-Day pressed on. The man did not know when to keep his trap shut.

"So why do you work here?" Ten-Day leaned closer to the bull cook who pulled on holey socks. "In town you could put your feet up once in a while."

Pokey cast a sharp eye on Ten-Day. "Don't you worry none about the whys and wherefores." He stood to his feet. "Me and Starkweather have an understanding." He winked one eye. His tongue hung through his whiskers. "Empty wood boxes. You boys fill them up or go hungry tonight."

Nels buttoned his coat and turned to go outside.

"Wait up, boys," Pokey said. "Gather up these toenails before you go."

"Why for?" Ten-Day said.

"Take them to the cookshack. Irish will boil them up for soup." Pokey laughed until a spasm of coughing robbed his wind.

Nels and Ten-Day stepped back out into the cold. Behind the bunkhouse they found a jumble of wood in various lengths, shapes, and sizes. They loaded a wooden wheel barrow, the sap still sticky on its handles, as the jacks filtered in from the cut. Skinners drove oxen toward the barn. The oxen lowed in anticipation of grain and water.

"I'd rather be an ox skinner than an axman," Nels said.

"Not me," Ten-Day said with disgust. "Smelling cow farts and dodging shit?"

They filled the wood boxes and started to take off their coats.

"My bones predict bad weather." Pokey gestured to an empty corner opposite the filled the wood boxes. "Doesn't hurt to have a little extra wood inside."

When they finally satisfied the bull cook's appetite for firewood, Nels gathered his courage and chose his words with care. "Is Pettibone the bull of the woods?"

"Him?" Pokey snorted. "Hell no." He glanced over his shoulder. More men trickled in the door. "Pettibone is Mr. Starkweather's errand boy." He laughed a silent, wheezy laugh. "I'd stay clear of him."

"Who's the push then?" Ten-Day's voice carried in the cavernous room.

"Who wants to know?" a tall man said in a thick Swedish accent. Snow dusted the shoulders of his red mackinaw. He brushed it away with leather mitts. A sharp jawline showed beneath a bushy red beard. He pulled a knitted hat from his bald pate. "I'm the one pushing you lazy bastards."

A low rumble of griping and curses as lumberjacks dragged in from work and draped wet socks from bed frames and rafters. The room turned rank with the stench of wet socks and dirty bodies. A thin man asked for the push's help with a gimpy ox. The push shoved on his cap and went outside with the man.

"What do they call him?" Ten-Day said. "The push."

"Paulson," Pokey said.

"Hey Pokey," a man called Fish said. "Isn't it time to blow the Gabriel? I am so hungry I could chew the ass off a skunk."

"I'll blow the Gabriel when I say it's time to blow the Gabriel." Pokey grumbled, slipped into a mackinaw, and shuffled out the door.

"What's the boss like?" Ten-Day said to Fish.

"That bull of the woods would work his own mother into the ground," Fish said. "Decent enough, I suppose, but Starkweather rides him hard. Everything for the almighty dollar."

"Who's the man who fetched him?" Ten-Day said. "The thin fellow."

"The barn boss. Everyone calls him Barrister. Used to be some high fangled lawyer back in England," Fish said. "He's the smartest man I've ever known."

The men came in all sizes and ages. Some were near-deaf and talked loud enough to be heard back in Aitkin. Others had bad eyes, stoved backs, and scarred faces. Ten-Day hastened to get acquainted.

"Where does Pettibone bunk?" Nels determined to keep as far away from him as possible.

"Pettibone?" Fish spat a glob of tobacco in a nearby sandbox. "He's too big a toad for this swamp. Bunks with the filer."

Nels was about to mention his bad blood with Pettibone when the dinner horn blasted. The bunkhouse snapped into life. Men streamed out the door like grain pouring out of a sack. Nels's belly cramped with hunger. It had been a long time since Solveig's cookies. He joined the others heading to the cookshack. Lights from the windows guided them along the path. Snowflakes spat into Nels's face and down the neck of his coat.

Two tables stretched from the stove to the door of the log building, but only one table lined with dishes. Nels looked for an open seat.

"I need room for my south paw," Ten-Day whispered.

Nels and Ten-Day moved to seats nearest the door as Solveig and Irish hustled food to the tables. It would have been impossible to keep a conversation going in such clatter, had it been allowed. The metal bowls and spoons clanked louder than the threshing machines at the bonanza farm.

The platters emptied half way down the table. Solveig rushed to refill them, her red face dripping with sweat. The platters moved down the table at a snail's pace. Next time he would make sure to sit closer to the serving end. Ten-Day could fend for himself.

The hierarchy of the camp was never more obvious than at table. The scaler and surveyor sat at the end nearest the cookstove, along with the pencil pusher, the bull of the woods, the toploader, and the smithy. Pettibone swaggered in. Nels expected him to sit with the big shots since his nose was up Starkweather's ass. Instead, Pettibone came toward them.

"Move," Pettibone said to Ten-Day, his grin a surly smirk.

Ten-Day ignored Pettibone and reached for the johnnycake. Pettibone grabbed the plate, holding it high above Ten-Day's head.

"You must not have heard me," Pettibone said in a menacing voice. "I'm left-handed and need this spot."

The cacophony stopped. Every man stared, some with spoons half way to their mouths. The silence louder than clatter of tin on tin. Nels expected one of the big shots to toss Pettibone out on his ear. It was against all the rules to speak in the cookshack.

Ten-Day's face turned beefy red. Nels held his breath and saw it for what it was. Pettibone was out to get rid of them.

Pettibone screamed into Ten-Day's face. "Move your sorry ass out of my spot."

A vein in Ten-Day's temple visibly throbbed. Someone should stop Pettibone. Nels looked around for help, but saw no one leap to Ten-Day's defense. Nels placed a restraining hand on his friend's shoulder. Somehow Ten-Day kept his wits and tongue, though his jaw worked and the vein kept throbbing. Ten-Day stood to his feet, took his plate and spoon, and moved farther up the table.

The cook grabbed a meat cleaver and stomped to the end of the table. He glowered at Pettibone without a word. Nels hunched over his plate. The sounds of tin on tin thundered again. Irish stood by Pettibone until the men streamed out of the building.

Nels once heard of a cook who threw a meat cleaver at a blabber-mouth during breakfast. Killed the jack right in front of everyone. The cook had been too valuable to hang, so they buried the man behind the crapper and never told anyone about it. Of course, it could be leg-end, like Paul Bunyan and his blue ox. Jacks were worse than women when it came to gossip and tall tales. Even so, Nels wished Irish had thrown the cleaver at Pettibone when he had an excuse.

Nels looked back as the cook jawed with the bull of the woods. He pressed close to Paulson's face while waving his cleaver in Pettibone's direction. The bull of the woods shrugged his shoul-ders and plodded toward the blacksmith shop. It seemed Paulson's shoulders slumped under the weight of Irish's tongue lashing.

"I don't understand why Pettibone has the run of the place," Nels said.

"I'll get him." Ten-Day muttered dark threats until Nels grabbed him by the arm.

"No!" Nels said. "You'll make it worse."

"I don't care," Ten-Day said. "He thinks he's Julius Caesar."

"Julius Caesar!" Fish snorted. "That's the name for him."

Nels was already sick of working at Starkweather Timber, and he had not started yet. He climbed up on his bunk and tried to adjust to his new surroundings. Two men played checkers across the room. Fish pulled out a mouth harp and played along with Pokey, who wheezed a melancholy tune on his accordion.

An Indian joined the crew, his black hair hanging in long braids. Ten-Day was quick to greet the man after Pokey showed him to a bunk near the door. A few others dragged into the bunk-house before lights out.

"Chief said he's looking for steady meals through the cold of winter." Ten-Day stretched out beside Nels on the bunk. "And that Latvian is here for the vittles, too."

"You should be a preacher," Nels said. The straw prickled in all the wrong places. "Always sticking your nose in other people's business. Didn't your folks teach you manners?"

"I have two goals in life: springtime and suppertime," Ten-Day said. He dismissed Nels's rebuke with a wave of his hand. "Pay is the same wherever you go."

By the time Pokey blew out the lamp, Ten-Day snored like a locomotive. Nels lay awake, his arms on fire from poling the *Mud Hen*. The wood frame creaked and groaned whenever anyone turned or twisted. Nels squeezed his eyes and tried to sleep.

He could handle the work, but Pettibone put his nuts in the cracker. One word, one misstep, and Nels would be out on his ear. Nels had worked with all kinds of men since coming to America. Julius Caesar, indeed. Pettibone had set himself up as chief tyrant and tormentor. Nels refused to be his victim.

It was only a half day's walk around the lake and another mile or two to Weyerhaeuser's camp. But the black list. Ten-Day pulled the blankets away. Nels jerked them back. A drink would calm his nerves. One little drink would make him sleep like a baby.

A lumberjack lived with a swarm of men, short and tall, fat, or thin, stupid, or clever, friendly, or not. A man learned them by heart and blessed the ones who kept their mouths shut and their noses clean. Someday Nels would possess a life away from men like Pettibone and Pinchpenny. He would own a little place where he could sleep in peace. His stash of barley pop, like Irish, would bring him comfort after a hard day's work. A man deserved a drink once in a while.

God, his mouth felt dry as chaff.

Chapter 15
Sister Magdalena

Sister Magdalena squeezed her eyes tight in concentration. The mournful bleating of a ship's whistle drifted in from the harbor. The whistle reminded her of home and family, maybe because of its sadness. She had not seen her family in years. Soon the harbor would freeze and the ships would be gone.

Her knees hurt. She was too heavy to kneel for long. God must understand. She hefted herself to the pew, rubbing, and stretching her legs. She polished her shoe with the inside of her skirt. Much better.

Whisking scrub brushes sounded outside the closed door. Postulants at work. The wind off Lake Superior rattled the window panes. Funny how minutes dragged in the silent chapel.

Sister Magdalena contemplated Jesus on the crucifix with his face contorted in agony. She knelt again, the floor pressed her tender knee-caps in all the wrong places. She prayed an *Our Father*, trying to imagine God's Kingdom on earth. She prayed for Sean Murphy's wife, the new school in International Falls, and for herself to hear from God.

She did not want to be a nurse. She was tired of the laundry. She was not a teacher. She did not want to work in the orphanage. She did not want to be the Novice Mistress. She did not want to work in the kitchen.

She could not bring a list of all the things she did not want to do to the meeting. Mother Superior expected results. What could she say? That a boat whistle reminded her of home? That the sound of scrub brushes in the hallway made her thankful she was no longer a postulant?

Sister Magdalena would carry her cross, even if it meant being a nursing sister. She prayed fervently for more conversion in her inner life. More light. More understanding. More dying to self.

Nonsense. Saint Francis heard specifics when God directed him to build and repair the House of God. It would be handy to be a saint. She imagined herself as Saint Magdalena of Duluth, so righteous and holy that God spoke directly to her. Her sanctity would be a light to the community and a witness for Jesus. She shook herself back to reality. Ridiculous. She was far from sainthood.

Again, Sister Magdalena heard the silent whisper that all should pay a little for the greater good. She refrained from throwing her prayer book across the room. She turned to Psalm 36, "For with You is the fountain of life, and in Your light, we see light. *Lord, send your light. Heal my spiritual blindness.*"

The bell rang for mid-day prayer. It was no use. She felt as exhausted as if she had been hauling wash water. Someone else should be given the task to hear from God.

The sisters filed into the chapel. Sister Lucy sat next to Sister Magdalena. They sang as one voice from Isaiah 30, "And thy ears shall hear the word of one admonishing thee behind thy back; This is the way, walk ye in it; and go not aside neither to the right hand, nor to the left." Almost one voice, Sister Magdalena corrected herself. Poor Agatha's voice stood out like a squeaky shoe.

The reading was from Exodus Chapter 13, "And the Lord went before them to shew the way by day in a pillar of cloud, and by night in a pillar of fire; that he might be the guide of their journey at both times."

A gentle peace settled her spirit. God would continue to lead them as He had through the centuries. They had trusted Him then and they would trust Him now.

After the noon meal, Sister Magdalena returned to the chapel with a lighter heart and a certainty that God would send guidance. She spent the afternoon in silence. Nothing.

Her confidence evaporated by the time of the meeting. She was spiritually deaf. She must swallow her pride and admit that she failed to hear God's voice.

God humbled the proud and exalted the weak. She would ask the sisters to pray for her and beg pardon for her hardness of heart.

The meeting was scheduled in the refectory directly before the evening meal. Each sister stood behind her chair. A figure of the Blessed Virgin graced the center of the table. The room smelled of fried onions.

Mother Superior stood at the head of the table, her black and white habit immaculate, as always. Her rosary draped from her pocket in graceful blue-beaded spirals. Not a hair showed around her coif. Although her face was serious, Sister Magdalena had the feeling that a twinkle hid just behind Mother Superior's eyes.

Mother Superior urged the sisters to spend a few moments in silent prayer. Then she invited them to be seated.

"There is a need for hospitals closer to the logging camps. There are concerns about the costs. We're here today to begin the discussion," Mother Superior said. Then she seated herself and nodded for the sisters to begin.

Sister Lucy stood to her feet. "By the time many of the injured loggers finally arrive in Duluth, it is too late. Timely care would save lives and undue suffering."

Sister Lucy sat down. No one else spoke. The silence grew awkward.

Sister Hildegard struggled to her feet, winced and held her crooked back. "And how are we to pay for new hospitals? We barely keep afloat now," she said. "Besides, where would we find doctors to serve in the wilderness?"

"Patients cannot afford their bills." Sister Bede Marie adjusted her round spectacles. She served as bookkeeper for the hospital and community. "We struggle to balance our books."

"But the suffering is great." Sister Lucy leapt to her feet. She lost her sour expression and tears filled her eyes. "God will send doctors. He has never failed us." She sat down with a plop.

Mother Superior stood to her feet. "The need does not necessarily constitute the call. Didn't Jesus say that the poor would always be with us?"

"Yes, Mother." Sister Lucy stood back on her feet. "But Saint Benedict said that before and above all things, care must be taken of the sick, that they be served in very truth as Christ is served."

Others spoke of the need, the call, and the direction they felt the community should take regarding outreach. Sister Magdalena's heart sank. They were impoverished. They had nothing to offer but themselves.

"We have sacrificed everything for this hospital," Sister Hildegard said. Her face carried a gray sheen of ill-health. "What more can we give? We scrimp every penny to continue what we are doing now. The orphanage needs a roof. Some sisters wear habits so thin that mending is impossible. Our shoes are patched on patches. We should bolster our foundations before attempting expansion."

"Thank God, a recent donation will cover our most pressing needs here in Duluth," Mother Superior said. "But you are correct in stating that the need far outweighs our ability to provide what is required." Mother Superior turned to Sister Magdalena. "Saint Benedict reminds us how the young often bring words of wisdom." She nodded encouragingly. "Sister, please share your discernment with us. Perhaps the Lord has given you direction."

Sister Magdalena slowly rose to her feet, pushing her black veil behind her shoulder. She swallowed hard, wishing she had a great revelation to share, something to lift their spirits. She hesitated, thinking to confess her prideful lack.

Instead, she felt a sudden urge to share what she had been given. It was plain and simple. Nothing miraculous. It might be a wild idea of her own imagination. But it might be a small fish to feed thousands. It was not her responsibility to know. Her community of sisters would discern which it was.

"What if each lumberjack purchased an inexpensive chit that would pay for hospital care in case of injury or sickness?" Sister Magdalena said.

A low murmur rolled over the room like a breeze ruffling the waters in the harbor.

"There are only a few injured men from each camp," Sister Magdalena said. "If all paid a little, there would be enough to pay for those few."

Sister Magdalena sat down. Her heart beat in her throat. What would they say?

Several sisters stood to their feet at the same time.

"One at a time, Sisters," Mother Superior said.

Silence settled over the room.

"It would never work," Sister Hildegard said. "Loggers won't pay money for care they might need. Men never expect to get hurt. No one does."

"It might work," Sister Lucy said slowly. "Someone could go from camp to camp selling the chits at the start of the season."

Another murmur.

"The men could buy tickets at the beginning of the season," Sister Magdalena said. Hope rose again and her words rushed out in a torrent. "And later, after they see how others benefit from the tickets, they will be eager to buy the following year."

"Money left over at the end of the season will build hospitals closer to the logging camps," Sister Bede Marie said. "Thirty thousand men in the woods at even a dollar a man would pay for a lot of expansion."

In amazement Magdalena uttered a silent prayer of thanks. She believed she was not hearing God, and yet His voice had been speaking all along. That quiet voice. That voice heard only in the silence of one's heart.

"The owners might be persuaded to promote the plan," Sister Lucy said. "It is in their best interests to keep their crews healthy."

"And drunken brawls?" Sister Hildegard said. "The men come to us with as many broken heads from fighting as falling trees." She sniffed. "Paying for their care would promote immorality."

Sister Magdalena thought of Nels, the young logger from the train cars.

"Of course," Mother Superior said, "we'd cover only injuries or sicknesses sustained on the job."

"Would a priest sell these chits?" Sister Hildegard said.

"We cannot expect priests to do our missionary work," Mother Superior said.

"The bishop approves new ventures only if we do the foot work."

"I'd be afraid," Sister Hildegard said. "It's not safe for a decent woman in such places."

"Sister Magdalena wouldn't be afraid," Novice Maria said with a triumphant tone in her voice. "She's not afraid of anything."

Sister Magdalena had not considered that she might be the one to sell chits. She had not thought that far ahead. But visiting the camps would be almost like seeing her brothers. She was not afraid of rats or rascals.

"What would you do if one of those lumberjacks accosted you?" Sister Hildegard said with a shudder.

The answer popped out of Sister Magdalena's mouth without thought. "Why, I'd pray to Saint Michael the Archangel for protection."

"But what if the man persisted?" Sister Hildegard stood to her feet and leaned forward. "What if he made indecent advances in spite of your vocation?"

Although it was not a holy answer, one formed on Sister Magdalena's tongue. She stood to her full six feet and squared her shoulders. "If any man dared to disrespect me in such a way," she said. "I'd sock him in the nose." She took her seat.

With that, the meeting ended. Mother Superior announced another for the following evening when they would vote on the issue.

Mother Superior looked toward Sister Hildegard. "We will not go forward unless we are in unity."

The smell of onion soup wafted from the kitchen. "And now let us thank God for our supper."

The cook brought the kettle and Sister Lucy began reading the next chapter from Thomas a' Kempis. The Great Silence descended like a comforting cloak.

Chapter 16
Solveig

Solveig looked around the kitchen before she headed to bed. The tables readied for breakfast. Coffee pots lined the back of the stovetop alongside a pot of oats. Beans soaked in a cauldron. Prunes and dried apples softened in their designated pans. Queenie kept watch for rodents.

Fatigue stooped her shoulders. Her bunions throbbed and her back ached. She had boasted of youth and endurance. She felt as old and used up as the old bull cook.

She had done her best. No doubt Mr. Lillo would find fault, as he had done with everything she had touched. She took the lamp into her room and closed the door behind her.

She sat on the lower bunk and eased out of her shoes. Using her paring knife, she slit the shoe leather over her bunions. Perfectly good shoes ruined, but she had no choice. She had to save the farm.

She draped her apron over the window. No telling who might be looking in. That business with Pettibone had rattled her. She could not imagine threatening anyone with a cleaver.

She rummaged in the trunk for her hatpin. Not that she could take a lumberjack with it, but it would do for an unexpected threat. She would keep it in her braids during the day. Starkweather Timber held many surprises. So far, none of them to her liking.

No lock on the door. She dragged the trunk in front of it. She pulled her nightgown over flannels and petticoats, added another pair of wool socks and a knitted nightcap, and slipped Rasmuss's old shirt over the nightgown.

Solveig held the lamp to peer into the cage. No eggs yet, but Gumbri was sure to provide a daily offering. Irish had eyed the hens with suspicion.

"They can stay tonight, but tomorrow they have to go," Irish had said. "Barn boss might keep them."

She climbed into bed. How good to stretch out on her own sheets and blankets after her long journey. Sleet peppered the windows. The stove pipe popped in the kitchen. An open door would allow more heat into her room, but the front door was unlocked for the fire tending. Anyone could walk into the cook-shack. She would keep her door shut with the trunk in place.

The walls creaked. A strange rustling in the corner. The few strands of straw did nothing to cushion her hips.

She would be all right. Everything worked out in the end. Memory rose like sour milk in her throat. She had broken no promises. Halvor had.

Starkweather Timber was a perfect name for this desolate place. She fell into a fitful sleep tallying the numbers, figuring to the dollar how she would pay the banknote.

A sound woke her in the night. The wind was a dull roar in the treetops outside her window. She held her breath. Footsteps echoed on the wooden floors near the cook stove. Pokey stoking the fires? No clank of stove lids. No clunk of wood. The rustle of someone in the cupboards. The steps paused outside her door.

Solveig grabbed her butcher knife. She heard rough breathing, but could not tell if it was her own or that of the intruder. With shaky hands she lit the lamp.

"Who's there?" she said with a firm a tone. "Leave at once."

Quiet. Someone stood beyond the door.

She grabbed her hat pin. God help her. If he tried coming into her room, she'd jab him in the eye and kick him in the crotch.

"Go away," she said. "I mean it."

Footsteps sounded and the door slammed. Solveig peeked out the window. Only swirling snow against a world of white. She slept with her hatpin in her hand and woke to the sounds of

Pokey slamming stove lids. Almost morning. Solveig dressed and ran a comb through her hair.

"Don't worry," she whispered to her girls, still asleep in their cage. "We'll be fine."

Solveig greeted the old man who drank yesterday's coffee at the work table. No sign of Irish. She began grinding coffee beans. It was all about getting organized. Pokey had filled the reservoirs the night before.

Queenie rubbed against Pokey's legs and arched her back.

"We've needed a cat around here," Pokey said.

"How about chickens?" Solveig explained her predicament.

Pokey rubbed his whiskers. "Maybe with Barrister."

"I'll bake a cake if you work it out," Solveig said. "I have two eggs, and my recipe won a ribbon at the Wilkin County Fair."

Pokey grinned showing gums and tongue. "Yes, ma'am. I have not had cake since Hector was a pup."

Solveig mixed batter, expecting Irish to burst through the door at any moment. Stewed prunes sat on tables. She sliced side pork until her hand fell asleep, frying the strips in a huge skillet. Where was Irish? She was not sure how much to make. She turned the fatty strips in the sizzling grease and piled the golden slices onto platters. She sliced a cauldron of cold potatoes into the fat. She glanced out the window as she salted and peppered the potatoes. The men would be in soon and no sign of Irish. It was time to start the pancakes. How good the boiling coffee smelled. She sipped a cup while she fried flapjacks.

Pokey asked if it was time to blow the Gabriel.

"Where's Irish?" she said. "I'm not sure what to do."

Pokey rubbed his hands. "Logging berries in the morning and dried apples at noon. Fetch the syrup. Butter in the cold box." He rummaged in a covered box in the corner and brought out two plates of butter. "One on each end. Side pork and taters."

Solveig needed at least three more sets of arms. At home she always served cold buttermilk with flapjacks. If there was buttermilk, she did not know about it.

"I'll blow the horn," Pokey said. "Damn Irish."

Solveig faced fifty hungry men alone.

She filled the coffee pitchers and set them on the table along with the heaping platters. Tinware clattered. She flipped pancakes as fast as she could, but could not keep up. Pokey tried to help by dishing bowls of oatmeal. He spilled more than he spooned.

Irish dragged in as the men were leaving. He reeked of liquor and stared rheumy-eyed from a haggard face. He was younger than Pokey, but acted older.

"I did my best." Solveig wanted to give him a threshing he would never forget. He earned more than she, and yet he left her doing all the work. She took a deep breath and tried to sound calm. "I have questions."

"Do whatever you want." He slumped onto a bench and slurped coffee right from the pitcher, spilling it down the front of his shirt. He burped and sprawled his legs. "They eat like hogs. Don't matter what slop you put in front of them if there's plenty of it."

"Would you please tell me your menu?" Solveig said. "And I need to know which facilities I might use."

"What are you talking about? The outhouse?" He snorted. He pulled the makings out of his pocket and rolled a cigarette. "There it is." He pointed through the window to a small out-house behind the cookshack. "Your own personal crapper. Are you happy now, Lady of the Kitchen?" He struck a match to the bottom of his boot and tobacco wafted through the room.

"You must have a root cellar."

"Let me smoke in peace," Irish said. "Finish up and I'll show you."

Solveig washed the dishes and reset the tables. Queenie rubbed against her skirts, and scooted off, returning with a mouse.

He muttered about varmints, two legged females, and four legged foes out to destroy him.

Solveig seethed. He had no reason to bitch.

Solveig had eaten nothing all morning. A few cold pancakes lay on a platter but the side pork and fried potatoes were gone. She scraped a dish of oatmeal from the bottom of the pot. Tomorrow she would eat before serving the men. She needed her strength.

Frost etched the windows. A constant flow of wood was needed to keep the stove going, but the wood box was empty, and no Pokey in sight. Irish slumped on the bench, even after he finished his smoke, and stomped the butt on her clean floor.

"Did you come to the cookshack during the night?" Solveig said around bites of oatmeal. It was almost warm. "Maybe to check on the fire?"

"Not me," Irish said. "Bull cook's job."

She told him about the footsteps.

He rubbed his cheek with the side of his hand. "The filer keeps busy with the saws. Doubt he would be out. Zeke and Stinky work most nights. More likely Pettibone."

"Why do you say Pettibone?" Solveig remembered the cleaver from supper.

"He's Starkweather's darling," Irish said with a snarl. "Thinks he owns the place."

Nels had told her about Pettibone's light fingers. "I'd hate to be blamed for something missing," Solveig said.

"Knew this would happen if I wasn't sleeping in the cook-shack." Irish cursed his way to the shelves and counted the sup-plies. "Maybe a sack of logging berries, but I could be off tally. A man must be backed up in the bowels to snitch prunes."

"Valuable commodity," Solveig said. "Worth money in selling or trading."

Irish's jaw worked and he swiped a hand across his forehead as if trying to put the missing pieces together. "By God, you're right. Someone running a side business, maybe selling to the Injuns." He jammed a fist against the wall. "God, I hate a thief. Give me a slacker over a thief any day of the week."

Solveig finished eating and hurried to follow Irish into the snowy morning. Irish pulled an empty sledge behind him. A few flakes lingered in the air, but the morning sun melted the snowy ground into a slushy mess that clung to her shoes and balled the hem of her skirt. The path showed no footprints. They came to the dugout cut into the side of a hill. A rough wooden door concealed the opening. Irish pulled an iron key out of his apron pocket and situated it in the heavy lock.

"No thief will get in here," Irish muttered.

"We could lock the kitchen," Solveig said. She raised her voice over the sounds of chopping axes and crashing trees from beyond the hill.

"Quit nagging!" Irish held his head. "Give a man a little peace."

Solveig could report his drinking. She did not want trouble. She only wanted to do her job and pay the mortgage.

The door swung open to more goods than were carried at the general store back home. Barrels of flour stacked high alongside cut oats, navy beans, kegs of molasses, salted pork, tea, coffee beans, lard, salt, vinegar, and pickles. Bales of salted codfish piled below hanging beef and smoked hams. There were gunny sacks of onions, rutabagas, and carrots hanging from the rafters. Squash and pumpkins stacked besides sacks of potatoes. Solveig figured at least a hundred bushels or more.

"Thank God for a full storehouse," she said.

"Won't last through January," Irish said. "When we're running a full crew, they'll eat three bushels of potatoes, a hundred pounds of beef, thirty pies, forty pounds of side pork, a couple gallons of molasses, a half barrel of flour, twenty loaves of bread, a bushel of cookies, twenty-five pounds of liver, two gallons canned tomatoes and coffee, tea, and beans. Rutabagas, onions, and carrots. Apples and prunes. That is only one day."

Solveig's mouth dropped open, and Irish laughed.

"We're counting on Pettibone to bring in enough meat to make do. Good Lord." Irish slumped onto a keg of molasses. He hung his head and groaned.

Solveig loaded supplies as Irish barked orders and recited menus and schedules. Breakfast over by 5:30 am. Noon meals served off the swingdingle, whether the men were outside the cookshack or miles away. Cooks loaded the swingdingle for the bull cook to take out to the cut. A firebox kept the food hot in the swingdingle.

"Measly skinflint gets his money's worth," Irish said with a glower. "Jacks mostly eat standing up. All day in the woods and they can't even rest their legs at noon. Supper after dark. Fish on Fridays or the Catliks will revolt." He eyed her with suspicion. "You're not Catlik, are you?"

Solveig shook her head. Irish made no move to help her load the heavy barrels or haunches of beef. Her back cramped.

"Should be four cookees and a flunkey for a crew this size. Look what we got." He snorted in disgust. "Petticoat. Who heard of such a thing?"

He locked the door behind them, testing the lock to make sure it held.

"A lock on the cookshack would thwart a robber," Solveig said.

Irish snarled. "You want to get up and fire the stove? You want to fetch the wood and fill the reservoir?" Irish said. "I'm not traipsing over to Skunk Hollow to ask favors of old Starkweather. He spends all his time at that roadhouse."

"We can't let a thief rob us blind," Solveig said.

"Keep a tally. I need facts before I go running to Starkweather for anything." He swore again. "God, I hate a thief."

Solveig lugged the heavy sledge while Irish ranted about thieves and skinflint bosses. He made no move to help pull the load, not even when it hung up in a drift of snow. Irish fell into a surly silence beside her.

"It's a terrible amount of prunes every day," Solveig said. "Do they need so many?"

"Did you see where they shit?" Irish said. "A pole over a trench. They freeze their arses unless they do it quick." He guffawed with a leer. "The jacks raise hell if they don't get enough logging berries. And no one would blame them."

Solveig had a lot to learn.

Inside the cookhouse, Jacob Pettibone lounged at the clean table and stretched dirty boots across Solveig's floor. His hands and mackinaw showed dried blood.

"What were you two doing?" Pettibone leered. "About ready to come looking for you."

"Fetching supplies," Irish mumbled. "Don't get your drawers in a knot."

In her opinion, Pettibone had no business loafing around the cookshack.

"Brought something for you," Pettibone said with a twist of his chin toward the window. "Fresh meat."

A bear hung by his hind paws from a scrubby branch. There were not many bears on the prairie, and Solveig studied its pig-like snout and long claws. She suppressed a shudder.

"That's fine," Irish said, though his voice lacked enthusiasm.

Pettibone swaggered out. Rasmuss would have named him a blowhard.

"Injun food," Irish spat out the words. "Any hunter worth his salt dresses it himself. Today of all days, and supplies to unload."

He turned to the bread bowl. "You start the bear." He avoided eye contact.

Solveig had been on her feet since before dawn and was worn down to the nub. She had hoped to check on her girls and bake Pokey's cake, maybe put her feet up a bit.

Instead, she swathed in Rasmuss's old mackinaw and tied another shawl around her head. She fetched a hatchet and butcher knife. She collected pails and dishpans.

"Don't worry about the hide," Irish said.

She had never eaten bear meat nor dressed one out, but as a farm woman, Solveig had butchered hogs, beef, sheep, chickens, ducks, and wild game. Of course, she could dress a bear. She set her jaws. Nothing could stop a determined Norwegian.

She stepped outside where the wind roared in the treetops. She paused and lifted her face, letting it blow away the heaviness she carried. She was losing everyone and everything she loved.

She slit through the tough hide as the wind whipped her skirts and petticoats, exposing the legs of her drawers. Snow fell from the branches overhead, landing on her face and hands. A nuisance more than anything. The wind numbed her fingers. The knife turned clumsy in her hands. The hide resisted her efforts.

"Wait," Pokey came out hanging onto his hat with both hands. The wind grew stronger, howling across Stink Lake. "It's too cold to work out in the open."

Together they dragged the bear into the wood shed. Though mostly filled with kitchen wood, it blocked the wind. Together they stripped off the hide and hacked the meat away from the bones. The meat, darker than beef, reminded her of the ducks Rasmuss had shot on the swampland behind their property. She sniffed. Meat was meat. She should be glad for it.

Irish showed up when it was time for Pokey to haul the Swingdingle to the cut. "Hang the meat from the rafters, and make damn sure the door is tight against wolves," Irish said. "Bring the liver and heart along with a haunch for supper."

Pokey lugged the meat on his shoulder while Solveig carried buckets of organ meat. Her hands smeared with blood and her apron needed a good boil up. She trudged into the cookshack, feeling old and crippled.

"Start peeling spuds," Irish barked. "At least a bushel."

He chopped bear meat into a huge cauldron along with a peck of onions. He sliced potatoes as fast as Solveig peeled them. He added rutabagas and carrots.

He took off his apron and laid it across the back of a stool. "Not feeling very well. I am going to have a little lie-down," he said. He did not make eye contact. "Keep the fires burning." He was almost out the door when he turned and spoke. "Start the biscuits when you finish."

Solveig bit her tongue to keep from giving him a piece of her mind. He could at least carry his weight. She pulled a stool next to the table. If she were in charge, she would boil taters in their skins to cut down on the workload. She was not in charge. Queenie rubbed against her legs.

"Catch another mouse," Solveig said. "Earn your keep."

Pokey stomped snowy boots by the door. "Brr," he said. "Winter settling in for good." He stuck his hands under his armpits and flapped his arms to get the blood circulating again. "More snow coming down." He wiped his nose on his sleeve. "Dirty dishes in the swingdingle."

"Bring them in," Solveig said with a groan. She filled the dishpan. "The water reservoir is near empty." She looked to the dwindling wood box. "And I need more wood."

Pokey dragged himself out to fetch the dishes, water, and wood. At this rate she would be up all night. The tasks prioritized in her mind and fell into place. She sliced a few more potatoes into the cauldron and gave it a stir. Then she rinsed the remaining potatoes and put them in a separate kettle to cook in their skins. To hell with Irish. If she had to do it alone, she would do it her way. They would be tomorrow's fried potatoes.

Pokey tottered in, looking ready to collapse. He pulled two eggs out of his pocket with a flourish. "Hens are doing fine, ma'am. Barrister has them under his wing. Like pets, they are. He talks to them like a dog." He coughed and sputtered, his color like burned flour. Solveig wondered when the old man had eaten.

"Sit down for a spell" She brought him a plate of hot biscuits and a pitcher of molasses.

The boys deserved the best she could give them. Once the dumplings were in the pot, she decided it would be easy enough to use the eggs for gingerbread. She needed her own key to the root cellar, especially if Irish proved unreliable. She slid the gingerbread into the oven.

"Thank you, ma'am," Pokey said. His ragged shoes showed holey socks. The poor man would freeze his feet with such poor footwear.

"Bring your socks to the kitchen after supper, and I'll darn them for you before bed," Solveig said as she filled pans with batter and slipped them into the oven. "Won't take me long."

"Thank you, ma'am." Tears welled in his eyes. "It's been a long time since anyone has shown me kindness."

"It's nothing." Solveig refilled his cup and patted his shoulder. Instead of wasting energy fussing and brooding over Irish's poor showing, she would treat others the way she wanted to be treated. That was how she had been raised.

The afternoon flew by with cooking and baking. No sign of Irish. Solveig ground coffee beans, at least a chance to get off her feet for a while. She set the pots to cook on the back of the stove and filled a plate for herself. The bear meat tasted gamey, but not disagreeable. She had eaten worse.

Pokey blew the Gabriel. The tables were set, the food ready, and this time Solveig knew what to expect. She filled the coffee pitchers and brought heaping trays of biscuits to the tables. Then scooped huge bowls of bear stew with dumplings.

A sudden joy welled up within her. She was young enough to work, and had enough strength to help someone else. She may be widowed and on her own, but she still had a life to live.

Chapter 17
Nels

Before the morning was half over, Nels's muscles screamed a protest. The push partnered Nels and Ten-Day with Dutch, an experienced axman. Contrary to what the pencil pusher promised, they were to limb, measure, and buck the logs plus keep a path open for the ox skinners to collect the logs. Not enough men hired to divide the work. They were supposed to do all that and keep a day ahead of the ox skinners. Impossible.

Nels leaned on his ax, caught his breath, and wiped freezing sweat from his neck. The wind swirled white clouds around them. They heard the dull crack of axes and the zing of saws. The roar of the wind in the pines, the crack of splintering timber, the calls of skinners. The fellers were to keep a safe distance from other jacks, but accidents happened on windy days. It took skill to aim a tree where it was supposed to land. A wrong angle, careless wedge or wind shift sent gigantic pines onto the heads of other workers or animals. Even worse, trees hung up on other trees only to come crashing down later when least expected, killing the poor sot stupid enough to be in its way. A man could not let his mind wander if he wanted to survive the winter.

A tree wobbled and trembled. "Timber!"

Nels hoped the fellers knew what they were doing. He stepped out of the way watching the great tree waver and fall. The splinter of the trunk and whoosh of pine branches falling hard crashed like a gunshot.

Nels headed toward the fallen tree and struck a blow on a lower branch. Dutch and Ten-Day topped it off. He chopped close to the trunk and tossed the branches aside. Only the trunk was harvested. Beautiful wood from larger branches was left to rot in the woods.

"How are we supposed to keep up?" Ten-Day said. "Takes twenty minutes to fell a tree, but two hours to buck and trim."

"Keep chopping," Nels said. It was his bad luck to get stuck with the yapper.

Dutch measured the trunk with an eight foot-three-inch measuring stick. Nels and Ten-Day bucked the trunk into sixteen foot-six-inch logs using a two-man misery whip. Misery indeed. Nels hated that cross-cut saw above all else. The edge wore off before noon.

"Hell," Ten-Day said with a burst of vapor before his mouth. "We could chew through the wood faster with our teeth."

"The dentist at Gull River knew how to put an edge that lasted. This filer doesn't know his ass from a hole in the ground," Nels said.

Dutch looked over his shoulder to make sure the push was not watching. He stopped to catch his breath. "Good God, I'm out of shape."

Nels joined Dutch in taking a breather, sitting on the heavy log, and resting his aching arms and back until the push headed toward them. They jumped to their feet and began working.

"Less jawing and more butchering," the push said. "Not paying you to sit on your asses."

Nels seethed. He was not a trained monkey to jump to commands. He lopped off the next branch with one blow of the ax while pretending it was the push's bald head.

Fish dragged the logs, one by one, to the shores of Stink Lake. Later, when they worked farther away, Fish would pile logs in the woods for the toploader to collect on sleighs. After freeze up, the logs would be piled on the lake. In the spring thaw, the harvest would float down the Skunk to the Mississippi and then on to sawmills downriver. No ice yet, but winter would remedy that soon enough.

"This ax work is killing me," Nels said to Dutch as the horn blew for nooning. "I thought I was in good shape from pitching bundles." He stowed his ax and headed toward the swingdingle. The woods silent after the morning's commotion.

"Ax work isn't learned in a day," Dutch said. "Limbing and bucking is harder than being a road monkey." He spooned stew and stuffed a whole biscuit into his mouth. "You're going too fast." He washed it down with coffee. "Find an easy rhythm and work like you've got all day."

Nels gobbled his food and stretched his hands toward the fire. His fingers ached as the circulation began to flow again.

"You were at Gull River Timber," Ten-Day said. "You slept in the other bunkhouse."

"I did. Rented out my team to the bastards. Barn boss did not believe me when I claimed my horse took sick because of overwork." Dutch spat in the snow leaving a brown streak of tobacco. "I won't never hire out a team again unless I'm there to take care of them, even to a high-ball outfit."

"Anyone seen Julius Caesar?" Nels said.

"I heard he got fired for talking in the dining hall," Dutch said. "Irish threatened his privates with a meat cleaver."

"Oh, Pettibone's around," Frenchie said. "He went hunting early this morning."

"You're both wrong." Pokey told them that Mr. Starkweather and Mr. Elliot were off fetching men from Duluth. "Took the Weyerhaeuser spur." Pokey made a slow wink and cocked his head in a comical manner. "Heard Starkweather had good luck."

The men laughed. Nels remembered the whispered rumor that Starkweather cheated at cards. Unsettling to know his paycheck depended on a cheater.

"Lord knows we need more help," Ten- Day said. "Look at us. This rate we'll be chopping trees until judgement day."

"Time to get back to work," Paulson said. "Starkweather wants more board feet."

Nels dragged back to the cut. Usually, a cold snap was followed by a warm up this time of year, but no sign of higher temperatures.

They worked all afternoon without a break. Dutch knew what he was talking about. Nels took his advice and the afternoon went smoother.

They trudged back to the bunkhouse in deep twilight and peeled off their wet clothing.

"Pokey, play us a tune on your accordion." Frenchie said. "Something lively."

"Can't, though you sorry bastards could use some livening up," Pokey said. "Time for supper."

"I soak my ax handles in kerosene to put a little limb into them," Dutch said on the way to the cookhouse. "It's a filer's trick that spares your bones. We'll drop our axes off after we eat, and leave our misery whips to be sharpened."

"Smells good," Nels said. "I'm starved."

Irish was nowhere to be seen. Solveig ran between the table and stove, serving food, unable to keep up with the hungry men. She struggled to carry a heavy kettle to the table, almost dropping it in her haste. She was like a drowning woman. Even Pokey was not around.

Nels moved to a seat nearer the stove. He looked around, half expecting Pettibone to come out of nowhere to raise a ruckus. Mr. Elliot was gone. Paulson was not in the cookshack. Pettibone gone.

Nels took it as long as he could. He got up and helped deliver platters and bowls. The room grew silent as a stone.

The men resumed eating when nothing happened. Nels finished passing out the food. The clamor of metal on metal created such commotion that no one heard Solveig's soft thank you.

"Go ahead and eat," she said. "I'm caught up."

She rested her hand on his shoulder for the briefest of moments. For a long time, he felt the imprint of her hand.

The food disappeared. Solveig ran for more. She refilled the coffee pitchers. Then she brought the gingerbread to the ends of the table with a flourish.

Solveig broke the no-talking rule. "Gingerbread tonight, boys. You deserve it."

And then the reaching of hands, grunts of satisfaction, and deafening clatter of forks on plates. The pans emptied. Solveig limped to the door and stood like a queen. She nodded to each man leaving the cookshack.

Thank God, none of the bosses were around.

"Thanks, Ma," Ten-Day said as he stepped out the door.

It was the first time Nels heard Solveig's camp name.

"Where were you, and where the hell is Irish?" Ten-Day said as they met Pokey coming from the bunkhouse. "Ma can't do it all on her own."

"You're right. She's not so young these days," Pokey said. "I'll give a hand."

Nels caught a whiff of liquor from Pokey that roiled a thirst in Nels almost strong enough to drop him to his knees. Something was cock-eyed with the whole outfit. Why, back in Gull River Timber, not a drop of liquor was to be found. But here, it was as if a few men did whatever they wanted. Not everyone, but a few.

"Pokey should have been helping Solveig all along," Ten-Day said.

"He and Irish should be horsewhipped." Dutch was all for giving them a good threshing. "They'll work Ma into her grave if we let them. She don't deserve it."

The men discussed the punishments they might mete out to the miscreants. Nels did not want to cause trouble. He did want to find Irish's hidden bottle.

Fish slid out the door as if going to the backhouse. He came back a good quarter hour later, rubbing a bruised knuckle.

"Where you been?" Ten-Day said.

"Saw a man about a dog," Fish said with a wink.

"And the dog?" Nels said. "How's he doing?"

"He's sobering up," Fish said. "Promises not to do it again."

Nels hoped not.

Chapter 18
Sister Magdalena

Dear Lord, I promise to obey whatever is decided, but please do not let it be nursing.

Sister Magdalena took her place in line between Sister Lucy and Agatha as the nuns walked single file into the refectory. She was not hungry. The smell of fresh bread. The gentle swish of cotton skirts. The tap of soles upon the wooden floor. Sister Magdalena fingered the roughness of an inside seam of her wide sleeves where she dutifully hid her hands. The room filled with black and white habits scattered with novices wearing gray and postulants in black dresses.

The direction of her life would change within the next few minutes. Either she would begin traveling the north woods or take a different role in the monastery. She might end up as a nurse, God forbid. She braced herself. *Not my will but thine.*

Sister Magdalena had taken vows of obedience, stability, and chastity. Perhaps God meant to test her commitment. Her brother's warning lingered in her mind. She lassoed her wandering thoughts and forced herself back to the reality of the moment.

A painting of the Madonna and Child splashed color on the far wall. Sister Magdalena's eyes rested on the blue folds of the Virgin's robes. The bright eyes of the Child Jesus looked approvingly on the flock of women. Each sister waited in silence behind her chair.

Sister Hildegard's lips pursed into a distinct frown. Sister Lucy nodded at Sister Magdalena. Agatha chewed her bottom lip.

"Before the Great Silence, we will vote on building more hospitals closer to the logging camps," Mother Superior said. She did not invite them to be seated, an indication there would be no discussion. "This expansion would provide care in a timelier fashion. All funded by the sale of hospital chits." She nodded at Sister Magdalena, and then Sister Bede Marie.

A clattering wagon and clopping hooves sounded outside the window. Children called in the street. Somewhere a dog barked.

"Sister Magdalena suggests that all loggers pay a little to provide for those who need care. This program spares financial hardship for both men and their dependents."

Brief whispers until Mother Superior raised her hand. Silence. The sound of wheezy Sister Dorothy's asthmatic breathing and the beating of Sister Magdalena's heart. Agatha hiccoughed, then covered her mouth as her face reddened.

"Remember Sisters," Mother Superior said. "This community has seen God's provision every step of the way. He, not we, built this hospital and orphanage. He, not we, built the schools. We are His vessels. He makes it possible. Without Him we can do nothing."

She looked kindly upon the face of each sister. "Your service and sacrifice are not forgotten, dear sisters. Once again, we discern His will in the face of great need. Fear not, little flock. Do not be ruled by doubt, but by His holy will."

Sister Hildegard pressed her lower back with a look of misery on her face, leaning to one side as if she might fall. On a good day, Sister Hildegard could be contrary. Sister Magdalena's hopes wilted. Even one negative vote meant the sisters would not go ahead with the expansion.

Of course, the decision must be unanimous. Such sacrifice could only be sustained by unity among its members. Amazing things were being accomplished by religious communities across the world. Everyone had an opinion, but in the final decision, the good of all must come before the will of any single person.

"Our supper waits," Mother Superior said. "We have prayed and discerned God's will. Raise your right hand if you agree with the plan to expand health care into the north woods by the sale of hospital chits."

Sister Magdalena and Sister Lucy were the first to raise their hands. One by one habits swished as hands raised and sleeves fell back over forearms. All eyes turned to Sister Hildegard who stood motionless. When she realized that she was the only abstention, Sister Hildegard took a deep breath, and raised her hand.

The decision was unanimous.

Mother Superior nodded to Sister Hildegard. "I am happy to report that our community will be receiving another substantial donation in the coming months. I have spoken to the bishop. He agrees an outreach to the loggers and their families is needed."

Then she crossed herself and led the meal prayer. *Bless us O Lord, and these thy gifts which we are about to receive from thy bounty through Jesus Christ our Lord, Amen.*

Chairs scraped across the floor and everyone sat. The postulants served the soup and bread. The Great Silence descended as Sister Lucy read another chapter.

Sister Magdalena could not concentrate on a' Kempis. She tasted her soup with a tongue thick and dry. It was really happening.

What had she been thinking? She knew nothing about being a drummer. She had never sold a thing in her life. How would she find the camps scattered all over Minnesota in the winter time? What would she say when she found them?

This is how it must feel to have a baby. Women waited for months, but when it finally arrived, the mother faced the responsibility of raising the child to adulthood. Families faced struggles much greater than Sister Magdalena's small endeavor. Her thoughts flew to Sean Murphy and his wife. Sister Magdalena took comfort knowing the Blessed Mother must have been assailed by anxiety so far from home with a new baby.

Fear not.

God's will, God's bill, as Mother Superior once told them. He would intervene on her behalf. He would protect her in her travels. He would put words in her mouth. She would ask the priest for a special blessing to sell hospital tickets. She could depend on the community's prayers. She would ask the saints and angels to intercede for her venture. She was not alone. The Body of Christ and the Benedictine Community worked as one.

Agatha jabbed Sister Magdalena with her elbow and pointed at the plate of soup before Sister Magdalena, still untouched.

Sister Magdalena picked up her spoon and dipped the lukewarm soup. She would face the future with courage, whatever came of it. First, she must finish her supper. It was her turn to do the dishes.

Chapter 19
Solveig

Solveig finished the supper dishes and set the tables for breakfast. Where was Irish? Damn Finlander. At this rate she would be up all night. Pokey's accordion music sounded from the bunkhouse.

Solveig thought to send for him, but reconsidered. After her years on the silent prairie, Solveig welcomed music. Let the poor man get some rest.

She hummed along as she set the sponge for flapjacks and put a kettle of beans to soak. She filled a pot with rock-hard prunes and set them to stew overnight. Then, though her feet ached and stabs of pain went through her lower back, she rolled lard and flour into huge crusts and filled twenty pie plates with softened apples and sweetening. Fresh pies for the breakfast table.

The floor tracked mud from fifty pairs of dirty boots. If only they had a flunkey to help with the chores. While her pies baked, Solveig mopped the worst parts and headed toward her room. She stashed the finished pies in the pie safe overnight. Mice would foul anything left out in the open. Queenie rubbed around her legs.

"Get to work," Solveig said.

Wearily, she lit a candle stub and removed her heated bed stone from its place under the stove. Frost etched the outside walls, and her teeth chattered as she put the hot stone between the covers to warm her bed. She shivered into night clothes, adding Rasmuss's flannel shirt and a knitted cap. She wore her heaviest woolen socks and both layers of underwear. She climbed into bed and pulled the quilts over her shoulders, listening to the moaning wind. Ice pellets tinkled on the glass pane.

Thoughts of Halvor nibbled at her peace. She hoped he hated living in town. Then she hoped that he found happiness in town. He was her son, even if he no longer considered her his mother. As for his wife. Solveig wrinkled up her nose.

The bunk was rock hard, nothing like the feather bed at home. She counted her blessings. She had a job. Gunnar cared for Young Bob and Buck. She had health and strength. She refused to think of the future. Something would work out in the end. It always did.

Mr. Starkweather might bring the mail when he returned. Maybe a letter from Halvor begging her pardon. Maybe not.

She slipped into an exhausted sleep. In the middle of the night, she woke with a start. Someone was in the kitchen. She fumbled for a match and lit the candle. The wind moaned and snow dusted the top of her quilt. Footsteps and the clank of metal. Pokey firing the stove?

The pies. Someone was stealing pies. She pulled the hat pin from her pincushion and stuck it into her shawl. She grabbed her butcher knife and a stout piece of firewood used to prop her door. Her heart pounded in her ears. She would not put up with it any longer. "Who's there?"

No answer.

"Get the hell out of here or I'll scream loud enough to wake the camp."

Hesitation.

"I mean it." She banged on the wooden door with the club. "Help! Help! There's a thief in the cookshack!"

Footsteps. The front door slammed. Holding the knife in one hand and the club in the other, Solveig stepped into a melted puddle of snow outside her door. Her feet wet through her bedsocks.

"You should have chased him away," Solveig said to Queenie who rubbed around her legs. Her heart returned to normal rhythm. "I'd be better off with a watchdog."

She peeked out the door. Footprints in the new snow led toward the scaler cabin.

The door to the warming oven hung open. Two pies sat on the table. Solveig counted and recounted, but one was missing. She raised the candle and examined the pantry shelves. A sack of dried apples gone. She tallied again. No question. The thief had struck again.

She shivered in her wet socks. A skiff of ice covered the water buckets by the work tables. Where was Pokey? She stuffed wood into the stove and held her hands over the flames. She could be accused like Nels at Gull River Timber. Then what would she do? Go directly to the poor farm? She replaced the pies in the safe and secured the door. Queenie yowled a reminder of her empty dish.

Solveig spooned a bit of mush from the kettle. She knelt and petted her cat as it lapped the food. "Nice kitty. Pretty kitty." She set her jaw. She would not let a thief rob her future.

To hell with Irish, the sot. Not only would she demand locks, but she would report the thievery to the pencil pusher. She would go to Mr. Starkweather, if necessary.

Exhaustion weighed as heavy as the thefts. She could not continue doing Irish's work as well as her own. It was not fair. She would report his drinking on the job.

No, she vowed to speak to Irish privately. Then, if his behavior continued, and only then, she would bring down the wrath of Mr. Starkweather upon him.

Rasmuss always knew how to handle difficult situations. She returned to bed and fell into a restless sleep until she heard Irish rustling in the kitchen. Solveig pulled on her clothes and hurried to her chores.

Irish looked gray as paste except for a purple bruise the size of a fist on his jaw.

"Glad to see you made it."

"Quiet." Irish winced. "Can't a man work in peace?" He made no explanation for his absence the previous night nor bruised face.

"Who else sleeps in the scaler's shack?" She must tell him about the thievery, even if he did not want to hear.

"Shut your trap, damn you." He slammed a fry pan onto the stove. "Yapping skirts have no place at a logging camp."

"Listen, I'm trying to tell you about the thief." Heat rose her neck. She would not be intimidated. "I scared him off and foot-prints headed in that direction."

"Didn't hear nothing," Irish said. "Are you sure?"

"He nipped a pie and a sack of dried apples," Solveig said. "Is Pettibone around?" If he was with Mr. Starkweather, he was in the clear.

"He's around."

They worked until the men streamed inside, bringing an arc-tic blast with them every time the door opened. They devoured every monkey blanket, piece of side pork, logging berry, and apple pie on the table.

Several jacks tipped their hats toward Solveig as they left the building. They did not speak, but she felt their appreciation. A glimmer of light showed on the eastern horizon. Another day at Starkweather Timber. How did the jacks stand the brutal cold?

Irish rubbed his bruised cheek. "You should have baked more pies. None for us."

"I did, but the thief stole it." Solveig said. "We've got to report it to the office. I won't be blamed for thievery."

"You're right," Irish agreed. "You report it. I'm feeling under the weather."

Of course, he could not report it. Drawing attention to his bruised face or hung-over condition might cost him his job. "You must have been poorly last night, too." She held her tongue, but oh, how she wanted to give him the sharp edge of it.

"It won't happen again," Irish said.

He got to his feet and slammed dirty plates into soapy water. Solveig half expected him to go back to bed and leave her with the work, but he scrubbed the dishes and began mixing bread dough.

"I'd like my own key to the root cellar," Solveig said. "In case you're poorly again."

"Take it up with the pencil pusher when you see him," Irish said. "Go now before the swingdingle comes. I'll cover here."

Not exactly an apology. She wrapped in her heaviest shawl and ventured into the winter weather. Cold pierced to her bones, freezing her lungs and nose hairs. She pulled the shawl over her face until only her eyes showed. Frost collected on her lashes.

At least Halvor worked inside this year. Though she was cold, she felt a thawing in her heart toward her son. Maybe today a letter would come.

Chapter 20
Nels

The weeks dragged by and winter set in for good. Nels counted himself lucky to bunk near the stove. He and Ten-Day caulked the log wall by their bed with old rags to cut down the draft, but the wind off the lake proved stronger than their efforts.

"Want to play checkers?" Ten-Day said. "I'll tell you what Barrister said about gold mining in the Dakotas."

Nels walked over to the checkerboard sitting atop an old barrel near the amen corner where Pokey sat with his squeeze box. At Gull River Timber they had played parlor games, usually aimed toward greenhorns. The games were always cruel, though not mean-spirited.

"Watch out for snow snakes, boys." Pokey stretched out an ominous chord. "They'll wrap around your leg and pull you down under the drifts." The accordion moaned as if in distress. "Lost a man last year. Snake hooked around his leg and pulled him down. Didn't find his body until spring thaw."

Alfie, a young farmer from Wadena, took the bait.

"Snow snakes? What do they look like?"

"You won't see them until it's too late," Pokey said. "They're near invisible in the snow."

He paused and looked at Alfie eye to eye. "Too bad they don't give warning like rattlers. Would save lives."

"Are they poisonous?" Alfie said. "Never heard of them before."

"We only lose a few men every year," Pokey said. "Nothing to worry about."

"But if you can't see them," Alfie said.

"You'll see their pink tongues against the snow," Pokey looked at Nels and Ten-Day as if for validation. "Isn't that right, boys?"

Nels shrugged. He was not about to fill that poor boy's head with lies.

"Tell us about the olden days," Ten-Day said. "When you worked on the Rum."

If Pokey were a cat, he would start purring, he was so pleased to be asked. He puffed out his chest and licked his lips. "You boys don't want to hear all that business."

"I do," Ten-Day said. "Listen up, everyone. Pokey's telling stories."

The worst part of living in the bunkhouse was all the blathering. Nels grew tired of it mighty fast.

"When I was a young pup, I worked oxen down on the Rum River. Well boys, one year I needed work and went into town to find it." Pokey rolled a wad of tobacco in his mouth and spat in the spittoon. He stretched back and took a breath. "A walking boss came by and saw me holding my ox goad. He asked me if I knew how to skin an ox team. I says yessir, I do." Pokey paused for effect. "That man dropped down on all fours and yelled, he says, 'I'm an ox—drive me.'" Pokey stopped and waited for the jacks to react.

"Drive him?" Ten-Day said. "He got down on all fours?"

"Why, I was a might shook up," Pokey said. "I was a young pup, like I said, and just talking to a walking boss made my mouth pucker."

The bunkhouse grew quiet.

"'Hurry up', he says. 'Drive me,'" Pokey said. "Somehow I found voice enough to call out gee and haw." Pokey shook his head. "But the man wasn't satisfied. He says to me, 'Son you don't know nothing about skinning ox.' He went on his way and I was left standing with my goad in hand."

"What happened next?" Alfie said.

"Why," Pokey said, drawing out his words in a slow drawl. "He came back the next day and I was still looking for work. 'Son,' he says, as if he had never laid eyes on me before. 'Son, can you drive an ox?'"

"He said that?" Ten-Day said. "Just like before?"

"He says to me," Pokey said. "'Can you drive an ox?' I nodded and he dropped down on all fours.' I'm an ox, he says, drive me.'" Pokey paused. There was not a sound except for the hiss of boiling water in the barrel on top of the stove.

"So, what did you do?" Ten-Day said.

"I didn't say a word," Pokey said. "I just took my goad stick and drove the nail a half-inch into his fat ass."

Nels grinned and the jacks gasped.

"The man leapt to his feet, rubbing his hinder. He says, 'you're hired,'" Pokey said. "I worked for him a good spell and we always got along."

The men whooped and guffawed. It was always the same. The tallest tales were always generous to the jacks and hard on the bosses.

Pokey began another tune. He did not smile, but there was a sparkle in his eyes. Pokey was a master story teller and a good bull cook, even though he was rough as a cob and not above throwing his weight around.

Pettibone swaggered into the bunkhouse and called for a game of hot-hand. Nels left the amen corner and climbed into his bunk. He wanted nothing to do with it.

Pettibone plopped on the deacon's bench with a hat in his lap. "Who will be the first to give it a try?" Pettibone looked from man to man, hoping for a victim.

"How do you play?" Alfie said.

Nels scoffed. Hard to feel sorry for someone so gullible. Most of the men headed back to their cards or games, but Ten-Day and Fish gathered around Pettibone.

"It's fun," Pettibone said. He told the rules of the game, notorious to experienced jacks. Alfie would bend over with his head in the hat. "That will leave your southern exposure prominently displayed." The men would take turns giving a spank. After each swat, Alfie would guess who slapped him.

"Name the man, and he takes your place," Pettibone said. "It's harmless fun."

Alfie rubbed his curly head and looked from face to face before he finally agreed. Once he had his face buried in the hat, Dutch climbed to the top of his bunk and pulled out a flail on a leather strap. Instead of feeling the men slapping his buttocks with an open palm, poor Alfie got a flailing that raised blisters. Again and again, he turned, red faced and sputtering, trying to point out the man who had smacked him. Pettibone laughed until he turned purple.

Nels turned his back in disgust. The jacks would not think it funny if they were the ones taking the hiding. Alfie would not be able to sit down for a week.

The jacks were rude, rough, boisterous, and cruel. They were crude talkers and hard drinkers. At one time Nels sought to fit in with them, to be one of the crew. Not anymore. He had had enough.

The whole thing made him thirsty. Nels covered his ears with his pillow and shut his eyes as tight as he could. God, what he would give for a drink.

Chapter 21
Sister Magdalena

Sister Magdalena awakened to the wind rattling her window. The bell had yet to ring for morning prayers.

Today she would leave the confines of the convent and go out into the world in the Name of Christ. Today was her chance to do something for God.

A niggle of worry wormed into her thoughts. What if she failed? What if she disgraced herself and her religious community? Her father had cautioned that her behavior reflected on her family.

She knelt by her bed, shivering, as she prayed the morning offering, *"My God, I adore You, and I love You with all my heart. I thank you for having created me, made me a Christian, and preserved me this night. I offer You the actions of this day. Grant that all of them may be in accordance with Your holy Will and for Your greater glory. Protect me from sin and from all evil. Let Your grace be always with me and with all my dear ones. Amen."*

She splashed cold water on her face and rubbed salt over her teeth. Then she reached for her tunic, the long-sleeved black dress, reciting the prayers that went along with dressing.

"Clothe me, O my God, with thy holy religious practices so that I may appear before Thee such as our habit and profession require."

She attached the girdle around her waist. *"Unite me to Thee, O my God, in an intimate union and attach me to Thee in the bonds of charity the links of which may never break."*

Then came the toque, the tightly fitting white hat that covered her head, and the coif which framed her face and neck in white. *"Consider, O my soul, the whiteness of this toque represents the purity of conscience you should have in order to please God. O Lord, grant me this grace, to die rather than to defile my soul by any sin. Purify it in Thy Precious Blood and grant me perfect contrition for my sins."*

Then came the scapular, the double-sided apron that covered front and back. *"Lord grant me the grace to carry with joy and love Thy yoke and burden all the days of my life."*

Then the mantle. *"Oh, spotless Lamb of God, adorn Me with the purity with which all those are adorned who follow Thee."*

Then the veils. First the white and then the black. *"The veil should teach me, Lord, that I should die to the world and to myself so as to live no longer but for Thee. Grant me, therefore, the grace that nothing of this miserable life may remain in me, which prevents my union with Thee."*

It would have been helpful to have a looking glass. Sister Magdalena felt for strands of hair showing around her coif. Sister Hildegard and the other sisters were always immaculate in dress and demeanor. She sighed. Why was perfection always out of reach?

She eyed the neat stack of hospital tickets on her bedside stand. She tried to imagine speaking to a room of strange men, trying to convince them to spend money on a concept rather than a tangible product. Her mouth turned dry just thinking of it.

Holy Spirit, fill the hearts of your faithful.

Sean Murphy had died the previous week. Sister Magdalena remembered vague directions to his wife's dwelling on the waterfront. There might be time for a short visit before she left for the woods. Sister Magdalena could offer nothing but sympathy and prayer, but she could at least visit the young woman.

Sister Magdalena prayed for the widow at Morning Prayer. Sister Magdalena faced a long journey and needed her strength, but her porridge lay like paste in her mouth.

After breakfast, Mother Superior and the sisters prayed a blessing over Sister Magdalena. Sister Lucy squeezed Sister Magdalena's shoulder as she passed by on her way to the ward.

Mother Superior motioned Sister Magdalena into her office where she handed her a cloth knapsack. Inside was a special pocket to hold the hospital chits, and another to hold the money. Both pockets secured with buttons. There was room for clean stockings, night-gown, handkerchiefs, and a change of underwear. Another pocket for her prayer book. Mother superior handed her two silver dollars.

"For emergency use only. Trust in God's provision, Sister," Mother Superior said. Her eyes twinkled. "Please restrain from unnecessary violence."

Sister Magdalena felt a flush rising in her cheeks. "Of course, Mother."

"The owner of Starkweather Timber is in Duluth recruiting employ-ees." Mother Superior gave her a handbill from Starkweather Timber. Mother stood to her feet and tucked her hands in the sleeves of her gown. "Father Pattullo says Mr. Starkweather expects to transport new workers by train to his camp on Stink Lake." She nodded encouragingly. "Mr. Starkweather will allow you to travel with him and address his workers." She took a step toward the door, and Sister Magdalena followed. "Makes sense to start farthest west and work your way toward home." She gave instructions about other camps in the area, trains and boats going out to the different camps. "Avoid expense. You must address the camps at the beginning of the season to sell as many tickets as possible."

"Yes, Mother."

"The train leaves in two hours."

Sister Magdalena stepped into the hall and broke into a smile. God was at work. She would have just enough time to visit Mrs. Murphy.

The cold snatched the air out of her lungs as the wind off Lake Superior tangled her long veil. A skiff of snow glazed the streets. She was glad for the extra set of long underwear and woolen stockings that Mother Superior had insisted she wear. A heavy woolen cloak covered her long habit. The fabric was thick enough to block the Minnesota winter. Sister Lucy had knitted sturdy mittens. Sister Magdalena untangled the veil and tucked it inside her cape. She hastened down the hill to the waterfront, careful lest she slip on the cobblestones.

She could not resist reading the handbill as she walked. Starkweather Timber needed workers of every description. If she were not a professed sister, she might work there. Not cooking, of course, heavens no. But washing dishes and doing chores. Logging camp fare was legendary. Her mouth watered at the thought of sugar, butter, eggs, cream, pies, cakes, and cookies.

Her cheeks numbed by the time she reached the rattletrap building where Mrs. Murphy lived. Sister Magdalena climbed a rickety stairway, stepping over a slop bucket on the step, sniffing urine and sour milk, surprised by a rat racing down the stairs. Sister Magdalena stomped the rat and kicked it over the side of the stairway. She prayed a silent prayer for wisdom, then knocked at a door labeled *Murphy*.

Sister Magdalena took a quick breath when Mrs. Murphy opened the door. Mrs. Murphy stood at least a foot shorter, and her dark, curly hair hung loose over her shoulders, framing a heart-shaped face with rosy cheeks. Her startling blue eyes rimmed red from weeping. A worn apron hid any sign of a baby. When Mrs. Murphy saw the nun at her door, she burst into loud wails and pulled Sister Magdalena into the small room.

"Thank God," she said between sobs, "I prayed someone would come."

All her life, Sister Magdalena recognized herself as homely and gawky. It did not matter at the convent, but being in the presence of this beautiful woman made Sister Magdalena feel like an ugly toad. Sister Magdalena stood tongue-tied.

The room, stark and dreary, almost squeaked with cleanliness. A crucifix hung over a crude table. A bed with a patchwork quilt stood in the corner. A braided rug lay on the floor by the door. Sister Magdalena had not thought what she might say once she got there.

The Rule of Benedict instructed to listen with the ears of your heart. If nothing else, she could lend a sympathetic ear to the distraught woman before her.

Sister Magdalena laid aside her feelings of inadequacy and folded Mrs. Murphy into her arms as if she were a relative.

"What will I do?" Mrs. Murphy wailed. "My Sean is dead. What is to become of us?"

Mrs. Murphy's tears dampened Sister Magdalena's scapular. Time was slipping away. The train would be leaving soon. She did not see a clock.

"I'll make you a cup of tea," Sister Magdalena said. "Sit and tell me about it."

The words poured out as Sister Magdalena found the boiling kettle on the stove and added the last bit of tea leaves from a jar. The dishes, though mismatched and cracked, stacked neatly on a shelf. The entire kitchen stood orderly and clean. The sugar bowl was empty. A dried heel of bread was the only food in sight.

"I can't pay the rent. I can't find a job." Mrs. Murphy picked up her cup but set it down again without tasting it. "I have no family here or references. No money to go home." She began sobbing again, laying her head on the table. Her black hair spread across the mended linen cloth. "What am I to do, Sister? The baby comes the end of May."

Sister Magdalena was taking a chance and probably making a big mistake. She should have consulted Mother Superior before even visiting Mrs. Murphy. Sister Magdalena knew that pretty widows like Mrs. Murphy sometimes ended up working in the brothels along the waterfront.

Sister Magdalena pulled out the advertisement from Starkweather Timber and smoothed it on the table in front of Mrs. Murphy.

"Look, Mrs. Murphy," Sister Magdalena said.

"Call me Gertie," she said.

"Starkweather Timber needs workers. I'm on my way there right now. The logging camp is west of here." She felt as if she were walking on thin ice. She must consider not only this young woman's future, but her baby's future, too. What would Mother Superior say?

"They need kitchen helpers. I can see you have a clean hand. No doubt you would be perfect for the job." Sister Magdalena took a breath. "The camp is filled with rough men, and the days will be long and difficult. Not easy when you are in the family way."

Great tear drops hung on the ends of Gertie's eyelashes, dripping down the bridge of her upturned nose.

"It would be a roof over your head and a chance to earn money before the baby comes. Travel with me. You won't do it alone," Sister Magdalena said.

Gertie sniffed and blew her nose. She looked around the room, as if trying to decide if she could leave it or not.

"But the baby," she said in a small voice. "They'll never hire me once they know I am with child."

"It's not a lie unless they ask you outright," Sister Magdalena said. It was not something she had learned in religious formation, but a saying of her brothers. "Keep yourself to yourself. What they don't know, won't hurt them. Once they figure it out, the season will be almost over."

"When do we leave?" Gertie said in a voice so low and hopeless that Sister Magdalena leaned closer to hear her.

"Now. Pack your things and put on your warmest clothing," Sister Magdalena said. "The train leaves in less than an hour."

The girl would turn heads. Every man in timber country would fall in love with her. "Wear your plainest dress and shawl. Two sets of underwear and three petticoats. And tie a kerchief over your hair."

It did not work. Even a drab dress and extra layers did little to disguise Gertie's beauty. Sister Magdalena crossed herself as they stepped out into the cold.

The clock in the square showed the lateness of the hour. It had taken longer than expected. Everything hinged on her connection with Mr. Starkweather. Her future and Gertie's depended on it.

"Run," Sister Magdalena said. She took Gertie's valise. "We'll miss our train."

Gertie hung on Sister Magdalena's arm, and pumped her short legs to keep up with Sister Magdalena's long strides. It was uphill from the waterfront. The cobblestones were slippery and the wind whipped around them. Sister Magdalena's veils swirled into a whirlwind of black and white that slapped Gertie's face.

"The veil must be a bother," Gertie said, pushing the veil away.

"Whoever invented the religious habit did not consider Duluth winters," Sister Magdalena said.

She glanced at her young companion, tears frozen on her cheeks, eyes red and sad. Later she would take the time to explain to this young woman how much being a sister meant to her. Sean had said Gertie once considered joining a religious community. Sister Magdalena would share the beautiful prayers that accompanied dressing in a habit. Someday. Not now.

Finally, they arrived at the low depot built along a winding track. Sister Magdalena clutched her aching side and leaned forward to catch her breath. Seagulls swarmed around the women. A train chugged at the depot and a line of straggly men filed into the car. An elderly gentleman wearing a swallow-tailed jacket and top hat stood aside, examining his pocket watch.

"Mr. Starkweather," Sister Magdalena said, trying to catch her breath while untangling her veil. She needed to look presentable, as an ambassador for Christ and the Benedictine Convent. "I'm Sister Magdalena, here to go with you to your logging camp."

He eyed her with a raised brow. He tucked his watch back in his pocket. He did not remove his hat or introduce himself.

Then he noticed Gertie. The wind had colored her cheeks. Her eyes as blue as a June day. Mr. Starkweather removed his hat with a sweeping bow.

"My pleasure, Miss...

"Mrs.," Gertie said. "Mrs. Murphy."

"My pleasure, Mrs. Murphy." Mr. Starkweather took her hand and kissed it, formal as a prince greeting a princess. It sickened Sister Magdalena. He had barely looked at her. He must be a Protestant, having so little respect for a religious sister.

"Mrs. Murphy is answering your advertisement for a kitchen helper in your camp," Sister Magdalena said. She had a strong urge to stand between this powerful man and the vulnerable young widow. "I can vouch for her habits."

"Yes," Mr. Starkweather said, eyeing Gertie up and down. "We are indeed looking for kitchen help."

"And I will speak to the lumberjacks about hospital tickets," Sister Magdalena said. "As Father Patullo inquired about."

"Yes, of course, the hospital chits," he said. He seemed preoccupied and distracted. "But not until the work day is finished." He frowned. "Not a word to the men until after supper."

The whistle blew. He gestured for the women to board the train car.

Sister Magdalena guided the young widow into the car that was half-filled with men. Some in flannel shirts and blue overalls, others in wool suits and jackets, some ragged. They were mostly young, though a few older faces scattered among the crowd. All eyes turned toward the women as they found their way to a seat near the back of the car. The men doffed their caps as Sister Magdalena passed. Catholics, they were, or perhaps they acted out of deference to the beautiful widow following close on her heels.

Wind rattled the windows and the engine puffed oily smoke that made Sister Magdalena cough. A spindly man poked firewood into the pot-bellied stove near the front of the car. No warmth reached the back seats.

Sister Magdalena planted herself on the aisle beside young Gertie, feeling like a guard dog, wondering all the while how she had gotten herself into the situation. She had left the convent with the sole intent of selling hospital tickets. Not even two hours later she had taken on a helpless widow. Perhaps she was leading the young woman into greater dangers.

The Rule of Benedict clearly said to ask for advice before beginning a new venture. *Lord have mercy*. She pulled her rosary.

"I'm scared, Sister," Gertie whispered. "I've never worked out before."

"I'm scared, too," Sister Magdalena said. What a relief to say it aloud. She told her of the plan to sell hospital tickets to lumber jacks.

"I wish Sean would have had a ticket," Gertie said. "He worried so about the money."

The train jerked forward. Someone played a harmonica. A few men leaned into the aisle for a card game. Mr. Starkweather glanced back from his seat at the front of the car until his eyes rested on Gertie.

Sister Magdalena pulled her cloak over Gertie like a blanket, trying to shield her from leering eyes. "Lean against the window and take a rest," Sister Magdalena said. Mr. Starkweather did not look away.

Two young brothers shivered in the seat ahead of them. They were thin and ill-clad for the weather. They were too young to be out on their own alone, too young to work in a logging camp. People suffered, especially poor people. They lost their money, lost their health, lost loved ones. They made poor decisions, made mistakes, and dug themselves deeper into their misery. Each person in the railroad car carried a story. Even Mr. Starkweather, richer than anyone Sister Magdalena had ever known, must carry secret heartaches.

Before she began the Glorious Mysteries, she petitioned for help for herself and each person on the train. She pulled out her biggest weapon:

Saint Michael, the Archangel, defend us in battle. Be our protection against the wickedness and snares of the devil.

Chapter 22
Solveig

Solveig's shoes, though sturdy, pinched in all the wrong places. It did not help that Irish failed to show up for breakfast the next morning.

"He's in the cups again," Pokey said with a shrug. "You know how it is."

Solveig nodded. Pokey did his best to help, but spilled more coffee than he carried to the tables. He was underfoot, asking what to do next. She finally sent him for water. The reservoir should have been filled long ago. Pokey could best help by doing his work without being told.

Solveig seethed as she flipped monkey blankets. Irish was a whirling dervish at making them, boasting that he could fry a hundred pancakes in five minutes on a hot stovetop. Solveig was getting faster, but still nowhere near as quick as Irish. She piled the flapjacks on platters in the warming oven. She ladled logging berries into serving bowls. The men filed inside and took their places. She ran back and forth between the stove and tables. She had forgotten the molasses. The clatter of tinware almost drove her to insanity.

Damn Irish! He had promised never to do it again. She missed her chance to tattle on him when she was at the office about the locks. The pencil pusher had asked her directly about Irish's behavior.

"Everything is all right," she had said. "We're short on help."

The pencil pusher assured her that Mr. Starkweather was bringing more workers. That had been two days earlier. Starkweather was overdue.

The jacks shoveled their food and left. The pencil pusher looked her way but did not say anything. Of course, there was no talking during meals.

Nothing as quiet as the end of scraping and banging tin. Solveig collapsed to a bench. It was all she could do to keep from bawling. Queenie jumped into her lap. Pokey brought her a plate of food and a cup of coffee and dropped to a bench beside her.

"Damn Irish," Pokey said. "He never pulled this shit before— excuse my French, Ma."

She had wanted a job, and boy did she have one. She had worked hard all her life, but never such long hours without a rest. The demanding, physical work that took every bit of energy she could muster. The tables mounded with dirty dishes and she must ready food for the swingdingle. Not to mention supper. They were low on bread. The men deserved better.

The kitchen was too much for two and impossible for one.

Solveig pulled herself to her feet. "How are my girls doing today? I had hoped to have a minute to visit."

"Tolerable in the cold. Only one egg today," Pokey said.

Pokey cleared the dirty dishes as Solveig started the food for noon. She stirred a batch of cornbread for the swingdingle, adding her egg to the thick mixture. She put leftover stew on the stove to heat. She would add potatoes and onions to stretch it out for noon. They would fill up on cornbread and molasses.

Her legs and feet felt like fire. If Irish dared show his face in this kitchen, she would give him a piece of her mind. She was done mollycoddling a grown man. Bottle fever. Hmph. She would show him bottle fever. She would break an empty bottle over his head and see how he liked that. She would slap him into next week.

A sound at the doorway. She turned to wage war on Irish.

A tall nun stood at the door with a shivering young woman at her side. It was the religious sister from the train. The pencil pusher followed them and directed the women to the stove to warm themselves.

"Hello, Ma." Mr. Elliot said. "Where's Irish?"

What could she say? Her words would mean Irish's job. Before she could answer, Pokey spoke up.

"He's drunk as a skunk, and it's not the first time." He reported the times Irish had left Solveig with the work.

A quick tear gathered in Solveig's eye. God bless Pokey, no doubt repaying her for mending his socks. A good deed returned, as her grandmother always said. The truth out in the open, at last. Whatever happened now at least was not of her making.

"We'll see about that." The pencil pusher clamped his lips and worked his jaw.

"I've brought help," he said. "Mrs. Murphy is your new flunkey. We've hired two dozen new men, starved down with traveling. They need breakfast before they head out to the woods to join the others."

He left without further comment. A swirl of frigid air entered the room with the open door. Pokey followed, making a slight bow to the nun as he passed, though staring the whole time at the younger woman.

That was all Solveig needed. A pretty girl would turn heads and disrupt work.

"Please call me Gertie, ma'am," Mrs. Murphy said with a curtsy.

Pokey stuck his head through the door. "Hungry men coming this way, Ma."

Solveig's head whirled. Too much was happening too fast. Solveig had no time to greet the flunkey. She had no time to ask why the nun was in the cookhouse. No time to hunt down Irish and force him to do his share. She had men to feed. No time to wait for the corn bread to bake. The stew was needed for the swingdingle. Better make more pancakes. She mixed and stirred as fast as she could.

Gertie removed her shawl and began setting the empty table with plates and cups. Thank God, she knew her way around a kitchen.

"What can I do?" the nun said.

She looked big, strong, and capable. Help was help, and Solveig needed it.

"Stoke the fire." Solveig kept flipping flapjacks. "No time to grind coffee. Boiling water is in the kettle for tea." She told Gertie where to find the flatware, and how to refill the molasses pitchers. "Apples on the stove go in the serving bowls. Two bowls should be enough." She kept flipping pancakes until she filled a huge platter. The first shift had eaten all the side pork. No time to fetch more from the root cellar.

The nun finished her tasks and began washing dishes. The men straggled in the door. They did not look promising. City dwellers, by the look of their clothing. Many were immigrants. Rasmuss had told of greenhorns who knew nothing about logging.

Two boys were in the mix, too young to be working in the woods. They looked alike. They stuck together, finding seats near the doorway. The younger was no more than twelve or thirteen. The older not yet shaving. Their bare faces would be frostbitten before the morning was over. They wore low shoes and insufficient jackets. Rasmuss's old clothes would hang on the boys, but she could cut them down to size. Poor kids had no business at Starkweather Timber.

Solveig carried the pancake platters to the table. The men ate as if they had not seen food for a week. Solveig made more pancakes. The men shoveled them down as fast as she fried them, and looked for more. Gertie passed the cooked apples. When she saw them disappear, she reached for the prunes.

"Logging berries are for the swingdingle," Solveig said. She scraped the last of the batter as she spoke. "They'll have to do without."

Mr. Elliot stepped into the cookhouse and motioned for the men to follow him. They filed out the door like prisoners being led to the hang rope. Gertie cleared the table. Dark curls poked out from her kerchief. Her clothing looked worn, but clean. Pretty though she was, this girl knew how to work. It was only morning, and Solveig was exhausted. The women looked tired, as well. The nun reached for the broom.

"Have you two eaten?" Solveig said.

The women shook their heads.

"Neither have I," Solveig said. The cornbread should be done by now. They would cut into one of the pans. "We'll take a few minutes."

Mr. Elliot returned with red cheeks and a dripping nose. His eyebrows scrunched together. He headed for the stove and rubbed his hands together over the heat. "I see you met," he mumbled. He motioned Solveig aside.

What did he want now? She limped behind him to the far corner of the room. Thank God for the women's help. Any rope for a drowning person.

"I'll be quick about it. Irish is no longer employed at Starkweather Timber," Mr. Elliot said. He swallowed hard enough to bob his Adam's apple. "Mr. Starkweather does not tolerate intoxication on the job."

What? Irish fired?

"Mr. Starkweather has been pleased with your diligence. He offers you the cook position," Mr. Elliot said.

A surge of hope, stronger than fatigue, flowed through Solveig's veins like a shot of hard liquor. Her tongue stuck to her front teeth, and she managed to croak. "Me?"

"Yes, you." Mr. Elliot pulled his lips into a grimace. "It's what you wanted."

Solveig's mind raced. A cook was responsible for everything.

"Of course, it comes with a pay raise—to thirty-five dollars a month."

Her mind tallied the figures. She would pay off the mortgage and have just enough for a train ticket home.

"Irish made forty dollars a month," Solveig said. It was not fair that they would pay her less because she was a woman.

"Irish had experience," the pencil pusher said as if reading her mind. His voice squeaked. He bobbed his head, as if in apology. "The brains wanted to pay you thirty-two dollars, but I convinced him to go a little higher." He looked at her pleadingly. "It's the best I could do."

"Thank you, Mr. Elliot," Solveig said. "I accept."

"That's that, then." He looked relieved. "Mrs. Murphy will bunk with you. The Sister will be here overnight." He turned to leave.

"Wait." Solveig tried to sound confident. She had questions. She barely knew what was expected. "Irish and I couldn't keep up with fifty men, and now the work load has increased."

"You have Mrs. Murphy," he said.

"I need a cookee," Solveig said. "And two or three flunkeys." Solveig's thoughts became logical and orderly, a step-by-step plan falling into place. "Gertie can take my position as cookee. I noticed two brothers too young to do much good in the woods."

Mr. Elliot shook his head. Solveig saw the refusal coming. She also reasoned that she had him over a barrel. No food, no men. No men, no timber harvest. No timber harvest, no money for Mr. Starkweather's bank account. She chose her words carefully.

"I'm not as young as I used to be, Mr. Elliot," Solveig said. "I doubt I'd last the winter without more help." She sighed. "And then where would you be?"

The pencil pusher paused and took a deep breath. "The younger lad, maybe. He's all I can spare, Mrs. Rognaldson."

The clerk did not use her camp name. He was not happy. No doubt he would have to defend his actions to Mr. Starkweather, the old tightwad.

It felt good to have a voice again, to have some leverage. "Two flunkeys are needed." She might have just saved their lives, such dangerous work in the woods. "And another if you can scare one up."

Mr. Elliot pursed his lips into a frown and shook his head. "You don't know what you're asking." He tugged his collar and stuck his hands into his pockets. "You'll have the younger boy and Mrs. Murphy can take over as cookee." He turned and left. Even his footsteps sounded angry on the puncheon floor. "Make it work."

A blast of wintery air came in with his exit.

It was not until later that she remembered the mail. Mr. Elliot brought nothing for her.

Chapter 23
Nels

Nels sunk his ax into a branch and stretched his back, squinting at the rising sun. The day had barely started and would never end.

"He's almost a hermit," Ten-Day said. "Hasn't been to town for three years and doesn't plan on going this summer either."

"Who's that?" Dutch said.

"Barrister, of course," Ten-Day said. "He's a genius. Studied in Oxford, that's someplace in England."

Nels turned back to his ax. He did not know the barn boss, and did not need to. Ten-Day was worse than a woman when it came to gossip.

Fish came with his ox team. He talked so fast that saliva flew from his mouth and froze on his beard. "She's a vision, boys, a high-stepper."

"What you talking about?" Ten-Day said.

He blurted the news. Another woman was hired for the cook-shack. Irish was out on his ear. Ma was promoted to cook.

A woman in camp? That was all Nels wanted to know. He and the other two men drew closer to catch every detail.

"She's the prettiest thing you ever saw," Fish said. "A real lardy-dardy."

"Back to butchering wood," Paulson growled as he walked by. "This ain't no sewing circle." He brought the new men with him. They were a ragged lot, for the most part, some in city clothes. It was best to keep a low profile and hope Paulson tagged someone else for the dirty job of training greenhorns.

The bull of the woods introduced two brothers from Estonia who spoke little English. Cosmos and Stefan bowed and smiled. "They're hired on as fellers," the push said.

"Best to pair new men with experienced workers until they get the hang of things," Dutch said in a low voice as the push showed the new men where to start cutting.

"Maybe they come with experience," Ten-Day said. "I'll ask."

"At least we're not stuck with them," Nels said.

A team of matched Percherons passed by with the toploader standing behind the driver like a lord. The horses tossed their heads and swished their tails, lifting hooves to plant their iron calks into the ice-covered trail. God, they were beautiful animals.

"Who's the toploader?" Nels said to Fish who wrestled tongs to the end of a log.

"Name of Hungry Mike, a real pooh-bah," Fish said. "Starkweather brought him back with a bunch of new men. We're almost full strength."

Nels should have studied up before asking to work on the load team. "Hey Ten-Day, what's a fid hook?" Nels said.

"Barrister says it's part of the cornerbind holding the load on the sledge," Ten-Day said. "He knows everything there is to know about logging."

Next year Nels would know better. He watched with a sigh as the team pulled out of sight. Then he turned his thoughts back to the cookshack.

A woman in camp. The news flew from tongue to ear like water down a sluiceway. Whispers of porcelain skin and red lips made Nels chomp at the bit. He had not seen a woman since coming to camp, except for Ma, and she really didn't count. His imagination raged as he bucked logs with Dutch on the other end of the misery whip. Maybe she was the one he had been waiting for. Although he had not laid eyes on her, Nels was almost in love.

And if that was not enough, Pokey brought a message from Mr. Starkweather as they gathered around the swingdingle at noon. The gloom had lifted and bright sun sparkled on the snow, glittering and blinding.

"A nun is coming to the bunkhouse tonight to talk about hospital tickets," Pokey said. "The brains says be on your best behavior."

"And keep your drawers on," someone said. The men hooted and guffawed.

"What's a hospital ticket?" Ten-Day said.

Pokey shrugged. "Dunno."

"You've seen her. Tell us what she's like," Nels said. "We hear she's pretty."

Pokey rubbed his whiskery cheek and pushed out his cheek with his tongue. "She's tall." His eyes sparkled and a toothless grin spread across his face. "Favors black and white, but from what I know, she ain't interested in men—her being the bride of Jesus H. Christ hisself."

"Not her! The other one," Nels said as men roared with laughter. "The young one."

"She's fine," Pokey said. "A belle. A rose among you shitty asses."

All afternoon, Nels imagined a girl, tall and willowy, with blond braids wound around her head. She would look at him, and their eyes would lock, blue on blue. She would smile only at him. He jogged to the bunkhouse when the Gabriel finally released them from the cut.

The other men must have had the same idea. There was jostling and pushing at the washbowl, a preening of hair, a smoothing of beards. Nels changed into a clean shirt and smoothed the wrinkles best he could. A woman. A beauty. A lardy-dardy.

Nels and the men stampeded to supper, eager to see the new girl. She was not there. A rustling of disappointment went through the room without a word spoken. A slump of shoulders. Sighs. Then she stepped out from the pantry, and a collective gasp came from the jacks.

She carried a pail of molasses, lugging the heavy bucket with both hands, her fingers dainty and small as a child's. Petite and lovely, too fine for heavy work, her skin white as milk. Freckles scattered across a perfect nose. Black curls poked out from beneath her kerchief. She turned rosy-pink and lowered her eyes. A decent woman, a real lady who blushed when strange men stared.

What had brought such a girl to Starkweather Timber? He had to talk to her. Nels hardly noticed a tall nun passing food down the tables until he realized it was Sister Magdalena from the railroad cars. She kept a steady trot between the stove and tables, toting platters, and bowls.

A kitchen boy shoved a hat on his head and headed outdoors with empty buckets. Nels tried to catch the younger woman's attention, but she kept her eyes downward. Only Sister Magdalena returned his gaze with a nod. His rotten luck.

It seemed the jacks dawdled, reluctant to leave the cookshack. Paulson pushed to his feet and Nels knew he must leave with the others. If only he could help with the dishes, or fetch stove wood. Impossible. The cookshack was off-limits to the jacks except for mealtime.

The nun followed the men out of the building after supper, and her veil caught the wind off Stink Lake, billowing stark white against the darkness. The pencil pusher walked beside her, the pantywaist, strutting with self-importance. The boots of a hundred men squeaked in frozen snow to the bunkhouse. A white owl hooted from the trees.

"Mr. Jensen," Sister Magdalena said to him as he walked close to her. "We met on the train."

Nels choked to hear his name. He stood taller as he greeted her, noticing the pencil pusher looking at him with respect. Sister Magdalena paused at the threshold of the bunkhouse and crossed herself. Nels removed his hat. She acted like it was the most normal thing in the world to enter a bunkhouse full of lumberjacks.

Nels beelined for the stove hoping for an opportunity to ask the nun about the new woman in the cookshack. Sister Magdalena ducked between wet clothes hanging from the rafters, unruffled by the long underwear or fetid socks, heading for the amen corner behind the pencil pusher. If she was afraid, she did not show it.

"No one knows anything about hospital tickets," Ten-Day mumbled at Nels's elbow. "Not even Barrister."

"Attention!" Elliot's voice cracked. "Mr. Starkweather says to listen to Sister Magda, or is it, Marguerite?" He turned to the sister as the men tittered.

"Sister Magdalena from the Duluth Convent." She looked around the room, nodding and smiling. "I'm a farm girl acquainted with hard work. I know better than to keep you from your rest."

Pokey moved the lantern above Sister Magdalena, framing her face in halo. The men removed hats as a mouse streaked across the floor and underneath her long skirts. A mouse would not matter to a man, but Nels's own mother leapt on chairs to escape a scurrying mouse, though she wasn't afraid of ornery boars or mean ganders. Nels held his breath.

"A mouse," Ten-Day said in a loud whisper. "Under your dress, Sister."

Sister Magdalena stepped aside and stomped the rodent. If she was bothered by the commotion, she did not show it. She kicked it aside. Without pausing, she continued speaking.

"You can see I don't put up with botherations," Sister Magdalena said.

Everyone laughed. The tension lifted.

"Growing up with eight brothers taught me to hold my own." Sister Magdalena paused as laughter tittered across the room. "My community built St. Mary's Hospital and plans for more hospitals. You know how dangerous it is in the woods."

She paused for a breath.

"Many jacks get injured every year. The expense is a hardship for the man and his family." She held up a small slip of paper. "This is a hospital chit. Buy one and your care is free if you need it."

The lamp flickered as someone entered the building. Jacob Pettibone swaggered over to the amen corner, pushing closer to Sister Magdalena. Nels's belly clenched just to glimpse the braggart.

"A chit costs a dollar," Sister Magdalena said. "A hospital stay is thirty dollars a month and most injuries take longer. A chit is a bargain."

"Waste of money, boys." Pettibone called out. "Pissing in the wind."

"Perhaps," Sister Magdalena said with a grin. "I'd prefer to think of it as a dollar less for the tavern."

Nels let out his breath. A wave of laughter swept over the room, guffaws, and elbow poking. She was a woman to reckon with. He would like to see her stomp Pettibone like that mouse.

"Buying a ticket helps the men who aren't lucky," she said. "Any money leftover will build more hospitals."

Pettibone spat into a spittoon and wiped his mouth with the back of his sleeve. "A lot of bull, if you ask me. Another scheme to get our wages."

"Julius Caesar will get his comeuppance," Fish whispered. "You don't treat a religious like that and get away with it."

A rumble of discussion drowned out Sister Magdalena.

"Let her talk," Ten-Day said. "She's not finished."

"I'll talk if I want. You man enough to stop me?" Pettibone said.

The room grew silent. Ten-Day was past due for a good fight. Mr. Elliot rapped on the stovepipe with his pencil.

"Let her talk," Mr. Elliot said.

"Every cent will care for the injured now and build more hospitals later. Everyone benefits," Sister Magdalena said. "All for a dollar."

Another wave of argument swept through the room, drowning out Sister Magdalena.

"Pipe down!" Mr. Elliot drummed his pencil on the stove pipe for emphasis. "Mr. Starkweather left orders for every man to hear her out."

Nels swallowed his disgust. Instead of dealing with Pettibone, the root of the problem, Mr. Elliot barked at all the men. A shotgun blast instead of a single shot.

"We need every man on board." Sister said. "Together much good can be accomplished."

"How long are the tickets good for?" someone called out.

"The ticket provides care during the logging season. You must behave. It will not cover injuries from brawling or drinking."

"Sounds jiggy to me," Pettibone said. "Don't trust nothing Catholic. She'll send the money to the pope, and we'll never see a bit of good from it."

A flush colored the nun's cheek and her jaw clenched. She purposely turned away from Pettibone.

"Raise your hand if you want a ticket," Sister Magdalena said. "You'll be helping yourself and others."

No one responded. Nels almost raised his hand out of pity. Common sense prevailed. He had no family to worry about. It would be a waste of money for him.

"The hospital ticket may be charged at the company store," Mr. Elliot said. The man gripped his ledger closer to his chest. "A small investment to protect your family."

"I work too hard to throw my money away," Pettibone said. A murmur of approval swept the room. "And I'm too good looking to get hurt."

The braggart. Nels's blood surged.

"I've never been hurt," Ten-Day said. "Don't plan on changing my ways."

Sister Magdalena picked up the dead mouse by the tail and threw it into the firebox. Nels felt sorry for her, so large and awkward, kind-hearted.

"We'll end with Night Prayer," Sister Magdalena said. "I'll come again tomorrow night. Give you time to think about it." She pulled out her prayer book and dropped to her knees. Some knelt with her, and others stood shifting their weight from one foot to the other, looking down at the floor.

The sound of a woman's voice came as a reminder of home and religion. An unexpected tear burned Nels's eye. When she prayed the *Our Father*, men joined in many languages. Nels whispered the words in Danish. She ended with *God grant us a restful night and a peaceful death.*

"Good night, boys." Sister Magdalena lumbered to her feet. "Don't let the bed bugs bite."

Nels smiled. Others were smiling, too. Nels could tell the men liked her, but not enough to buy a chit.

"I'll take letters out when I leave. No doubt your wives and mothers would like to hear from you," Sister Magdalena said. "Have them ready tomorrow night." She grinned. "And I'm willing to do a little mending while I'm here. I'll wait at the door to collect it and return it tomorrow night. Minus the lice."

"How much does it cost? "a jack called out.

"Not a thing," Sister Magdalena said. "I try to be useful."

The men eyed each other, trying to decide if she meant it. A few hustled to fetch socks or pants. Nels handed several items to her, apologizing for the stink.

"I've brothers and know all about socks," she said with a cheerful wave of her hand. "Though it's a good idea to take advantage of the boil up when you can," she said. "Cleanliness next to godliness, you know."

She treated them as brothers. Sister Magdalena was a welcome visitor, Catholic or not. She left the bunkhouse with Mr. Elliot.

"Only sensible to get a ticket," Pokey said.

"You're ready for the boneyard and need it," Pettibone said.

"I'm still in the vigor of youth." He flexed his biceps. "Not wasting my cash."

The men crawled into their bunks without the usual tall tales, a few staying up to scrawl letters home by the light of the lamp.

"I'll buy one," Ten-Day said. "I'll pay a sawbuck now and sell it later to someone who needs it. Make a little money."

"You'd try to make a buck off your own mother," Nels said. "They keep a list of who paid for tickets. They're not for resale. Didn't you see the pencil pusher's ledger? Our very lives are in that book."

"No wonder she's a nun," Ten-Day said with a whisper when they settled in their bunk. "She's as plain as a mud fence."

"Shut your trap," Nels said. "She's mending your drawers."

"I'd not add to your sins by talking like that," Fish said to Ten-Day. They were only about a foot apart, Fish on their top bunk and Ten-Day on his. "You don't want to tempt God." Fish pulled his blankets over his shoulders, then scratched his neck. "Maybe God sent Sister Lumberjack to help us."

"Lord knows we need it," Nels said. Sister Lumberjack was a good name for her. He grinned in the darkness. "We need all the help we can get."

Chapter 24
Sister Magdalena

Lord, make haste to help me.

What would Mother Superior say? She had tried to act holy but ended up being only herself, teasing and joshing, the sister from the vegetable gardens and laundry room. It was as bad as Agatha's burned veil. As botched as that spilled soup.

Not a single ticket sold. She was glad her mother and father were not alive to know her failure. The heckler's words rattled in her head. A waste of money. A flim-flam. She would like to take that man aside and put the fear of God into him.

And on top of it all, she had promised to stay another night. For what? To do their mending? Pride and arrogance had led her here. Who was she to think she could change anything?

Mr. Elliot excused himself at the cookshack, no doubt to report the bad news to Mr. Starkweather. Sister Magdalena pushed the door open, almost stepping on Stutz who was wiping up puddles from the floor. Mrs. Rognaldson fried doughnuts. Gertie washed dishes, looking white-faced and drawn. The boy finished the floor and began setting the tables for breakfast, the clatter of tinware adding to the burden of fatigue washing over Sister Magdalena. Sleep must wait.

Gertie fetched a heavy sack from the pantry. She stumbled, faltering under the weight. Sister Magdalena hurried to help her.

"Mrs. Rognaldson," Sister Magdalena said after she deposited the sack on the work table. "I've a strong back and a willing heart, but you'll have to tell me what to do."

Mrs. Rognaldson cracked a smile and gestured for Sister Magdalena to take a doughnut. "Call me Solveig. Gertie will finish here. Come with me to the root cellar."

They bundled up and headed into the darkness. On her way out the door, Solveig told Stutz to head to the bunk house.

"Time for bed," she said. "Pokey will wake you in the morning."

Stutz rolled his eyes. Sister Magdalena winked at him.

Solveig pulled the heavy sledge and Sister Magdalena carried the lantern. The moon glimmered through scattered clouds, and tufts of snow clung to the needles on every pine. Stumps and slash cast ghostly shadows in the moonlight.

They were almost to the root cellar when a sound echoed across the clearing. They stopped and listened. It came from the direction of the office where lights blazed in every window. A woman's laughter, a hooting shriek more like despair than joy. Male voices boomed boisterous and loud. The sound of an accordion. Someone singing. More female laughter. More than one female.

Howling wolves sounded as eerie as the voices. Sister Magdalena shivered and reached for the St. Benedict medal around her neck, the touch comforting in the darkness.

"Mr. Starkweather and Mr. Elliot live in the back rooms of the office," Solveig said, her voice barely a whisper. She continued toward the root cellar.

"I've heard Mr. Starkweather preys on young women. Gertie is vulnerable," Sister Magdalena said. "Lost her husband last week. There's a baby on the way, but not until summer." She had no choice but to trust this woman.

Solveig snorted and pulled a key from around her neck. She fumbled with the heavy padlock on the root cellar door. Sister Magdalena lifted the lamp, and the door slowly creaked open. She hung the lamp on a nail and loaded the sledge with beans, potatoes, a hanging slab of beef, a ham, side pork and a box of sausage. More prunes and dried apples topped the heap. Solveig added two cabbages.

"This should get us through another day or two," Solveig said. She fastened the lock and picked up the sledge-rope.

"My turn," Sister Magdalena said. "You carry the lantern."

Laughter screeched from the office. The sound of crashing glass. More laughter.

"I beg you to watch over young Gertie." Sister Magdalena said. "She's a good Catholic girl, far from home, and alone in a strange country."

"I know the sorrows of widowhood," Solveig said. "Too well, I know them." She slipped on an icy spot and grabbed hold of the sledge to steady herself. "Don't you worry none. She's safe with me."

"And the baby?"

"Nobody's business," Solveig said. "She's a good worker. That's all that matters." She lifted the lamp and cast a feeble path before them. "Now then, let's visit my girls."

Sister Magdalena thought perhaps she was referring to the women in the office. Instead, she led Sister Magdalena to the barn. Solveig motioned for her to leave the sledge and enter the log building.

Oxen lowed in a wooden pen to the right of the door, and on the left, another held work horses and a smaller horse. Stacks of hay and sacks of grain lined the ends of the barn.

The homey smells brought a lump to Sister Magdalena's throat.

"Here they are." Solveig lifted the lamp and pointed to three hens perched on top of the wooden gate. "My girls." Solveig reached out and stroked the back of a hen with more tenderness and affection than Sister Magdalena had seen in the stoic woman. "Aren't they beautiful?"

"You two share the top bunk," Solveig said when they finally retired for the night.

Sister Magdalena eyed the thin blanket. It was cold enough to see their breath. Gertie pulled a quilt and pillow from her bundle. Sister Magdalena spread her cloak. Solveig pushed the yowling cat into the kitchen.

"Pokey fires the stoves several times a night." Solveig sounded tired. "Don't be alarmed to hear him clanking around. We've new locks on the pantry, but the front door is left open."

How strange to sleep with a stranger, to neglect the Great Silence, to be away from the Community. Sister Magdalena knelt on the floor by her bed and chattered through her prayers.

"Why are you here, Sister?" Solveig said when Sister Magdalena finally climbed into bed. "You didn't come as chaperone to our new cookee."

Sister Magdalena giggled. "I am not the best chaperone. I'm headstrong, and quick to get into trouble." She told Solveig about the hospital tickets and the plan to build more hospitals. "Lives would be saved if men found treatment earlier. And families spared heartache."

The wind moaned around the chimney, and wolves sounded in the distance. Solveig blew out the candle and the room plunged into darkness. Gertie fell asleep at once. Sister Magdalena knew she ought to observe the silence, as was her custom, but she could not sleep.

"I've made a mess of everything," Sister Magdalena confessed. "Not a single jack bought a chit. I didn't know it would be this hard to convince them."

"Don't worry." Solveig's sleepy voice came from the bottom bunk. "Everything works out in the end."

Platitudes, maybe, but comforting to Sister Magdalena in the darkness of the night. Solveig was old enough to be her mother, and Sister Magdalena needed a mother. Of course, she had the Blessed Mother, but it felt good to hear a real voice. Solveig carried a sadness about her, but Sister Magdalena knew better than pry.

"I'll try again tomorrow night," Sister Magdalena said. "It's up to God. If I can't sell tickets, I'll go back to the laundry like a whipped pup."

The walls cracked in the cold, and the stove pipe popped. Queenie meowed. Sister Magdalena fell into a restless sleep.

Chapter 25
Solveig

Solveig could not sleep. The bunks quaked every time some-one shifted position. Probably unwise to put the nun on the top bunk, considering her bulk. Young Gertie called out in her sleep. Sister Magdalena snored.

But all these things did not keep Solveig awake. It was the date on the calendar.

One year ago, a slipped ax gouged Rasmuss's leg while on a limbing crew. Halvor brought him and the team home by train. His telegram came first. *Pa hurt. Coming home.*

Solveig had gone berserk. She had not slept one wink from the telegram until Rasmuss's death. What if he had possessed a hospital chit? The cook at the camp doctored him as best he knew, but Rasmuss arrived home delirious with fever, and with a leg rotten with gangrene.

She had begged to send for the doctor, but Rasmuss refused. "It's too late," he said. "Don't waste our money. A sawbones would take my leg." He grasped her hand and looked into her eyes. "What good is a farmer without a leg?"

It might have been too late for a doctor to do anything, but Solveig was still angry at her husband for not letting her try to save him.

Every jack ought to buy a chit. If Sister Magdalena could not convince them, then someone else must do it. A simple plan mapped in her mind.

The next morning, the nun was on her knees when Solveig awak-ened. Pokey banged around the kitchen, adding wood and shaking down the ashes. Solveig's first thought was of Irish making breakfast. Then she remembered. She was the cook now. She was in charge.

Darkness covered them. Her nose felt as cold as ice. Solveig tiptoed around the praying nun, and shivered as she pulled on her clothing. She nudged Gertie awake. In the kitchen, Stutz sat by the stove, bleary-eyed and half asleep.

"Your young prince." Pokey pointed at Stutz with a frown. "Here in body, if not in mind."

Stutz yawned and shivered. How thin he looked. Poor boy.

"First thing in the morning, help yourself to porridge." Solveig pointed to the porridge pot on the back burner. "Eat before the commotion starts."

The boy dragged to the stove with open disdain.

"What are you so owly about? Be glad you're inside," Solveig said. "You wouldn't last a day in those clothes."

"Better pay as a road monkey," Stutz said. "I'm almost fourteen, too old for kitchen work. Ma needs the money."

Solveig had not considered the boy might rather be out in the woods. Her concern did not last more than a second. She sniffed. His mother would appreciate what she had done for the boy, even if he did not.

"Road monkeys shovel shit all day long. You're missing nuthin'," Pokey said. "We need water and wood hauled in. Be quick about it."

"First finish your porridge," Solveig said. "Add some sorghum for sweetening."

Queenie laid a dead mouse at Solveig's feet and rubbed against her legs. Stutz was all eyes. "Is that your cat, Missus?"

"Queenie is her name," Solveig said. "Call me Ma. I like boys, and we'll get along if you do your chores."

The nun ground coffee beans and added the grounds to huge pots of water. Solveig had been wise to set filled pots on the stove overnight. Organization was the key to keeping afloat. She needed water reservoirs full and the stove always fired hot, dishpans of water in the oven whenever it emptied. Water pails and wood boxes kept full. Stores inside before they were needed. As many breakfast chores as possible done the night before.

"What can I do?" Gertie said.

"Slice the side pork," Solveig said. "About 150 slices—a little more if you have the strength."

Gertie placed a huge iron skillet on the stove to heat, away from the griddle area. Gertie dropped the strips of meat into the frying pan as soon as the slices were ready. By the time the skillet was filled, the first strips were finished. Gertie put them on a tray and covered them with a cloth in the warming oven. Gertie was a step up from Irish's surly attitude and his cigar ash dropped in the food. Not to mention his romance with the bottle.

With the extra help, it looked like Solveig might find time for a rest in the afternoon. Maybe it was the mortgage off her back that lightened her heart.

The nun busied with serving bowls and pitchers. Solveig wanted to discuss something with the sister, but a horde of hungry men would swoop in from the cold in a quarter hour. It would have to wait.

Breakfast came and went in a flash. Once again, the men watched Gertie wherever she went. Solveig took pity on the poor girl and put her to work frying flapjacks. At least she could keep her back to their prying eyes.

The kitchen help ate in silence. Gertie put a cauldron of beans to boil. Stutz cleared dishes. Sister Magdalena pulled out the dishpan. Solveig planned doughnuts and stew for the swingdingle at noon. Pork gravy and potatoes for supper. She pulled down the bread bowl and mixed dough for twenty loaves.

There was a lull before the swingdingle would need to be loaded. Sister Magdalena took out the mending. Stutz checked on the chickens. Solveig fetched Rasmuss's turkey from her trunk. Just the sight of her husband's clothing brought a flood of grief. Stutz needed warmer clothes, though the boots and coat were much too large for his slender frame.

"Do you think we might cut this down for Stutz?" Solveig held up a flannel shirt. "He'll freeze to death in what he's wearing."

Gertie looked it over. Then she rose to her feet and went into the bedroom. She returned with a much smaller shirt.

"This was my Sean's," Gertie said. Her white face showed no expression, but Solveig saw her grief.

"It'll fit," Solveig said. "Kind of you to offer."

Stutz's eyes shone when he saw the warm shirt, then looked down.

"Can't take charity," Stutz said. "Ma would skin me if I did."

It would not do to contradict the boy's mother.

Sister Magdalena intruded. "Who said anything about charity?" She nodded toward Gertie. "When you are paid in the spring, you will pay Gertie forty cents for the shirt." The nun looked at Gertie for approval.

"Fifty cents." Gertie thrust her upturned nose into the air and steeled her jaw. Fat tears gathered in her blue eyes.

"Fifty cents it is, then," Solveig said. "And a deal at that. A new shirt in the office costs a whole dollar."

Solveig felt her admiration for Gertie go up a step. Gertie was pretty and sensible, a rare combination. Of course, Gertie needed every cent for herself and her little one. She had done the right thing to demand what was due.

Sister Magdalena suggested the long shirttails be made into a muffler. "Might as well put the extra fabric to use."

Stutz beamed as the women cut and stitched, sitting close to the lamp on the dreary day.

After the supper rush, Sister Magdalena prepared to go out to the bunkhouse. Solveig whispered instructions to Gertie and Stutz, then followed after Sister Magdalena and the pencil pusher, pulling her shawl over her head in the cold.

The work was being done whether or not she was in the kitchen. There were advantages to being the cook, more than just the wages. Solveig would never talk about it, lest she sound boastful, but the satisfaction of being promoted to cook filled her ribcage. If only Rasmuss knew.

The stink slapped her face as she entered the bunkhouse. She gathered her skirts lest she collect bugs. When Rasmuss came home from lumbering, he undressed outside and left his clothes on the stoop. After wintering alone, Solveig met him with almost delirious joy. She heated water for an all-over bath and cut his hair down to the scalp to make sure he brought no lice into their home. He brought stories of loggers, comical occurrences, and strange happenings. He brought gifts and new ideas for improving the farm. But she had seen to it that he did not bring bugs.

Every man removed his hat at the sight of the women. They stood around the amen corner, shuffling feet and spitting tobacco, murmuring among themselves, not making eye contact.

Sister Magdalena placed the mending on a bench, and the men sorted through the stack to find their items. They bobbed their heads in thanks. One man knelt before Sister Magdalena and kissed her hand, asking for a blessing. Several men carried rosaries.

"You know why I'm here," Sister Magdalena said. Her hands rested inside her bell-shaped sleeves. "Hospital tickets provide care if you get hurt or sick on the job."

She had a strong voice and a merry wit, but the men were not quick to part with their hard-earned money.

"Only a dollar," Sister Magdalena said with a shaky laugh. "You'll spend at least that much at the saloon, won't you now?" Embarrassed laughter. No one volunteered to buy a ticket. "Reconsider, for your families' sakes." Her voice quavered at the end. How defeated she looked, draped in her yardage of black and white, chin quivering.

Solveig took a breath and stepped beside the sister. Solveig rarely knew a woman taller than she, but Sister Magdalena's eyes were at least three inches above hers.

"Boys," Solveig said. "I want to tell you something."

All eyes turned her way, surprised, and interested. They worked so hard. They came in almost too exhausted to eat. She loved them, she realized with surprise. She wanted what was best for them.

"Last year about this time, my man got hurt in a logging camp west of here."

She had their attention. Not a sound but the wind whistling around the rafters and the hiss of melting ice from wet socks dripping onto the wood stove.

"He worked on a limbing crew and took a gash from a slipped ax." Her lip trembled and she bit it hard. "The cook treated him best he could, but my man got worse instead of better." She grasped onto a bedframe to steady herself. "Our son brought him home to die. Half wages for both and for their team hired out to the company. His leg mortified."

A quick intake of air. Every eye riveted on her. "There was no hospital or tickets. No one knows if a sawbones could have saved him. We'll never know."

Solveig blinked a burning tear. "I'm here at Starkweather because he's gone." Solveig could have told them about the mortgage, but her words had run out. She stood for a long while. "If you care about your families," she said in a low voice, "buy a ticket."

No one moved. It grew silent as a church. Beads of sweat dripped around the nun's face.

"Sister Magdalena," Solveig said. "Cooks get hurt, too. I'll be the first to buy a chit."

"I'll take one," Pokey said.

The men looked at Pokey, and then at each other. Fish and Ten-Day followed. Soon half the men stood with raised hands. Sister Magdalena handed out the tickets as Mr. Elliot jotted their names in his tally book. Their dollar would be deducted from their wages and paid directly to Sister Magdalena by Mr. Starkweather.

"Thank you," Sister Magdalena said to each man as she handed him a ticket and told him where to sign his name. "May God watch over you and keep you safe."

A miracle unfolded before Solveig's eyes. Men showed respect to Sister Magdalena, as well they should. Solveig had never met such a wise and holy woman. But to her surprise, Solveig felt the same respect shown to her. The men shook her hand as well, and expressed sorrow for her loss.

"Thank you, my friend," Sister Magdalena whispered when the tickets were passed out. "You made the difference."

Sister Magdalena dropped to her knees for night prayer. Knees thudded to the floor around her. Sister Magdalena sang in a firm voice, not quite on tune. *Praise God from Whom all Blessings Flow*. Men joined in. Solveig blinked tears.

If only life were simple again, like it had been with Rasmuss. Work and sleep and church on Sundays. If only Halvor hadn't married that town girl. Even though she was paying the mortgage, she felt no comfort without Rasmuss.

She had work to finish before bed. Pokey chorded *Abide With Me* on his squeezebox. *Help of the helpless, Lord, abide with me.*

Solveig did not like feeling helpless.

"What kind of flim-flam you got going with the papist?" Pettibone jeered as she opened the door to leave. "You getting a cutback on this operation?"

Solveig stopped short.

"You tell the sob story and she rakes in the cash?" He grinned. "You've got a good thing going, I can see." Then his grin twisted into a sneer. "I'm not so stupid as to fall for your racket like these rubes. Not on your life."

Solveig stood taller and pulled her shawl tighter around her shoulders. She would not get in a pissing match with Jacob Pettibone. She had a mortgage to pay.

Chapter 26
Nels

Nels hung back from the others as Sister Lumberjack gave her spiel. If he had a wife, he would be the first to buy a ticket. If he was married to Gertie, he would buy a chit, by God, maybe two. Gertie, beautiful Gertie. He had bribed Pokey into revealing her name. Pokey said she was newly widowed. He said she was a good woman. Nels knew that much by looking at her.

Solveig stood and began talking about her husband's death. So, what, that he had worked on a limbing crew. It did not mean Nels was in danger. He knew to be careful of widow makers, to cut around knots, and to keep a sharp edge on his ax. Solveig's story meant nothing. Everyone died. There was no way around it.

A memory of the poor stiff in Brainerd came to mind. The tragedy was that no one knew who he was. Nels had made Ten-Day promise to send word to his folks if something happened to him. That is what mattered.

The women left and Pokey stowed his accordion. A few men went to their bunks. Others started card games or dominoes. A Latvian named Mack gave haircuts. Ten-Day yawned, scratched his belly and belched.

"You going to fall out of bed tonight?" Ten-Day said to Mack who had fallen from his upper bunk the night before. Mack carried a bruised face to prove it. Half the bunkhouse had awakened with the crash.

"Not tonight, boss," Mack said in his usual good-humored way. "I'm tying myself to the bedpost."

"Why did it happen?" Ten-Day prodded for more information. "Did you have nightmares or a dizzy spell? Maybe you had a conniption fit and don't remember it."

"Ten-Day, shut your trap!" Fish said from his bunk. "I'm trying to sleep."

Ten-Day shrugged and crawled into bed. Nels followed. Nothing came of jawing.

"Five minutes 'til lights out," Pokey said. "You boys need your beauty sleep."

"She made me homesick, that nun," Ten-Day said. "And I don't even have a home."

Nels turned his back. He did not want to talk about homesick. He didn't want to talk about hospital tickets or nuns or Solveig's dead husband. His number came up, that was all.

Ten-Day snored like a pig. Nels jabbed his side to make him turn over.

The darkened bunkhouse was a living thing. Strangers crowded together like animals in a barn. Snoring, turning, farting, belching and men talking in their sleep. Once someone called out, "Gertie." The place reeked of smoke, piss, sweat and unwashed bodies. Drafts blew in around the door and windows and between the logs. Sometimes a skiff of snow covered their blankets in the morning. A fire would kill them all. Too many men would not escape out of the single door, and being so close to the stove meant he would be one of the first to die. The wooden structure and flimsy stovepipe posed a real danger. Heck, sleeping in the bunkhouse was as dangerous as working in the cut. It did not matter to Nels. He figured when a person's number came up, it came up. It made no sense to worry or buy a hospital ticket or anything else.

He fixed his thoughts on Gertie. If only he could speak to her. He was certain that she would love him in return if they only met. She would look at him through those dark lashes. She would see him for who he really was. His loins melted at the thought of holding her close, kissing her face. She would be someone he could introduce with pride, someone his mother would love like a daughter. They would have children, many children. He would get a toehold and make a life for them. By God, his wild days would end if she were by his side.

He fingered the blue stone around his neck. He imagined slipping the thong over her beautiful hair and seeing her eyes match the gem.

If only Myron Pinchpenny had not robbed him. If only Jacob Pettibone hadn't framed him and ruined his chances. Gertie would understand. She would take his side.

God, he needed a drink.

Chapter 27
Sister Magdalena

Sister Magdalena left the bunkhouse with a lighter step. *Thanks be to God.* Sixty-eight men purchased tickets. It happened with God's help and Solveig's testimonial.

The big dipper hung in an inky sky. She found the north star, fixing the direction of the Weyerhaeuser camp. God had brought her this far, and He would guide her the rest of the way.

She hurried to the cookshack where Stutz wielded the broom. He wore his new shirt with the muffler wrapped around his neck in a cozy fashion. His eyes drooped and he smiled around a yawn. Gertie rolled pie crust while Solveig finished them. The smell of cinnamon and apples filled the room. Sister Magdalena hurried to lay breakfast tables.

"I have a favor to ask," Sister Magdalena said when she finished. Solveig was crimping the last of the pies, a smudge of flour across her nose. "Your story convinced the men," Sister Magdalena said. "May I share it other places?"

Sister Magdalena loaded the oven with pies and closed the door with a bang. "I wouldn't mention your name," Sister Magdalena said. She knew Solveig to be a private person and braced for a refusal.

Instead, Solveig gave a reluctant nod. "Suppose it would be all right."

Thank you," Sister Magdalena said. "I will guard your privacy."

Pokey brought in an armload of wood.

"Don't forget to fill the reservoir," Solveig said. "Need all the hot water I can get."

"I know, I know," Pokey said. "Keep your drawers on." He slapped slips of paper on the table. "Too busy playing mailman to do my chores. The jacks are all afire for Gertie. See these love notes? I could make a lot of money on delivery fees."

"They go right in the fire," Solveig said. "Tell that to the jacks."

Gertie glanced at the notes piled on the table. She turned and went to bed. Pokey and Stutz left for the night. Sister Magdalena was tired. Mr. Elliot had lined up a ride the next morning with the surveyor. She expected another long day.

"Do you want a cup of tea?" Solveig said. "Have to wait for the pies."

Fatigue weighed on Sister Magdalena's shoulders. Back home, the sisters enjoyed the peace of the Great Silence. However, the Rule of Benedict said to greet guests with the love of Christ. Although Sister Magdalena was a guest in Solveig's kitchen, Solveig was also Sister Magdalena's guest in this present moment.

"A quick cup," Sister Magdalena said.

They sipped the brew and warmed their hands on the cups. Sister Magdalena spoke of growing up on a farm, longing for an education, and the satisfaction she knew as a sister.

"Your pa didn't force you to take the veil?" Solveig said. Her chapped fingers tapped the cup in nervous staccato.

"I begged to go to the convent. The only men interested in me were widow men with big families and farms to work. Religious life was my escape."

"I was surprised to marry," Solveig said. "Came to America as an indentured servant."

"Children?"

"An adopted son," Solveig told of finding him in the middle of the Indian war. "We were newly married, just starting out." She twirled her cup with one finger. "He was a boy without a mother."

Sister Magdalena was about to ask more, but Solveig got up and took the pies from the oven. The delicious aroma made Sister Magdalena's mouth water.

"How about a slice before bed?" Solveig said. "We've earned it."

The next morning Stutz stumbled into the cookshack wearing his old shirt.

"Where's your new shirt?" Sister Magdalena said.

"It's real cold in the woods." Stutz fiddled with a button. "I borrowed it to my brother."

Of course. His brother. She whispered the situation to Gertie who fetched another shirt and a sweater. "You'll pay for both at the end of the season. What size boots does he wear?"

Stutz grinned his thanks. He left with empty buckets. Sister Magdalena saw the snow falling straight down. No wind. A good day for travel.

The men came for breakfast. Gertie did not look up from frying pancakes. Even so, the girl needed a gunny sack over her head to stave their gazes.

In the middle of the meal, the mouthy man from the bunkhouse provoked an argument with a slim man minding his own business. The slim man had bought a chit the night before, and had introduced himself as Mack, from Latvia. The bully squeezed close to Mack and elbowed for more room. Mack obliged, moving over, and taking his plate with him. The bully was the same man who had heckled her during the chit sales.

The bully was not content with the extra space. He stabbed a sausage from Mack's plate, shoving the whole thing into his mouth, and reached for another.

Mack shielded his plate with his shoulder and kept eating, trying to ignore him. The bully snatched the pie from Mack's plate. Sister Magdalena watched helplessly. She looked toward Mr. Elliot to do something.

"Stop it. Eat your own food," Mack said.

Those few words were barely audible above the clanking tinware, but Mr. Elliot rose to his feet. Silence descended as forks paused between plates and mouths.

"Mack, you know the rules." Mr. Elliot pointed at the sign on the wall. "Draw your pay and get out. You're fired."

The color slipped away from the poor man's face. The air went out of the room. The faces of the other jacks slackened as if in disbelief. Sister Magdalena gasped.

Mack protested, but the pencil pusher jabbed a thumb toward the sign. Mack slammed his fork on the table, pushed away from the bench and stomped out of the cookshack, muttering Latvian curses.

He was given no second chance, no opportunity to explain himself. Sister Magdalena witnessed the injustice before her very eyes. If anyone should be fired, it was the bully who provoked the altercation. Surely Mr. Elliot misunderstood what had happened.

The tinware banged as the men resumed eating. No one looked up from their plates. Even Gertie had lost her appeal. The jacks finished their meal and hurried out of the building.

She could not keep the surveyor waiting. Mack's firing was not her business, and she suspected it would be imprudent to say anything, but the injustice stuck in her throat like a fish bone. The Rule of Benedict demanded she at least attempt to right a wrong.

She would speak to Mr. Elliot when she collected the money from last night's sales. It was her duty. If he were unreasonable, she would go to Mr. Starkweather with her complaint. Right was right, and wrong was wrong. Sister Lucy would never miss an opportunity to right an injustice.

Sister Magdalena collected her things. She hugged Gertie and promised her prayers.

"Thank you, Solveig," Sister Magdalena said. "For everything."

Solveig acted as if they had not shared confidences the previous night.

"Dress warm," Solveig said. "My bunions predict bad weather."

"If I wore any more layers, I'd waddle," Sister Magdalena said with a laugh. She turned to leave, but Solveig touched her arm.

"It's a sad day," Solveig said. Her shoulders slumped and the light had gone out of her eyes, that hopeful light that had shone so brightly after her promotion. "Mack deserved better."

"I know," Sister Magdalena said. She was almost to the door when she turned. Solveig was at the stove with her back toward her. "Who was that bully who caused the trouble?"

Solveig did not turn around. "Jacob Pettibone."

Sister Magdalena hurried to the office. A scattering of white clouds flittered overhead. She tucked her hands into the sleeves of her cloak. Thank God she did not have to walk to Weyerhaeuser.

The dim room reeked of tobacco and liniment. Mr. Elliot leaned over a ledger.

"Sister." His voice squeaked and he touched his throat, stroking his Adam's apple. "We've a little problem."

"Are you referring to that poor man at breakfast?" Sister Magdalena stepped closer and glared with what she hoped was righteous anger. She towered over him and outweighed him by at least two stone.

"If anyone should be fired, it's Jacob Pettibone," Sister Magdalena said firmly. "I saw the whole thing. Pettibone provoked the man. He wanted him fired."

"Now, Sister," Mr. Elliot squirmed and pulled at his neck. "There's more behind the story." His cheeks flushed. Sister Magdalena smelled a lie.

She did not avert her eyes. Let him squirm. She pressed closer until her face was inches from his. Mr. Elliot fluttered his hands and looked away.

"The problem," he squeaked, "is that Mr. Starkweather left on urgent business and is not here to sign your bank draft."

"But you said," Sister said with a sputter. What would Mother Superior say if she came home without payment?

"A minor delay," Mr. Elliot said with a wave of his hand. He pushed the ledger toward her with the list of names and the tally at the bottom. "Stop later in the season." He looked up. "We'll have it ready then."

"But you know the difficulties of travel," Sister Magdalena said. Her mind whirled with indecision. How would she get back to Starkweather Timber?

All the joy from last night evaporated. They might mail the draft, but Mr. Starkweather proved unreliable. Better to pick up the payment herself.

Sister Magdalena glanced out the window to see the Latvian heading toward the lake with his turkey on his back. "What about poor Mack?"

"Forget about it. It's done," Mr. Elliot said. He did not look happy. "Lardass, I mean the surveyor, is waiting for you." He pulled a pair of snowshoes from the wall. "Take these for your trouble with our regrets."

Sister Magdalena poked her fingers through the webbed lacing. "I'm not a small woman."

"Yes, ma'am," Mr. Elliot said with a grin. "And I doubt the world has seen a penguin on snowshoes."

Sister Magdalena chuckled all the way to the sleigh. Maybe Mr. Elliot was not such a bad egg after all. A penguin on snowshoes. It would be a lark to go tromping through the woods. Her brothers would laugh themselves sick to see her. She must send a sketch with her next letter. She giggled. Penguin indeed.

The surveyor waited by a small cutter hitched to a single black horse. Sleigh bells jingled with every shake of the beautiful beast's head. He was a short Frenchman with a pigeon-like chest and a wide, heavy bottom. Dark eyes glittered beneath a red stocking cap with a long tail. A glint of sun bounced off a medal dangling from his neck. A Catholic. She relaxed.

"Hello, Sister," the surveyor called out. "Ready?"

She climbed into the sleigh dipping the runners on her side into the snow. The horse whinnied and stomped, but the uneven weight made it impossible for them to move forward. Sister Magdalena climbed out and lifted the runner back onto the frozen path.

"What is your Christian name?" Sister Magdalena said as she pulled a horse hide blanket across her lap.

"You know my nickname?" he said around a wad of tobacco. "I was baptized Louis La'Valley."

"Then Mr. La'Valley, I'm ready to leave."

Once underway, she dared voice a question. "Shouldn't Mr. Starkweather keep good workers instead of training new men?"

Mr. La'Valley shrugged. "There are always three crews at a logging camp, Sister." He flicked the lines and steered the horse around a pile of logs. "One working, one leaving, and another coming."

He spat a stream of brown juice into the snow. A burst of wind splattered it back across his coat and onto Sister Magdalena's cape. Sister Magdalena flicked away the freezing drops of slime.

"Did you see that poor man fired this morning?" She pointed to the Latvian floundering in the deep snow. "Where do you suppose he is going?"

He hedged before answering. "The little settlement across the lake, no doubt."

"I didn't know of a settlement," Sister Magdalena said.

"Not exactly a settlement," Mr. La'Valley said. "A roadhouse."

"A saloon?" Sister Magdalena remembered the women's laughter the previous night.

"Mr. La'Valley shrugged. "They sell liquor."

"And women?"

Another shrug. "Maybe." Mr. La'Valley slapped the lines. "Of course, women."

"So that poor man was driven from honest work into vile temptation," Sister Magdalena said. "Mr. Starkweather will have much to answer for."

The horse plowed through the snowy drifts, snow churning around his hooves. The bells rang out across the frozen lake. They passed the Latvian. No room to offer a ride.

Hot tears stung her eyes. There was nothing she could do. Sister Magdalena swallowed hard. At least she had helped Gertie to a place of safety.

If Starkweather Timber was a safe place.

Sister Magdalena crossed herself. *St Michael the Archangel, by the Power of God, cast into hell satan and all the evil spirits who prowl about the world seeking the ruin of souls.*

Chapter 28
Solveig

She should have done something. Last time Pettibone caused trouble, Irish squelched it with his cleaver. Even Mr. Elliot had no business speaking in the cookshack. Solveig must think and act like a man if she wanted to keep her job.

She turned the bread dough and added a handful of flour. It was her kitchen, but the pencil pusher would not back her up when it came to Pettibone. Nor would Mr. Starkweather.

Gertie proved a good worker. Stutz grumbled, but his young legs saved Solveig countless steps. Too bad Sister Magdalena had to leave. Had time allowed, they might have become friends.

Ridiculous. Solveig was not at Starkweather Timber to make friends.

"Mack was always friendly. Sully said he worked hard," Stutz said from the dishpan. "He was one of the first hired on."

"How long ago was that?" Gertie said.

"Almost two months," Stutz said. "He came early to work on the road crew."

"No use talking about it," Solveig said. "What's done is done."

The wind puffed a burst of smoke from the stovepipe.

"I heard voices last night, on my way to the bunkhouse" Stutz said. "Were you and Gertie in the office?"

"No," Solveig said. "We were here where we belong."

"I heard women," Stutz said. "A party, I think. I spied Pettibone and Lardass's sleigh. Tonight, I'm going to sneak over there, and look in the windows."

"You will do no such thing," Solveig said. "Peeking in windows will cost you your job."

Stutz pouted. He was about to say something else when Pokey came in with more water. He tracked snow across the floor. Solveig sighed and fetched the rag.

Chapter 29
Nels

God, it was cold. He and the others slipped into the woods like gray ghosts in the twilight between dawn and sunrise. Old Starkweather got his money's worth from the crew, damn his sorry hide.

"Colder than a witch's tit," Ten-Day said. He hunched his shoulders and buried his face in the folds of a wool scarf wrapped around his neck. "My God, what will Mack do?"

"They shut down if it's forty below," Nels said. He hoped to steer the conversation to the safer of the two topics. Griping about Pettibone would only lead to trouble. His nostrils froze together with every breath. His lungs burned. "Cold weather is too hard on the teams."

"That's a comfort," Ten-Day snorted, pumping his arms to warm himself. "Did you see a thermometer this morning?"

Nels shook his head.

"The bull of the woods hides one in the dentist's cabin," Ten-Day said. "It's not forty below until he says it's forty below."

Nels shrugged. Cold was cold. It did not matter once they started working. The air penetrated his heaviest woolen clothing. Some of the newcomers wore city jackets. They might buy winter clothing on credit, but that meant leaner paychecks in the spring.

The oxen plodded before them, switching their tails and snorting bursts of cloud. A rim of frost covered their noses, and Fish stopped to break ice away from their nostrils.

"You ready for this?" Ten-Day said to Fish.

Nels suspected Ten-Day talked to the trees if no one else was around.

"Ready to have this beast farting in my face all day?" Fish said. "Warm air keeps the chilblains away." As if on cue, an ox released a groan of fetid air. "See what I mean?" Fish said. "Convenient."

Branches and slash scattered here and there, a monument to yesterday's labors. Nothing pretty about logging except the paychecks.

"Hurry up, boys," Paulson hollered. "Daylight's burning in the swamp."

Nels hated the snow more than the cold. Snow made it harder to walk, harder to skid timber, harder for the limbers, and harder for the sawyers to cut the trees low enough to prevent a dressing down from the bull of the woods. Wasted board feet meant slimmer earnings, and there was no doubt in anyone's mind that their goal was to make Mr. Starkweather richer.

The push snowshoed from one crew to the other, barking orders. "They're cutting a hundred thousand board feet a day at Weyerhaeuser. Starkweather expects the same here."

"Starkweather can kiss my frozen ass," Ten-Day said as soon as the push was out of ear shot. "I'd like to ask him why he let Pettibone goad Mack that way."

"Not if you want to keep your job," Nels said. He waded through snow up to his knees to a lower branch. The frozen wood popped under his ax. Icy pellets sprayed into his face from the shaken needles.

They chopped as chips scattered and piney smells filled the frigid air. There was no wind. Nels's heart pounded. His breath labored. Sweat gathered under his arms and trickled down his back. Nels kept a rhythm. If he lost focus, he might feel the bite of the ax in his leg or lose a hand. Stray branches might poke out an eye. The branches were heavy enough to crush a man's bones or cave a skull.

They had no time to pile the slash. The bosses did not care. They would be gone before the fires came in the spring. Camp shut down long before the snow pack melted from the forest.

If he were the boss, Nels would do things differently. Crews would salvage the tops and larger branches, not prime wood, but still valuable. At the end of the season the woods would be neat and orderly. Maybe he would replant the trees taken. Lofty thoughts, not befitting a brush ape who did what he was told, filled his imagination. Nels sunk his ax into the cleft of a branch. Useless to think about it. No one waited in line for his opinion.

Besides, there was a never-ending supply of white pine in the north woods. Everyone knew that.

Exhaustion set in after an hour's work. Nels found his second wind around mid-morning. Once he hit his stride, he kept going until his growling belly demanded dinner.

The swingdingle pulled in at noon. Nels did not have to be called twice. The stew froze to the tin plates before the jacks had a chance to finish. Fish and Ten-Day perched on rocks around the campfire. Dutch dragged a log over for a bench.

"My granddad ruined his kidneys by sitting on rocks during the War of Rebellion," Dutch said. "He was pissing needles during Antietam."

Nels fetched another log. He wanted nothing to do with pissing needles. Besides, once Nels stopped swinging his ax, his sweat started to freeze. The sooner he ate and returned to work, the better.

They gobbled their food. A few men relieved themselves behind bushes. The men stood around the fire, warming first their hands, and turning to warm their backsides.

Pettibone swaggered out of the woods, dragging a moose calf behind him. He shoved his way to the fire, complaining how little food remained.

"Get here on time," Pokey said with a sour curse. "First to the trough gets the most."

Pettibone pushed his face into Pokey's. "I'm the one bringing in meat for this camp," Pettibone said. He pushed Pokey in the chest, and the old man stumbled. "I deserve a little respect."

Nels held his breath. Pokey was no match for the braggart. Nels stepped forward.

"Leave Gramps alone."

"You stay out of it," Pettibone said in a loud voice. "Watch your pockets, boys. Fingers robbed us blind last year at Gull River Timber."

"You robbed everyone," Nels said. The blood rose until he felt the throb of each heartbeat. "And set me up to take the blame."

The push stepped between them. "Back to work, men," Paulson said. "This ain't no ladies aid society."

"We just got here," Ten-Day said.

"Time to go," the push said. "Get off your sorry ass."

Pettibone and Nels glared at each other. It was hopeless. One way or the other, Pettibone would get Nels fired. Maybe Pokey, too.

"Forget it," Ten-Day said as they headed back to the cut. "Everyone knows Pettibone's true colors."

Nels hurled a thousand curses at Pettibone as he topped a pine and bucked the logs.

"Isn't it time to quit?" Ten-Day said.

The sky showed purple behind the forest, the tall pines spires against the colored sky.

"It's time when the push says it's time," Nels said. "And not a minute sooner."

The Gabriel blew and the men trudged back to the bunkhouse, a weary line of gray coats and colored mackinaws. The men grumbled, calling hellfire and damnation down upon the bosses. The griping always turned to women, and their lack of them. Men poured over old newspapers, reading the romance adverts aloud.

"The dentist said you can't trust a woman, no sir," Ten-Day said as they entered the bunkhouse. "They'll find a baby wherever they want, and the man none the wiser."

The small huddle of men looked their way and whispered as Nels peeled off wet socks and outer clothing. Nels clenched his jaw and pretended he had not noticed.

How does a man defend himself from slander?

At supper, Gertie ignored him. Pettibone sneered from across the room and made a cutting gesture across his neck with his finger. Ma put the food on the table without a glance his way.

Nels returned to the bunkhouse too tired to talk. Pokey lit the lantern over the amen corner and perched on an old stump. He cleared his throat for story telling as the jacks gathered around. Some whittled or darned socks. One jack sharpened a saw blade, unwilling to trust it to the dentist.

"Old Paul Bunyan once lassoed the moon," Pokey drawled. "It happened like this…"

Nels's arms and back ached. He climbed into his bunk, but when he pulled back the blanket, he discovered a sack of logging berries on his side of the bed. Pettibone was setting him up to be a thief. Why else would a sack of prunes be in his bunk? Nels would be fired if he were discovered with stolen goods.

The more Nels had defended his innocence at Gull River Timber, the less others believed him.

"Babe, his blue ox," Pokey continued from the amen corner. The tale ambled on.

Ten-Day scribbled a letter to his mother. A few jacks climbed into their bunks. Loud growling came from someone already asleep. Pokey finished his tale.

"Pokey," Nels whispered. "Come here."

Pokey shuffled over to the bunk, cursing, and grumbling. "What now? Can't a man go to bed in peace without being bully-ragged by some lazy, good-for-nothing brush ape?"

He grew quiet when he saw the contraband.

"Look," Nels whispered. "Pettibone is trying to set me up as a thief."

Pokey's gaze sharpened. "Why Pettibone? Did you see him?"

"He swore he'd get me fired." Their prior history poured out in a whispered jumble.

"Hmm," Pokey said. "What would he gain by making you out a thief?"

"Dunno," Nels said. "But I've got to get this back to the kitchen before Pettibone starts accusing me."

Pokey rolled his tongue around the inside of his mouth, pouching out his cheek as he considered Nels's words. "I don't want to get caught in the middle," Pokey said. "But I can't abide the braggart, and you stood up for me today." Pokey looked off into the distance as if weighing his options. The bunks groaned as men settled for the night. The water in the wash barrels sizzled on the stove. "I'll take care of it." Pokey tucked the sack behind the wood box.

"By God," Ten-Day shivered and pulled blankets to his side. "I need more logging berries. I swear, my shit came out frozen solid."

"Shut your mouth, you dumb Polack," Nels said in a whisper. "Whatever you do, don't mention prunes."

But Ten-Day was already asleep. One minute jabbering, the next snoring. The bunkhouse settled into its nighttime symphony of snores, mumbling words and bodily sounds. All the beans, Nels figured. The men had a reason for calling them blanket lifters.

Nels expected Pettibone to barge in at any time and make a scene.

Voices woke him when it was almost morning. Someone talking to Pokey.

"We need every man," Pokey said in a loud whisper. "Can't you wait a few more days until the new men are trained in?"

"Elliot says we can't wait."

It was Jacob Pettibone up to no good. Nels recognized their voices. Ten-Day turned in his sleep and flopped an arm across Nels's chest.

"Elliot says go," Pettibone said. "Straight from Starkweather hisself."

"I don't like it," Pokey whispered, his voice barely audible. "Wait another week. They're just making a dent in the woods. New men don't know shit from shingles."

"It's happening whether you like it or not," Pettibone said.

Whispering. Footsteps across the wooden floor and a burst of cold air with the open door. Pokey slammed wood into the firebox, cursing and kicking a stray boot across the floor.

Nels crawled out of his bunk, taking his clothes to the barrel stove to dress. "What's the matter?" he said to Pokey in a low voice. "Get up on the wrong side of the bed?"

"Sometimes I wonder," Pokey said. "That nun tries to help people, and the rest of us shit where we eat."

"It can't be that bad."

"Mind your manners if you know what's good for you," Pokey said.

"Always do," Nels said.

Pokey grabbed Nels's collar and pulled his face closer. "I mean it, boy. Hightail it to the cut, work like the devil, and for God's sake, don't say a word if Pettibone tries to pick a fight. Keep your head down."

"What do you mean?" Nels said. Something was very wrong.

"Mind me." Pokey said. "Forewarned is forearmed."

Pokey grabbed the Gabriel and blew a short blast to wake the men. Nels watched to see if Pokey might warn any of the other men, but as far as he could tell, Pokey spoke to no one, though his face glowered and a steady stream of profanities poured from his lips.

Nels sidled up to Ten-Day and shared Pokey's warning.

"I've heard of shenanigans like this," Ten-Day said in a low voice. "Fine print in the contract robs a man of his wages if he's fired before a certain date. Did you read your contract?"

Nels shook his head. He had been glad to get the job, not worried about the fine print. Would he never learn? Nels ground his teeth. It could not be happening. What would he do if he were out on his ear without wages?

After breakfast, the bull of the woods made a big production about Mr. Elliot inspecting the work site. It was unusual for the pencil pusher to leave the warmth of his fire.

Nels and Ten-Day were first to the cut. Nels's ax carried a perfect edge, and the overnight soaking in kerosene limbered it up just right. He trimmed a magnificent pine the fellers had dropped the previous afternoon, dodging the prickly under branches.

Ten-Day and Nels rode the misery whip as Dutch measured the trunk. The sawdust flew. Nels saw neither Pettibone nor Mr. Elliot during the morning hours. Fish skidded the logs, his oxen snorting against the chains.

"Did you hear?" Fish said as he clamped the tongs to another log. "Old Julius Caesar tangled with Pokey."

"What now?" Nels said. His mouth turned dry as he considered the implications. "Pettibone was ragging about something and Pokey got right in his face," the skidder said. His laugh gleeful. "Good for the old man, I say."

Nels attacked the next tree. His ax never slowed. Sweat ran down his back and his body begged for rest, but he kept going.

For all he knew Pettibone hid out in the brush, conjuring a reason to fire him.

He was done playing the fool. This time he would outsmart Pettibone.

Dutch topped another tree and together they bucked the logs. A bolt just two inches less than the required sixteen feet-four inches thrown aside to rot. A waste. He threw off his scarf and kept working. He topped another tree while Dutch measured more logs.

"Hear that?" Dutch said. "Those greenhorns don't know what they're doing. Listen to their rhythm."

Someone else's problem. They would figure it out. Nels poured every ounce of strength into his ax. His bones jarred. Sweat poured down his face. He threw off his jacket, his body a fiery furnace. He did not notice Pettibone sneaking up behind him.

"What do you think you're doing?" Pettibone said with a snarl. "Slacking again."

"Butchering wood," Dutch said. "Our fifth tree this morning."

"I count only one," Pettibone said.

Nels gritted his teeth.

"The skidder took the logs already," Dutch said. "Count the tops if you doubt my word—or ask Fish."

Pettibone itched for a fight. However, he could not fire anyone. Only Mr. Elliot or the push carried that authority. The pencil pusher walked across an open area, his mackinaw like a red bird against the snow.

"Nipped any logging berries lately?" Pettibone said with a leer.

Nels attacked the branches like one of his Viking ancestors gone berserk. He bit his tongue until he tasted blood.

"You'll regret your laziness," Pettibone said.

"Goddam you," Dutch said. "Count the tops."

"Save your excuses," Pettibone said. "Elliot!" The pencil pusher did not look their way.

"Has he gone deaf?" Pettibone bellowed Mr. Elliot's name again. With a curse, Pettibone charged after him, floundering through snow, calling out Elliot's name. The men watched as Mr.

Elliot joined Pettibone. The two men hurried back toward them. The wind shifted.

Nels saw it for what it was. He would be fired. All his work was for nothing. Almost two months wasted. Nels cursed Jacob Pettibone until he ran out of breath. Nels drove his ax into the tree trunk and put on his jacket and scarf. No use wasting another breath for Starkweather Timber. Everything was lost. Again.

Hellfire, he needed a drink. A sudden gust of wind

"Timber," echoed behind them at the same moment as the Gabriel announced the swingdingle's arrival.

An explosion of crashing branches. Then screams. Horrible, ear-splitting shrieks that turned every jack toward the sound. Nels followed the rush of men hurrying toward the noise.

"Who caught it?" Nels's heart pounded and he struggled for breath. He thought he knew. Could it be?

Pettibone lay tangled in the branches of a gigantic pine. "Help!" He reached one hand through the prickly branches and screamed. "My leg."

"By God." Pokey huffed so hard that Nels feared the old man might keel over. The veins bulged on the sides of his temple and the old man's hand trembled as he pointed to a glimpse of red mackinaw beneath the heavy trunk. "It's the pencil pusher. My God, Mr. Elliot."

Mr. Elliot's ledger lay aside in the snow. During the chaos of men rushing to aid the fallen men, Nels grabbed the ledger and tucked it inside the front of his coat.

The two new fellers came white-faced and distraught. "I'm sorry, it was an accident." They repeated it several times. "The wind shifted. An accident. So sorry."

"I'll fetch blankets," Nels said to no one in particular. Saws bit into the branches, axes chopped, shouts, and commands to free the injured men sounded throughout the woods.

Nels ran to the bunkhouse and scanned the ledger, holding it up to a window for light. He found the list of men to be fired that day. Mack's name was on the top with a check by it. Then a long list of names also on the chopping block.

His name, Ten-Day's and Dutch's were there. Frenchie and Alfie. He had been right. Their asses were in a sling. They were the next to go.

Nels hesitated. While it was doubtful either of the injured men would survive, perhaps someone else knew about the list.

Nels had nothing to lose. He tore the page out of the ledger book and dropped it into the stove. It flared and disappeared to ash. Nels tucked the ledger back into the front of his jacket and jogged back to the cut, grabbing blankets on the way out.

Nels tossed the ledger under a tree when he was sure no one was watching. He hurried to the cluster of men around the victims.

"Took you long enough," Pokey muttered. "About ready to send out the cavalry."

"How are they?" Nels said.

"See for yourself," Pokey said. "You ain't blind."

Mr. Elliot lay at an odd angle on the firewood sledge. Blood pooled from the side of his head. He was alive, but barely. Nels breathed easier. Nels was no doctor, but he predicted the pencil pusher would not last the day. The best of luck. Too-good-to-be-true luck.

Pettibone's hands fluttered around his chest. A white bone stuck out of his bloody leg. The color had drained from his face. Except for the constant fluttering of his hands, one might have thought he was a goner.

Surely, an answer to his mother's prayers.

Chapter 30
Sister Magdalena

Already across the lake, Sister Magdalena spied a side-trail leading into the woods. A plume of smoke hovered above the trees. The roadhouse.

"I'd like to stop at the tavern," Sister Magdalena said. She craned her neck to see down the trail, with an impulse to visit the women who lived there. Perhaps they needed help.

"No, Sister," Mr. La'Valley said. "It's no place for you."

"I'll be the judge of that." Sister Magdalena sniffed. "We will stop," Sister Magdalena said with more firmness than intended. Men thought they knew better because they wore trousers. "I know my duty."

Mr. La'Valley groaned. "Sister, you don't understand..."

"I will stop." Sister Magdalena had no time to explain, and no obligation to do so. The laughter from the other night compelled her to see for herself. The women needed spiritual care as much as any lumberjack. They might be innocents like Gertie, trapped through circumstances. "Let me out. I will go the rest of the way on foot."

"But..." Mr. La'Valley squirmed on his side of the cutter. "It's a rough place."

He was a good man, but he should mind his own business. "I will go," she said. "Whether or not you take me is up to you."

Mr. La'Valley turned the sleigh toward the roadhouse. Poor man. Sister Magdalena was hindering his work. The morning sun was half-way up the sky.

The trail littered with cigar butts and whiskey bottles. Tobacco froze dirty stripes in the snow. A log building peeked through the trees. The wind was rising, and each puff sent a shimmering wave of icy snow from the branches of the overhanging pine. Sister Magdalena snugged her cape tighter around her neck.

"I won't be long," she said while climbing out of the sleigh. "I'll snowshoe the rest of the way to Weyerhaeuser, if you'd rather." She hoped it was not far away.

"Leave you at a whorehouse?" he said. "How could I explain that on judgment day?"

Sister Magdalena ignored the angry clench of his jaw. He followed her to the door but did not enter the building, or knock on the door.

Sister Magdalena hesitated and pounded on the door herself. Nothing. She pounded again. A muffled call. Footsteps.

The door creaked open and a man stuck out a tousled head. "Go away. We're closed." He wore a ragged sweater that hung down over red underwear faded pink. The sweater was buttoned wrong and gave him a lopsided look.

"Hello, Lardass," he said. "What in the hell are you doing here so early in the morning?" He glanced toward Sister Magdalena, rubbed his eyes, and sputtered an apology for his language.

He sprang to attention, holding the door open, and motioning them inside. His feet shuffled in ragged carpet slippers. He waved them toward a barrel stove in the center of the room, urging them to warm themselves. He threw wood in the fire. The stovepipe smoked, and he fiddled with the damper.

The building stank of stale beer. Peanut shells littered the sawdust covered floor. A chair lay on its side alongside a tipped table. Playing cards scattered around the room as if a game had been interrupted. A shotgun lay across the bar made from a split log balanced on two barrels.

Sister Magdalena lifted her habit above the peanut shells.

"Sister, Clarence Mortimer, owner of this establishment," Mr. La'Valley said. "Sister Magdalena. We're going to Weyerhaeuser."

"Starkweather win another poker game?" Clarence laughed, then coughed a fearful jag. He emerged red-faced, wiping phlegm on the sleeve of his sweater.

"I'm here to visit the women who were at Starkweather the other night."

Mr. Mortimer blanched. He stuttered, rubbed his whiskery chin, and looked toward Mr. La'Valley for help. "They keep late hours, ma'am, Sister."

"We'll come back later," Mr. La'Valley said. He acted relieved as he took her elbow to guide her out the door.

Sister Magdalena pulled away and dropped to her knees on the filthy floor despite what might be crawling under the peanut shells. She pulled out her rosary.

"Hail Mary full of grace." She peeked out of one eye. The Blessed Mother was a fierce weapon against evil.

The men stood with jaws gaping open, about as stymied as Sister Magdalena had ever seen a man stymied. She closed her eyes, suppressing a giggle. She prayed out loud, fingering the beads.

"Sister," Mr. La'Valley said. "We have to go."

"Blessed art thou among women," she continued in a louder voice.

"Rosy, Delores," Mr. Mortimer called into the loft. "You've got company."

Sister Magdalena stood to her feet, still holding her beads.

Two women peeked down, messy-haired, and bleary eyed. The yellow-haired woman wore a nightdress that barely covered her chest. Her buck teeth chattered with cold. The dark-haired woman wrapped in a striped blanket.

Poor things. What lives they must lead.

"I will speak to the women in private," she said. "You may step outside."

Mr. Mortimore stared. An angry flush turned his face red. He sputtered a reply. Sister Magdalena held up her rosary and prepared to kneel again.

"It won't take long," she said.

Mr. Mortimer screwed his mouth and spat in the overflowing spittoon next to the bar.

"Make it fast," Mr. Mortimer said.

"What's going on, Lardass?" the yellow-haired woman said.

"Sister Lumberjack wants to talk to you," Mr. La'Valley said.

"Sister Lumberjack? Is that my name?"

"Yup." Mr. La'Valley jerked his mitts on and headed outside. "Come, Clarence. The sooner she yaps, the sooner I can go."

The women climbed backwards down the ladder.

"You're not dressed for company," Sister Magdalena said. "Warm yourselves." Sister Magdalena added more wood. She would not take time to empty the ashes, though it would have been a Christian gesture. The women shivered

"What do you want?" The dark-haired woman reeked of perfume that did little to mask a musky smell. "It's freezing and I'm tired."

Sister Magdalena had better talk fast or she would lose her. She had not thought what to say. "I heard you laughing at Starkweather the other night. It had a hollow ring to it." Sister Magdalena brushed peanut shells off her cassock. "I'm here to help." As soon as the words were out of her mouth, she knew they sounded more condemning than friendly. "You could leave this life and do something more worthwhile." Holy Mother of God, even worse.

The dark-haired woman snorted and started up the ladder.

The other woman stared at Sister Magdalena as if she were from another world. Sister Magdalena fumbled for words. Everything was coming out wrong.

"I always make a mess of things," Sister Magdalena said. "I've never been in a place like this before and I'm a little nervous. I only meant to say that perhaps, because your laughter at Starkweather sounded unhappy, you might be interested in finding a line of work that is of more service to mankind."

"Oh, we service mankind." The dark-haired woman's voice dripped sarcasm. "You needn't worry yourself about that."

A giggle rose in Sister Magdalena's throat. She swallowed. She could not have chosen more unsuitable words if she had tried. The giggle turned to laughter, then rib-shaking mirth that made tears roll down her cheeks. "That's a good one!" she said between gulping breaths. "Servicing mankind, indeed!"

The two women stared as if at a monkey in a zoo. This made Sister Magdalena laugh harder. A penguin, not a monkey. Sister Lumberjack on snowshoes. The yellow-haired woman smiled politely. The other stared with disdain.

Sister Magdalena regained control. She wiped her eyes and nose and straightened her coif. "Let's try again, shall we? You can see that I'm a disappointment to God, Mother Superior, and everyone."

She took a breath, aware of their full attention.

One of you is Rosy and the other Delores," Sister Magdalena said. "Which is which?"

The yellow-haired girl introduced herself as Rosy. That left the other girl as Delores, though she did not offer the information. Sister Magdalena introduced herself as from the Duluth Convent.

"A nun? How do you stand wearing that get up?" Delores rubbed her eyes and stifled a yawn.

"Yes, I'm a Benedictine, but you've seen for yourself that I'm a poor example. As far as my clothing, I could say the same of you." She chuckled. "It appears both of us dress differently than polite society."

"Good folks do not welcome us into polite society," Delores said. She looked older than Rosy. Fine lines surrounded startling green eyes.

It was true. She suspected even Sister Hildegard would have a hard time extending mercy toward these women. A wave of affection flooded Sister Magdalena, a gift from the Holy Spirit. On her own, Sister Magdalena was without charity.

"I heard you laughing," Sister Magdalena said. "A mournful, desperate sound." Sister Magdalena paused. "I invite you to leave this place."

"Where would we go?" Rosy said.

"A roof over our head and three squares a day," Delores said. "It's not so bad."

They looked at each other for a long moment.

"Can I pray for you?" Sister Magdalena said. "And you pray for me that I will learn to live without judgment."

Delores started back up the ladder.

"Please, Sister," Rosy said. "Pray for my little boy in the Duluth orphanage."

"Of course." Sister Magdalena's heart leapt under her ribs. Angels had guided her to this place. Her convent ran the only orphanage in Duluth. "What is his name and age?"

"Jimmy...James Jackson," she said, her voice strangling at his name. "He's four years old."

Sister Magdalena remembered trousers with scuffed knees. She had replaced missing buttons on his shirt. A sign. She was being guided by God's mysterious will, the divine plan that defied logic.

Sister Magdalena knelt again in the sawdust. Rosy knelt beside her, but Deloris stayed half-way up the ladder, leaning back and glowering at Sister Magdalena. Delores acted tough, but wasn't the Lord near to those broken-hearted and crushed in spirit? Sister Magdalena prayed aloud for their health and safety, for more love and charity. Then she prayed for young Jimmy.

Rosy's tears dripped onto the peanut shells. Delores sneered.

"Return with me to Duluth...to visit your son," Sister Magdalena said.

"I'm no good for him," Rosy said. "He's better off with the sisters."

"No one loves like a mother," Sister Magdalena said. "I'm named for a sinner. Jesus, the Christ, lifted her out of her misery. It can happen for you, too."

"A little late for us," Delores said.

"Never too late," Sister Magdalena called after her as she climbed up into the loft.

"Thank you, Sister." Rosy's nose dripped. She fumbled for a handkerchief.

"Think about it," Sister Magdalena said. "I'll stop again."

Mr. La'Valley did not speak when she came out. Mr. Mortimer spat in the snow as she walked by. The cheery sleigh bells sounded again as the horse pulled them through the forest.

Poor Rosy separated from her son. Poor James away from his mother. No mention of a father. Men did not consider the pain and heartache they left behind.

Perhaps Rosy could work at the orphanage in exchange for room and board. No money, but at least she could be with little James.

Sister Magdalena would approach Mother Superior with the suggestion. The Rule of Benedict said to seek counsel before acting. Every instinct within her wanted to scoop Rosy into her arms and carry her away from the life she lived.

"Be careful," Mr. La'Valley said, startling Sister Magdalena out of her thoughts. "Those girls belong to Clarence, and he won't like you interfering."

"You're wrong," Sister Magdalena said. A phrase of her brother's popped onto her tongue. "Mr. Lincoln freed the slaves."

"Don't want you getting hurt," he said with a grunt. "That's all."

Sister Magdalena doubted even Mr. Mortimer would dare to lay hands on her. She had the Blessed Mother at her back. Besides, she outweighed the little pissant.

Weyerhaeuser Timber lay a mile north of Stink Lake, on the banks of the Skunk River. Crashing timbers, the calls of teamsters, chopping axes and whining saws greeted them. The camp bustled with efficiency. She counted six teams pulling loaded sledges from different parts of the surrounding woods.

"Warm up in the cookshack," the man in the office said after her brief introduction. "I received a letter from your Mother Superior informing us of your visit. Come back after you eat, and we'll discuss the particulars." He pointed the way. "And I've mail for Starkweather. Lardass, I mean..." he looked at Sister Magdalena and floundered for the right words. "What is your name anyway?"

"I'll take the mail," Mr. La'Valley said. "Everyone calls me Lardass."

Mr. La'Valley told her to leave her belongings in the sleigh. "You can ride back with me tonight if I finish my work," he said. "Pick up your check."

Sister Magdalena hurried the short distance to the cookshack on shoveled and sanded paths. Stacks of kitchen wood piled in a woodshed convenient to a side door.

The smell of baking bread greeted her. She stood on newspapers spread across the floor. The cook, a big man with a handlebar mustache and salt-and-pepper colored hair, turned in surprise when she walked into his domain. He had gray eyes and a firm chin. A white apron wrapped around his middle. He was as neat and clean as Sister Hildegard in the hospital kitchen, and clearly in control.

"Sister? You must be frozen," he said. "Irish, fetch the sister some swamp water."

A skinny man wearing a towel around his waist brought a steaming cup of tea. He scurried back to peeling potatoes, keeping his head down. Sister Magdalena smiled when he looked her way.

"We've had sky pilots, but never a nun," the cook said.

Sister Magdalena explained the hospital tickets. "I'm visiting all the camps."

He invited her to share the noon meal with the kitchen staff. The bull cook left with the loaded swingdingle and Irish scooted beside her at the table.

"You came from Starkweather?" he said just loud enough for her to hear. "I was their cook until a few days ago." He looked around and his Adam's apple bobbed. "Who replaced me?"

Solveig had complained about this man's drinking. He looked the part. Sister Magdalena hesitated. "Two women work in the kitchen," she said. "I know nothing about it."

It did not seem appropriate to help with kitchen chores. She was in the way. Not like Starkweather Timber.

She returned to wait in the office. Blue jays and whiskey jacks chattered in the trees. She watched logs unloaded onto the frozen river. It took God a century to grow such trees. Men took them in hours. Even the sisters needed lumber for hospitals and schools, but all at the price of the beautiful forest.

She entered the office and explained how she spoke to the men at Starkweather after supper, and how the company handled the chits. She did not mention the delinquent payment.

"Smart," the pencil pusher said. "Injuries are a distraction." He drummed his pencil stub on the wooden counter. "Ties up the cook and sets everything back. Not to mention how it upsets the men." He opened his ledger book to a blank page. "Your name, Sister?"

"Sister Lumberjack," Sister Magdalena said with a grin. She had thought to make a joke, but he gave her no opportunity. He wrote across the top of the page in a bold hand: *Sister Lumberjack Hospital Tickets.*

He pointed to a stack of newspapers in the corner. "Try to stay out of the way."

Sister Magdalena perused the headlines. The government was to broker peace with the Mormons over polygamy. The economic forecast was grim.

"Is there a locomotive going to Aitkin anytime soon?" she interrupted.

The pencil pusher looked up from his figures with a frown. "Tomorrow or the next day," he said. "It depends on the weather."

She prayed a rosary for Rosy and Delores, but found it hard to concentrate. Sister Magdalena suspected Mr. Starkweather arranged for the women to visit the camp. Their laughter lingered in her mind.

Sister Magdalena prayed for Gertie, Rosy, Deloris and all women in vulnerable positions. She prayed for men who took advantage of women. *Forgive us our trespasses as we forgive those who trespass against us.*

The afternoon dragged. She woke up with a start when the horn blew for supper. She had fallen asleep sitting upright in the chair. No one else was around. She pulled on her cloak and hurried to the cookshack.

She took a seat among the men. She was used to the clang of tinware. The sisters at the convent dined on soup while she feasted like Christmas. The meal ended. She followed the men to the bunkhouse with the pencil pusher at her side.

This bunkhouse carried the same rank odors as Starkweather, but was better lighted and of sturdier construction. Triple bunks lined both sides of the long building with three large barrel stoves: one at the far end, one by the main door and another in the middle. Kerosene lamps hung around the room. A stack of extra blankets folded on a bench. Wet work clothes hung everywhere. Some things were the same.

She faced the jacks with more confidence than she felt. God had brought her this far. She could count on Him now.

Once again, it was Solveig's story that broke through their reserve. To her amazement, Sister Magdalena sold one hundred and nineteen tickets. She shook each man's hand as she handed him his ticket. They doffed their hats in her presence. A Mexican kissed her hand, speaking in rapid Spanish. Many knelt on the hard floor for Night Prayer. Others gawked or mocked as their consciences dictated.

Sister Magdalena prayed for each one, those who knelt and those who did not. All were children of God.

Afterwards, Mr. La'Valley waited outside the bunkhouse, pacing back and forth to keep warm. "It's late, but I'm heading back to Starkweather," Mr. La'Valley said. "There's a full moon." He scanned the skies. "Might as well sleep in my own bed. Ride along if you wish."

Mr. Starkweather might be there to sign the draft. "I have to go to the office, but I'll be right back," Sister Magdalena said.

"I'll hitch the sleigh," Mr. La'Valley said.

The pencil pusher presented Sister Magdalena the check without hesitation. She secured the draft in her pocket. Money to be used for good.

The moon drooped like an orange in an indigo sky. The sleigh bells jingled. Sister Magdalena had enjoyed evening sleigh rides with her brothers. Thoughts of home curled through her mind as ethereal as the vapor from her breath.

Mr. La'Valley hurried past Skunk Hollow. Sister Magdalena chuckled. He acted as if he were afraid she might insist on another visit. Lights showed in every window and smoke poured from the chimney. She carried an image of Rosy in her flimsy gown, a mother with a son reduced to such circumstances.

Sister crossed herself and prayed for all women tangled in such a trade. Then she prayed another for little Jimmy as they crossed Stink Lake. The runners jolted over the frozen drifts. The horses raced toward the feed trough waiting for them.

"Look!" Sister Magdalena pointed to the north where wave upon wave of undulating greens and yellows filled the heavens. "Northern lights."

Mr. La'Valley slowed but the horse was not interested in the mesmerizing sky. It pulled at the bit and snorted great clouds. Mr. La'Valley fought the lines, but finally let the horse have its way.

"No use, Sister" he said. The horse charged across the lake. It skirted round the piles of logs at the landing and stopped in front of the barn.

Sister Magdalena craned her neck to watch the lights as long as possible. Didn't the Holy Scriptures say that the heavens declare the glory of God?

Sister Magdalena unfolded her long legs out of the sleigh and thanked Mr. La'Valley for the ride. She was about to thank him for stopping at the roadhouse, a touchy subject, when Barrister stuck his head out from the barn.

"Thank God you're here, Sister," Barrister said. "There has been an accident. One man with a broken leg, but the other..." He shook his head. "They're in the cookshack."

Mother Superior should have sent someone who knew how to deal with injured men. Why hadn't they considered this dilemma?

Chapter 31
Solveig

Solveig swallowed a smirk when she first heard the news. Pettibone deserved what he got and Mr. Elliot had done nothing to curb Pettibone's tyranny. Justice served on a plate by Almighty God.

But when the jacks carried them into the cookshack, she changed her mind. Elliot's breaths came in gurgles and groans. One eye hung half out of its socket and his head split like a melon. Pettibone screamed and cursed with every movement.

"Where do you want them?" Pokey said.

Solveig did not want them. She grabbed the edge of the table to steady herself. "In the corner," she whispered.

Everyone expected her to know what to do. She had no idea. She would not wish a logging accident on anyone. If she had felt animosity toward the cook who doctored Rasmuss after his injury, she let go of it at that moment. Of course, the man had done the best he could.

All Solveig knew to do was to keep them warm, and offer sips of broth. Solveig covered Mr. Elliot with her own quilt, and used pillows to prop Pettibone's leg. Pettibone screamed and demanded whiskey. The afternoon inched toward suppertime. The men ate with downcast eyes and left like snakes slithering to their dens. It could happen to anyone.

Solveig steeled herself to keep watch overnight. Perhaps Pokey might spell her for a few hours later. She was too anxious to sleep. She propped her feet up and prayed for all of them.

She must have drifted asleep because she woke up praying for Rasmuss. In her dream, Rasmuss slept in the corner, injured. She drifted back to sleep and dreamed Sister Magdalena touched her shoulder. The nun's voice called her name.

Solveig startled awake. It was very late and the room was cold as ice. Sister's face shone in the lamplight as she bent over the injured men. Solveig took a breath. Was she dreaming?

"It's freezing in here," Sister Magdalena said.

Solveig stumbled to the stove and filled the firebox, feeling the welcome woosh of flames. Pokey had neglected his duties, exhausted after the day's events, but she had fallen asleep on watch.

The nun uncovered Mr. Elliot's face and quickly covered it again. Sister Magdalena made a gagging motion. Her face turned as pale and green as Pettibone's. Solveig felt the same way. A helpless, sickening sensation.

"Get some rest," Sister Magdalena said. "I will keep watch. Tomorrow's another work day for you."

"Where did you come from?" Perhaps this was all a dream. A nightmare. Pettibone thrashed and called out in his sleep.

"Finished up at Weyerhaeuser's and rode back with Mr. La'Valley." Sister Magdalena knelt and pulled out her beads.

Solveig could have kissed her. To be freed from the death watch was a gift. God had sent her to help them. Solveig mumbled her thanks and stumbled off to bed.

Later, Pokey's raspy voice and the clang of stove lids woke her. Solveig's foot hurt and her back ached. Solveig pulled herself out of bed and wrapped in an afghan to check on the injured men. The nun still knelt by Mr. Elliot. She stood to her feet when she saw Solveig, the rosary beads swinging in the folds of her long habit.

"I'm Sister Lumberjack now," Sister Magdalena said with a laugh. "That's what the jacks call me."

"We are christened anew at Starkweather Timber," Solveig said with a grin. "Some names better than others."

"Like poor Mr. La'Valley," Sister Magdalena said.

Sister Lumberjack sank onto a bench and Solveig spread the afghan over her shoulders. Solveig poured yesterday's coffee, a brew strong enough to choke an ox.

"Will they live?" Solveig handed a steaming cup to the nun.

"Mr. Pettibone might survive if he gets to a doctor," Sister Magdalena said. Sister pointed her chin toward Mr. Elliot. "He's bad."

"What can be done?" Solveig whispered.

"A train leaves Weyerhaeuser today. They might allow the men to ride out for medical care if we get them there in time."

Solveig thought to return to bed, but instead joined Sister Magdalena in keeping watch. Queenie jumped into her lap and purred. The minutes passed. Solveig, usually reticent, confided Halvor's reluctance to return to the woods. Sister Magdalena listened without comment.

"I'm sorry," Solveig said. Her grandmother had taught her to keep family business in the family. It was bad manners to burden others. She had spoken her mind. No, she corrected herself, she had spoken her heart. "I shouldn't bother you."

"Nonsense," Sister said. "It helps to share with a friend."

Solveig's voice choked. She had felt friendless since Inga's death. Of course, she knew neighbors and named them friends, but friendship with Inga had been different. Letters connected them through the years. Their visits, though infrequent, bolstered Solveig's resolve to persevere through the hardships of life. Inga's death had been a blow. She needed another friend like Inga.

In the dim light, Solveig whispered Halvor's betrayal, her desperation to keep the farm, and her fear of living without son or husband. Solveig finished, exhausted with emotion. They sat as the cat purred and moans sounded from the injured men. Solveig expected a reprimand, an exhortation to be more religious, more dedicated, more something.

"Mercy flows from the pierced wounds of Jesus's Sacred Heart." Sister spoke in a matter-of-fact fashion, as if it were the most ordinary thing in the world to bare one's soul to a near-stranger. "And Jesus speaks to us through the wounds we receive in this life." She looked into Solveig's eyes. "Sounds to me like Jesus is speaking to you, my friend."

"What do you mean?" Solveig said. "What would God say to me?"

"Listen with your heart," Sister Magdalena said.

Ridiculous. Solveig stood to her feet. She should have kept her mouth shut. A Catholic nun could not understand the pain of losing a husband or son. No one understood. Jesus speaking through wounds in her heart? Catholic gibberish. Martin Luther warned of superstitions.

Mr. Elliot gasped. His arms flailed. Sister Magdalena turned to tend him. Solveig hurried to the stove. Stutz stumbled into the kitchen rubbing sleep from his eyes. Gertie's footsteps sounded in the side room.

"He's gone," Sister Magdalena said. She covered Mr. Elliot's face with a blanket and crossed herself.

The Gabriel blared. "Another day in the swamp." Pokey's voice, most unwelcome in the frigid darkness, reverberated through the camp.

Mr. Elliot had taken her request for higher wages to Mr. Starkweather. He insisted that Irish make room for her and had negotiated higher pay when she became cook. And he had sent Stutz as flunkey. He had not been so bad.

Pettibone should be the one who died.

Pokey and Sister Magdalena carried Mr. Elliot's body out of the cookshack. A relief to have him out of sight. The frozen ground allowed no grave digging. Starkweather's problem, not hers. If only Pettibone had somewhere to go, too. He rambled and thrashed in his sleep, cursing, and calling out.

Solveig could not help the man. She had work to do. Gertie and Stutz started their morning chores. The men would be hungry. Solveig had no time to think.

Chapter 32
Nels

The bull of the woods carried a ledger to breakfast. Nels's belly roiled. It might be another list of names to be fired. If so, he and the others were sunk. But maybe the push had not known what Elliot and Pettibone were doing. Pokey knew, but the old man would keep his trap shut.

Before the food was served, the bull of the woods stood to his feet and reported Mr. Elliot's death.

"Mr. Starkweather is unavailable," Paulson said. "I need someone to drive Pettibone and Sister Lumberjack to the Weyerhaeuser spur." He looked around at the stunned men. "Sister Lumberjack will accompany Pettibone to the hospital in Duluth, but I need someone to drive the cutter there and back to camp. I need a volunteer."

Nels needed to stay out of the way for just a few more days. The deadline for firing him without pay was approaching. He saw his opportunity.

"I'll do it," Nels said.

Paulson raised an eyebrow, but shrugged. He directed Pokey to fetch the sleigh. The clatter of tin started as the jacks dug into their food. Afterwards Nels hung back, waiting for Sister Lumberjack who was talking to Paulson. He could not help overhear.

"Sorry," Paulson said. He jammed on his cap and readied to leave. "He might be playing cards at Weyerhaeuser's." He hesitated a bit. "Sometimes he goes to the roadhouse."

The uncomfortable words dangled in the air. She straightened her veil and fidgeted with her sleeve. Nels sensed her outrage.

"Will there be anything else?" the push said. He acted nervous, as if anxious to get away from her, or maybe it was Pettibone moaning on his pallet that made the push uncomfortable.

Sister Lumberjack took a deep breath. She crimped her mouth. Nels waited for harsh words.

"Yes," she said. "There's something else." She asked for the ledger the push was holding.

Nels held his breath. Had Sister Lumberjack known about the list?

Paulson shrugged and handed the ledger to her. A stubby pencil attached by a string.

Sister Lumberjack turned to the page with the list of hospital tickets. She added another name and handed it back to Paulson. Nels caught a glimpse before she closed the book. *Jacob Pettibone*. She was giving Pettibone a chit. Of course, he would pay for the ticket out of his wages, but still it was a gesture that defied imagination.

Pettibone had called her a fat cow behind her back, a Holstein in black and white. He did everything he could to thwart her efforts to sell chits to the men. His other comments about the good sister came to mind. She should be crossing his name off the list rather than adding it.

"He doesn't deserve it," Nels said. She did not realize how wicked Pettibone was. She did not understand.

"No," Sister Lumberjack said. "He doesn't." Fatigue etched her face and added years to her appearance. Nels wondered if she had been up all night. "None of us deserve anything."

Pokey drove the cutter to the door. The horse snorted and pranced, his mane sparkling with ice crystals in the lamplight. A finger of color showed on the eastern horizon as men and animals headed to the cut.

"Keep it quiet, will you?" Sister Lumberjack said. "My superiors wouldn't like me adding names." She smiled a crooked smile. "I'm always getting into trouble."

Nels gaped. She was perfect in his estimation. But what did he know about Catholic nuns?

"We'd better brace that leg before we move him," Sister Lumberjack fetched a stick from the wood box. "Don't try to straighten it—just protect it from jarring."

Pettibone screamed when they touched him, He screamed louder and cursed when they braced his leg. Old Julius Caesar flailed a curled fist at Sister Lumberjack's face as they lifted him off the floor.

"Get away, goddammit," Pettibone said. Sweat beaded on his blanched face. "You're killing me."

"Shut your mouth," Nels said. "She's trying to save your life, you knucklehead." He jerked hard. Pettibone screamed. Then silence.

"Is he killed?" Nels said.

"Swooned, thank God," Sister Lumberjack said. "Hurry before he comes to."

Pettibone was dead weight between them. Gertie ran to open the door, and Nels tried to catch her eye or say a word, anything to connect with the comely girl. She looked away as he and Sister Lumberjack lugged Pettibone to the cutter.

"Thank you," he called back to Gertie as they stepped out into the cold. The door was already closed.

There was room for only two and Pettibone sprawled both sides.

"Move over, you idiot," Nels said. "Someone has to drive."

He and Sister Lumberjack tugged and pulled and made room for a driver. Nels caught his breath and surveyed the situation.

"You drive, Sister." Nels had to drive the cutter back. "I'll walk beside you."

"My brothers rode the runners when we were kids."

Nels shrugged. The horse was rested. He supposed it would not hurt. Sister Lumberjack took the lines and he stepped on the rear runners behind Pettibone. The horse floundered, but pulled forward as Sister Lumberjack urged them toward the lake. They made better time on the ice. How strange to hear the axmen in the woods without being part of the crew. He pulled his scarf over his face.

Sister Lumberjack urged greater speed. They reached the opposite shore and bounced up the steep bank, jolting over frozen drifts and dodging boulders. Nels gripped tighter lest he be vaulted into the air. Pettibone called out in pain.

"Hang on," Sister Lumberjack said. "We have a train to catch."

Nels had not been north of Stink Lake. It seemed they were going to higher ground, leaving the tamarack swamps behind. A trail veered into the forest.

"What's over there?" Nels leaned forward from his perch.

"Sin and hell," Sister Magdalena said. She snapped the lines and surged forward, the end of her veil flapping in the wind.

So, Skunk Hollow was a real place, after all, the place jacks whispered about in the bunkhouse. Nels was thirsty beyond thirsty. No one would know if he stopped on his return trip.

"Promise to stay away from that place," Sister Magdalena said as if reading his mind. The rising wind snatched her words and flung them to the skies. Nels leaned closer. "I remember you from the train," she said.

Nels shrugged. It was none of her business. She slowed the cutter and turned half way around in her seat to look him in the eye.

"Please," she said. "Stay away from liquor. It will destroy you." She picked up the lines again. "I'm coming back to Starkweather for unfinished business. I'll ask you then if you stayed away."

"I'm broke. No need to worry about me." It was not true. He had coins for a glass of beer, thanks to his undertaker money.

"You must have a little money."

"Pennies." Nels squirmed. If only she would shut her mouth and get going.

"Ask Saint Augustine to intercede for you. Resist temptation."

Nels did not know anything about saints. He said as much to Sister Magdalena.

"Do you have family in America?" Sister Magdalena slapped the lines and the horse jerked forward, causing Pettibone to shriek.

"No," Nels said. "My family is in Denmark."

"You're not alone anymore," Sister Magdalena said with a triumphant tone. "I will call upon the angels and saints for you." She grinned. The tired lines around her eyes disappeared. "Your drinking days are numbered, my friend."

Did she have a crystal ball? He had tried to quit too many times to count. Still, Sister Lumberjack was a holy person. She would not lie.

She held back a hand. "Give me your money for safe keeping."

"Are you crazy?"

"Make no provision for the flesh," she said. "Hand it over."

Nels hesitated, then pulled out his pennies, thinking to hold back the nickel. Maybe a few cents would shut her up.

"All of it," Sister Lumberjack said. "Every last cent."

Nels dragged the nickel out of his pocket and handed it to her. The cutter lurched in a rut and Pettibone screamed.

"I'll keep it safe."

Nels sighed. With his luck, he may have run into Old Starkweather himself at the tavern. There would have been hell to pay then. Of course, the sister was right, but he deserved a drink after all his troubles.

Just one beer.

Chapter 33
Sister Magdalena

Sister Magdalena heard the train before she saw it. She hurried the cutter toward the puffing engine, relieved to have made it in time, and terrified they would be refused. If they were allowed on board, she had no idea how to get Pettibone from Aitkin to Duluth. He might not live. Then what would she do? She imagined being stuck with a dead body in a strange place.

They hit a frozen drift. Pettibone's scream raised the hair on her neck.

"Shut your pie hole," Nels yelled.

Her brain fogged with fatigue. She turned to prayer, clutching her faith with every ounce of strength. What would she do if the cars had already left? *Holy Mary, Mother of God, pray that Weyerhaeuser will bring us to Aitkin.*

Perhaps there was a doctor in Aitkin. If not, she would purchase train tickets to Duluth for him to receive medical care. She must take fare from the collection in her pocket. She did not know if Mother Superior would approve.

Mr. Pettibone would be the first jack to take advantage of a hospital chit. Not exactly, she chided herself. He had a chit only because of her duplicity.

She climbed out of the cutter and approached a porter hefting bags into the caboose. He looked up in surprise, and touched his cap in greeting.

"An injured man needs a doctor. Who do I ask for permission to ride the cars?"

The porter pointed toward the clerk she knew from the previous day. He stood with a tally book, counting barrels and baskets.

"Sir," she said, breathless from running. She explained her predicament.

"We're not a public railway service."

"A man's life is at stake. He needs a doctor."

He hesitated. The engine puffed and the men were finished loading the cars.

"Please, sir." She felt herself losing control. She had not a wink of sleep the night before. "I would do the same for you."

"I believe you would," he said. "We have room going out." He signed a paper with a flourish. "We'll have Mr. Starkweather and a crew of men on our return trip."

Sister Magdalena's spirits lifted through the fog of fatigue. She would nab the old skinflint in Aitkin, and save herself a return trip.

Pettibone regained consciousness when she and Nels carried him to the caboose. His body trembled and his face carried a sickly sheen. The men loading the cars gawked their way, mumbling among themselves as to what might have happened.

"You're a giant of a woman, aren't you?" one man said to her.

"Shut your mouth." Nels stepped forward with a balled fist. "Show a little respect."

"He's right," Sister Magdalena said as she restrained her friend. "I'm tall and strong." She pointed to the stack of crates yet to be loaded. "I can lift as much as any man."

The man looked at her, shrugged and returned to his work. She ignored his comments and sneers. Fact was fact. She was a near-giant of a woman. Her cross to bear. Some days it was harder than others.

The porter fired a stove in the back of the car. The radiating heat came as a welcome relief. Nels helped her move Mr. Pettibone closer to the fire and they snugged quilts around him. Pettibone screamed curses.

"Another inch and you'd be squashed like the pencil pusher," Nels said. "Too bad."

She held animosity toward Mr. Starkweather because he had not honored his commitment to pay what he owed. She blamed Pettibone for Mack's firing. "We must learn to forgive," she said.

"When hell freezes over," Nels said. "Pettibone got me black-balled from the big outfits and the better jobs I deserved. Because of him, I'm stuck as a swamper."

"Your cross to bear."

"You don't know the half of it," Nels said.

The whistle blew.

"God bless you." Sister Magdalena grasped Nels's hand. "You were my guardian angel to get us here on time." She needed more angels for the journey ahead.

Nels held his cap in both hands. "I did it for you, Sister. Don't care a lick about him."

He reminded her of her brothers, so tough on the outside and soft-hearted on the inside. She touched his shoulder.

"Forgive with the help of God," Sister Magdalena said. "For your own sake."

She waved as Nels climbed into the cutter and watched him head south toward Stink Lake. The train belched smoke and jerked forward. She grabbed hold of a crate, giggling to imagine herself sprawled over the floor of the caboose.

She leaned against a mailbag and pulled out her rosary. As she finished meditating on the Joyful Mysteries, she lifted the people she had met on her journey. She had broken all kinds of rules when she added Pettibone to the list of ticket-buyers. Another kneeling pardon at refectory, no doubt. Sister Magdalena sighed. A heaviness closed her eyelids. Her beads fell to her lap. She slept until the train squealed to a stop at the Mississippi River.

"Is he dead, ma'am?" the porter said. "He's awful quiet."

She rested her hand on Pettibone's chest. His heart fluttered.

"He lives," she said. If there ever was a man unready to meet his Maker, it was Jacob Pettibone. "Is there a doctor in Aitkin?"

"Yes ma'am," the porter said. "Old Doc Hamilton."

Taking Pettibone to the closest doctor was the best she could do.

Chapter 34
Solveig

Seeing Mr. Elliot's crumpled body transported Solveig back to Rasmuss's death. She was tired to the point of exhaustion. She felt guilty leaving Gertie to load the swingdingle, but decided a few winks would not hurt.

Solveig dozed a few minutes and woke in a panic. She dreamed her horses were injured and unable to work. After that, she could not get back to sleep, so she returned to the kitchen.

The wood box stood empty. "Thunderation." The water buckets were empty. "Good Lord." Solveig caught a sliver in her finger as she fired the stove. She yanked the sliver and sucked the bloody spot.

"What's wrong, Ma?" Stutz said. "Your hands are shaking."

Solveig stuck her hand into her apron pocket. She was falling apart.

"I need fresh air." Solveig reached for her shawl and grabbed *Peer Gynt*. Gertie's eyelids drooped and the younger woman rubbed her lower back. No one had slept well the previous night. "Take a rest after the swingdingle goes out," she said to Gertie.

Solveig escaped into the cold. Sun dogs hung on both sides of the sun, casting eerie shadows on the snow. Her shoes squeaked.

Barrister was filling the troughs for the ox teams. Solveig waved as she entered the barn. The hens perched on the gate. Solveig cooed and called to them, "Hear chick, chick." Gumbri flapped her wings and hurried over, expecting a treat. Solveig's shoulders relaxed.

Back in her prairie home, Solveig was the boss of her universe. She went to bed when she wanted and got up as she pleased. She organized her work for times of rest and reading. She cared for the animals. Everything was orderly and pleasing. Nothing like Starkweather Timber. Here she was Starkweather's slave. Chaos was the routine, not the exception.

"No use worrying." Her words were clouds before her mouth. "I'm a foolish old woman."

Gumbri pecked against her hand, a gentle request for more grain.

"You pig," Solveig said. She sprinkled more grain. The hens flapped and scratched. Her hands no longer shook. Her pulse slowed. She had once believed in God's goodness. That was before Rasmuss's death. Before Halvor's marriage. Before everything went to hell.

"Little by little our days go by, short if we laugh and long if we sigh," she said to the hens. It was something Rasmuss quoted when a blue mood fell upon her. She remembered the look on his face, the sound of his voice. She caught his scent. The memory snugged like a caress in the gloom. She touched the cuff of his red flannel shirt worn under her dress.

"If only you were here," Solveig said. She opened Peer Gynt, but her eyes blurred with unshed tears. She bent and kissed the page, knowing Rasmuss had touched it so many times. Then she navigated the icy path back to the cookshack. Work remedied most things.

"Gloomy, we are," Gertie said when Solveig returned. "The whole lot of us is down in the mouth."

"Elliot dead," Stutz said. "Pettibone hurt bad. It might happen to Sully."

"How is your brother?" Solveig said.

Stutz shook his head. "Yesterday he slipped while putting hay under the big sled. Escaped by a whisker."

Stutz was not exaggerating. Hay was needed beneath sled runners to prevent the loads from overrunning the team. She had noticed Scully's face scabbed with frostbite at breakfast. He seemed like a serious and capable young man. A pity he was not her flunkey.

Pokey fetched the swingdingle and left for the cut. Gertie pulled Solveig aside, glancing around to make sure Stutz wasn't within hearing.

"I need your advice," Gertie said.

"Stutz," Solveig said. "Fetch more water."

Stutz pulled on his coat and headed out the door with a grumble. He dragged his feet, banging the empty buckets on his leg.

"Mr. Starkweather sent word for me to come to the office after supper," Gertie said as soon as Stutz was out the door. "He left word with Paulson to tell me. Mr. Starkweather is coming back tonight. He says he has something to talk about." Her lips trembled and her face paled. "I'm scared. Maybe he found out about the baby. Maybe he'll fire me."

"Don't worry," Solveig said. That old scoundrel. She knew what he wanted. "We'll go together."

"I don't want to go," Gertie said. "I'm scared of him." She shuddered. "There's something about the way he looks at me."

"Then you won't go," Solveig said. "I'll take care of it." She thought a bit, thinking it best not to face the old fart alone. Stutz returned with the water. "Stutz, you and I are going to the office tonight to help Mr. Starkweather. Bake the pies after supper, Gertie. Unwise to leave them unattended."

Chapter 35
Nels

Nels slowed the cutter to a crawl. The trees would still be there whenever he got back. No one to dock his pay with the pencil pusher dead. He laughed out loud. A tree falling out of the sky. He could not have planned it better. Served the bastards right.

By God, his luck had finally turned.

How brilliant his quick action to tear the page from Elliot's ledger. He wanted to crow about it. The jacks should know how he saved their bacon. He could not risk idle talk, but oh how he wished he could tell them all.

He hunched under the horse-hide blanket. Even so, it felt luxurious to ride instead of swinging an ax. He deserved a rest after near-rupturing himself the day before.

A drink would warm his blood and reward him for his amazing feat. When he came to the roadhouse, he turned the horse into the lane.

At least he could warm up by their stove. By God, he was thirsty.

Maybe someone would float him a loan or buy him a drink. One drink would not hurt anything. He would get back to Starkweather in plenty of time. He should have refused to hand over his money to the nosey nun.

He tied the horse behind the woodshed out of the wind. He would not be long. It was too hard on the animal to be out in the cold. The trees burdened with heavy snow like folded umbrellas. He would like to take Starkweather's umbrella and wrap it around the old geezer's neck. Old Starkweather was as bad as the Dirty Dog Saloon. Lowdown thieves stole from honest working men.

He skidded on the icy path past the outhouse on his way to the tavern.

Sounds of weeping halted him in his tracks. Someone was crying in the outhouse. A woman's voice. He was sure of it. He paused and was about to keep walking when the weeping turned to wailing. Something was wrong. Maybe she was sick. Nels could not ignore someone in trouble, especially a petticoat. He mustered his courage and knocked on the door.

The wailing stopped with a hiccough.

"Ma'am, is something wrong?" Nels said.

No answer. Nels knocked again. "Do you need help?"

The door opened a crack. Then wider. A woman wrapped in a blanket stood inside. Bruises covered her face and blood dripped from her nose. She had a cut over one eye and a bloody spot on her scalp where it looked like a hank of yellow hair had been ripped out by the roots.

"What happened?" Nels said. He searched for a handkerchief to staunch the blood, but found only empty pockets.

"I've got to leave." Her words came in great hiccoughs. "I've got to get away before he kills me."

"Who did this to you?" Nels would find the bastard and beat the shit out of him. "Your husband?"

"He's not my husband," the woman said. She burst into loud weeping again, her thin shoulders heaving, her sobs building mountains of cloud.

Nels stood flatfooted. His throat gasped for a drink. It was someone else's problem.

"Can you help me?" she looked at him with sad, begging eyes. She wasn't pretty, not like Gertie, but she was fetching in her own way.

It was not his business.

"Please?" Tears dripped down her face. "It's my only chance."

Nels did not know what to do. He could bring her back to Starkweather. He dismissed the thought at once. He would be fired for bringing a woman into camp.

But who would know? The pencil pusher was dead. Pettibone was gone. Ma and Gertie bunked alone in the cookshack. No one would know if the girl stayed with them. She could keep out of sight and help Ma with the chores until they figured out what to do with her.

Nels licked dry lips. No time to both help the girl and beg for a drink. He had to choose between them.

"Come, then," Nels said. No good came from helping strangers. "Hurry up."

He pulled the blanket around the shivering girl. She wore carpet slippers insufficient for deep snow. Nels picked her up and carried her to the cutter, stumbling over the icy ruts. She felt like an armful of feathers. Her head tucked under his chin. She clung to his neck like a little child, her hair tickling his chin and blowing into his mouth. The horse shied away.

"Whoa, girl," Nels said. He tucked the woman into the cutter and pulled the lap blanket over her. "Get down and cover your head."

Nels turned the cutter down the lane. Behind them a door slammed.

"Rosy, goddam you, get in here," a rough voice called. "Get in here or you'll wish you did."

Nels pulled his hat lower over his face and slapped the lines. The horse broke into a trot.

"He can go to hell and shovel coal," the girl said. "Dirty bastard will kill us both if he catches us."

"I doubt it," Nels said. He did not have a weapon but he was strong as a bull from swinging an ax. "I'm not so easy to kill."

She peeked out from under the blanket, shivering with cold. "Where are we going?"

"Starkweather Timber," Nels said.

"I know it," she said in a dull voice. "Mr. Starkweather won't let me stay. He and Clarence are in cahoots."

Nels did not answer. Pettibone sometimes bragged about bringing women to the camp. Nels had brushed it off as boasting. The horse kicked spurts of snow, cold sprinkles that settled on his face and chest. The winter sun hid behind heavy clouds.

"I'm Nels," he said. "You must be Rosy."

"I'm dead," Dark eyes smudged her face. She dabbed at her bleeding nose. "No use learning my name." The tears started again. "I may as well slit my throat and get it over with. My poor boy. My poor Jimmy."

They slid down the bank and began to cross Stink Lake, the horse whinnying and anxious to get home. The Gabriel echoed over the frozen water. On the other side of the boom, men streamed toward the swingdingle. Nels paused behind a pile of logs, out of sight of the men heading in the opposite direction.

"Look, Rosy," Nels said. "There's a woman cooking here, a good woman. She'll hide you until we figure out what to do."

"I talked to a nun," Rosy said. "Real tall."

"Sister Lumberjack," Nels said. "I know her."

"She said she'd help me back to Duluth," Rosy said.

"We'll hide you until she comes back," Nels said. He had a strange sensation that he was doing something bigger than himself. He shook it off. "Stay down. We're almost there."

He figured ten minutes to get her into the cookshack before the bull of the woods was on the prowl again. Ten minutes to convince Ma.

Chapter 36
Sister Magdalena

Thank God, the Mississippi was open enough to cross, though they had to break through ice near the banks at Aitkin. Sister Magdalena stretched her aching muscles and ignored the hunger gnawing her insides.

Mr. Pettibone crumpled on the bottom of the boat. The men scurried to their work. Only the man in charge stepped forward to help her.

"We're in a hurry, and will dock long enough to load supplies and collect our passengers." The man helped her carry Mr. Pettibone ashore. "We must get back to the spur line before the river freezes over. Expect no more help from us."

They had been more than generous. Sister Magdalena thanked the man and promised prayers for their safe return.

"Where's Mr. Starkweather?" Sister Magdalena said. There was no one in sight.

"Damned if I know," the man said. "Won't wait for him if he don't show up."

He bawled orders at the crew. Mountains of barrels and wooden boxes waited on the shoreline.

Reality stared Sister Magdalena in the face. She was alone with a man who may or may not survive. She knew no one in Aitkin. She had no idea where to find Doc Hamilton. She was on her own.

Fatigue draped like a gray shroud. She cached her snowshoes and satchel in the bushes alongside the trail. She was not alone, she corrected herself. Her help was in the Name of the Lord God Almighty.

She dropped to her knees. *Thy will be done on earth as it is in heaven.* She roused the unconscious man. "Stand on your good leg, Mr. Pettibone." His eyes flickered dull and listless.

"You've got to help me," She bent to pull him up, but he fell back onto the snow.

He groaned. If only she could get him on her back. He was not a small man, but he did not weigh more than a side of beef. At least not much more. She had toted many a hog and beef to the hospital kitchen.

"Wake up, Mr. Pettibone. Hang onto my neck." Sister Magdalena placed his arms around her neck and scooted her weight under him. She hoisted him onto her back like a sack of flour. He screamed, and Sister Magdalena felt his bones shift. He reeked of urine and dried blood. "Hold tight."

She bent under the burden. The trail up the bank was compacted with snow. She needed both hands to hold Pettibone's legs. "Stay awake, Mr. Pettibone!" If he let go, he might fall backwards and hurt himself even more. Her coif slipped and Pettibone's arms tangled with her veil. She gritted her teeth and kept going, praying that she would not drop the man.

A nun toting a grown man was humorous. She might have laughed had it not been his life at stake. If she had not been so tired and worried. If she had time to think. She reached the top of the bank. Her muscles burned.

A well-worn trail stretched before her. She shifted his weight on her back and caught her breath. She came to a sign advertising *Jack's Liniment*. She would need liniment after such a day. An arrow pointed to a low building. *Popescu's General Store, Ivo Popescu, Proprietor.* Thank God. Civilization.

She stumbled to the store. Mr. Pettibone's weight pressed hard on her back and shoulders. Sweat poured down her face and her coif and veil were askew. Impossible to open the door. No breath to call out. No one in sight.

She refused to give up. Sister Magdalena balanced on one foot and kicked the door with the other until the proprietor came to the door. The effort took all her strength. She had nothing left.

"What's the matter?" Mr. Popescu said in a thick Romanian accent. His eyes bulged. He wore a butcher's apron streaked with blood. His bearded face accentuated his balding pate. "Josue! We have a sick man here."

He helped Sister Magdalena to a wooden bench, and lowered Pettibone off her back. His wife came from the back, wiping wet hands on her apron. She straightened Pettibone's legs. He screamed, swore, and cursed before landing a weak fist on Mrs. Popescu's jaw. She backed away, rubbing her face.

"Logging accident on Stink Lake," Sister Magdalena gasped. Her hands trembled as she adjusted her coif and straightened her veil. Her back felt as if someone had taken a knife to it. She struggled to catch her breath.

"You're a strong woman to carry him like that, Sister," Mrs. Popescu said. "A saint to put up with the likes of him." She rolled her eyes toward the sick man who growled curses and threats. "How far have you come?"

"Just from the landing," Sister Magdalena breath settled and the shakiness left her voice. "Need a doctor."

"Doc Hamilton," Mr. Popescu said. "Just saw him going into the saloon."

Sister Magdalena took a breath but did not hesitate. She stooped low to collect Pettibone again. Mr. Popescu held out a restraining hand.

"Leave him here, Sister," he said. "I'm in the middle of butchering, but Josue can watch him while you fetch the doctor."

If only one of them had offered to fetch the doctor. A customer demanded Mrs. Popescu's attention. Sister Magdalena bowed to the will of God as she bundled again against the cold. Pettibone was her cross. A barrel of apples stood by the door. She thought to purchase one to tide her over until her next meal, whenever that might be. Instead, she offered up her hunger as a fast for Mr. Pettibone's life.

Lord, come to my assistance. Make haste to help me.

Chapter 37
Solveig

A clatter at the cookshack door interrupted Solveig's routine. She turned from the bread bowl to see Nels Jensen with a blanket-swathed woman in his arms. Good Lord. Now what?

"Ma," Nels said. "We need your help."

Solveig motioned them toward the stove. The woman, a girl really, wore no hat or mittens. Thin carpet slippers covered her feet and bare legs showed beneath a thin gown. No long underwear. She had a cut on one cheek, a black eye, and a bruise on her jaw the size of a fist. Her eyes darted around the room, cringing as if she expected another blow to fall. Solveig pulled a stool closer to the stove for her to sit down.

"What happened?" Solveig tucked a blanket over the woman's legs, pulled the warming stone from beneath the stove, and placed it under the woman's feet.

"Found her on the trail coming back from Weyerhaeuser's," Nels said. He pulled Solveig aside and whispered. "She's from the roadhouse. Sister Lumberjack promised to help her get back to Duluth."

"Sister Lumberjack, you say? The roadhouse?" One of the laughing women in the night. "Stutz, bring a cup of tea," Solveig said. "Gertie, fetch another quilt." Solveig knelt on the floor and rubbed the girl's icy feet. A miracle if she escaped pneumonia. "You're frozen, child."

"Will you hide her until Sister Lumberjack comes back?" Nels said, fumbling for words. "She's in trouble." He shrugged his shoulders. "She needs to lay low."

Leave it to a man to shove his responsibilities on a woman. Solveig glared at Nels. She had enough to do without taking on charity cases.

"Her name is Rosy."

Solveig was not a rescue mission, no matter what Sister Lumberjack thought. First Gertie, although she proved to be a godsend. Now this woman? The jacks would go wild. A saloon girl, a loose woman would set them on fire. Solveig sniffed in disgust. Men were pigs, just like Irish said.

There was no one to ask with Mr. Elliot dead. Mr. Paulson knew only wood butchering. Mr. Starkweather was out galivanting. And the work grew heavier every day. More men coming.

Rosy might be a help in the kitchen, but she would have to hide in the back during meals. No one could know. Nels would not blabber. She could browbeat Stutz into silence. Gertie never spoke to anyone. Pokey would have to be in on it. Solveig thought she could trust him with the secret. It would not be for long until Sister Lumberjack returned to collect money from Mr. Starkweather. Then it would be up to the nun.

Solveig weighed the pros and cons. Rosy could work off her meals and board. Sharing a bed with Gertie would be no skin off Starkweather's butt.

Hell. She might as well do it. She had a strong argument that she needed the help and the girl needed work.

Solveig took a breath and made her decision. "Against my better judgement."

Nels grinned. "Thanks, Ma." He leaned over and bussed Solveig's cheek. "I knew I could count on you." He hurried back to work.

Solveig touched her cheek. The curse of widowhood to admit how much she craved human touch.

"Not one word to anyone," Solveig said. It was simpler to act crabby. "That means you, Stutz," He was the weak link in their secret. "Not a word to your brother or anyone in this camp."

Stutz promised with wide eyes.

"I mean it," Solveig said. "I'll box your ears if you breathe a single word about our new kitchen girl. Now back to chores."

"Thank you, Missus," Rosy said. "I'm sorry to cause trouble."

"Call me Ma," Solveig said. The girl was someone's daughter, someone's child. "You'll earn your keep."

"I don't know what to do." Rosy's shoulders heaved and fat tears sprouted from her eyes.

She was no older than Halvor. But her eyes, behind the bruises, reminded Solveig of Inga Jacobson. Funny, the two women looked nothing alike. Rosy's eyes were blue and Inga's had been brown, but both carried a sorrow beyond their years.

"You'll be safe if you stay out of sight," Solveig said. "Go with Gertie and find something to wear."

Solveig turned back to the stove. She was placing her farm in danger for someone from a road house. Her father always said to wind back her neck and mind her own business.

Queenie meowed around her feet. Stutz slopped greasy dishwater across the floor. Frost climbed the log walls. Icy fingers of homesickness wrapped around her throat. She had no hope that things would turn around. Troubles only got worse with the years. Like the mortgage due. Like Rasmuss's death. Like her sore back and bunions. Like Halvor's wife.

Would somebody come after Rosy and make trouble?

Good Lord, she was in it up to her neck.

Chapter 38
Nels

Nels joined the men around the campfire next to the swing-dingle. Pokey frowned and scraped the stew pot. The gloomy sky matched Pokey's frown. Everyone talked about the accident, and Fish made wagers about Pettibone's chances of survival with anyone flush enough to throw a half-dollar into a hat.

Ten-Day toasted bread on a stick over the fire. Nels sidled toward him with his plate.

"Did you get to the spur in time?" Ten-Day said, turning his bread to toast it evenly. "I would have dropped him in the woods for the wolves."

Nels did not trust his voice to answer. He had been so close. His hands trembled. He could have talked someone out of a drink at Skunk Hollow. He had done the right thing, but wished he had not. A drink would have been better.

Nels gobbled the stew though it was icy cold. Ten-Day divided the toasted bread and handed Nels half. Ten-Day stuffed prunes into his mouth. Pokey slammed dirty dishes and urged the men to hurry up.

"They split up the teams after you left. Every greenhorn is put with a seasoned jack," Ten-Day said. "Typical Starkweather—day late and a dollar short."

The last thing Nels wanted was to train in a newcomer.

"Nah, not on our team," Ten-Day said when Nels asked. He pushed out his chest and crowed like a rooster, high stepping around the campfire until all the men were laughing. "Knew better than bust up their best ax team."

"Back to butchering wood." Paulson did not laugh at Ten-Day's antics. "This ain't no whist party."

The men dragged away from the fire, tossing their dishes into the swingdingle as they passed.

"Hey Nels," Dutch said as they headed back to the woods. "Is it true that Sister Lumberjack added Pettibone to the hospital ticket list?"

Nels nodded. Paulson must have said something. "She did. Too soft hearted for sense."

"She's a do-gooder," Ten-Day said with a snort. "Baptists don't have to work their way to heaven."

"What do you know about Baptists?" Dutch said.

"My mama is a Baptist. Yes, she was dunked in the Pomme de Terre River down by Appleton. Only the good die young, my mama always says." Ten-Day launched a long story about a riverboat accident where only gamblers and confidence men survived. "Only the good die young, that's what the Baptists say."

Nels stepped up his pace to leave behind their talk of religion. Religion always led to arguments. He wondered how Rosy was getting along. He might catch a glimpse of her at supper if he was smart about it.

He turned his attention to the work at hand. What if Pettibone recovered and raised hell? No, Pettibone was out for the rest of the year, if he survived at all. So far, Nels had survived the Starkweather massacre of men to be fired. Nels hurried his pace. His blood would warm with the swinging of his ax.

Chapter 39
Sister Magdalena

Sister Magdalena located the Stumptown Saloon, its rickety sign hanging lop-sided over a weathered door. She steeled herself as she entered. *Be my protection from the snares of the devil.* Sawdust clung to the wet hem of her habit. Every eye turned to stare as she made her way to the bar. It was as if they had never seen a nun before—at least not in a saloon.

What would Sister Lucy say? Sister Magdalena swallowed a chuckle. She held up her skirts and went to the bar. She was there to save a man's life. Nothing improper about it.

The barkeeper washed glasses in scummy water. The bar itself was a pine log split lengthwise and nailed to empty barrels. She leaned forward, the wood rough to her touch. Pine sap stickied her fingers.

"I need the doctor." Sister Magdalena wiped the sap on her cassock. "It's an emergency."

The barkeeper jabbed a thumb toward a rear table where a man sat alone with his back toward them. A bottle of whiskey and a pair of leather mitts lay on his table. He wore a frayed wool jacket. A plaid cap covered gray hair that curled around the brim. Doc Hamilton looked more like a lumberjack than a doctor.

Sister Magdalena walked over to his table. He did not budge when she called his name.

"He's deaf as a post," the barkeep called. "Give him a jab."

Sister Magdalena touched his shoulder and repeated his name.

The man startled and leapt to his feet. His mouth gaped when he saw her. "Good Lord, is this the end?"

"No," Sister Magdalena said with a smile. Guffaws sounded around the room. "I'm Sister Magdalena. There's an injured man at the store."

"What?" Doctor Hamilton wore a look of alarm on his lined face. "Are you here for me?"

Sister Magdalena smiled. Doctor Hamilton looked around the room and realized his foolishness. "Scared me to death." He rubbed his eyes. "Must have dozed off."

Sister Magdalena yelled into his face. "There's a man at the store who's hurt real bad."

With that, the doctor pulled on his mitts and followed her outside, grabbing her arm. "What's a man to think?" he mumbled. "I thought my time was up."

"Angels of death don't wear black and white habits," Sister Magdalena said.

"What was that?"

She screamed into his face to make herself heard. Mother Superior would frown upon frivolity in public.

"I think my hearing might be going," Doctor Hamilton said.

Sister Magdalena smiled. She was certain the man was right in his diagnosis.

They reached the store as the sun dipped behind a fringe of pines in a blaze of pink and purple. Sister Magdalena had done her best to save Pettibone's life. It was out of her hands.

"He's in a bad way," Doc Hamilton said after checking Pettibone over. Mrs. Popescu lingered nearby wearing a worried look. "One leg will go. The other is broken. A concussion. Maybe a broken back."

"Can he travel?" Sister Magdalena yelled. "He has a ticket for St. Mary's Hospital." The words tickled her tongue. Yes, a kneeling confession awaited her return to the Mother House.

Doc Hamilton clucked his tongue and shook his head. "He wouldn't survive the trip." He scrutinized Pettibone's leg again, holding up the lamp. The sheen of bone glinted in the dim glow. Sister Magdalena looked away. "Sooner it comes off the better his chances," he said.

"How much will that cost?" Sister Magdalena said.

"Does he have any money?" Doc Hamilton said.

They searched Pettibone's pockets and found a silver dollar and odd change.

"Will you help him?" Sister Magdalena said. "Until he's well enough to travel to Duluth?"

"Don't do charity work." Doctor Hamilton brightened. "I'll take the dollar as down payment. He can pay the balance later, if he lives."

"St. Mary's Hospital will pay the difference," Sister Magdalena said. She told him about the hospital chits. She was not sure he heard. She scribbled the information on a scrap of paper. "All medical expenses are covered by his hospital ticket."

Complications followed lies. She imagined the alarm on Sister Bede Marie's face when she heard about her promises to Doc Hamilton.

The doctor scribbled Sister Magdalena's name and address in a ragged tally book kept in his back pocket. He tucked the dollar into his vest with a stiff nod. "Guess I can trust a nun to keep her word." He shook Sister Magdalena's hand. "You scared the life out of me."

"I'm no angel," Sister Magdalena said as loud as good manners dictated. "Perhaps God is sending a message."

"Maybe." Doctor Hamilton shuffled his feet. He spoke so low that Sister Magdalena leaned forward to catch his words. "Haven't been to church since Lincoln's war," he said.

"What would your parents say if they were here to advise you?" Sister Magdalena said.

His voice was low, almost contrite. "Ma was always harping at me to get to confession."

Mr. Pettibone groaned. An old woman entered the store, and Mrs. Popescu hurried to attend her.

"There must be a priest in town," Sister Magdalena said. "Don't delay." It was not something she wanted to shout for the whole world to hear. It was in the hands of God.

"I'd appreciate if you'd help spread the word about the hospital tickets," she said in a louder voice, a more appropriate topic to broadcast.

"I'll see what I can do," Doc Hamilton said. "Logging is damn near as dangerous as soldiering."

Doc Hamilton went for a stretcher. Sister Magdalena said her goodbyes and made plans to collect her satchel and snowshoes. The sky was spitting snow. She must find shelter for the night. Fatigue stumbled her steps and fogged her thinking. She felt near starved and her muscles quivered from carrying Mr. Pettibone. Perhaps there was a Catholic Church in town where she might find help.

"Sister," Mrs. Popescu said. "Do you need a place to stay? We have a cot in back and beans on the stove. Nothing fancy, but we would share it with you."

Sister Magdalena blinked tears. "Thank you, Mrs. Popescu." She hurried to fetch her pack, marveling at God's provision. Perhaps she would catch Mr. Starkweather at the landing.

The scow was gone. She had missed her chance for payment. She must return to Stink Lake before the season ended. She dreaded the long walk.

Sister Hildegard said that faith made things possible, not easy. God would not abandon her. The Rule of Benedict said to pray earnestly for God's help before endeavoring any difficult project.

She knelt in the snow.

"And please help Mr. Pettibone live," she added. "Although he doesn't deserve your mercy." She stood to her feet, but her conscience drove her back to her knees. "Forgive me, Lord. Neither do I deserve your mercy."

Sister Magdalena returned to the store. Her body ached. She was famished and exhausted. Mrs. Popescu showed her to the cot.

"Help yourself," Mrs. Popescu said. She handed Sister Magdalena a bowl and spoon. "We'll talk at breakfast."

Sister Magdalena's feet hung over the edge of the bed. She did not mind. She was off the ground, in a warm building with a thick quilt. God was good. She fell asleep while thanking Him.

The next morning, Sister Magdalena found Mrs. Popescu to be a wellspring of information. She knew the location of all the logging operations, even the jobber camps. She knew the names of the managers and owners. Mrs. Popescu sketched a map on the back of an old campaign poster. PROTECTION and HARRISON showed through the thin paper. She marked the best trails to each camp.

"They all come here for mail or supplies," Mrs. Popescu said. "You missed Mr. Starkweather yesterday while you were off fetching Doc Hamilton."

"Horsefeathers," Sister Magdalena said. Would she never corner the man?

"You'll hitch a ride to another camp if you wait around," Mrs. Popescu paused for a breath. She looked Sister Magdalena up and down. "Stay with us whenever you want. No sense for a religious to be sleeping rough."

Chapter 40
Solveig

Solveig plodded through the afternoon in a muddle. Mr. Starkweather was up to something. Why else would he ask for Gertie? She scrubbed the work table as she contemplated his shenanigans. Solveig was pretty sure she knew what kind of shenanigans they were.

Gertie was no match for the old Billy goat. Solveig splashed suds on the floor. She reached for the floor rag. Solveig was not afraid. She would march over to the office and set him straight. Of course, she would take Stutz along. It was imprudent to face him alone. But she would go, by jingo. If Starkweather so much as looked at her crossways, she would tell him what she thought. Without risking her job, of course. She would be diplomatic, though firm. She practiced as she stirred codfish gravy. *No, Mr. Starkweather, Mrs. Murphy is busy. I cannot spare her from her work.*

By supper, Solveig had worked herself into a self-righteous frenzy. She served the meal with as much disregard as Irish, so frazzled her mind. Starkweather had no business chasing the young widow.

Solveig readied to go, directing Rosy to do the dishes. She might tell Mr. Starkweather about Rosy working for room and board until Sister Magdalena returned. Solveig frowned and fastened her shawl with her hatpin. No doubt, Mr. Starkweather knew the wayward woman. Telling him would only cause problems, and put Nels in a bad light. Her mind whirled. Too much had happened with too little sleep.

Solveig was in no mood for monkey business.

She and Stutz followed the path to the office. The moon hung low over Stink Lake, transforming slash piles and stumps into ghostly shadows. "Hang onto my hand," she said to the young boy at her side. "We'll keep each other from falling." Solveig needed the comfort of the boy's presence. Much depended on how she handled the situation.

Mr. Starkweather opened the door when she knocked. He raised an eyebrow, but bade them come inside. His face sagged. Though he looked neat as ever, a slump in his shoulders suggested fatigue.

"Mrs. Rognaldson," he said. "And Master Stutz."

So, he remembered their names. Starkweather was a smooth one. A gambler. A man who broke his word to a nun. A lascivious and carnal man who frequented houses of ill repute. Solveig sniffed.

"You may wonder at my invitation." He showed them to chairs near the stove where he adjusted the draft.

"May I smoke?" he said.

At Solveig's nod, he lit a cigar. The comforting scent of burning tobacco wafted in the air as he settled in an easy chair next to them.

"I returned tonight with seventeen new men and find myself without a clerk. Mr. Elliot's tragic death places me in in an inconvenient conundrum. I thought perhaps Mrs. Murphy might take over his duties."

Solveig stared in disbelief. Had she misjudged the man? No, something smelled rotten about the whole thing.

"Mrs. Murphy has not had the advantage of an education." Solveig did not know if this was true or not, but the words came easy. "Besides, I need her in the kitchen, especially with new men. We're understaffed as it is."

"Ah yes," Mr. Starkweather said. He rubbed the side of his jaw in thought. "Perhaps you know of someone else with skills to keep accounts, run the store and manage the payroll."

"My brother, Sully," Stutz piped up. His voice squeaked in excitement. "He's a whiz at tallying. First in his class. Won every spelling bee and got a medal in penmanship."

Solveig relaxed into a smile. Sully needed to get out of the woods before he was killed. Yes, Sully would be the answer.

"I'll fetch him for you, sir," Stutz said. His eager voice squeaked again.

Mr. Starkweather nodded. "Please bring him at once." He turned to Solveig. "I worried needlessly."

Stutz left. Solveig considered following, but Mr. Starkweather spoke again.

"You are to be commended, Mrs. Rognaldson." He straightened his watch fob and checked the time. "The men are well satisfied with your cooking."

"Thank you, sir," Solveig said. "Irish predicted the supplies will not last through the season." Here was her chance. "And now we are without Mr. Pettibone bringing in game."

"Ah yes," Mr. Starkweather said. "Pettibone. I am wealthy on paper, but strapped for cash. The panic, you know."

"Like farmers," Solveig said. "We invest everything into land and equipment. The reason I am here."

Solveig was surprised to discover common ground. Logs shifted in the stove. The wind played harps in the treetops. She almost told him about Rosy.

"Do you want me to economize?" Solveig said. "I know how to skimp."

"No, no, definitely not," Mr. Starkweather said. "I'll bring supplies."

Sully and Stutz came running into the office. A blast of frigid air entered with them along with the smell of sweat. Sully's face scabbed with frost bite and he wiped his nose on his sleeve. Greasy hair hung over a pimply forehead. A blessing for the poor boy to use his brains for a change. No doubt he would get a pay raise. She must draw him aside and urge him to go to the boil up. Perhaps Gertie had a more suitable set of clothing to fit the lad.

"Come Stutz, we must return to work," Solveig said as Mr. Starkweather began to quiz Sully about his abilities in mathematics. "Sully has much to discuss with Mr. Starkweather."

The cold weather blasted ice into her lungs. A clear sky and a million stars overhead. She rested her eyes on the peaceful expanse of lake.

"Sully gets all the fun," Stutz said. "I wish I could be a pencil pusher."

"Hush, boy," Solveig said. "Run ahead and fetch the sledge. I will be at the root cellar."

Solveig fingered the key around her neck. She bent low to enter the storage room. It smelled of damp earth. She calculated the supplies to feed the extra mouths. One hundred twenty-nine men. The stores dwindled. Thank God, she had insisted on locks for the pantry to stop the pilfering. Those missing supplies were needed now. Would Mr. Starkweather keep his word to bring more?

It was only as she left the root cellar that she came to her senses. She, Solveig Rognaldson, had been hoodwinked by that scallywag. Her cheeks burned. Mr. Starkweather had invited Gertie to come to his quarters before he knew of Mr. Elliot's death.

Solveig snorted and jerked her shawl around her shoulders. She knew better than be taken in by a smooth-talker. By God, Starkweather would bother neither Gertie nor Rosy. She would see to that. And economize, she would, despite his grand promises. The men would not notice if she did it right.

Chapter 41
Nels

Nels woke up when the new men stomped into the bunk-house and stumbled toward the stove. Someone tripped in the darkness, landing just inches from Nels's bunk.

"What the hell is going on?" Pokey lit a lantern and held it high. "How many are you?"

"Seventeen souls," one of the men said through chattering teeth. "Starving and frozen stiff. We walked all the way from Weyerhaeuser."

"Find beds," Pokey said. "Wakeup at 4:30. Breakfast half hour after the horn."

"But we're starved," someone said.

"This ain't no hotel." He directed the men to bunks. "Get some sleep."

Nels seethed. Seventeen on the list to be cut. Seventeen men hired to replace them. Damn Starkweather. Damn him to hell.

A brute of a fellow, muscular, and bearded, mounted the empty bed that had belonged to the Latvian. Pokey blew out the lantern leaving only the glow around the door of the barrel stove and the light left burning by the door.

"Where you from?" Ten-Day said.

"Arizona Territory," the man said.

"Arizona! Good Lord! What you doing so far north?" Ten-Day said. "Your blood is too thin for this country."

"Shut your trap, by God," Pokey said from the bottom bunk. "Or I'll shut it for you."

"I have a friend in Yuma prison," Ten-Day said. "Calls it a hell-hole."

"I know it," the man said. Nels got the impression that he would tolerate no nonsense. "Every damn inch."

"You were locked up?" Ten-Day's voice rose. "Maybe you knew my friend." Ten-Day was impressed with cowboys in dime novels, especially the outlaws.

"Shut the hell up," Pokey growled from his bunk. "I won't chew my cabbage twice. One more word, and you are out on your ear."

The man rolled over, turning his back to them.

"Must be on the run," Ten-Day whispered to Nels. "Why else would he come north? Earning a few sawbucks before heading to Canada out of reach of the law."

"Watch out. He'll slit your gullet while you sleep," Nels whispered.

With that, Ten-Day shut up and began to snore.

The air breathed thinner in the bunkhouse with the additional men. Nearly every bunk was filled. Nels lay wide awake. The bunks creaked with every slap or scratch. Nels was used to the stench, like a man got used to shoveling cow shit or cleaning a hen house. Still, he smelled the dirty socks, unwashed bodies, wood smoke, and sour clothing when he thought about it. He tried not to think about it.

Starkweather was worse than Pettibone, as bad as the Dirty Dog. He was a swindler, plain and simple, a chiseler and bilker. They had trusted him to keep his part of the contract, and all along he had no intention of doing so. He belonged in Yuma Prison, if anyone did.

Nels imagined a jolt of whiskey, the slippery calm of liquor greasing his throat and soothing his mind. He could have begged a drink at Skunk Hollow except for Rosy and her sad face. He clenched his fists just thinking of the dirty bastard who had done that to her. He might sashay over to Skunk Hollow and teach that bum a lesson.

Sounds of whimpering came from somewhere near the door. Maybe one of the new men. Muttered curses and the clunk of someone throwing a boot. "Quit your bawling." The bunk house settled back to the usual snores, belches, scratching and rustling.

Rosy deserved better than Skunk Hollow, even if she was not a beauty. Nels turned and pulled the blanket over his shoulders. If only he knew how she was getting along with Ma.

His eyes snapped open. Sometimes his own stupidity amazed him. Stutz spent his days in the cookshack with the women.

Nels crawled out of the bunk, shivering when his foot touched the floor. He crept to Stutz's bunk and shook the boy awake. Stutz awoke with a start, bumping his head on the bunk overhead.

"Is it time to get up?"

"How's she doing?" Nels whispered.

"Who?" Stutz said in a whisper, rubbing his eyes and yawning. He lay back down on the pillow. Sully rolled over in his sleep and threw an arm across his brother's chest.

"Rosy," Nels whispered. "Who else would I mean?"

Stutz was about to speak but clamped his lips tight. "I don't know what you're talking about, mister."

"The hell you say." Nels wanted to throttle the boy. "I just want to know about Rosy."

"Leave me alone," Stutz said. "Ma told me to keep my mouth shut or else."

So that was that. Ma was the boss. Nels crept back to bed in disgust.

It seemed Nels had just closed his eyes when the Gabriel blew. The sound roused him from a good dream about Gertie that slipped beyond reach and memory.

"Daylight in the swamp," the bull cook called as he went from bunk to bunk prodding the men awake. "Breakfast in twenty minutes. Ten below zero. Dress warm and eat hearty."

"Where's Yuma?" Ten-Day said as they dressed.

"How should I know?" Nels said. "You'd be wise to keep your distance from that one."

Before they could say more, they were interrupted by an announcement from the bull of the woods. "Veterans, teach the ropes to the new men. We do not want another accident."

An audible groan arose in the bunkhouse.

Nels cursed. Ten-Day and Dutch were not the greatest com-
panions, but at least he was used to them.

"Listen up," Paulson said. "I'm only saying this once." He read the
names of the new men and new teams. Paulson placed Dutch with
a couple of Norwegians who did not speak English. The Arizonan,
named Arnold Edinburgh, ended up with Ten-Day and Nels.

"There's been a mistake," the Arizonan said. "I am a teamster. Don't know one end of an ax from another."

"Come along, Yuma," Ten-Day said. "That's the genius of
Starkweather Timber. We're all working jobs we know nothing
about." The man's camp name settled easy on the new man.
"Hurry. Ma sets a good table."

Yuma cast a cold look but followed along. "This is one hell of a
deal. Mr. Starkweather promised me," Yuma said once on the icy path
to the cookshack. "I did my share of teamstering back in Arizona.

"Before prison?" Ten-Day said. "What were you in for?"

"I wasn't a prisoner," Yuma said. The veins in his neck bulged.
Nels feared he might take a swing at Ten-Day.

"Look," Nels said. "I had my heart set on teamstering, too,
but ended up an axman." Nels tucked both hands under his armpits to warm them. Damn cold went right through his wool mitts.
"They'll promise you anything to get you signed up. Everything
is upside down here."

"Sounds like home," Yuma said with a shake of his head.
"The whole world is on a greased slide to hell."

Their conversation ended at the cookshack. Gertie looked
plump and pretty with flushed cheeks. She wore a white kerchief
over her dark curls. Every man eyed her movements.

Ma looked like she had been drinking sour milk. There was
no sign of Rosy. Maybe Starkweather found out and sent her back
to Skunk Hollow. Maybe Ma was in trouble. Maybe Starkweather
would fire the lot of them. Nels had to know.

But breakfast ended, and they trudged to the woods. Yuma
followed, still muttering about teamstering. A pink sky was a
backdrop to butchered pines and slash piles. A wolf howled in

the distance. Coarse laughter drifted back from a knot of men ahead of them.

"Is your blood freezing?" Ten-Day said. For a man worried about the cold, Ten-Day had not even put his mittens on yet. He placed both hands between his legs to warm them as he walked, creating a knock-kneed gait that would have been funny on a warmer day. "What do you think of our weather?"

"Fresh." Yuma's teeth chattered. "I like it."

"You'll warm up once you start," Nels said. Ten below zero, his eye. Ten below zero by Starkweather measurement. The bull of the woods added about ten degrees to his daily forecast or Nels did not know hot from cold. Anything to get the money into Starkweather's bank account. "This is the most miserable part of the day. It gets a little better when the sun comes up."

Ten-Day pulled his earflaps down over his ears and stuck his hands back in his crotch. "You like horses, Yuma?"

"Worked with horses all my life. Hauled freight to the army camp from my pa's ferry. Good living until the railroads ran us out." He spat on the ground. "Then I skun mules at a copper mine until everything went to hell. Governor sent the army to break up a strike." He shivered and rubbed his hands together. "Ended up a prison guard."

"Bet you knew all the big names," Ten-Day said. "Jesse James? Cole Younger? Billy the Kid?"

"Train robbers, thieves, forgers, confidence men," Yuma said. "I knew that scum like the back of my hand. Hell, they locked up Mormons, too, though they seemed like decent enough folks. They never caused trouble."

Ten-Day's eyes bulged and he pressed in to hear Yuma's answers. "I heard the Mormons have horns on their foreheads and fire blazing out of their eyes."

"Not the ones I knew," Yuma said.

Nels knew better than pester a man. It showed poor upbringing. Why his parents would have given him a whipping for stretching his neck into someone's business. Ten-Day had no manners. He kept a constant line of questions as they bucked their first log. Nels took pity on Yuma and took him aside to show him how to limb, leaving Ten-Day to work alone.

"You're right," Yuma said as he paused to wipe his brow. "A man works up a sweat swinging an ax."

At noon, the bull of the woods made an announcement as the men gathered around the swingdingle. The smoke from the campfire went straight up, a sure sign of cold weather. Thank God there was no wind in the shelter of the forest. Nels bent low over his stew, eating before it froze to his plate.

Paulson hollered in his loudest boss-voice. "New men go to the office and sign your contracts. Hurry along. Don't keep the brains waiting."

"Where's the office?" one of the men said in a heavy Irish accent. "We might end up lost in the forest."

"Jensen will be your guide," Paulson said. "Boss wants to see you, Nels. No dawdling. There are trees to butcher."

"Why does Nels get to go?" Ten-Day said. "He skipped work to take Pettibone to the spur. It isn't fair."

Paulson shrugged. "Back to work."

A knot pressed hard on Nels's windpipe. Not even Mr. Starkweather could blame Nels for the tree that Cosmos and Stefan dropped on Elliot. Nels took a deep breath and led the way to the office.

It was a half hour tramp through the mangled forest. Slash and stumps and bolts scattered across the landscape. A lightning strike, a careless match and the whole thing would go up in smoke. Forest fires might take the whole north woods.

Not to mention the waste. An ambitious man might salvage that timber and make a good living. Even this jobber camp left enough bolts to make it worthwhile.

"Ugly," Yuma said. "Mining is the same. Rich people always ruin the land."

Nels gazed up at a standing tree, the white pine boughs feathery against the blue sky. God, he hated the men doing this to Minnesota. Not the ordinary men, like himself. The brush apes working in the woods were just trying to survive. He hated the rich men who gambled for power and skimmed the best for themselves. They cared nothing about the loggers. Like the bonanza farm owners. Like the people running the Devil Dog Saloon and Skunk Hollow. Like Mr. Starkweather.

It was not fair. The common man did not have a chance.

Mr. Starkweather sat at the same table as before. Sully sat beside him with Mr. Elliot's ledger opened before him. The younger man fidgeted, straightened the ink pot, and whittled the nub of the pen.

It seemed Nels had been at Starkweather forever, but it had only been two months. Hell, it was not even Christmas. Time stopped the day he had signed the contract.

Nels could barely look at Mr. Starkweather without gritting his teeth. He stepped to the rear as Starkweather handed out the paperwork. Mr. Starkweather motioned Nels to approach the table as the men read the flimsy pages of their contracts. Yuma read it aloud for those unable to read. It was obvious that many of the men did not understand a word of it. They whispered to each other in foreign languages.

"Mr. Jensen." Starkweather stood to shake his hand. "I wish to express my gratitude for your assistance with the emergency yesterday."

Nels, recoiled by the touch of the rogue's soft hand, tried to interpret his comments. Starkweather must know about the missing ledger page. Nels waited to be fired. He felt it coming. He clenched his teeth.

"Mrs. Rognaldson told me how you helped the good sister transport Jacob Pettibone for medical attention."

Nels resisted slamming a fist in the old geezer's face. He only did it to help Sister Lumberjack. He should have let the weasel die.

"You saved his life," Starkweather said. "Heroism in the face of tragedy."

Nels balled his hands into fists.

"I need a replacement for Mr. Pettibone," Mr. Starkweather said. "A hunter to supplement the larder. Someone to run errands and fetch supplies. Perhaps you are that dependable man."

Nels had never shot a firearm, but it had to be easier than swinging an ax. Better than listening to Ten-Day's babbling. It would be a chance for peace and quiet, and best of all, a daily visit to the cookshack when he delivered the meat. It was a golden opportunity to get acquainted with Gertie.

If he were a better man, he would sock old Starkweather in the snoot and warn these new men to get the hell out of there. He should make a big stink about the Latvian's firing on the day of the accident.

"I'll do it." Nels felt like a traitor, like a rat burrowing into a manure pile, like a beaten dog licking his master's shoes.

"There's a small pay increase," Mr. Starkweather said, though he made no mention of dollars or cents nor did he offer a new contract. "Pettibone's rifle is in the surveyor's hut."

Yuma interrupted. "I've a question about this here contract, Mr. Starkweather." He spoke with authority, as if he were representing the group. "This line about no wages paid if fired before sixty days of employment?" He laid his contract on the table in front of Mr. Starkweather and jabbed a thick finger at the page. "What kind of rogueries are you pulling?"

Every eye fixed on Mr. Starkweather. The boss's face drained of color.

"What's your scheme?" Yuma said. "I've seen dirty dealings in the copper mines, but this is the lowest yet. You planning to bilk us out of our pay?"

"No, of course not," Mr. Starkweather said. "You misunderstand." He adjusted a pair of spectacles and leaned over the papers. "Starkweather Timber is law abiding to the utmost."

"It says right here," Yuma said. He read the sentence aloud.

"An irregularity in verbiage, I assure you. My lawyer's mistake in phrasing. An innocent error. Firing someone without pay is something that would never occur at Starkweather Timber."

The liar. The cheat. Seventeen men would have lost their jobs, including Nels, had not God rescued them.

"I'll not sign the contract unless that line is blacked out," Yuma said. He looked around at the other men as if encouraging their agreement. "None of us will."

"Understandable," Mr. Starkweather muttered. "Thank you for bringing it to my attention." He crossed out the line using Sully's pen dipped in black ink, blamed the error on his attorney, and deflected all personal responsibility. The men signed their corrected contracts. "Nothing like this has happened before, nor will it ever occur at Starkweather Timber."

Good for Yuma who caught the old buzzard by the balls and called him out on it.

Mr. Starkweather's shoulders sagged.

"Thank you, gentlemen," Mr. Starkweather said as he dismissed the men. "All of our fortunes depend on the logs harvested from this site."

With that, the boss stood up from the table and left the room, leaving Sully to gather the contracts.

"How much was Pettibone making?" Nels asked in a whisper.

"How should I know?" Sully made a neat stack of the signed documents.

"It's in the ledger." Nels said. "Look it up."

"Not everything is in the ledger," Sully said.

"Find my name and put down today's date and raise," Nels said.

"Are you crazy?" Sully glanced at the door where Mr. Starkweather had exited. "I'll end up back as a road monkey."

"You won't," Nels said. "Mr. Starkweather is getting old. Heck, even my memory is losing ground. I don't want him to forget."

Sully shrugged and began arranging the contracts in alphabetical order, no doubt to add the names to the ledger.

"What's the hold up?" Yuma called through the door.

The men were waiting in the cold. Nels did not have time to argue.

"Do it, goddam it, or I'll knock your teeth out."

Sully glared at Nels. Then he laid the papers aside and grabbed the ledger. He paged through it until he found Nels's name. He made a notation with shaking hands. Then he slammed the ledger shut and folded his arms in front of him. "Happy now?"

A shout and crash in the distance as another white pine hit the ground. A flush warmed Nels's neck and cheeks. Sully was just a scared kid trying to send a few bucks home to his folks. It was not his fault. Nels had acted like Pettibone, all bluster and threats. Good Lord, what would become of him?

"It will be all right," Nels said in a humbler tone. He did not know how to apologize but knew that he should. "If there's trouble, I'll take the blame. You have my word on it."

On the way back to the cut, Nels congratulated Yuma on confronting Starkweather.

"Him?" Yuma said with a snort. "In the end all bosses are as tame as a chicken under a Slav's table."

Nels considered telling him about the massacre that almost happened, but decided against it. The line on Nels's contract was not blackened out and he did not trust Mr. Starkweather as far as he could throw an ox. The old carpet bagger might still find a way to fire him.

"Do you know how to shoot?" Nels said.

"Hell, I was a prison guard," Yuma said. "No one escaped on my watch, at least no one got very far." His face set hard as rock as if remembering something unpleasant. "I fought Apaches a time or two. I can shoot."

"Think you could teach me?" Nels said.

"You don't know how?" Yuma said. "Starkweather should have hired me as hunter."

Nels shrugged. It was the truth. "Tomorrow is Sunday. We could practice behind the outhouse."

Yuma did not answer at first. "If you can get that yapping fool to quit talking my ears off, I might." Yuma tucked his hands in his arm pits and shivered.

"Ten-Day is curious," Nels said. "Doesn't mean nothing by it."

"I've known men like him," Yuma said. "Sooner or later, someone shuts them up." He raised an eyebrow in Nels's direction, and pulled his collar up against the wind. "You shut him up and I'll teach you how to shoot."

Ten-Day would quit jabbering when he quit breathing. Threats and warnings had not worked up to this point. Nels nodded and led the newcomers back to the cut. An eagle soared high above, stretching wings and gliding across the sky. Drifts of snow covered their tracks.

Nels avoided the bull of the woods who was bawling out a feller crew for sawing too high on the trunk. Paulson would not like his promotion. Old Starkweather could break the news.

The sun gleamed on the white snow. Squirrels chattered. It felt good to take a breath without someone breathing down his neck. He wanted to head to the cookshack and visit with Gertie, but knew better. There would be time for that later. He imagined bringing in a magnificent buck and Gertie's admiring glance.

First, he had to learn how to shoot. The surveyor's hut stood next to the filer's cabin. Nels stuck his head in the doorway and asked Lardass where Pettibone kept his rifle.

"How should I know," Lardass said. "Nothing in here. He moved in with the filer a while back."

The filer's cabin was next to the blacksmith shop. The filer was a wizened, older man rarely seen without a pipe hanging from the corner of his mouth. He was owly on his best days and downright cantankerous on the others. Ten-Day said the filer's given name was Gus Patterson. Everyone in camp called him the dentist.

Nels tapped on the door. No answer. He leaned closer and heard snoring. He grinned. The dentist was up all night sharpening blades and axes. He slept during the day. Even his snores sounded like a rasping saw.

Nels tiptoed inside. The front of the shack held the filer's bench, a foot-propelled grindstone and every imaginable sharpening tool arranged in orderly fashion. A barrel of kerosene sat by the door. Axes, cross-cut saws, hatchets, and butcher knives hung from pegs on the wall, sharpened and ready for use. A wooden box filled with more to be sharpened.

On the backside of the room were two bunks. The snoring came from one. The other had a rifle hanging next to it. Nels took the rifle, careful not to wake the sleeping filer.

No ammunition in sight. Nels searched through Pettibone's turkey. He had few belongings, as most of the jacks. A suit of ragged underwear. A tin of liniment. In the bottom of his knapsack was a tintype of a man in a uniform and a pretty woman. It was hard to believe Pettibone had a mother.

The dentist woke up with a start. "What you doing in here?"

Nels squirmed. He had nothing to feel guilty about. He explained his new position. "Looking for ammunition."

"Pettibone had nightmares about it catching fire," the filer said. "Stored it in the tool shed. Get out of here and let me sleep."

Nels hefted the rifle to his shoulder and made ready to leave.

"You taking his bunk?" the dentist said.

"Nah." Nels would not sleep in that reprobate's bed.

"Thank God," the dentist said. "Maybe I'll get some sleep."

He was snoring before Nels was out the door.

Sure enough, Nels found a leather pouch of ammunition hanging on a nail in the tool shed under a frozen bear hide. He hung the pouch around his neck and turned back to the hide, rubbing the thick fur. Snarly yellow teeth showed in its mouth. Long claws stretched from its paws. Nels suppressed a shudder. Bears hibernated over the winter. He had nothing to worry about.

Already darkness fell over the camp and the top loaders navigated their loads to Stink Lake. Fish skidded a final log to the turn-about as the jacks streamed back from the cut.

"Where were you?" Ten-Day said. "How are we supposed to keep ahead of the skinners with you gallivanting?"

"Didn't Yuma tell you?" Nels said.

"He don't say nuthin," Ten-Day said. "He's unsociable, that one."

Nels told Ten-Day about his new job. Ten-Day's eyes grew wide.

"By God," Ten-Day said. "You hit the jackpot."

After supper, the men gathered round the stove. A few waited in line for a Polander who gave a good haircut for a nickel. Frenchy tried to beguile the new men into a game of hot hand, but no one fell for it. Nels had seen enough of bunk house life to last a lifetime.

It was as if they all waited for something to happen. The Polander finished the haircuts and pulled out a mouth harp. Yuma had a battered guitar. Pokey played his accordion. Together the men sang the old songs, *Annie Laurie, Lorena, Tenting Tonight, My Old Kentucky Home* and *Home Sweet Home.* The voices sounded plaintive in the glow of the single lamp, lonely men far from wives and sweethearts.

Gertie and a little farmstead filled Nels's thoughts. They would build a cabin and raise horses. The rest swirled into a blur of longing and desire.

"Enough blubbering," Pokey said. "Tamarack down, boys! Tamarack down." He switched to a lively melody, and the guitar and mouth harp followed suit.

Frenchy and Ten-Day dipped exaggerated bows to each other and began to dance. Nels howled with the others when Ten-Day pretended some mock impropriety and slapped Frenchy across the cheek. The others joined, singing with the musicians. Cosmos pretended to be a flirtatious female in Stefan's arms as they danced around the bunks. The roar of laughter and ribald jokes made them forget the drudgery of camp life.

They collapsed around the fire, and Ten-Day begged Yuma to talk about the Arizona prison. Yuma told of a criminal imprisoned for "seduction with promise to marry." The men hung on every word, asking about the heat, the prisoners, and the infamous warden.

"Why, the warden's wife was bolder than her husband," Yuma said. He stroked his beard that showed streaks of gray among the red. "She was an educated female. Even started a library for the prisoners." He stretched his feet toward the glowing barrel stove. "But that did not stop her from taking up a gatling gun during a riot. She mowed 'em down, boys. That she did."

"Don't believe a word of it, boys," Pokey said. "I know a tall tale when I hear one."

Pokey, the usual story teller had his nose out of joint. He made ready to launch into one of his yarns, but Yuma interrupted.

"All truth," Yuma said with an indignant huff. "A woman prisoner taught me to play this guitar. Her voice echoed down the cell block those hot summer nights. Drove the men wild."

Frenchy fired the stove, forgetting to open the draft and sending a plume of choking smoke into the room.

"What was she in for?" Ten-Day leaned forward, his eyes glittering. "Train robbery?"

"No." Yuma waited a bit, everyone hanging on his words. "She stuck a knife into her man's gullet when he came home drunk and started knocking her around. Said she had had enough."

Nels would never hit a woman. He was not a good man, but he was not a bad man, either. He drifted somewhere in the middle.

"Why did you leave if you liked it so much?" Ten-Day said.

Yuma shrugged. "The Mormons, for one thing," Yuma said. "They started sending decent men to prison for their religion. So what if they had more than one wife? The women did not mind. Figured it was nobody's business."

"Sounds like a good religion to me," Ten-Day said with a leer. "I'd like a dozen women to warm my bed at night."

"Not me." The Polander crossed himself. "I'd be afraid of going to hell."

"That's the beauty of it," Yuma said with a slap on his thigh. "When you're in Yuma Territorial Prison, you're already there."

The men roared and the accordion started again.

"What's the other reason?" Ten-Day said, raising his voice over Pokey's tune. "You said you had more than one."

"My little brother," Yuma said. "Ben Edinburgh homesteaded in the Sandhills of Nebraska. Went bust in the drought and worked the wheatfields of Dakota. Last we heard he was heading to the timber camps. I would like to find him."

No one knew Ben Edinburgh. Thirty thousand men scattered across Northern Minnesota.

The next morning, they woke to a bitter wind and overcast sky. Pokey filled the barrel for the weekly boil up. Nels was not about to risk his health. It made no sense to take a bath and put on the same louse-ridden clothing, though some of the men wrapped in blankets and washed drawers and trousers.

"Yuma," Nels said in a confidential tone. "I've got to start pulling my weight."

"Later," Yuma said. "I'm writing a letter to my ma."

"You promised," Nels said.

Yuma complained that Ten-Day was still yapping. He edged off his bunk and pulled on his coat. "You'd better catch on quick."

Frenchy and Ten-Day tagged along and placed wagers on Nels's chances of hitting the target. The odds were against him.

Nels lifted the bulky rifle in his hands, unsure what to do next. It smelled of gunpowder and an oily sheen felt slippery on his fingers.

"Press the butt into your shoulder," Yuma said. "Caress it like a woman. Close but not too close." He pointed to the sites on the barrel. "Fix both sites on the target and squeeze."

Nels's first shot grazed the edge of the target, but the buck of the gun pushed him backwards into the frozen snow. Ten-Day and Frenchy guffawed until tears ran down their faces.

"That's all there is to it," Yuma said with a yawn. "Practice until you get it right."

Nels shot a few more rounds. Men gathered to jeer and gamble. Even though it was Sunday, Nels donned snowshoes and trudged into the woods. If he brought game into the cookshack, he might speak to Gertie.

The wind played harps in the treetops. Small hoof tracks showed in the snow. A rabbit streaked by in the underbrush. Nels aimed and shot, but missed. A porcupine chewed bark off a tree. Nels took aim but hesitated. How would a man dress out the prickly animal without hurting himself? The new job was not as easy as he had thought. Other men lounged around the bunk house while he was freezing to death in the woods.

Nels wandered around until he saw an Indian gutting a moose on the west side of Stink Lake. The man had worked at Starkweather for a few days at the beginning of the season, but disappeared without a word. He dressed in a leather shirt and denim jeans. His hair hung in long black braids.

Nels called out a greeting. The Indian grunted a reply and returned to his work. Entrails spilled across the snow in steaming piles. Crows circled overhead, anxious for the scraps. The Indian eyed the rifle.

"You coming to make war?" he said. "I left my warpaint back at the cabin."

Nels introduced himself. At camp the Indian had been called Chief. "What's your name?"

"Gilbert Peterson. Pa is a Norske. Ma is from the Red Lake Band."

Nels chuckled and relaxed. A Norwegian Indian who spoke English seemed less of a threat.

"Where's Pettibone?" Gilbert said.

"In hell, I hope." Nels told him about the accident. "He's too ornery to die, though he looked half-dead when he left camp."

"I've got his moose."

So that is how he did it. Pettibone pilfered from camp to trade for game. "Did he often make trades?" Nels said.

"Had to," Gilbert said with a glint in his eye. "That fool couldn't hit the broad side of a barn."

Nels had nothing to trade. He would not survive without his coat or mitts. He needed the rifle and snowshoes. Then he thought of the turquoise stone hanging around his neck.

A beam of weak sun reflected off the blue gem as he held it out for Gilbert to examine. Nels had thought to keep it for a wedding gift for Gertie. But fact was fact. Unless he kept Ma happy, he had no chance to win Gertie's hand.

"It's a big critter," Gilbert said. "About eight hundred pounds of meat."

"An old buck, tough as shoe leather," Nels said. "We'll need forks and knives to eat the gravy." He pressed the stone into Gilbert's hands. "Look. I've never seen anything like it."

"Hell," Gilbert said after looking it over. "Why not?" He hung the cord around his neck. The turquoise looked brilliant against his leather shirt. "But I keep the antlers and hide."

Nels nodded and sealed the deal with a handshake. "Help me get it to the cookshack?"

Gilbert shrugged. "Not for nothing."

Nels had a red bandana handkerchief, none too clean. He would soon be naked and bankrupt at this rate. Gilbert tied the bandana around his upper sleeve. They each grabbed a hind leg and slid the animal over the top of the frozen snow.

They arrived at the camp, sweaty and exhausted. They hefted the carcass on a tree branch, out of reach of critters but convenient for removing joints of meat. Gilbert peeled off the hide and trotted off. Nels hacked a haunch for the kitchen.

There was little time to talk to Gertie, Ma saw to that, although he expected to win her over by the end of the season. But that was the rub. He was still a home seeker. No place to bring a wife. No money to get one. Damn Pinchpenny. Damn Pettibone.

"How would you like a Christmas tree in the cookshack?" He had to find a way to get the women's approval.

"No room in here for a tree." Ma snorted. "Do your job and supply meat."

But Gertie smiled behind Ma's back. He was on the right track.

Chapter 42
Sister Magdalena

Mrs. Popescu was right about traffic into the store. A clerk from Anderson Timber came the next morning before Sister Magdalena finished breakfast. Sister Magdalena begged a ride and sold chits at the camp that night. There she found an orderly camp and jacks eager to purchase hospital tickets. Word had filtered around about the accident at Starkweather Timber. The clerk paid without hesitation and arranged for her ride to another camp.

Sister Magdalena visited many camps through the middle weeks of December. She caught rides with surveyors or staff going into town for mail and supplies. Sometimes she hiked on snowshoes to nearby operations. The button strained on her money pocket. She was doing it. She was helping loggers and their families.

"Where next?" Mrs. Popescu said when Sister Magdalena returned to the store.

Sister Magdalena had walked at least thirteen miles on snowshoes and her legs felt like jelly. She wanted to eat and go to bed.

"I'll return to the convent for Christmas," Sister Magdalena said. She owed a little conversation, at least, to repay this woman for her generosity.

"A mistake to go back to Duluth," Mrs. Popescu said. She mentioned a camp beyond Stink Lake. "Now's the time to sell tickets. After Christmas, the jacks will figure the season is too far gone to shell out their hard-earned cash."

She was right. Perhaps she should disregard Mother Superior's orders and keep selling. She might beg a ride to Weyerhaeuser, and travel the rest of the way on snowshoes. She needed to stop at Starkweather's again, anyway.

As she stretched out in bed and felt the delicious relief of sleep, the Rule of Benedict made her decision. She would return to Duluth out of obedience, as Mother Superior commanded.

Her brothers had warned the vow of obedience would be a stifling, impossible thing. "You're too independent," they said. Yes, she was both stubborn and independent, but Sister Lucy once compared the vow of obedience to a locomotive. "A train goes faster when it stays on the tracks," she had said. Sister Magdalena chuckled and felt the burden of decision lift.

Jesus, I surrender myself to you. Take care of everything. Tomorrow she would leave for home. Mother Superior could decide whether Sister Magdalena sold more tickets.

Doc Hamilton's office situated on the path to the train depot. She had time to visit Jacob Pettibone before catching the train back to Duluth. Sister Magdalena debated. Mr. Pettibone had maligned her, the Pope, and the Church. She wanted to throttle him, not visit him out of Christian charity. She could walk right by the doctor's office, and no one would ever know.

Forgive us our trespasses, as we forgive those who trespass against us.

Sister Magdalena sighed. She had enough to confess when she got back to the convent. She would do her duty.

She grasped the rickety rail on the outside stairway that led to Doctor Hamilton's office above the saloon. A blast of wind pelted bits of ice and sleet into her face. The steps wobbled, slippery with ice beneath her feet. How easy it would be to take a tumble.

She hiked her skirts and climbed the teeter stairs. Every step caused the wooden structure to shudder and sway.

Sister Magdalena gripped the rail with one hand and her skirts with the other. The whole thing might collapse beneath her weight. She had eaten too many meals of potatoes and milk gravy while in the woods. She chuckled, imagining how she would grab the support beam on the wall and dangle like a giant bat in her black and white habit. The drunks would rescue her.

Or else, she would plunge to her death. Her tombstone could say *Death by Corporal Acts of Mercy* or *Sister Lumberjack, Killed by Poor Craftsmanship*. Puffing and sliding, she laughed until the tears streamed down her face.

A hand-painted sign nailed by the door said: *Doctor Hamilton might be asleep. Knock Loud as you Can.* Underneath tacked a piece of brown paper written in pencil: *Doc Hamilton can't hear worth a damn and is usually drunk. Walk in.*

Sister Magdalene swallowed a chuckle and pushed open the door. The dim room reeked of antiseptic and sour bodies. On one side was a bed where Jacob Pettibone lay. On the other side was a table and cookstove. The morning sun shone through a dirty window onto Doc Hamilton napping in a wooden chair by the table. He startled and leapt to his feet, rubbing sleep and squinting toward the door. As before, a half-empty liquor bottle stood on the table.

"Good morning, Doctor. No need for alarm. It's just me," she said.

"I didn't hear you knock," Doc Hamilton shouted as he snapped his galluses over his shoulders. He wore a filthy white shirt with spots of blood down the front. His boots sprawled under the table and his big toe wiggled through a hole in his sock. "I think my hearing is going. You'll have to speak up."

"I'm sorry to bother," Sister Magdalena yelled.

"Why yes, it is cold. December in Minnesota. What did you expect?" Doc Hamilton said. "I was up all night with a lying-in."

"That's not what she said, you fool," Pettibone yelled across the room. The log hanging from his leg banged against the bedframe.

Doc Hamilton ignored his patient, or maybe he did not hear the man. "Almost froze to death on my way home. Yes, sirree, it's cold out." He added an armful of wood to the firebox. "Twins, can you believe it? Injun mother and Welsh father. Big, healthy boys. Faces round as plates with fat rolls around their fists. They'll have one hell of a life in this country. Excuse my French, Sister."

Doc Hamilton ground coffee beans in a rusting grinder.

"How long will it take for him to heal?" Sister Magdalena said. She repeated herself several times before Dr. Hamilton understood.

"A few more weeks, if I don't kill him first," Dr. Hamilton said with a dour shake of his head. "The orneriest cuss I've known." The fragrance of freshly ground coffee filled the air. "One leg off and the other slow to heal."

"Get me out of this torture chamber." Pettibone's log slammed again.

The ungrateful wretch. Sister Magdalena walked toward his bed. The stink of him was enough to make her gag. She pulled a handkerchief to her nose and tried to sound pleasant like Sister Lucy. "How are you?"

"Terrible," Pettibone said. He shifted, making the log swing and bang. "Going crazy laying here day after day. All I do is count my troubles and tally my bills. I'll end up in the poor farm." He twisted again, sending the log banging against the bedframe.

"Lie still," Doc Hamilton said. "I'll take the other leg, too, goddammit. Quicker."

Pettibone slumped back on his pillow.

"May I pray for you before I go?"

"Hell no," Pettibone said. He punched out with his fist as if to knock her down. "Don't need no papist muttering psalms over me."

"Shut your mouth," Doc Hamilton yelled. "Have breakfast, Sister? Don't waste your breath on the likes of him."

Sister Magdalena sighed. Sister Lucy would know how to tame the wild man. Sister Magdalena had thought to ease his mind by telling him about the hospital ticket, the one that would save his bank account and get her into trouble. His behavior changed her mind. Let him worry a while longer.

Doc Hamilton slapped strips of side pork into a filthy frying pan. "Time for breakfast, Sister?"

"No, thank you," Sister Magdalena said. "I've got to be going." She had felt so cocky about selling tickets, but Pettibone brought her back to reality. Any nun worth her salt knew how to deal with a sinner.

"Sister Lumberjack, wait." Mr. Pettibone gulped hard. Drops of sweat glistened on his pale face beneath his messy hair. "I lost my leg."

She could promise to pray for him and go her way, easier than resuming the conversation. He looked so pathetic lying on that filthy bed with pulleys and logs dragging on his mangled body. Love of her brothers made her return to his bedside, though it was a poor reason to offer Christian charity. She must confess her lack of love when she got home. She lowered herself to her knees beside his bed, her skirts dragging across the filthy floor.

The front of his shirt stained with spilled food, and crumbs collected in his beard. The man never stopped squirming during the entire prayer. Maybe he had pinworms.

Our Father, who art in heaven…

"Sister," Pettibone said when she got back to her feet. He wiggled beneath her gaze. A piano started an off-key tune in the saloon below. "Is it true that you carried me out on your back?"

"Just from the river. Like a sack of grain," Sister Magdalena said with a laugh. "Thank God, I'm tall and strong and grew up with brothers." Her words came near boasting. "You can thank Nels Jensen for getting you to the spur line." She paused for breath. "And Mr. Weyerhaeuser allowed you passage to the river and the keelboat man floated you down the Mississippi between ice floes."

"What?" Pettibone's eyes widened. "Nels wouldn't help me."

"Love of neighbor, Mr. Pettibone." His gratitude would have felt good. She made the sign of the cross. "Christian charity makes a better world."

"Don't go." The log banged as he strained to sit up.

First Pettibone wanted to punch her and then he begged her to stay. One leg hoisted high with the swinging log underneath. His other a lump beneath the covers.

"Yes, modern inventions make the world a better place for everyone." Doc Hamilton rambled on about something in the newspaper. He made no sense. The sign on the door was right. He could not hear a thing. The patient squirmed, causing the log to bang harder on the bed frame. Pinworms for sure. She swallowed hard and bit her lip.

It was too late.

Laughter bubbled up inside of her. Pettibone demanding first that she leave and then begging her to stay. He could not make up his mind. Doc talked of modern inventions. She mopped tears with her veil. Doc Hamilton and Jacob Pettibone stared as if she were a lunatic escaped from the asylum. The more she tried to quit laughing, the more she could not stop.

"What's so funny?" Pettibone's log banged. "Are you mocking me?"

Sister Magdalena swallowed as hard as she could, shaking her head. "No." She sniffed and steadied herself on the bedframe. Pettibone leaned to the side and the log banged again.

"I broke the rules," she said. The truth always paid off. She gasped for breath. "I added your name to the list of hospital chits. Your bill is paid."

His jaw dropped. "Why would you do that?" He took a quick breath. "I made fun of you behind your back. Called you names. I did everything I could to make you fail."

"I know. I disliked you, but I felt sorry for you," Sister Magdalena said. Jesus said to take out the log in her own eye before she worked on the splinter in her brother's eye. "Because we're so much alike."

"How are we alike?" Pettibone said.

"I'm always getting into muddles, saying the wrong thing, and making things worse. Just like you. We are both sinners," she said. "Rule breakers who need the mercy of God."

A horse and wagon lumbered down the street. The sounds of children playing. A dog barking. Somewhere a whistle blew long and low.

"Will you get into trouble for helping me?" Pettibone said.

"Maybe, but I get in plenty of trouble on my own."

"Speak up. Can't hear a word you say," Doc Hamilton said. "I think my hearing is bad, and it is mighty inconvenient. Did you want breakfast or didn't you?"

She fumbled in her pack for a leather-bound prayer book containing the Psalms and Proverbs. It was all she had. She passed it to Mr. Pettibone with great reluctance. Her brothers had given it to her at her final vows. "You've time on your hands. Use it wisely."

Jacob Pettibone's face showed complete astonishment.

Only when she was on the train, did she fully relax. Home for Christmas. She had reached eight logging operations. A pittance compared to all the camps scattered through Minnesota, but a good start. She carried almost seven hundred dollars. Eight hundred if she figured the money still owed by Starkweather Timber. Sister Bede Marie would be pleased. Mother Superior would be overjoyed. The money burned in her inner pocket.

Sister Magdalena liked the freedom of riding trains, snowshoeing through the woods, visiting logging camps and selling hospital tickets. She had vowed to stay with the Duluth community all her life, and she had been content with her decision. Something had changed. She had grown independent. For the first time she imagined a life away from the convent, a life of her own.

The train chugged through acres of decimated timber. Hideous stumps and scattered slash piles littered the landscape. She meditated on the Sorrowful Mysteries, and considered all the homes the lumber would build, and all the men earning good livings in the woods.

The train pulled into the Duluth depot near noon. A gray sky hung low over the city and snowflakes boiled in the wind. She patted the fat pocket holding the money. She hiked to the convent from the railroad depot to save the few cents it would cost to hire a cab. The cobblestones sheathed with ice. She slipped and slid, holding her arms out for balance. The wind swept in from Lake Superior, swirling her veil and snatching her breath away.

She arrived at the convent during noon prayers. She paused outside the chapel, listening to the murmur of voices. *"God is the strength of my life."* An unexpected rush of tears sprouted in her eyes. These were her sisters. How she had missed them. Together they worked, prayed, and sacrificed for the love of Christ. She would never abandon them. They were her life.

Sister Magdalena crossed herself but did not go in. She stank as bad as Jacob Pettibone. Her cassock soiled with sweat and engine smoke. She headed toward her room to clean up before dinner. How good a hot tub of water would feel on her feet. She sighed. It would take too long to haul water for a bath. Her stomach growled in protest.

She would freshen up as best she could, eat and bathe later.

Mother Superior's eyes brightened when she saw her at table. Everyone smiled and nodded her way. No talking during meals, of course. The greetings must wait.

The nuns hurried off to their work when the bell released them from the table. Obedience guided their steps. Sister Magdalena understood. They would visit during recreation hour. Not until then.

Mother Superior motioned for Sister Magdalena to follow to her office.

"You're back," Mother Superior said. She directed Sister Magdalena to sit. "Our prayers have been with you."

"Thank you," Sister Magdalena said. "I felt them."

"You're looking well," Mother Superior said. "The fresh air agrees with you. You have fleshed out during your travels."

"All that cream gravy and potatoes," Sister Magdalena said with a laugh. "Pies, cookies, cakes, bread, butter—Christmas every meal at a lumberjack's table."

Sister Magdalena placed the lists of hospital chits along with the cash and bank drafts on Mother Superior's desk. Mother counted the money, keeping tally with a pencil stub on a scrap of paper.

"Amazing. The Lord has blessed you," Mother Superior said. She sat back in her chair with her two index fingers before her smiling mouth. "I want to hear all about it."

A wave of fatigue washed over Sister Magdalena. Where would she start? The miles and camps and faces swarmed into her thoughts. Best to first admit the hardest part.

"I have sinned," Sister Magdalena said. "I broke the rules and added Jacob Pettibone's name to the list after he was injured." She told of Mr. Pettibone's verbal attacks against her and the Catholic Church, his injury, and the death of his companion.

"Why did you add his name?" Mother Superior said.

Sister Magdalena took a breath. "I did it because of my great dislike for the man. He did not deserve it, but I did it anyway."

"Out of charity for Mr. Pettibone? Or penance for your lack of love?"

The sound of a crashing metal tray sounded from the refectory. The Blessed Virgin looked down from her shelf.

"Both," Sister Magdalena admitted. A miserable start to her report if there ever was one. "I did it because of my lack of charity, and because of charity." She gulped. "I will pay the dollar myself, if you prefer. Perhaps I could ask my brothers for the money."

"Mr. Pettibone did not pay?" Mother Superior said.

"No," Sister Magdalena said. "He will pay eventually. It will be docked from his pay at the logging camp."

"So, he did pay for his chit," Mother Superior said. Her eyes danced though her face remained stern. "It seems you did nothing wrong."

She did everything wrong, putting her foot in her mouth, making horrible blunders that Sister Lucy would never consider doing. "Starkweather Timber still owes payment for the chits sold there."

Sister Magdalena described her problem with collecting from Mr. Starkweather. "Mr. Starkweather claims he is log rich and dollar poor. Rumor has it that he gambles for money to operate the camp. I must go back to collect."

Their conversation moved to the other camps she had visited, how she had prayed with the men, and carried Mr. Pettibone to a doctor's care. Sister Magdalena's tongue slurred and her thoughts blurred. Fatigue weighted her eyelids. She stifled a yawn.

"Well done," Mother Superior said. "What's next?"

"A bath," Sister Magdalena said. "I stink like a lumberjack."

"You will give a short report to the sisters before supper," Mother Superior said. "Spend tomorrow in retreat to rest and hear how God is leading. We will talk again after Christmas."

How good it felt to be home. As she entered her cell, she realized she had completely forgotten to mention her visit to the brothel.

Chapter 43
Solveig

Rosy slopped dishwater on the path instead of into the woods, making a quick journey to the backhouse a treacherous risk of limb. She left the broom in the middle of the floor, the task half-finished. Great gobs of unmixed flour remained in her batter, and she fired the stove either too hot or let it die out entirely. Stutz showed more common sense than Rosy.

Solveig was breaking all kinds of rules, and Rosy was not worth the risk.

One morning, Solveig put Rosy to peeling spuds after breakfast dishes. A half hour later potatoes covered only the bottom of the kettle. Rosy cut too deeply and wasted too much. And the stores diminished day by day.

"Help Stutz set the tables." Solveig picked up the knife and attacked the tubers like the Vikings attacking Ireland. She twirled the knife, skinning only a thin layer.

Rosy laid the table as haphazardly as she peeled potatoes. They needed every place with the number of men on the crew. Rosy left spots without any dishes and others without cups.

"Gertie," Solveig said. "Show Rosy how to lay the table—again."

Rosy burst into tears and fled into the back room. "I can't do anything right."

Solveig sighed, blaming Nels for sweet talking her into harboring the girl. Who knew when Sister Lumberjack would return? Enough was enough. That girl had to go. She was only trouble.

Rosy sat on the bottom bunk holding Queenie close to her chest.

"What's your problem?" Solveig's patience withered. Either Rosy carried her share of work as agreed upon, or she would leave the camp and find her own way. "I want to know, and I want to know now."

"It's Christmas Eve," Rosy said. Her voice blubbered and snot ran down her face.

"So what?" Solveig said with a start. She had forgotten. Of course, there was no calendar in the cookshack. The bull cook had not mentioned the holiday. No plans for a celebration. At home she would have baked *julekake*, Norwegian Christmas bread. Their country church always had midnight services.

"It's Jimmy." Rosy wiped tears and cat hair off her face with her apron hem. "My little boy's birthday is today."

Solveig's anger drained away. She had not known Rosy had a son. She did not want to hear her sad story. She had enough troubles of her own. It was Solveig's first Christmas away from home, her first Christmas without Rasmuss and Halvor. Who cared what Rosy was going through? Solveig was not Sister Lumberjack who offered a shoulder to cry on to every miserable wretch in her path.

"Where is the boy?" Solveig said after an awkward silence.

"An orphanage in Duluth." Rosy's shoulders slumped. "He deserves better." She looked up with red eyes. "I could not take care of him. I tried, but I couldn't do it on my own."

"His father?" Solveig said.

"Him?" Rosy's face hardened into an ugly wedge. "Dirty son of a bitch left and never looked back."

Part of Solveig wanted to give her a hug. Instead, she hardened her heart against the young tart. She was right. The boy was better off without her.

"Bawling won't help," Solveig said. "You made your bed, and now you have to put up with the bugs." She had no time for dilly-dallying. "I'll tell you once, and I won't tell you again. Carry your load or get out."

Rosy startled as if she had been slapped. She swallowed hard, wiped her face, and scurried to the kitchen. The front door opened as Pokey came for the wanigan. Outside was as cold and dreary as Solveig felt.

"I'll take over here," Solveig said to Gertie. "Show Rosy again the correct way to lay the tables."

Gertie rolled her eyes, but obeyed.

"Plate upside down, bowl upside down on the plate, cup upside down on the bowl. Nice and neat," Gertie said as she showed Rosy what to do. "About two feet between place settings." Gertie's growing belly made it harder for her to reach across the table. "Fill both tables."

Someone rattled at the cookshack door, and Rosy disappeared into the backroom. It was Nels holding a brace of rabbits in one hand and his rifle in the other. He grinned in Gertie's direction. How young he looked when he smiled, no older than Halvor.

"Rabbit pie for supper," Nels said.

Gertie barely looked up from her work. The lovesick boy sought Gertie's attention whenever he showed his face in the cookshack. The day before, Solveig overheard him telling her that he was saving up to send for his parents in Denmark.

"Gertie, fetch Nels a plate." Solveig sighed. Rabbits were stringy and tasteless, nothing like a haunch of beef or hog. Solveig called into the back room. "It is only Nels. Get back to work."

Rosy came out with Queenie rubbing around her legs. She tripped over the cat, but regained her footing, and headed toward Nels.

"Get busy," Solveig said. "No time to mill about."

"What do you want me to do?" Rosy said.

Solveig bit back a harsh retort. Rosy should know without being told. "Damn it!" Solveig slammed a kettle, and felt a little better. "Chop the damn onions and rutabagas, and be quick about it. Gertie, roll the pie crust. Stutz, peel more potatoes." They scurried to their tasks.

One rabbit would only flavor the pies. Solveig sighed. Codfish gravy over mashed potatoes again. She glared at Nels. "This is a piss-poor Christmas supper."

"I know," Nels said. "The woods are empty. Met an Injun willing to trade for game."

"Starkweather holds the purse strings," Solveig said. "Tell your troubles to him." She had to have meat, and she needed it right away. "I'm tired of your excuses."

"Roll more crust, Gertie. We will bake apple pies for supper, too," Solveig said. It was the only thing she had for a Christmas treat. She could not spare the time for doughnuts.

"Not enough pie pans," Gertie said. "It will have to be something else."

Solveig searched her mind for a recipe. "Gingerbread, then. I've a few eggs from my girls, and it is Christmas Eve. The boys deserve a treat."

She turned back to Nels. She would set him on the straight and narrow if it was the last thing she did.

Chapter 44
Nels

Nels felt long fingers gouge his arm.

"Young man," Ma hissed. "You and I need to talk."

She gave him a tongue lashing that would have earned a punch in the nose had she been a man. Nels hunched down and took it. She had helped him out with Rosy. Was it his fault that hunting was near-impossible in the dead of winter?

"I need meat, and I need it today," Ma said. "Bring something for the kettle."

"If I had something to trade." Nels pulled away from her grip. "A bale of fish or a bag of salt..."

"I told you before. It ain't mine to give," Ma said.

"It's not stealing to trade for something else," Nels said. "It all goes down their gullets."

"I'm not risking my job for your convenience."

Where was the nice old lady who made doughnuts for the keelboat crew? Ma had turned into a troll. Nels grabbed his hat and stomped out of the cookshack. He was not a miracle worker.

If only he had something to trade. Anything would do. The filer's tools would be missed if he filched them. Pettibone's belongings were not worth anything. He stepped into the barn and eyed the row of barrels containing oats for the horses. No sign of Barrister. Nels eyed the hens. A missing chicken would be blamed on a brush wolf. It would serve Ma right if she lost one of her precious hens.

Nels wavered, but kicked the hen aside. He had been called a thief, but had never stolen anything before. Taking the grain would not be like snatching one of Ma's chickens. He walked away in disgust. Jacob Pettibone, Myron Pinchpenny and Starkweather Timber were turning him into someone he did not want to be. Ma, and the rod up her ass, made it worse.

He imagined the burn of whiskey down his throat. He would like to swim in the stuff. An idea came to him where Irish might have hidden his liquor. He searched the woodshed, growing thirstier with each passing minute. He would be fired unless he brought in more meat. He needed something to trade.

The bear skin hung in the woodshed. Thank you, Jacob Pettibone. The hide belonged to Starkweather, after all, so it was not stealing to use it in trade. He draped the frozen hide over his shoulder, and went in search of Gilbert. The long claws clacked by his ear. The hide smelled like dirty socks.

Nels found Gilbert on the other side of Stink Lake. The man crouched in the reeds holding a bow and arrow pointed upward. A pile of rabbit entrails lay on the ice as bait. An eagle circled overhead, and swooped down toward the bait. Nels had not seen an eagle up close before, nor had he known its huge wing span. The twang of the arrow string. The majestic bird snatched the bait and soared away, avoiding the arrow.

"It was a slim chance," Gilbert said with a sigh. "Those feathers are gold at Red Lake." Gilbert sighed and pinched tobacco from a leather pouch. With great dignity he scattered a few shreds of tobacco to the four winds. Only then did he sit back on his haunches and examine the bear hide. His eyes widened as he touched the long teeth.

Nels offered to trade for a deer or moose. Gilbert nodded. Nels had bargained too quickly. "Two animals," Nels said. "Two animals with lots of meat on them."

Gilbert hesitated. "My cousins up north go wild for shit like this. They make necklaces out of the teeth. Rugs out of the hide. Big medicine."

They shook hands as a white swan glided across the open patch of water. Supper. Nels aimed and pulled the trigger. The rebound against his shoulder knocked him back on his behind.

The bird flew away in a flurry of flapping wings. He had missed. Of course, he had missed. He was a miserable hunter.

"You need a shotgun for birds." Gilbert threw more tobacco to the four directions with a muttered prayer. He pointed to a porcupine clinging to the lower trunk of a nearby pine. The animal looked at them without fear. "There's meat for today," Gilbert said. "I'll bring the bigger animals soon."

"Porcupine?" Long quills covered every inch of the animal's body. "How would I clean it, even if I could shoot it?"

Gilbert laughed and picked up a stout branch. "Watch and learn, white man." He walked toward the porcupine and swung the club, smashing the porcupine's head. It dropped to the ground without a shot being fired. "Good eating," Gilbert said. "Lots of fat."

Nels bent to pick it up, but Gilbert stopped him.

"Touch him, and you'll regret it."

"How do I dress it out?"

"I told you to watch and learn." He built a fire. "I've been doing this since I was a boy."

Using two sticks, he picked up the dead animal and lowered it into the flames. He singed the quills until the animal was charred and naked. Gilbert lifted it out of the fire and lay the porcupine on the ground. He grinned and trotted away with a promise to deliver deer or moose to the camp.

Nels's feet and hands ached with cold. No doubt, he could learn a lot from Gilbert. He cut a small pine tree for Christmas. Piling the porcupine on top, he started back to the cookshack. The charred meat did not look appetizing. Ma would complain about it. She always complained.

That evening, Nels punched holes in chewing tobacco lids gathered from the crew. Ten-Day looped bits of thread through the holes and hung them on the Christmas tree. No candles, but the dangling tin reflected the lamp light.

Pokey squeezed a few chords on his accordion. "Did I ever tell you about the feller on the Rum River who froze his manhood?"

The jacks gathered round the barrel stove, waiting for the joke, elbowing one another in anticipation.

"What's a manhood?" Stutz said.

"Shut up." Sully glared a warning at his brother as the others laughed and jostled.

"His manhood?" Pokey said. "Why, it's the most important treasure a man has." He teased a long note from his squeeze box. "He was a young feller, not much older than you." He nodded toward Stutz. "Careless, he was. An Icelander saved his bacon, yes sir, he surely did."

"Careless with his ax?" Stutz pressed closer.

"Careless with fire. Hung his trousers too close to the barrel stove." Pokey said.

Nels marveled how Pokey used the accordion to add drama to his yarns.

"You can never be too careful with fire in a place like this." Pokey pointed to the log walls. "The bull cook was keen to give him a hiding."

Even Yuma drew closer. Not a sound except the crackling of fire and sizzle of water in the lard can. Nels strained to hear.

"Well, now." Pokey stretched a long, wailing note on his accordion. "The crotch was burned away. They were his only trousers. The bull cook was a mean old bastard, unlike yours truly." Pokey pretended to put his accordion away.

"What happened next?" Ten-Day said. "What about the Icelander?"

Pokey pretended to be surprised. He picked up his squeeze-box and chorded a low melody. "The boy had no choice but to wear the burned pants the next day. He hightailed it out to the cut before the bull cook could give him the promised beating."

"What about the Icelander?" Ten-Day said.

"Almost forgot about him." Pokey chorded until Nels almost felt the cold portrayed in the music. "Bitter cold, that day. The boy had just a thin layer of underwear between him and the elements"

"Hurry up with it," Yuma said. "What happened?"

"The boy kept swinging the ax, hoping the exercise would warm him up," Pokey said. "At first he felt pins and needles in his privates—but soon he felt nothing at all."

"Then what?" Ten-Day said.

"At noon he stepped away from the fire to relieve himself," Pokey said. "That is when we heard a terrible screech. We looked for Red Indians coming with scalp knives." Pokey paused for effect, and stretched his feet toward the stove, in no hurry to continue.

"Spit it out, Old Timer," Yuma said. "It's bedtime."

"Hold your horses," Pokey said. "One thing you do not understand, Yuma, is that a yarn is meant to be spun out to the very end. You do not just blurt it out, and call it done. You tease it, like one of those saloon girls doing a dance." His eyes glittered and he looked at the Arizonan in triumph. "That's why you'll never be a story teller, here or back in the territory."

"Tease it out, then," Yuma said. "Just get it said."

Pokey glared at Yuma for a long minute. "You just don't know how it's done."

The jacks started fidgeting in their seats. "Just tell the story," Ten-Day said.

"He could not pass a drop. Frozen solid, he was. Hurt like hell," Pokey said.

"Frozen solid?" Ten-Day said. "It couldn't be."

"Saw it myself," Pokey said. "Froze his nether regions. We thought he was a goner, for sure."

An uncomfortable anxiety rustled across the bunkhouse. A few men shifted the front of their trousers.

"What about the Icelander?" Ten-Day said.

"We had this old Icelander cook with the name of Flinch. He was a peppery fellow, fond of knitting. Many a jack had his nose bloodied for teasing him about it." Every man leaned forward in his seat. "Flinch took one look at the poor boy and took him back to the cookshack."

"Did he live?" Yuma said.

"Flinch treated him for frostbite, just like you would a foot or cheek. Rubbed him good with snow and soaked him in cool water. He got the piss flowing, by God. That cook was a wonder. Then he knit him a special mitt to cover his jewels so it would not happen again. And it never did."

"No," Ten-Day said. "That never happened."

"You calling me a liar?" Pokey said. "I've still got the mitt to prove it."

The jacks roared with laughter.

Merry Christmas. At home Nels's family processed by candle-light to the little country church. Afterwards, the aunts and uncles and cousins filled their home to celebrate as Mother unveiled the lighted Christmas tree. They joined hands and danced around it, singing, and admiring its brilliant wonder. The women served herring, sandbakkels, pebbernodder cookies, rice pudding and roast goose. They ate until their sides ached.

His father always raised a glass to the Christ Child. "Skal!"

The women washed the dishes, their laughter and chatter like a flock of hens. The men and boys set out sheaves of grain for the wild birds to find in the morning, while sneaking more liquor out of womenfolk's view. Father measured extra feed into the animal troughs. The children waited at midnight to hear the animals speak in human voices, as tradition promised. Most of the chil-dren were asleep by midnight, sprawled across the haystack in the corner of the barn. They celebrated long into the night.

Here in the woods, they celebrated Christmas with tall tales about frozen manhood. The desire for home and family nearly choked him. He should have never left Denmark. But then he would have not met Gertie. Someday he and Gertie would give their children a Christmas to be remembered. He would butch-er a goose for dinner and take the children out to the barn at midnight. Nels drifted to sleep, scratching to the rumble of Ten-Day's snoring, and dreaming of being with Gertie after the chil-dren were asleep.

Chapter 45
Sister Magdalena

Christmas interrupted the dreary routine with bountiful sweets and succulent dishes. Sister Magdalena nibbled a cookie as Sister Lucy chorded Christmas carols on the piano. Sister Bede Marie and Sister Hildegard played checkers at the parlor table, while novices pulled taffy in the kitchen. The smell of popcorn wafted across the room.

"Isn't it glorious?" Novice Agatha said. "I wish it was Christmas every day." Her eyes shone as she pointed to molasses cookies baked with her mother's recipe. A local merchant had donated a crock of spicy pickles. A farmer delivered a barrel of sauerkraut. A parishioner brought a platter of smoked tullibees. The bishop sent chocolates. Sister Hildegard added a heaping plate of honey cakes to the sideboard.

The Christmas Liturgy, the glorious celebration after penitential Advent, the creche, the carols and Advent candles made Christmas come alive. Jesus born of the Blessed Virgin Mary. Jesus, fully human and fully divine, became God's mercy in flesh and bone. They would celebrate through the octave of Christmas.

Sister Magdalena's thoughts kept wandering back to Starkweather Timber. She still carried Nels's coins in her pocket. She suspected Solveig would make sure the jacks had a Christmas dinner. Then she lifted a quick Hail Mary for Jacob Pettibone, that his leg would mend along with his soul.

The doorbell interrupted their merriment. Sister Magdalena answered the door, swallowing the last bite of cookie and wiping crumbs on her skirt. It was Father Miller. A blustery wind off Lake

Superior caught his words. Father's face looked gray and drawn, and though Sister Magdalena knew he was only in his thirties, he appeared much older. Patches of frost clung to his black cassock.

He refused to come inside. "There's sickness by the waterfront." His voice cracked with weariness and he shivered in the cold.

"You must come in, Father. Warm yourself." Mother Superior joined Sister Magdalena at the door. "Sister Bede Marie, fix Father a plate. It is freezing outside."

"No." He stepped back from the doorway. "It's bad...typhoid."

It was if the air went flat. Mother Superior gasped, and stepped back from the door.

"A family is down with it." He shivered and tucked his hands under his armpits while stomping his feet to keep the circulation going. "Doctor Milton says it's virulent."

"How can we help?" Mother Superior said. She, usually so brave and resolute, braced one hand on the door frame to steady herself.

"Doctor Milton urges prudence lest folks panic," Father Patullo said. "The last thing we need is for people to scatter and carry the disease with them."

"No doubt it's the Irish," Mother Superior said. "Filth brings contagion."

Sister Magdalena doubted it was the Irish. Gertie Murphy was impeccable.

"Doctor Milton blames the rats," Father Miller said. "Nursing sisters are needed." He blew on his hands. "The waterfront is under quarantine."

Mother Superior dipped into silence. She crossed herself. "Sister." She motioned Sister Lucy to the door. The piano music stopped and the novices crept nearer, licking sticky taffy-lips.

Father Miller repeated the news.

"Of course," Sister Lucy said. "I'll bring my things and stay until it's over."

Brave Sister Lucy would walk into the arena of the martyrs if needed. She was saint-like in her dedication to the sick.

"Someone must go with you," Mother Superior said.

"Nonsense," Sister Lucy said. "No use in exposing anyone else."

Sister Magdalena knew she should volunteer, but it was likely that whoever went would get sick. What if Sister Lucy died? They were already short-staffed in the hospital.

Novice Agatha piped up, "I'll go with her, Mother."

Sister Magdalena imagined Agatha setting rooms on fire and spilling hot soup on sick people. She stifled a giggle. This was no joke. Sister Magdalena feigned coughing. Sister Bede Marie cast a warning look.

"Thank you, Agatha," Mother Superior said with a gentle smile. "This situation calls for experienced nursing sisters, ones fully professed."

The sisters shifted uneasily, glancing from one to another. It was clear that no one except Sister Lucy wanted the dangerous assignment.

Sister Hildegard stepped forward. "I'll go," she said. "I have lived my life. We need the younger sisters to keep the orphanage and hospital going."

Mother Superior grasped Sister Hildegard's hand and made a slight bow. Tears glittered in both of their eyes. This holy moment dropped a measure of guilt on Sister Magdalena as heavy as a load of logs. Sister Hildegard, even with her bad back, stepped forward while she, Sister Magdalena, the physically strongest of them all, did nothing except find it amusing. Try as she might, Sister Magdalena would never be as holy as they.

"May we have your blessing, Father?" Mother Superior said.

The women dropped to their knees, waiting for the priest's blessing.

"Of course." Father Miller made the sign of the cross and bestowed a blessing from the doorway. Then he prayed aloud: *"Watch, O Lord, with those who wake or watch or weep tonight, and give Your angels and saints charge over those who sleep."*

"Tend Your sick ones, O Loving Lord, rest Your weary ones," Sister Magdalena and the other sisters joined the ancient prayer of

Saint Augustine. *"Bless Your dying ones, soothe Your suffering ones, pity Your afflicted ones, shield Your joyous ones. And all for Your love's sake."*

"Amen," Father said.

The sisters stood to their feet.

"Father, when you get home, you must scrub your hands, take a full bath, and wash your hair," Sister Lucy said. "Use strong soap and vinegar. Boric acid is even better, if you can stand it. You might escape contagion."

"Is it that serious?" he asked.

"Yes, deadly," Sister Lucy paused to consider. "Burn the clothing that you are wearing and dip the soles of your shoes in carbolic acid."

"I'm but a poor priest," he said in alarm. "This is my only cassock, and I don't know how I'd replace it."

"It can't be helped," Sister Lucy was firm. "You must take every precaution."

"There was a typhoid epidemic when I was a child," Mother Superior said. Her voice carried a strange, strangled sound. "Our priest died after giving last rites to the victims."

Father Miller nodded. "You're right, of course."

Sister Bede Marie passed a plate wrapped in a cloth to the good priest, careful to stay far back from the man as she stretched her arm forward.

"Thank you and Merry Christmas." He turned and walked toward the rectory across the street, his footsteps heavy with weariness.

They watched him go until Mother Superior closed the door. They packed soap, carbolic acid, vinegar, clean rags and as much food as they could spare.

The whole time Sister Magdalena's heart fluttered in her chest, and she felt a slow burn in her cheeks. What would her parents think of her cowardly response? The Rule of Benedict gave priority to caring for the sick. Sister Magdalena must offer to help. She imagined her heroic efforts to kill rats, scrub the waterfront houses, and nurse the sick. Then she imagined the letter sent to her brothers telling of her virtuous death and gallant self-sacrifice. Maybe she would become a canonized saint, Saint Magdalena of Duluth, patron saint of rat killers. Sister Magdalena's imagination spurred her resolve. She sought Mother Superior who was kneeling in the parlor with her rosary.

Sister Magdalena cleared her throat, planning what she would say. Mother Superior did not pause from her prayers. Sister Magdalena's heart thumped. Sisters Hildegard and Lucy prepared to leave. She had to speak now.

"Mother, may I interrupt?" Sister Magdalena said. "I would like to volunteer to go with Sister Lucy to the waterfront. I am hopeless with sick people, I know, but I could tote water for bathing and do the heavy lifting."

Mother Superior started to shake her head, and Sister Magdalena pressed on before Mother Superior could refuse.

"Sister Hildegard has a bad back, and I'm strong as a mule."

"Pray with me, Sister," Mother Superior said.

Remembering her vow of obedience, Sister Magdalena pulled her mother's pink beads from her pocket and dropped to her knees beside Mother Superior. Sister Magdalena again had the sensation of riding the rosary to a place closer to God. Her head cleared and her breathing slowed back to normal.

"I've other plans for you," Mother Superior said, getting to her feet after she finished. "Come to my office after the sisters leave."

"But," Sister Magdalena persisted.

"Enough," Mother Superior said. "We will speak later."

Everyone gathered by the door to bid farewell to the nursing sisters. Novice Agatha pressed a bundle of her mother's cookies into Sister Hildegard's hands. Sister Bede Marie urged them to contact her if there was something needed for their ministrations.

Mother Superior embraced and kissed the cheeks of Sisters Hildegard and Lucy. "Thank you, dear ones, for taking up this heavy cross. We go with you in spirit, and will uphold you in our prayers."

It was as if the sisters were going to their deaths. Perhaps they were. If she were in charge, Sister Magdalena would have chosen someone younger and stronger than Sister Hildegard. She would send someone like herself. Sister Magdalena's dream of martyrdom for the cause of Christ drifted away like a soap bubble.

Sister Lucy was like a she-wolf with her pups when it came to protecting her patients. Sister Magdalena vowed to pray for both sisters to be spared contagion.

No one felt like celebrating after they left. Novice Agatha gathered the cookies and cakes to take to the refectory where a goose roasted in the oven for supper. Sister Magdalena sniffed the delicious fragrance on her way to Mother Superior's office.

Mother Superior urged her to take a seat and came right to the point. "You must return to Starkweather Timber before the disease spreads. Remain until Mr. Starkweather pays what he owes. Sell more tickets if you are able."

"But Mother," Sister Magdalena said. "What if I am stuck there until the end of the season?" She had hoped to stay at the convent through the coldest months, at least to welcome the New Year of 1894.

"Financially we are barely afloat. If the hospital is inundated with typhoid patients, we will go under. If pestilence strikes even one logging camp, the tickets sold would not cover the expenses," Mother Superior said. "It's desperate." She plucked a paper from the pile on her desk. "Here is the bill from Doctor Hamilton for the care of Jacob Pettibone. It is over thirty dollars and there is a note that says complications will keep Mr. Pettibone in bed longer."

Sister Magdalena gulped. She had added Mr. Pettibone to the hospital list. "And if Mr. Starkweather doesn't pay?" Sister Magdalena said.

"Then we'll abandon the ticket program," Mother Superior said. "And take it as a sign from the Lord that we acted in presumption."

Sister Magdalena took a deep breath. Perhaps she was not meant to be a nun. She made a mess of everything, as her brothers had forewarned. Had all her work been for nothing?

"Catch the morning train to Aitkin," Mother Superior said. Deep creases showed around her mouth and puffy eyes. She seemed older and very weary. "We take up our crosses and follow where He leads. At Starkweather Timber, you may be spared the contagion. Lord knows what you will find on your return."

"Tomorrow?" Sister Magdalena's brain whirled with the sudden change of plans. "Surely it won't be that bad."

"Maybe not," Mother Superior said. "But as a child, a typhoid epidemic took a thousand people in a fortnight."

Sister Magdalena sobered.

"My parents sent me to stay with my grandparents in another town. It was right after President Lincoln's election and all the election banners were still up everywhere. My life was spared, but my parents died." The words fell from her lips in quick staccato. She lived with her grandparents until she entered the convent. "Typhoid is deadly." Mother Superior stood to her feet, as did Sister Magdalena.

Sister Magdalena imagined returning in the spring to find the convent empty and the graveyard full. She imagined going to the bishop and pleading for more sisters to help carry on the work of the Benedictines.

"We abandon ourselves to God," Mother Superior said. "His will is mercy itself."

"Mother," Sister Magdalena said. "What if Mr. Starkweather refuses to pay what is owed?"

"Then the hospital tickets are not working," Mother Superior said. The bell rang for supper. Footsteps sounded as the others headed toward the refectory. "The rest is up to God."

Sister Magdalena left the next morning bundled in both suits of underwear, her warmest socks and rubber boots over her shoes. The sun peeked over the harbor in pinks and purples as she made her way to the depot. She craned her neck toward the waterfront. Spirals of smoke rose from chimneys. No sign of Sister Lucy or Sister Hildegard. Sister Magdalena hated to leave without knowing what was happening. She could not visit them and risk carrying typhoid to the woods.

She was the only woman among a scattering of menfolk on the train. A few tipped their hats, while others stared. Mostly they ignored her. A heaviness settled. She felt as if she were being banished. Nonsense. She had her work to do, as all the sisters did. The vow of obedience directed her. Sister Magdalena meditated on the Joyful Mysteries.

Mother Superior had given the ultimatum. Mr. Starkweather must pay what he owed, or the program would be cancelled. That is why Sister Magdalena felt a heaviness. It was not the typhoid epidemic, though that was serious enough. If things didn't go well with Mr. Starkweather, Sister Magdalena would be stuck back in the laundry, orphanage, or somewhere else.

She resumed her prayers with determination. Jesus must resurrect the hospital ticket program or it was doomed.

The train chugged into Aitkin as the sun reached its zenith. Sister Magdalena gathered her bedroll and knapsack, a quick anxiety rising in her chest. She must find transportation to Stink Lake. Even if she started walking before sunrise, she would not reach Starkweather Timber before dark on these short, winter days. She would freeze to death if she slept outside in the elements. There was a slim chance the spur line might be open, or perhaps a sleigh from another camp was going in that direction. She crossed herself and stepped out into the street. God would provide.

She passed the saloon and forced herself to climb the rickety stairs to visit Mr. Pettibone. It was only charitable. Funny, she volunteered to care for strangers with typhoid, but dreaded an obnoxious person she knew.

Sister Magdalena pounded on the door until Mr. Pettibone called out. She stepped inside where he lay in bed wearing his log sling. She greeted him without enthusiasm.

"Doc says I can leave soon," he said. "My leg is finally better."

The fire had died down, leaving the room almost as cold as the outdoors. Sister Magdalena fed wood into the stove and fetched a cup of water for the patient. She rummaged in the cupboard and found a tin of crackers and a half empty jelly jar. It was not much, but it would have to do for the man's dinner.

"Where's Doc Hamilton," Sister Magdalena said.

"Got called out to a place north of town," Mr. Pettibone said. "Don't know when he'll be back."

A comforting wave of heat came from the stove and Sister Magdalena held her hands toward it. Sounds of laughter came from the saloon below them. The smell of urine permeated the room. She put the coffee pot on to boil.

"What will you do after you leave here?" Sister Magdalena said. The man's remaining leg looked withered and shrunken. His leg might be mending, but that did not mean he could return to timbering. Every day he spent in this bed meant a bigger bill to Mother Superior. "Will you return to Starkweather Timber?"

"Everything I own is there. And there is back pay."

Sister Magdalena picked up a sour dishrag and poured scalding water over it. Then she wiped the sticky table and chairs, cleaned the crumbs and bits of wood from the floor and washed the dirty dishes piled in the dry sink. A saintlier nun would offer to give the patient a bath. Sister Magdalena was not saintly.

A rattle at the door and Doc Hamilton walked in carrying a wooden crate of food stuff. He stomped his feet on the doormat before placing the box on the table.

"Merry Christmas," Doc Hamilton said. "Surprised to see you back so soon." He looked approvingly at the tidy kitchen, warm fire, and boiling coffee pot. He busied with putting the food stuff in his cupboard as she told him about the situation in Duluth.

"Typhoid, you say," Doc Hamilton said. "Saw it during the war." They chatted about Mr. Pettibone's leg. "He can leave any time. He needs lighter work when he's able."

"Travel is hard this time of the year," Sister Magdalena said. "I'll work something out."

"The sooner the better," Doc Hamilton said. "I'll be glad to see the ornery devil go."

Chapter 46
Solveig

Solveig served fish gravy for the third day in a row. Nels loitered in the cookshack, complained about poor hunting, drank coffee, and cast calf-eyes at Gertie. There were squirrels aplenty behind the woodshed. Even a mess of squirrels would taste better than fish.

Solveig placed a lamp in the window, and left Rosy and Gertie with the supper dishes. Solveig pulled the shawl over her face and hurried toward the barn, careful on the icy path. She breathed air free of cooking grease. Accordion music wafted from the bunkhouse.

She missed her life of solitude. A visit with her hens usually calmed her mind.

Thick clouds quelled any hope of northern lights. Here in the north woods, she had witnessed the undulating colors several times. They always reminded her of her Norway.

There had been no sign of Mr. Starkweather since before Christmas. Of course, the bull of the woods made sure the lumberjacks kept harvesting the pine. But what would happen if she ran out of food? Solveig put little confidence in the gambler. He and his cronies were up to no good as evidenced by the Latvian's dismissal because of Pettibone's bullying. She pulled her shawl with a snap. Pettibone had left camp more dead than alive.

Back in the old country, Old Petra, a crabby widow, had terrorized the children sent to buy her cheeses. Bestemor said that Petra was to be pitied because she had lost both husband

and baby daughter in a mudslide only a year after her wedding. Bestemor said troubles embittered some people. Solveig did not want to end her life in sour misery like Old Petra. Once Solveig had been a positive person who saw the best in everyone. She did not like the person she had turned out to be.

The hens perched on Barrister's legs as he stretched out in the straw with a book held to catch the lamplight. Her girls knew how to keep warm on such a cold day.

"Any cackleberries today?" Solveig said.

"Not today," Barrister said. "Short days hinder egg production."

He held up his book, and the hens scattered. Solveig strained to make out the title: *Animal Husbandry and Farm Management.* Barrister was always reading. Yesterday had been Chaucer and the day before had been a book about steam engines. Pokey said he had a trunk load of books with him.

"Are you going into farming?" Solveig said.

"Too much work for me. But I like animals."

"Farming is a lot of work," Solveig said. "But satisfying to have your own land."

A flood of memories washed over her. Coming to Rasmuss's farm after their wedding. Riding behind Old Bob across the prairies on Sunday afternoons. The grasshoppers and dry years. Her thoughts spiraled to Halvor and Britt living the high life without her. She was no more than a shadow, not even a real person in their eyes.

She bade good night and hurried back to her work.

It was the lowest she had felt in her whole life. What was the point of it all? Even if she saved the farm, she was too old to keep it going. Rasmuss was dead. She had no other children and no kin folk in America. Her life was slipping away.

These dismal thoughts surrounded her as she trudged through the crunchy snow. Her bunions throbbed. Her back ached. The flour was running low. The meat was gone. The eggs were used up. They had potatoes and lard, and a few bales of fish. She listened to the wind like the steady roar of the ocean overhead.

Queenie welcomed her at the door, meowing and rubbing against her legs. She gathered her into her arms and headed toward her room. The day had worn her down. Let it end. She was half-way there when a sudden blast of cold air blew in behind her. It was Pokey bringing in an arm-load of kitchen wood and a sloppy bucket of water.

"Shut the door," Solveig said, still holding the cat. "Born in a barn?"

Pokey mumbled an apology and dropped the wood into the box with a clatter while spattering dirty snow and chips across the clean floor. "I'm doing my job." He filled the water reservoir and hooked his thumb in the empty bucket handle. "You'd bitch if I didn't." He clumped outside, muttering low threats.

"Stutz," Solveig said. The poor boy looked half asleep. "Get the broom and clean up this mess before you go to bed."

Another blast of air as the door opened again.

"Shut the damn door!" Solveig said.

She turned to give Pokey a tongue lashing, and almost dropped the cat. Sister Magdalena stood in the doorway, swathed in shawls and blankets, covered with frost and a dusting of snow. She toted a huge bundle on her back and carried snowshoes under one arm.

"My goodness," Solveig said, embarrassed to have sworn in front of the nun. "You are the last person I expected. Come to the fire." She composed herself. "Rosy, fetch a quilt off my bunk. Stutz pull a chair by the stove. Gertie, fetch a cup of hot coffee, and pour a drop of medicine in it for the sister." The medicine was a bottle of whiskey kept for emergencies.

"It's a cold night." Sister Magdalena shivered. She stomped her feet and reached for a broom to clean up her mess. She staggered, clutching the wall for support.

"Never mind." Solveig took Sister Magdalena's pack and snow shoes. The poor woman was as heavy laden as a mule. She helped her to the chair by the stove and opened the oven door. "Put your feet in the oven."

Sister Magdalena's teeth chattered and white spots showed on her cheeks. Her eyebrows and lashes frosted. She warmed her hands on the tin cup, sipping the steaming coffee, as frost melted down her face, dripped from the hem of her habit, and pooled by her feet.

"Chilblains on your face," Solveig said. "You'd best undress and check yourself for frostbite."

Sister Magdalena hesitated, then looked at Stutz in embarrassment.

"Stutz, call it a night." Solveig directed Rosy to prop a chair in front of the cookshack door and to remove Sister Magdalena's shoes and stockings. The sister's feet blanched blue and cold. "Fetch warm water with vinegar." Solveig chafed the feet between her hands. Gertie flurried to comply. Rosy rubbed snow onto Sister Magdalena's cheeks while Gertie placed Sister's feet into the basin with a splash.

"No frostbite, thank God." Solveig said. "Put hot bricks into the top bunk, Rosy. Gertie, warm Sister's night clothes by the fire."

"Rosy?" Sister Magdalena said. "How did you get here?"

"No time," Solveig interrupted. "Explanations later."

Solveig added hot water to the basin, swirled it with her hands and added a little more. One had to be careful. Too much heat made a bad situation worse.

"The Lord takes care of his foolish children," Sister Magdalena whispered. Her voice sounded frozen, too. Nothing like the boisterous Sister Lumberjack. "I thought I was a goner." She lay aside the cup and took the hot food from Solveig's hands, trembling so that the fork banged on the tin plate.

"What happened?" Solveig said. "Why are you out in such weather?"

"There's typhoid in Duluth. I hitched a ride with the Weyerhaeuser spur," Sister Magdalena said. Her words jumbled. "The locomotive got stuck in a snowdrift. I helped shovel. I did not remember it to be so far across the lake."

"Typhoid? Not at the orphanage?" Rosy's voice shrilled. "Is Jimmy all right?"

"No typhoid at the orphanage." Sister Magdalena drained her cup. "They have quarantined the waterfront. Mother Superior sent me away as a precaution."

"You passed Skunk Hollow," Rosy said. "Clarence wouldn't turn you out in this weather."

"I should have stopped," Sister Magdalena said with a weak smile. "Guess I was more afraid of Mother Superior than of losing my way. It got dark so fast. I wandered in circles until I saw a light in your window."

"Foolish," Solveig said. "You could have frozen to death."

"I know, I know," Sister Lumberjack said with a chuckle. "Foolishness is my besetting sin. Weyerhaeuser's warned me that I was taking a chance." She took Solveig's hand and held it tight. "I kept thinking of you, my friend. I like being here with you."

Gertie took Sister Magdalena's arm and helped her toward the back room.

"Look what I brought," Sister Magdalena said. "Mail."

"I'll send it out to the bunk house in the morning," Solveig said. Her mind was on the sleeping arrangements. Rosy and Sister Magdalena must share the top bunk.

Sister Magdalena half-covered a yawn, and dropped to her knees by her bed. That was a Catholic for you. Gallivanting in the wilderness, almost freezing to death, and then kneeling on the cold floor risking pneumonia.

"Two letters for you and one for Gertie," Sister Magdalena said.

One carried Halvor's scrawling penmanship. Maybe he had changed his mind. Solveig held it up to the lamp. Britta's father had been called to a church in Bismarck. Halvor and Britta were moving to North Dakota with them. They hoped to be settled by New Years. Someone in the new parish promised a job. Solveig was welcome to join them in Bismarck. She would be a grandmother in mid-summer.

The words fell like blows. Spoiled Britta had babies, while Solveig had been denied. It wasn't fair. Solveig saw through their polite invitation. Britta's folks would be the favorite grandparents, while Solveig would be an outsider, an embarrassment to the family, someone who did not know city manners. Awkward and gawky and in the way. Thrown aside like an egg shell sucked dry.

"To hell you say," she said aloud.

Her hands fumbled with the second letter. Something must be wrong with the team for Gunnar to write. Instead, he gave glowing praise and offered to buy them outright. *I can see a future working these animals.* He asked if she had a price in mind.

Ridiculous. She needed her team. How else would she put in a crop? But she could not put in a crop. There was no money for seed. No way to keep the team unless she rented them out again next winter. A vicious circle.

"Damn it," she whispered. "Damn it to hell."

Solveig shoved Queenie into the kitchen and slammed the door. Sister Magdalena climbed into the upper bunk without a word. Solveig blew out the lamp, and climbed into bed beside Gertie.

She had never expected things to go so wrong. Halvor moving to Bismarck? Gunnar wanting the team? What would Rasmuss say? She turned on her side, pulling the quilts over her back. She concentrated instead on her responsibilities. Larder running low. Starkweather gone with no promise of coming back. Half frozen nun sleeping on the upper bunk with a fugitive whore. Pregnant Irish widow sharing her bed. Exhaustion heavied Solveig's eyelids, and the wind lamented around the eaves.

The next morning, Solveig was shaken awake by Sister Magdalena climbing down from her bunk. The construction at Starkweather Timber was not the sturdiest.

"I'd like to get the mail to the jacks before they head out to the cut," Sister Magdalena said. She was back to her usual, energetic self. "Should I take it to the bunk house?"

"What would your Mother Superior say about you and those half-naked men?"

"Their mail will be like Christmas," Sister Magdalena said with a laugh. "Perhaps Stutz could bring it out."

Solveig fired the stove, put the coffee on to boil, mixed flapjack batter, and sliced the last of the side pork. The wake-up horn brought the younger women. Stutz trotted out to the bunk house with the mail.

"Did you get bad news?" Sister Magdalena cranked the coffee grinder, pausing to add more beans. "I heard your response."

Solveig could have crawled under the floor boards. She was making Lutherans look bad.

Chapter 47
Nels

A layer of frost prevented Nels from seeing out the window. He scraped with the back of his thumbnail, blew on the glass, and scraped again. Too dark to see a thing. Bitter cold penetrated the building and thickened his blood. He dressed by the glowing, red stove.

"Kokott, hand out the mail," Paulson said.

"Hell no. Won't have nothing to do with mail," Pokey said. "All that pissing and moaning? No sir. Jacks worse than a bunch of women when it comes to mail."

In the end, Sully got the job. Pokey was right. The ones with mail gloated over those without. Letters reminded the jacks of home and left them gloomy and cantankerous. Lots of pissing and moaning.

"Nels Jensen," Sully called out.

Nels had been daydreaming about a glass of whiskey and did not pay attention. Sully called his name again.

"Do you want them or not?" Sully threw two letters on Nels's bunk. "I do not have time to hand deliver mail to everyone.

No one knew where he was. Who could be sending mail?

The first listed Starkweather Timber as a return address. Nels's mouth turned dry and he ripped into it with shaking hands. Starkweather must have found another copy of the ledger page.

Instead, it held a terse note in Mr. Starkweather's elaborate script. Nels was to collect supplies at the Aitkin general store. Mrs. Rognaldson was to provide a detailed list, and Nels was to purchase only those items. Credit was pre-arranged. Nels should take the largest wagon, the draft team, and stay overnight at the boarding house.

Nels's spirits soared. A chance to leave this miserable place. Horses. A real bed and a hot bath. An opportunity for a drink if he could borrow some money. He licked dry lips.

The second letter was from the North Dakota District Court.

It is with great satisfaction that I report a conviction of Mr. Myron Pinchpenny and the Dirty Dog Saloon for fraud and theft. Mr. Pinchpenny has been remanded to the county jail for a period of one year. The Dirty Dog Saloon is ordered to repay what was stolen or face forfeiture. Enclosed is a bank draft for $50. The saloon will pay an equal sum annually until the debt is paid in full. Justice served by the North Dakota judiciary.

Fifty dollars. A whoop brought Yuma running to see what was wrong. Nels pumped his fist into the air and danced a jig around the bunkhouse, nearly knocking Pokey off his pins. God bless the great state of North Dakota. God bless the depot man who made him leave a statement of complaint. He read the letter again and ran the numbers in his head. It would take years to pay off the entire amount. He had lost one hundred and eighty-nine dollars. A fortune.

"Hey Yuma," Nels said. "Know anything about the law?"

"Hell, ya. Enough not to break it." Yuma pulled on a second pair of wool britches. "What else is there to know?"

Ten-Day pushed closer, reading over Nels's shoulder.

"Ask Barrister," Ten-Day said. "He used to be a lawyer."

Nels found Barrister sitting bare-assed on a pole stretched over the latrine. He could hardly expect legal advice from someone with a frozen hinder. Nels handed Barrister the letter as soon as he finished.

"Amazing," Barrister said. "Poor men rarely find vindication in courts of law."

"Will I ever get the rest of it?" Nels explained his situation in low tones. He did not want
    everyone knowing how he had been bamboozled.

"Unlikely," Barrister said. "If I owned the saloon, I would pack up and start over out west. Cheaper than paying it off."

Nels sighed. But fifty dollars was nothing to sneeze at.

"Here's your chance to go west," Barrister said. "I have been reading *The Prairie Traveler* by Randolph B. Marcy. It lists the best routes and advice for homesteading. Fifty dollars is enough for a start up."

On the way to the cookshack, Nels contemplated Barrister's advice. Yuma's brother nearly starved homesteading in the Nebraska Sandhills. Grasshoppers, drought, and poor prices had ruined him. A hell of a gamble.

"That's the government for you," Yuma had said, "Gives something for nothing that costs everything in the end."

Nels had more pressing matters on his mind. He would leave for Aitkin the next morning. A long day on the trail, one night in town, and another long day to return. He would find a bank in Aitkin for his windfall, and decide later how to spend it.

"Sister Lumberjack is back," Pokey said.

Life was going his way for a change. Sister Lumberjack could take care of Rosy. His load felt lighter already.

At breakfast, Sister Lumberjack lined a row of coins by his plate. It was enough for a beer in Aitkin without cashing his draft. Ma slammed pans and crockery without as much as a glance toward the jacks. She would cheer up to learn about the coming supplies.

But when he tried to talk to Ma after breakfast, she chewed his ass about the empty larder. Ma used to be a sweet old lady, tough as nails, but sweet tempered. Starkweather Timber had turned her into a mean, old crow.

Nels stomped out of the cookshack without telling her about Starkweather's letter. Let the old biddy stew a while. He did not deserve to be treated like a child. He had helped her find a job, after all. She should be grateful.

The sun glared off the snow. Not a breath of wind. Nels strapped on snowshoes and hiked out to the cut to tell Paulson about needing a team and sleigh.

"Like hell you will," Paulson said when Nels showed him the letter from Starkweather.

"From the boss's mouth," Nels said. "I take the wagon and team or the jacks won't eat."

"Dammit." Paulson threw his hat on the ground and stomped on it.

"Not my fault," Nels said.

"Starkweather will have my hide if we get behind." Paulson said. "My job on the line."

A tree fell to the west of them with a crashing roar. Nels startled.

Paulson jammed his hat over his bald head. The hat covered with bits of sawdust and pine needles. He tucked his long beard into his collar like a scarf. "What's a man to do?"

Nels would have negotiated use of Weyerhaeuser's spur if he were the boss, or at least purchased supplies before the season started. A haywire outfit. Nels had not realized he had spoken out loud until Paulson muttered agreement.

The push hurried off to his duties leaving Nels to marvel at his good fortune. He was going to town and driving horses. He would take his sweet time and get paid for it. Sounded like heaven.

He snowshoed out to Gilbert's trap line with a partial sack of oats pilfered from the barn. He found the Indian with six muskrats tied together with rope. Their yellow teeth protruded and they smelled rank. Nels scratched his head. Ma would bitch at how little meat was on a muskrat. She would bitch if she were the queen of England. Nels made the trade, and toted the frozen rats back to the cookshack. If he were lucky, he could sneak a visit with Gertie.

He imagined buying Gertie a present while he was in town, exactly what, he could not recall, but something so wonderful that she would look at him, call him by name, and smile. The daydream stayed with him as he dressed the game in the woodshed. The meat stank like old swamp. He tossed the pelts aside and hurried inside where he slapped the meat on Ma's work table.

"Meat," he said, unable to keep the gloating from his voice.

Ma scrutinized the game with a sniff. "We're eating rats now?"

"Meat is meat," Nels said. "Folks ate them all the time in the old days and were glad to get them."

"What do you know about the old days?" Solveig said. "It was the skins were valuable, not the meat." She turned to the stove and banged pots and pans, barking orders at Gertie and Rosy. Stutz cowered out of her way. "The hides were called Minnesota money. Rat meat was only for starving folks." She picked up a cleaver and pointed it at him. "Like we are starving now with your poor showing. At least Pettibone brought in game."

Nels backed away as if she had struck him. She was to blame for not giving him trade goods.

Ma hacked the stringy carcass, sending splatters over her apron and face. Nels stood there, not knowing what to do.

"I got a letter from the brains of the outfit," Nels said. "Told me to collect supplies in Aitkin. You are to send a list of what you need."

"When?" Solveig turned a quick eye toward him. "What kind of letter? Why didn't you say something?"

"Tried to tell you this morning. You were too busy insulting my character," Nels said. "I'm leaving in the morning."

Ma ordered Gertie to finish with the meat, and pulled an old Starkweather advert from the wood box. She started scribbling.

"I'll ride along if I may," Sister Lumberjack said in a low voice. Nels had not noticed her nearby. "I've business in Aitkin."

"What will we eat while you're gone?" Ma said. "These rats won't make a meal."

She would kick if she were being hung with a new rope. No wonder her son deserted her.

Gertie lifted a kettle off the stove and the effort pulled taught her apron. Nels gaped. She was with child. Why hadn't he noticed before? His good luck of the morning drained away at the reality. Marrying her meant raising another man's child. His mind whirled.

"It's time for prayer," Sister Lumberjack said. "I will petition God for meat." She hefted herself to her feet. "Do not worry, Mr. Jensen. It is our Father's good pleasure to bless His children."

Sister Lumberjack left the room. Ma glared thunderclouds and refused the younger women even a minute for conversation. Ma guarded them like a watch dog.

Nels stormed out of the cookshack in disgust. He met Pokey on the path to the bunkhouse. Overhead the ch-ch-ch rattle of a whiskey jack's warning.

"Where have you been?" Pokey leaned on the side of the woodshed to catch his breath. "Ox fell and broke a leg. Fresh meat laying in the woods."

Nels felt a grin crack his face. Sister Lumberjack's prayers answered, and in a hurry. An ox would keep Ma happy for a week. He hurried to the barn and asked Barrister's help in fetching the animal.

"It's bad luck," Barrister said once they were out on the cut. "The blacksmith fastened the cleat to this hoof all wrong. Shoddy work, if I ever saw it."

Nels focused instead on the miracle of answered prayer. Why hadn't he learned about it in Confirmation? Ask, and God gave you what you wanted. Nels wanted a place of his own with Gertie by his side. He wanted her baby to disappear. He wanted cash in hand to send for his parents before they were too old to travel.

They winched the ox to a tree limb and gutted it out. Crows pecked the bloody entrails scattered across the white snow. "Mind the heart and liver," Barrister said. "And brains, tongue, and kidneys. Do not forget the cheeks and tail." They piled the organs onto a sledge and hefted haunches of meat on top. Together they dragged the heavy sledge out of the woods, going around stumps and fallen trees. Barrister complained the whole time. "It was a gentle ox. A waste."

Sister Lumberjack had not named her Aitkin business. Nels did not care what she did. He hoped she did not preach or yammer about his drinking. He only wanted her to pray.

Chapter 48
Sister Magdalena

During the previous night, Sister Magdalena had thought she heard Solveig crying. The next day, the air crackled with tension. The mother always set the tone in the household, whether cook or prioress. Sister Magdalena had only to watch Stutz and the girls dodging out of Solveig's way to know something was wrong.

The letters held bad news. Why else would Solveig curse after reading them?

Sister Magdalena pondered ways to ease Solveig's burden. She carried out the slops, swept the floors, and set the tables for supper. Gertie sliced bread as Rosy loaded the swingdingle.

Solveig's face drooped haggard and gray. She limped toward the stove.

"Why don't you put your feet up for a spell?" Sister Magdalena said. "You can boss from your chair."

Solveig hesitated, dropped to a bench, and slipped out of her shoes. She propped her feet on the wood box. Sister Magdalena poured coffee as Pokey clattered wood in the wood box.

"Sugar?" Sister Magdalena said.

"Cream," Solveig said with a laugh. "And lemon cake with a dish of strawberries."

"Too bad you didn't bring a cow along with your chickens," Sister Magdalena said.

Pokey collected the swingdingle. The kitchen relaxed. Gertie pressed a hand to her back and said that she needed to rest for a few minutes. Rosy followed Gertie to the back room, jabbering all the way. That girl could talk the hind leg off a mule. Stutz dragged empty buckets outside for water.

"Tell me about your letters," Sister Magdalena said once she and Solveig were alone. "I fear you've had bad news."

The Gabriel called the men to the swingdingle. The cessation of axes and saws dropped a layer of silence over Starkweather Timber.

Solveig twirled the cup on the table. "Someone offered to buy my horses," Solveig said. "A young man I know."

"You dislike the man?" Sister Magdalena said.

"No, nothing like that," Solveig said. "My godson." She explained that he worked and rented out the team at Gull River Timber. "I cannot sell them. I need horses for my crops."

A blue jay scolded outside the window. The sound of Gertie's voice in the back room.

"But your son left," Sister Magdalena said.

"So what?" Solveig said. "The horses are mine."

"Of course, they belong to you." Sister Magdalena had touched a sore spot. Once again, she tasted foot in her mouth. "But you can't farm alone."

Solveig drained the cup and set it back on the table with a bang. Her eyes flashed and her chin tilted up. Small lines showed around pursed lips. "I'll do as I please."

Solveig limped to the stove in her stocking feet and stirred the stew. "Muskrat stew. I never dreamed of eating such."

"And the second letter?" Sister Magdalena might as well go all the way.

"From my son." Solveig said. She turned to the stew and stirred again. Sister Magdalena dared not prod further.

"Think I'll go out and see my girls." Solveig put her shoes on. "I need air."

"Take your time," Sister Magdalena said. "I'll hold the fort while you're gone."

Sister Lucy knew how to draw someone out, but Sister Magdalena did not. Alone in the kitchen, Sister Magdalena ground coffee beans as she prayed the rosary. She mentally fingered the beads with every turn of the crank, praying for whatever was bothering Solveig. She paused when Pokey returned with the swingdingle.

He plopped down on a bench nearest the stove and groaned, tramping wet snow over the newly swept floor. His whiskers frosted and he wiped his nose on his sleeve. "Cold to my bones," he said. "This winter will never end."

Sister Magdalena fixed his dinner plate and poured his coffee. She would finish the grinding, a never-ending chore, and slice more bread.

"Have you been in this line of work long?" she said as she returned to the grinder.

"Since the War of Rebellion," Pokey said. "Lied about my age and joined up when I was fourteen. Marched with Sherman and then followed him west to the Injun wars."

He spooned stew into his mouth and washed it down with coffee. "I lost my stomach for killing, and took up lumberjacking along the Rum River. Kept at it."

She had always thought him much older and was surprised that he was a few years younger than Solveig. Both were too old for the grueling, never-ending work. Sister Magdalena inhaled the fragrance of freshly ground coffee.

"Don't worry none about old Pokey," he said. A sly look crossed his face. "I have always got a place to live. Me and Mr. Starkweather got us an understanding."

Gertie and Rosy came out of their room and emptied the swingdingle. The clank of tinware drowned further conversation.

"I need a list for Nels," Solveig said with an apologetic smile when she returned to the cookshack. Sister Magdalena and everyone else relaxed at the smile. Bare cupboards and a crew of hungry men would make anyone nervous, and yet there was something more going on. Something with Solveig's son. "I'm heading to the root cellar to take inventory."

Solveig wrapped again in her shawl and headed out the door.

"Do you need help? "Sister Magdalena said.

Solveig nodded. Together they pulled the sledge over the icy tracks.

A downy woodpecker drummed on a dead tree next to the cookshack. Overhead the wind whispered in the treetops. The women followed the winding path to the base of the hillside. Solveig opened the lock. They stooped low to enter the root cellar. The smell of earth and fish met them.

The stores had vanished since Sister Magdalena's last visit. Bins of potatoes and bales of fish stacked to one side, but empty boxes marked prunes, dried apples, and beans filled the other. An empty molasses keg lay on its side next to a single flour barrel. Fresh haunches of the downed ox hung from the rafters.

"It's so empty," Sister Magdalena said.

"They're hungry," Solveig said. "Starkweather took off without a word."

"He's slippery," Sister Magdalena said.

"Never seen anything like Starkweather Timber," Solveig said. "Topsy- turvy in every direction."

They loaded what little they found, and Sister Magdalena pulled it back to the cookshack. It was mid-afternoon and the sounds of crashing timber, sawing, and chopping filled the air.

"Solveig," Sister Magdalena said. "I apologize for being nosy. Your mail is none of my business."

Solveig nodded. Sister Magdalena pressed a bit more.

"Families are touchy," Sister Magdalena said. "You should be a fly on the wall at our community sometimes. Put two women in the kitchen, and you have two dogs with one bone."

"You're right," Solveig said as they put away the supplies. "Families are difficult."

It was obvious that her friend did not want to talk about it. Sister Magdalena longed to be that peacemaker who helped people find their way on life's journey. She yearned to be wise, holy, and helpful. Instead, she stumbled along, making things worse rather than better. It seemed her spiritual gifts were stomping rats and toting dry goods.

Somehow, God came through despite her failings. Tomorrow, she would travel with Nels to collect Jacob Pettibone. Nels would not like it. Then a happy thought entered her weary mind. Supplies meant that Mr. Starkweather had money to pay his bills. Her bill. She would fetch Mr. Pettibone home, collect the money from Mr. Starkweather, and return to Duluth. Perhaps she might arrange a job for Rosy at the orphanage to be nearer her son. It might be possible if Rosy made a firm resolve to amend her ways.

Chapter 49
Solveig

Nothing to cry about, but tears sent Solveig fleeing to the backhouse before she made a fool of herself. Safe behind the closed door, Solveig bawled and sniffed until she regained control.

It was not about the supplies, though she had worried sick about the empty larder. Halvor's letter cracked Solveig's shell as if she were Gumbri's egg.

She gathered her composure and wiped her eyes. She returned to her work, chopping onions to hide the tears that refused to stop. Sister Magdalena was right. Family relationships were fragile. To think Halvor would treat her so unfairly, after all she had done for him. She had given him her life. But a grandchild. The tears flowed. Solveig chopped more onions.

She might send a letter with Nels to post in town. What would she say to Halvor? Go to hell? Good luck? But a grandchild. A baby to rock to sleep with Norwegian lullabies. A little girl to help in the strawberry patch, or a boy to fetch the cows. Britta and Halvor would not change, Solveig saw that now. She must bend or lose her family forever.

Bile rose in the back of her mouth, and the tears pressed again.

Solveig had learned from an early age to keep her feelings to herself lest she burden others. For the first time in her life, she felt unable to contain them. Rasmuss's death, Halvor's marriage, the unpaid note, and the realization that she could no longer manage on her own, left her undone. A thread had come loose. Her life was unraveling and her tears would not stop.

She returned to the root cellar on the pretense of finishing the list for Nels. She wanted to be alone, but the nun followed like a black and white dog, eager to please, and sticking her nose where it did not belong.

"Do you want me to bring the sledge?" Sister Lumberjack said.

"Might as well. I am finishing my list for Nels." Solveig did not encourage conversation. She stoked her anger against Halvor. The anger kept her tears away.

A nuthatch pounded for bugs in a pine. A pair of downy woodpeckers flashed red breasts from a hollow log. Above them the wind played its harp in the treetops. The air felt more like spring than winter. A nearby hillside that had been a glory of white pines just the week before, stood naked and ruined. The world was going to hell.

"Looks like good traveling weather," Sister Magdalena said.

"It's going to storm," Solveig said. It took a farm woman to tell the weather. "Feel it in my bunions."

"Really?" Sister Magdalena craned her neck upward, catching her veil on the brush along the trail. It pulled her coif askew and brought a deep guffaw from the nun. "I'm falling apart."

It was ridiculous to wear such headgear, anyway. Popish foolery. Everything about Sister Magdalena was excessive from her size to her dress to her incessant prayers. Solveig swiped at her eyes, and mumbled a feeble excuse about a cinder.

She opened the lock and lit the lamp inside the door with a match from her apron pocket. The light cast shadows across the earthen room. Coffee beans rattled in a near- empty keg. Solveig pointed her pencil stub at a barrel of salt pork and motioned for the sister to load it on the sledge along with the molasses. She added item after item to the list. More prunes and dried apples. More salt and flour. Sides of beef. Salt pork. Bacon and ham. More carrots and rutabagas. She figured enough potatoes to last until the end of the season, but how could she know? Too many supplies would be a waste. Too few meant disaster. Another two months of logging if all went well.

Mr. Starkweather would not be happy if she guessed wrong.

Solveig slumped down on a keg of vinegar. She was at the end of her strength. She covered her face with her apron.

Sister dropped to her knees beside her. Leave it to a Catholic to kneel in the dirt wearing a white apron. A wave of embarrassment swept over Solveig. She cleared her throat and got to her feet. There was no time for self-pity.

"Tell me," Sister Magdalena said. "You are so upset. It must be something terrible to bring such distress."

Solveig did not want to talk about it. Instead, she wept. She told Sister Magdalena about the letter, how Halvor chose Britta's parents over her, and about Halvor's betrayal of the promise he made to his father on his deathbed. She blurted out the worry over the mortgage and Gunnar's offer to buy the team.

"I can't do it," she said. "I'm too old to manage alone."

The earthen walls absorbed the words and emotions. They sat in silence. Finally, Sister Magdalena said, "No wonder you're mad. I would like to give Halvor a piece of my mind."

"It's Britta's fault."

"He is responsible for his own decisions. You raised him to be independent," Sister said. "Looks like you've done a good job."

"That I did," Solveig said with a laugh. "He has a mind of his own."

"He's a fledgling flown the nest, bound to make mistakes along the way."

"I suppose." Solveig blew her nose in a handkerchief from her apron pocket.

"Then bid him God speed and let him go with your blessing," Sister Magdalena said. "His dreams are not yours. Each must find his own journey to God."

What would a nun know about the grief of losing a son? It was easier without family entanglements.

"The Blessed Mother pondered all things in her heart," Sister said. "I've asked her to intercede for you."

A choking sensation cut off Solveig's response. She should correct the nun, and declare it superstition to call on Mary for intercession. She had needed a mother for so long. She doubted Mary heard Sister Magdalena's plea, but if she did…

A prayer from childhood flitted through Solveig's mind. Her grandmother's voice came from a place of deep memory. Solveig repeated the phrase. *"Gud gi oss din fred.* God, give us your peace."

"Amen," Sister Magdalena said. "It helps to let go."

Back at the cookshack, Solveig became overwhelmed by exhaustion. "I am not feeling well. I am going to rest my eyes for a bit." She was as bad as Irish. She had nothing left to give.

"Don't worry," Sister Magdalena said. "I'll help with supper."

Solveig lay in her bunk, too agitated to sleep. Halvor had broken his promise and her heart. Letting go of her anger toward him was only part of the problem. Britta would never allow Solveig to have a relationship with either her son or grandchild. Solveig knew it deep in her bones. A letter would not fix it. Her bunions throbbed. Her head ached. She lay abed pondering where her life had gone wrong.

To hell with them. To hell with everything.

She got up and wrote a note to Gunnar. She need not send it if she changed her mind by morning. Then she climbed back into bed. She drifted to a fitful sleep. In her dreams, Rasmuss came singing as he had sung to her so many times before. His voice off pitch, the melody a little different every time he sang the words from the Ibsen play. His brown eyes were sweeter than the words or music. She woke to the bang of pots and pans beyond the flimsy walls.

"Oh Rasmuss," she said. "Of course. Why didn't I think of it?"

She grabbed paper and pencil and scribbled a letter. She did not need to say anything except the words of his father's song.

Maybe both the winter and spring will pass and next summer, too, and the whole of the year—but there will come one day, that I know full well, and I will await thee, as I promised of old.

God strengthen thee wherever in the world you go. God gladden thee, if at his footstool thou stand. Here will I await thee till thou come again and if thou wait up yonder, then there will we meet again.

She signed her name with a flourish. Halvor would remember. If he had a heart, he would remember.

Chapter 50
Nels

The horses stomped and strained toward the men trudging to the cut. It was a mild morning with a soft edge in the air. Nels felt as eager as the team. No sign of Sister Lumberjack.

"These horses would rather work with their fellows than go off traipsing with you," Barrister said with a grin. He patted their noses and fed them stubs of carrots.

"Wally. Willy. Whoa now." Nels tossed a bedroll and lap robe into the wagon. He added a sack of oats, a rope, a lantern, and a hammer. At the last minute he packed the rifle. Not that bears were out of hibernation, but one had to be watchful of wolves.

"Be careful, now. I mistrust a January thaw," Barrister said. "And I mistrust a jack around saloons." He locked eyes until Nels looked away. "Careful, my friend. I heard about your windfall. I would stay away from those establishments." He kissed both horses on their noses and straightened the harness. "Think about it, my friend."

Nels drew back with a start. It was no one's business how he chose to spend his money. He was about to say as much when Sister Lumberjack and Ma interrupted their conversation. Ma carried a lunch basket and water jug.

"My bunions predict a storm," Ma said.

Nels eyed the skies. "We'll hurry."

"Look." Sister Lumberjack pointed to the horses still straining toward the cut. "Very Benedictine of the horses to love their work." She looked even fatter in all the layers wrapped around her. "Change their names to Benedict and Bernard."

Nels snorted. Wally and Willy were a matched team trained to their names. Only a woman would think of changing names in mid-stream. The trip had not started and he was already irritated.

Religious do-gooders were always sticking their noses into other people's business. Look at Rosy. Sister Lumberjack filled Rosy's head with impossible dreams of reuniting with her child. Everyone knew the boy was better off without a mother who made a living by lying on her back. Nels regretted bringing her to Starkweather Timber in the first place.

Sister Lumberjack hoisted herself into the seat with irritating cheerfulness. Barrister waved and returned to the barn. Ma limped toward the cookshack. Nels tried to recover yesterday's happiness. He carried money in his pockets. He was getting paid to drive a magnificent team. He licked dry lips. He turned his thoughts to Gertie.

Of course, men married widows with children all the time. But how could he love another man's son? A flurry of juncos trilled. Nels slapped the lines and the team jolted forward. He crossed Stink Lake, followed a trail past the dam, and turned back onto the frozen river.

"I'll spell you driving," Sister Lumberjack said. "I learned horses at home."

Nels grunted. He was responsible, after all, and had no confidence in her abilities. She jabbered about the weather and her brothers. Nels did not feel like talking. Sister Lumberjack shrugged her shoulders and picked up her rosary.

It was his opportunity to ask for prayer, but he could not form the words. He wanted to speak of his desire for liquor, and how he feared that he would end up like old Pokey—without a pot to piss in and no place to call home. Silly to worry about it. He could handle his liquor. He was not as bad as others.

"She's going to have a baby," Nels blurted out. It was an unheard of topic to discuss with another woman, and a nun at that, but safer than talking about his drinking. "Gertie is."

"I know," Sister Lumberjack said. "She's earning money to go home to her mother in Ireland before the baby comes."

Nels gasped. No doubt, she was right about Gertie, but if Gertie returned to Ireland, there was no hope for them to marry.

"Don't be upset," Sister Lumberjack said. "She's doing what's best for her child."

Nels slapped the lines. The team pulled harder. "The ox, yesterday," he said. "You prayed, and the ox went down."

"We serve a merciful God," Sister Lumberjack said.

"I need many things," Nels said. "Perhaps you could ask God for me."

Sister Lumberjack looked straight ahead as if trying to find an answer. Maybe she was praying. Hope sparked in his chest.

"Do you think to bring a list to God like Solveig sends to the store?" Her headgear fluttered in the wind. "We do not command God. He commands us."

He should have known it was too good to be true. God did not care about him. No one did.

"You want me to pray that Gertie will marry you?" she said.

Nels nodded.

"And that you'll get rich and successful."

Nels squirmed. He did not want to discuss it with Sister Lumberjack or anyone else. He wanted to confide in a bottle of good whiskey.

"I'll tell you something, Nels." Sister Lumberjack pointed a finger in his direction. "I would never pray that Gertie would marry you. No woman in her right mind marries a drinking man."

Nels restrained his tongue, though he wanted to throttle her. It was true. He had nothing to offer but a strong back and a loving heart. He would not drink once they were wed.

"I'll pray for you," she said. "Pray that you turn your life over to God and become the man any woman would be proud to marry."

He had heard enough of her bullshit. "You're a meddlesome old maid."

Sister Lumberjack burst into laughter. Her chortles startled the horses. Nels pulled back on the lines. Sister Lumberjack laughed harder, leaning forward, and holding her sides. Her face a startling red against the white of her wimple.

"You're right, my friend," she said, wiping her eyes and blowing her nose. "I know nothing about marriage or romance. Look at me. What man would want a six-foot penguin?"

"It's not funny," Nels said. The woman had lost her mind. Starkweather Timber had pushed her into lunacy.

"I'm the bride of Christ, hardly an old maid," she said. "As married as any woman, I assure you."

He did not know what that meant. He did not want to know. He hunched down into his shoulders and flicked the lines.

They traveled in silence until they came to the Mississippi River. It looked safe enough. Wagon ruts crossed the river in two places. Nels hoisted his ax over his shoulder and walked onto the river to make sure. He chopped into the ice a few places near shore to make sure it would hold the horses and wagon. Safe enough, though he felt the movement of water beneath the ice. Like his life, he realized with a start. The surface solid, but underneath a threatening current of bad luck and poor decisions.

"Aren't you going to go all the way across?" Sister Lumberjack said. "It might be rotten in the middle."

Damn her big nose stuck in his business. They did not have time to lollygag. The bank draft burned in his pocket. The saloon waited on the other side.

"Check for yourself, if you're so worried," he said.

She hoisted her skirts and climbed down the bank onto the ice, toting the ax over her shoulder like a lumberjack. She chopped a hole the middle of the river, walked to the opposite shore and waved him across. He told her it was adequate.

As they neared Aitkin, Sister Lumberjack's chatter faded to silence.

The team pulled like a well-oiled locomotive. Someday he would own horses. He would build a cabin for Gertie. The thought of her leaving America wrenched him from his dream.

"How much farther?" Sister Lumberjack said. "The wind has shifted to the north."

"We'll get there when we get there," Nels said with a growl. He licked his lips in anticipation. A night away from the crowded bunkhouse. A room to himself. A bath. A drink.

"Pokey told me about your money," Sister Lumberjack said.

Blabbermouths. He mumbled a reply.

"I worry," Sister Lumberjack said. "Don't lose it again."

"I'm opening a bank account," he said.

"Banks won't be open when we get there," she said. "I'll hold it for safe keeping."

She was reliable, but he imagined the slippery burn in his throat, the escape, the release. That giddy feeling as sensibilities changed to senselessness. Maybe he would have a woman. Most saloons had them.

"Make no occasion for the flesh," she said. "It is what I do with cakes, at least most of the time. Gluttony is another intemperance."

Cakes and whiskey were nothing alike. A cake did not have you by the short hairs. A cake did not make a nice girl like Gertie look somewhere else for a husband.

Sister Lumberjack had no business telling him what to do, and he told her so.

She acted as if she would take him to task over the issue, but instead settled in sullen silence. A dismal fog drifted over the river bed. An eagle screeched from a tall pine.

"You must cooperate with God to receive His help."

The lights of Aitkin showed through the gloom. Finally.

Chapter 51
Sister Magdalena

"Give this to the storekeeper," Nels said. "I'll pick up the order in the morning."

Sister Magdalena stood in front of the store and watched Nels drive off. He did not look back to make sure that she had lodging for the night, and made no effort to discuss the order with the storekeeper, as was his responsibility.

A bitter wind prompted Sister Magdalena to thank God for the Popescu's ongoing hospitality instead of having critical thoughts about her companion. Mrs. Popescu opened the door with candle in hand when Sister Magdalena knocked.

"Sister." She raised the candle for a better look. "Come in."

"Sorry to bother you," Sister Magdalena said. A faint odor of cooked cabbage filtered from the rear of the store. "I have brought Starkweather's order. We will head back in the morning."

"Tomorrow morning?" she said. "Oh my. I'll fetch Ivo."

She returned with her husband in tow. He wiped gory hands on his apron.

"Won't have the order ready for another day, and only if all goes well," he said. "Nothing but trouble this time of year. I've hired a boy, but it's a job to butcher two dozen hogs."

The storekeeper's face lined with fatigue. It was past supper time. Sister Magdalena glimpsed the cot in the back room and imagined hot soup and soft pillows. The wind rattled the shutters.

Sister Magdalena glanced out the window. It was not her responsibility to be concerned about Starkweather's order. She thought of fetching Nels, but did not have the stomach for it.

"I know how it's done." She hoped she looked more enthusiastic than she felt. "Butchering will go faster if we work together."

He looked at her with skepticism. "You're not dressed for it."

He was right. She looked down at her white scapular. Butchering was dirty work. She hesitated. The man was about her size. No one would ever know.

"Could I borrow some old clothes?" she said.

Mrs. Popescu looked askance, but fetched a pair of her husband's trousers, a chambray shirt, and a ragged sweater. Sister Magdalena had worn men's clothing at home during the harvest lest her skirts tangle in the threshing equipment, but it still felt strange.

"I keep a supply of used clothing in the back," Mrs. Popescu said. "People trade all kinds of things for provisions if they get hard up." She bustled back to her work. "You'd be surprised at the stories I could tell," she said over her shoulder.

Sister Magdalena slipped into the trousers and tucked the hems into rubber boots several sizes too large. The shirt buttons did not fasten around her chest. Sister Magdalena covered the gap with a canvas apron that smelled funny. She twisted an old towel around her head and pinned it tight. A denim coat stiff with dried blood came last. Sister Lucy would be scandalized, but even a nun must be practical. A habit was not convenient for catching hogs.

Before she left the small closet where she had changed, Sister Magdalena knelt and crossed herself. *God, come to my assistance.* It was going to be a long night.

Mrs. Popescu brought a cup of soup and a letter. "I almost forgot," she said. "Mail waiting for you."

Sister Magdalena's hands trembled as she opened the single page. Mother Superior shared the good news that the epidemic was over. She credited the prompt quarantine and the mercy of God. It was safe to return after she collected the money from Mr. Starkweather.

Sister Magdalena tucked the letter in a pocket with a prayer of thanks. She drank the broth. She needed her strength. Nels should be here and she should be heading to bed. It was his responsibility, not hers.

The slaughter took place in a fenced area behind the store. A huge iron cauldron simmered over a fire. The smoke from the fire blew into their faces. Johnny, the hired boy, scraped a hog on a table in an old shed by lantern light. Empty barrels lined the fence where hogs squealed and rooted in the snow. Ropes hung from a tree limb next to the pen.

Mr. Popescu tucked a pistol behind his back and lured a pig with a bowl of milk. "Here piggy, piggy," he said.

The pigs rushed toward the sound of his voice. Mr. Popescu opened the gate only a crack, allowing a single hog to the dish. When the pig pushed his snout into the milk, Mr. Popescu held the gun to its head and fired. The hog dropped to the ground in a gory spray of blood and bone. The other hogs squealed and scattered to the far side of the pen.

Sister Magdalena took a breath. She concentrated on pork roast and chops. She and Mr. Popescu dragged the animal to the tree and hoisted it with ropes around its back legs. Mr. Popescu slashed its throat with a butcher knife and propped an empty keg to collect the blood.

"Want the blood or intestines?" Mr. Popescu said. "Makes good sausage."

Sister Magdalena shook her head. No time for sausage making at the logging camp.

"Josue will be glad to get it." Mr. Popescu smacked his lips. "Folks are wild for it."

Mr. Popescu called out to Johnny as the animal bled. "How's it going?"

Johnny looked to be about twelve. He was too thin and wore ragged shoes and trousers far too short for his growing frame. His face pinched pale in the lamplight.

"I dunno," Johnny said. "Bristles won't come off no matter how I scrape."

"Damn this butchering in the middle of winter. Water cools too much. Excuse the language, Sister," Mr. Popescu said. "Johnny, stoke the fire."

Sister Magdalena stretched her back.

Mr. Popescu lit a wooden torch from the fire and handed it to Sister Magdalena. "Singe the hair," he said. "If that doesn't work, I'll cover the hog with straw and set it ablaze. Not pretty, but that is what my Romanian grandfather always did. Damn this weather and damn Starkweather for dallying. This should have been done in October."

Sister Magdalena wrinkled her nose at the acrid stench of burning hair. Johnny stoked the fire and returned to scraping. Twenty minutes passed on the first hog. It would take forever to finish. Mr. Popescu shot another hog and Sister Magdalena helped him hoist it on the ropes. He slashed its throat and positioned the keg.

"Watch how it's done," Mr. Popescu said. He used a sharp knife to make a shallow cut the length of the belly, starting near the anus and cutting all the way to the neck, careful not to nick the intestines or bladder. He pulled back the skin and poked a finger between the layers of fat until a loop of gray intestines bulged. Another tug and the intestines gushed out in a wave of stink. Johnny gagged as he positioned a washtub to catch the intestines. Mr. Popescu directed one of them to gut, and the other to continue scraping.

"Josue will take care of the intestines tomorrow." Mr. Popescu rinsed the cavity with clean water. Ice formed on the hooves and turned the area under the ropes into a skating pond.

Sister Magdalena salvaged the heart, kidneys, lungs, brains, and liver. She saved the massive head for headcheese and scrapple. The bones would be boiled for broth. The fat rendered into lard. The feet pickled. Her grandmother said that only the squeal was wasted during hog butchering.

"Short on time," Mr. Popescu said with a scratch of the head. "Cannot cut it up. You will have to do that at camp."

Sister Magdalena nodded. Let Nels do something for a change.

Mr. Popescu and Sister Magdalena stuffed the carcass into an empty barrel. She tucked the organ meats in the empty spaces around the pig. Mr. Popescu tacked a wooden cover on the filled barrel. He said the farmer had delivered the animals that afternoon.

Mr. Popescu wiped his hands, and hurried to slaughter another hog. "One pork barrel ready to go."

"Do you want to scrape or gut?" she said to Johnny.

Johnny looked a little green around his mouth. Sister Magdalena guessed he was new to butchering. It was one thing to clean a fish or dress a hen, but quite another to handle a steer or hog.

Sister Magdalena grinned. "I'll gut—unless you'd rather," she said.

"Oh no, Sister." He sounded relieved. "You do it."

They fell into a routine. Here piggy, piggy. Squeals. Gunshot. Drag. Hoist. Slash. Bleed. Scald. Scrape. Gut. Pack. It was almost daylight when they heard the final gunshot. Mr. Popescu and Johnny dragged barrels of intestines into the shed alongside the washtubs and kegs of clotted blood. His poor wife would face that disgusting chore the next day.

From time to time, Mrs. Popescu popped her head out the door to ask her husband about the Starkweather order. Much to be done before morning.

Sister Magdalena's fingers stiffened with cold, her eyes bleary. Finally, they packed the last pork barrel. Johnny's eyes lit up when Mr. Popescu handed him four bits for his labors. Johnny thanked him, grinned, and trotted away. He was a good boy. If she had chosen another path, she might have had a son like him. Her nephews were about that age, but she had never met them.

It was almost morning when Sister Magdalena collapsed into bed still wearing the clothes loaned to her, and drifted into the blackness of sleep.

A crowing rooster awakened her. She had just closed her eyes and it was time to get up. She struggled out of bed and dressed in her habit. Fatigue weighed heavy as she knelt for morning prayer. She had almost forgotten about Jacob Pettibone in the flutter of butchering. She could not keep Nels waiting. Perhaps he would have the wagon loaded when she returned with her patient.

Sister Magdalena tiptoed past the mountain of supplies ready for Starkweather's order. Snores came from the bedroom. Storekeepers worked hard to keep in business.

A glimmer of light highlighted a stand of tamarack on the eastern horizon, transforming them into ghostly shadows. It was cold enough to bring a chatter to her teeth, but the air felt softer, like snow.

She tugged her cloak tighter around her shoulders, the rough wool a comfort. Her shoes tapped on the wooden sidewalks. A person could break a leg on the icy patches. Smoke clouded the empty streets, and lights glowed in a barn where a farmer milked a cow. Morning in Aitkin.

She had not told Nels that Jacob Pettibone would return with them. Nels would not like it. She did not especially like having Pettibone return to camp either. He was a troublemaker and a ne'er-do-well. *Lord, increase faith, hope and charity in all of us.*

When she made ready to climb the stairs to the doctor's rooms, she glanced through the saloon window. A sign read *Always Open*. A man sprawled face forward on a small table. Empty whiskey bottles lay before him.

"Oh no," Sister Magdalena said. "Holy Jesus." She turned and entered the saloon.

A rough looking trio played cards in the corner and the barkeeper washed the bar. They acted as if it were a normal occurrence for someone to be drunk across a table. The place stank of stale beer. She marched over to Nels and shook his arm. He groaned but did not awaken. She shook harder and called his name.

"Leave me alone," he said.

Sister Magdalena's face grew warm. She had worked all night while he sat drinking in the saloon. The bum. The drunk. Christian charity deserted her.

"Get up," she said, this time louder. "It's time to leave." She shook him harder. He struck out with a weak punch. It did not really hurt, but his disregard stung all the same. She was a Benedictine sister. She was Sister Lumberjack and deserved respect. He owed her.

Two empty bottles. Where was his bank draft? She searched Nels's pockets and pulled out a few coins and two ten-dollar gold eagles. She checked his other pockets. Nels cursed and pushed her away.

Thirty dollars missing. She felt her heart sink. No one could drink thirty dollars of liquor in a single night. He should have listened to her.

Sister Magdalena tucked Nels's money into her pocket for safe keeping. She squared her shoulders and marched to the bar. "Excuse me, sir. How much is a bottle of whiskey?"

"That depends," he said. "There's whiskey and then there's whiskey. Some more expensive than others." The man shrugged. He was a little man, weasel-like in appearance with a sharp nose and small eyes. She was twice his size. Her coif and veil made her look even taller.

"I'd like to buy a bottle of whiskey like my friend bought," she said. "How much does it cost?" She locked eyes with him and refused to look away. He would tell her or she would shake it out of him. She was tired and hungry and behind schedule.

"A dollar," he mumbled.

"A dollar, you say? How many bottles did my friend buy?" Sister Magdalena said. "Certainly not thirty."

"Don't know lady, and don't care," he said. "I don't keep a tally book, it's all cash on the barrel head."

Sister Magdalena felt her blood rise and her cheeks flush. The pissant. The crook. She was too angry to control herself as the Rule of Benedict advised, as Sister Lucy would have done. As any of the other sisters would know to do.

Sister Magdalena leaned forward with both hands on the bar and hissed into the man's face. "Answer me or you will regret it. You do not want to get on my bad side." She leaned close enough to smell his sour breath. "I am Sister Lumberjack. You have no idea the connections I have."

The man dropped a bottle in his haste to step out of her reach. He bent to retrieve the shattered glass and cut his thumb on a shard. He stuck his thumb in his mouth, sucked blood, and wrapped it in a dirty rag. Sweat showed on his pale face. His eyes darted to the men in the corner and then to the door.

"So, the skooticks pay to cash a draft," he said. "Everyone does it. Even the bankers. Nothing illegal."

"How much did you charge my friend?" Her mouth tasted dust and her voice trembled. "Tell me." Her words came out slow and cold. "The exact amount you charged to cash his fifty-dollar draft."

He shrugged and avoided eye contact. A drop of blood showed on the rag around his thumb. The card players quit their game and were listening.

"The going rate."

"Which is?" she said. "Tell me at once."

"Thirty percent," he said in a low voice.

"You charged fifteen dollars on a fifty-dollar draft?" she said in a loud voice. "Thirty percent usury is robbery." She spoke to the card-players. "Wouldn't you gentlemen agree that it is wrong to charge thirty percent to cash a draft from a reputable source? This poor man worked hard for what he had. The draft was from the State of North Dakota, for goodness' sake. If we cannot trust the government, we are all in trouble. Blood suckers like him," she jerked her thumb toward the bartender who stood wide-eyed and quivering, "prey on the poor, rob their families, and steal their futures."

A murmur of agreement from the men.

"That leaves fifteen bottles of whiskey," she pressed. "I see only two bottles on his table. Where are the thirteen empty bottles?"

The bartender rubbed his whiskers and stammered. "The bottles were cleared away."

"Fetch them," Sister Magdalena said. "Bring out the empties, if you have them. Otherwise refund his money at once."

"By gawd, boys." One man threw his cards on the table. "Let us teach him a lesson. Get out the tar and feathers, and make him ride a rail through town."

The others muttered threats.

Things were getting out of hand. No need for violence. Sister Magdalena tried to calm herself. She needed to get back on the road.

"Return the money and I'll be on my way," Sister Magdalena said. "Twenty-eight dollars. That is only right."

"I'm trying to make a living." The bartender said. He looked like a boy caught with his hand in the sugar bowl.

"God sees." She glared at him. "God knows."

The man looked toward the card players, but made no move to return the money. The shutters rattled. The card players stood to their feet, ready to act.

She had connections, all right. The bartender was no match for the Blessed Mother's intercession. Sister Magdalena dropped to her knees with rosary in hand. She prayed aloud one decade. She peeked out of one eye. The card players gathered around her. She prayed louder.

"All right, all right," the bartender said. "You win." He counted out two gold eagles, a half eagle and three silver dollars. The coins clanked on the bar. Sister Magdalena stood up. She counted the money with a sigh of relief. Forty-eight dollars. She crossed herself and pocketed the money in her habit.

"Listen to me, and listen well," she said to the bartender. "If I hear of you gouging the jacks again, I will write letters to the newspapers, and expose your thievery. I will report you to the sheriff and demand that you be shut down and jailed. I will come back with all the sisters of my community. We will pray until God sends fire from heaven."

The bartender began scrubbing the bar as if his life depended on it.

The card players filed by. One tipped his hat as he passed. "Heard about you, Sister Lumberjack. You are the one who carried that jack out of the woods." He thumbed his nose at the bartender. "We're not through with you, yet," he said. "We'll be back."

She stood tongue-tied. It had only been a short way from the riverbank to the general store, hardly heroic. She did not want to become a tall tale told by homesick jacks. Any Christian would have done the same. The men left before she could explain.

The coins clinked in her pocket as she dragged Nels out of the saloon. Even the cold air did not revive the man. In frustration, she propped him by the stairway leading to Doc Hamilton's office.

"Nels, sober up. I will fetch the team." She had just saved his bacon. He should be grateful. Nels groaned, turned his head, and spewed vomit across the dirty snow.

Sister Magdalena turned in disgust. Let him sit in his puke. Served him right if he got frost bite. A lot of drunks lost toes or feet after a bender. She trudged up the stairs to the doctor's office and banged on the door. Jacob Pettibone welcomed her inside. He stood with homemade crutches made from spruce branches cut to size. Smaller branches served as hand grips. Old rags cushioned the tops. One pant leg pinned above his knee. Doc Hamilton was out on a call.

"We're leaving," she said. "Be down on the street in ten minutes." She turned without giving him a chance to reply. She had important things to do. She had no time to dawdle.

Fatigue shrouded like fog. She took a deep breath and swung her arms to keep awake as she hiked to the livery stable for the team. Nels was in no shape to drive back to camp. The supplies were needed. Pettibone could not manage a team in his condition. She would drive.

The empty wagon parked on the street. To her surprise, Johnny slept in a crude bunk next to the horse pen. Willy and Wally nickered to see her. Johnny did not rouse from his blankets. Poor boy. Up all night. It was warmer in the barn from the animals, but not much. He looked so peaceful in his sleep. He was a good boy.

"Johnny," she said. Where were his parents? Who watched out for him?

Johnny sat up and rubbed his eyes. He showed no surprise to see her. He jumped out of bed and brushed straggly hair from his eyes. He pulled ragged shoes over several holey socks. "You're here for your team."

He opened the gate and hitched lead ropes to Willy and Wally. Sister Magdalena helped lead the Percherons outside, careful to stay out of the way of their hooves and teeth. The horses snorted and stomped, their breath showing clouds of vapor before their noses. A wiggle of anxiety reminded her that she had never driven a wagon or team in town, nor turned a rig this size. The store lay in the opposite direction.

"These horses is real pretty, Sister," Johnny said. "I gave them oats and water when I got home this morning."

"You did well," she said. She could not resist. "How old are you?"

"Fifteen." He looked away as he spoke, fastening the harness.

"I'd guess you to be about twelve, the same age as my nephew."

A blush went up his cheeks. A bit of fuzz showed on his chin between a smattering of pimples. "I'll be thirteen in August."

"Your folks?" she said.

"I'm doing all right," he said. "I make my own way and I'm doing just fine."

She gave him half the flapjacks put aside for the return trip. His eyes shone as he shoved a whole pancake into his mouth. His hands trembled and he nearly choked on the food. The poor boy was starving.

She hesitated, then handed the remaining pancakes to Johnny. It would do her no harm to fast until she reached Solveig's table. The boy smiled until it seemed his face would split.

"Thank you, Sister."

"I need help." She fingered Nels's money in her pocket. It was not hers to give, and she must confess it later, but Nels's foolishness had gotten them into this mess. Nels could pay those who made up for his failures.

"I'll hire you to drive the team to the store and load the wagon," she said.

Johnny grinned even wider and jumped into the driver's seat. Sister Magdalena climbed beside him. He took the lines and turned the wagon toward the store. He knew horses. The team pulled together under his expert guidance. She said as much.

"They are real pretty," he said. "These horses are no trouble at all."

Sister Magdalena relaxed into the seat. *O Jesus, I offer you my prayers, works, joys, and sufferings of this day.* Back at the convent, the sisters were in chapel. How did she ever land so far from home?

More windows showed flickering lights. Men hunched against the wind as they beelined toward their jobs. A boy carried a pail of fresh milk, steamy in the cold. Johnny called out as he passed, proud to be seen driving a fine team.

Nels sprawled on the boardwalk. Jacob Pettibone was nowhere to be seen. She eyed the stairs and considered asking Johnny to fetch Mr. Pettibone, but reconsidered. Perhaps Doc Hamilton had returned. He might see her absence as an effort to avoid payment for Mr. Pettibone's care.

She sighed and lumbered down from the dray, her cassock catching on the box with a tearing sound as she pulled free. Everything was going wrong. They should be on the trail.

Jacob Pettibone answered the door, breathless with exertion.

"I'm sorry, but I couldn't get down on my sticks," he said. "Was hoping Doc Hamilton would come back."

She did not have the energy to scold. She guided Mr. Pettibone down the wobbly stairs. He leaned on her hard, and winced with each step.

"At least you didn't have to carry me on your back this time," he said. His efforts at cheerfulness did not cheer her.

"Looks like I may have to carry Nels." Another wave of disgust rolled over her.

She and Johnny hefted Nels into the back of the wagon. Then both Sister Magdalena and Johnny hoisted Mr. Pettibone in beside his old enemy. Mr. Pettibone landed with a hard thump and a muttered curse.

"Are you all right?" Sister Magdalena said. Lord only knew what Sister Bede Marie would say if there was a setback that required longer care in Aitkin. Mr. Pettibone was white as the snowflakes starting to fall from the sky, but said he had not injured himself.

"Can't wait to get out of this hell hole," he said.

The ungrateful lout. Doc Hamilton had saved his life. She thought to give him a piece of her mind, but the sleigh already bounced toward the general store. She held on and kept silent.

Mr. Popescu raised his eyebrows at the two men in the wagon box. "Looks like you'll need help loading up," he said. He needed a shave and his eyes were bloodshot.

Sister Magdalena swallowed hard. It was not her responsibility. She had only ridden along to collect Mr. Pettibone.

"Johnny will help me," she said with all the cheer she could muster. Inwardly she seethed. She was not a teamster.

Mr. Popescu took pity and rolled the barrels of pork outside where Sister Magdalena stacked them into the wagon box. Johnny toted sacks and crates. The snow fell steadily, though there was no wind.

"You'll have to move out of the way until we're ready to go," she said. "Go inside and keep warm." Mr. Pettibone climbed down and crutched into the store.

Nels lay where he had landed. She shook his arm and called his name. He mumbled, but did not stir.

"Nels," she said. "You are in the way. Wake up." She finally man-handled him into the driver's seat. Nels landed hard on the edge of the bench.

"Damn you," he said. "You're killing me."

"I might at that," Sister Magdalena said with a grimace. "Wake up and do your job. We are already late."

"My money," Nels said. "Where did it go?" He turned his pockets inside out and searched through his clothing. "Where's my money?"

"Gone," Sister Magdalena said. "You drank it all." Let him suffer. She would tell him the truth after he sobered up.

"Oh no," Nels said. "My money. It was my start-up. It is over for me."

"Not over," Sister Magdalena said. "It is not that easy. Hurry up, now."

Nels climbed down from the wagon box, holding his head, and cursing. He staggered toward the supplies waiting to be loaded, steadying himself on the crates. Sister Magdalena stacked the wagon as Johnny and Nels brought the goods to her. It took longer than expected. Nels acted grouchy as a dog with porcupine quills.

"You sure you want to be setting out?" Mr. Popescu eyed the skies.

Solveig's bunions were right. Mr. Popescu directed the question to her, though Nels should have made that decision.

"Nels is drunk," Mr. Popescu said in a confidential tone. "Wouldn't trust him to drive a pony cart, if I were you, good weather or bad."

They could wait until Nels sobered up and the weather cleared. Nels would welcome an extra day or two in town. But she had to catch Mr. Starkweather before he went shinning around again. That man was slippery as a wet fish.

Besides, thoughts of the convent with its routine of work and prayer, *ora and labora,* beckoned. The sooner she collected the money from Mr. Starkweather, the sooner she could go home.

"No use waiting on weather in Minnesota," she said, ignoring the shopkeeper's warning. "Might keep us here until spring."

Mr. Popescu shrugged and went into the store.

Sister Magdalena pulled Johnny aside while Nels checked the harness. She handed Johnny one of Nels's silver dollars. It felt good to give his money away, the sot. Johnny's eyes bulged.

"Thank you, Sister."

"You earned it," Sister Magdalena said. "If you ever need help, leave word for me at the store. Everyone knows Sister Lumberjack." She held back a strong impulse to embrace him. "Be a good boy and go to church. Say your prayers and keep out of trouble."

It was not enough. She was helpless. Even Johnny's dollar was from someone else. She took a breath. *In Christ we die, in Christ we live. Come, let us adore Him.* She climbed up on the box and took the lines. Nels slumped on his side of the seat like a sack of flour.

It was one thing to drive a team on a flat roadbed, but quite another to drive a loaded wagon down the steep bank and over the river. The load might push ahead and run over the team. The load might tip and be lost.

"You have to drive," she said to Nels.

Nels squinted, but dozed again, his head lolling on his shoulder. She would like to give him the back of her hand. Nels refused to do his work? Let him pay someone else to do it for him.

"Johnny," she said. "Could you drive the rig to the mouth of the Skunk River? A long walk back, but I will pay."

"Yes, ma'am." Johnny said.

They pushed Nels into the wagon box where he stretched out on sacks. He was asleep before his head hit the makeshift bed. Mr. Pettibone returned to the wagon.

There would be fireworks when Nels woke up and saw Pettibone was with them.

She thought of Jesus's agony in the garden. *Not my will but thine be done.* The boy maneuvered the great beasts down the trail to the edge of the riverbank without a hiccup. He paused, and then urged the team forward. The wagon jerked hard and swayed to the right. The horses neighed. Mr. Pettibone called out a warning, but Johnny righted the rig and drove on.

"Don't worry none," Johnny said as they reached the riverbed and turned north. "These horses are the best."

Maybe it was the frustration of overwork, her sleepless night, Nels's impudence, or the altercation at the saloon. A gray shadow swept over Sister Magdalena like a stormy wave on Lake Superior. Who did she think she was? She did not know how to drive a loaded wagon. She was not a teamster. It was too much. Her brothers were right. She rested her eyes and wished she were heading home.

The snow drifted down in gentle flakes that stuck to her veil and melted on her face. Overhead the sun glimmered through layers of gray flannel. The air smelled of pine and horse.

She tried to rest. Her body ached. If only Johnny could drive them all the way. He could not risk losing his livery job. She prayed. The words hollow and empty.

Mother Superior said it was better to pray what you could rather than what you could not. Surely God understood. Sister Magdalena dozed.

Johnny shook her arm when they reached the Skunk River. Sister Magdalena woke with a crick in her neck and a mouth as dry as chalk. It was late morning. They would be lucky to reach camp before nightfall. The snow had stopped, but a chill wind blew from the northwest.

"Well, then," she said. Both men snored in the back of the wagon. They slept while she did their work. It was not right. Pettibone was nothing but trouble. All of this could have been avoided if Nels had not refused her offer to hold his money. Instead, he went on a toot. She had rescued him, and this was her thanks. One word from her, and Nels would be fired. He deserved nothing else.

She handed Johnny another dollar from Nels's money. In for a penny, in for a pound. She might as well confess stealing two dollars as one. She had a strong urge to give the boy all Nels's money, but did not. Two dollars was enough to confess.

"Sister." His mouth gaped. "Thank you, a million times."

"Use it wisely," Sister Magdalena said. Poor boy had probably never had so much money before. "Mrs. Popescu keeps used clothing in the back. Ask her for a new coat and shoes. Maybe she would cut your hair."

She reached out to hug the motherless boy, but was too late. Johnny waved as he trotted across the river. It would have felt good to wrap her arms around him. He might have hugged her back. How long had it been since she had been hugged?

Instead, January wrapped around her with its cold arms. She should have left Nels to suffer the consequences of his actions. He had made her out to be the fool.

"Are you all right, Sister?" Mr. Pettibone's voice startled her from her spiraling thoughts.

"Of course," she answered. "Just tired."

With a mood as low as the overhead clouds, Sister Magdalena urged the team forward. She would not get lost if she stayed on Skunk River.

What was she thinking to pay Johnny with Nels's money? It was thievery, plain and simple. She made a promise to bring Rosy back to Duluth. Must she steal more money to keep that promise? She pondered the slippery slope of a single misstep. She needed to find a priest for confession.

The men in the saloon recognized Sister Lumberjack as someone doing good in the world. They did not know her or what a mess she had made.

"Good Lord." Nels sat up and wiped sleep from his eyes. "Where are we?"

"I'm driving the team because you're drunk," Sister Magdalena said. "You are a pitiful example of the male species, in my opinion."

"Shut your pie hole." Nels held his head with both hands. "Don't you ever quit talking?"

"Show some respect," Jacob Pettibone said. "You're talking to a nun."

Nels's eyes opened wide and he lunged toward him. Pettibone poked Nels in the chest with a crutch. They tangled into fisticuffs, cursing, and accusing each other, rolling on top of the sacks and crates. Someone would be killed.

"Enough." Sister Magdalena pulled the horses to a stop and turned around in her seat.

The men continued to tussle. Mr. Pettibone might bust open his stump.

"Stop at once," Sister Magdalena said. When they continued, she stood to her feet and grabbed the whip. She lashed out at the men, striking Nels across the back and shoulders, slashing Mr. Pettibone's cheek. "Stop, I said."

The men parted, but she kept the whip whistling down upon them. She lashed a red stripe on Nels's neck that oozed blood. "Stop, damn you! Have you lost your minds?"

The men gaped, too stunned to answer.

What had she done? She had struck them in anger. She had cursed. Sister Magdalena threw down the whip and stumbled clambered down from the driver's seat. She dropped to her knees in the snow.

"Lord, forgive me. I am no better than they. What have I done?" She dissolved into sobs.

Chapter 52
Solveig

Solveig peeked out the cookshack door and peered across the lake. Things were desperate. Ox bones simmered on the stove and the last of the beans baked in the oven. She drained the broth into a separate kettle and added rutabagas, onions, and potatoes. Bone broth was not filling, but her grandmother had sworn by it. Solveig added bay leaves and an onion. Thank God her hens gave enough eggs to make a batch of dumplings with flour scraped from the bottom of the barrel. Baked beans and dumpling soup for supper. Not much for working men.

She set Rosy to stirring up the dumplings. Stutz fetched more water. Gertie did not complain, but Solveig had eyes in her head. Gertie's feet swelled over the tops of her shoes. Solveig made her sit down and prop them up.

Gertie had been very quiet since her letter, Solveig realized with a start. Solveig had been too preoccupied with her own troubles to notice before.

"Did you hear from home?" Solveig said when Rosy took out the dirty dishwater.

Gertie nodded. Tears formed and dripped down her face.

"Bad news?"

"My father passed," Gertie said. "My mam wants me to come home to raise the baby."

Solveig felt a lurch in her chest. Gertie was also a widow, but without property or livestock to lean upon, and responsible for a baby. She had it much worse.

"At the end of the season?" Solveig said.

"Maybe," Gertie said. "I don't know how much it would cost. Only God knows."

"Go have a little lie-down," Solveig said. "I'll finish up here."

Solveig wished she had not asked. She could not help the girl. Her words felt feeble and late. She looked out the door again. Nothing in sight.

No doubt, the weather set them back. It was nobody's fault. Old Starkweather was too busy with cards and women to tend his business. Irish had warned about the lack of supplies, and Solveig had overlooked the warning. She was not without blame. The jacks paid the price for her timidity.

"Are they coming?" Rosy said from her dumplings when Solveig made another trip to the window. "This is the end of the flour."

"Then don't waste it," Solveig said. "You've got more on your face than in the bowl."

Didn't that halfwit gal know anything? Of course, Solveig knew the flour was low. Solveig thought of nothing but the pitiful stores. Molasses but no beans. Lots of potatoes, onions, and rutabagas. One sack of cornmeal, Two sacks of oatmeal. Plenty of dried codfish. No side pork. No bacon. No meat. No prunes or dried apples. No raisins. Solveig sighed.

She had asked Barrister for another ox that morning. He acted as if she requested his oldest child.

"You'll have to ask Mr. Starkweather about that," Barrister had said.

Since Sully's promotion, Solveig had not seen the brains of the outfit, though Sully took meals to Mr. Starkweather and returned with empty dishes. What would Mr. Starkweather think when he was served mush and fish?

She must sacrifice her hens. She had known this might be a possibility, but it left a bitter taste in her mouth. Her girls would make a thick soup that would at least be a meal. They could not live on fish.

Stutz must butcher the hens the next morning. She would spare herself that much. Damn it. Everything she loved was being taken from her.

Supper came and went. She set the porridge pot on the back burner to cook overnight and scrubbed potatoes for the oven. Tomorrow she would serve potatoes with fish gravy for breakfast along with mush and molasses. She dreaded being called a belly robber.

Solveig visited her girls before bedtime. They perched on the trough, huddled close for warmth. She stroked Gumbri who opened sharp eyes at her touch. "Go to sleep," she said in a whisper. "I've always loved you best."

Barrister would think her crazy to talk to chickens, but he did not look up from his book. She felt like crying. Instead, she squared her shoulders and headed back to the cookshack. They were livestock. She would buy more hens when she got her wages.

No stars showed through the dark sky. A north wind roared in the treetops. Icy snowflakes spat into her face. Her bunions did not lie. If Nels was out there in the night, he was in trouble. It was too cold to sleep rough, and too dangerous to drive without moonlight.

She lighted a lamp in the window facing Stink Lake. It was all she could do.

Stutz was banking the fire for the night when they heard the clatter of the team. It could not be. Solveig and Stutz ran outside with lanterns.

Sure enough, it was Nels with a full wagon. Ice crystals on his coat reflected the lamplight. He glittered like fireflies.

Sister Magdalena slumped beside him. She did not call out a greeting. Perhaps she was asleep. Jacob Pettibone poked his head up from the wagon box. So, the scalawag lived.

Barrister came from the barn. Gertie stepped outside. Rosy peeked out the window.

"Thank God, you made it," Solveig said. Snow fell in wet plops. "Come in by the fire. You must be frozen." She sent Stutz out to the bunkhouse to fetch Pokey. "We need a dozen men to unload supplies before the storm hits. Gertie, feed these travelers."

The wind picked up and the temperature dropped. Barrister and Stutz unloaded a few supplies for the cookshack.

"That's enough," Solveig said. "The rest goes to the root cellar."

Barrister drove the wagon and she rode along to unlock the door. The barn boss fussed about the team until Solveig grew impatient. "The supplies come first," she said. "It won't take long"

Afterward, Solveig returned to the cookshack. Her feet had turned into blocks of ice, but nothing could dampen her enthusiasm. Her cupboards were full.

Her hens were spared.

Chapter 53
Nels

Sister Lumberjack beelined to the backroom. Nels and Pettibone stopped to eat.

"What's wrong with Sister Magdalena?" Gertie said as she filled Nels's cup. Dark curls escaped her dingy kerchief, and steam framed her worried face.

Nels shrugged. He pulled his collar up over his neck to hide the whip marks. He did not want Gertie knowing that Sister Lumberjack had given up on him. Losing the money a second time proved his hopelessness. He imagined Gertie's face if she knew the truth. He did not deserve Gertie or any decent woman.

Pettibone acted as if nothing had happened. Nels sat far away from the man as Gertie busied with setting tables for the next morning. Rosie stayed out of sight. Stutz finished his chores.

Nels hunched down when Ma returned to the cookshack. One squeak from Sister Lumberjack and Nels would be out on his ear. She might keep her mouth shut, she was that kind of person, but Jacob Pettibone was sure to tattle.

It was not Nels's fault that criminals waited to rob hard-working jacks. A man deserved a drink once in a while. The sheriff should do something about the outlaws.

"Will be hard for me to go back and forth on my sticks," Pettibone said. His face wore a hopeful look, as if he wanted Ma to let him live in the cookshack.

"Ain't a sick house," Ma said. "You'll have to make do."

Nels would have felt sorry for anyone else, but Jacob Pettibone deserved every drop of misery. In the end, Ma shanghaied Stutz to help Pettibone to the surveyor cabin.

Stutz was shorter than Pettibone, and the cripple was dead weight on the boy. Stutz stumbled and Pettibone almost fell. Outside the snow was coming down in white curtains. Thank God, they had reached camp before the storm.

Nels saw his chance. One kick to his crutch would send Pettibone reeling. No one would think twice about a crippled man falling and freezing to death in the storm.

"I'll help," Nels said. "One on each side will get him there."

Ma called out as they were leaving the cookshack. "Nels, start cutting meat after breakfast. I'm not a butcher."

She did not even thank him for bringing the supplies.

"Is my bunk still open?" Pettibone huffed and puffed between Nels and Stutz. Nels felt the drag of his body and heard the grunt of pain with each step.

"How will you get by?" Stutz said. "You'll need help, even if Starkweather doesn't make you go out on the cut."

"Don't know," Pettibone said. "Starkweather owes me."

The snow fell thick and wet, filling their footprints. They reached the surveyor shack, Nels sent Stutz ahead to the bunkhouse. Then he turned to Pettibone.

"One word about me getting drunk and you're a dead man," Nels said.

"I won't say nothing." A look of fear crossed his pale face. He was not so high and mighty now. "I know to keep my mouth shut."

"I mean it," Nels said. "One word and you'll find yourself face down in the woods without your sticks." Nels relished the terrified look on Pettibone's face. "You got me blacklisted, spread lies about me, and drove me to drink." Nels grabbed him by the collar and twisted the cloth until a button popped out in the snow. "I'd love watching you grovel in a snowbank."

"Let me go," Pettibone said. "I'll call for help."

The wind grew into a steady howl overhead in the treetops.

"Go ahead," Nels said. He felt mighty as a toploader, as powerful as old Starkweather himself. "No one will hear you."

With that, Nels opened the door and shoved Pettibone inside. His crutches clattered on the wooden floor. Nels left him where he landed, slammed the door, and headed for the bunkhouse.

The snow turned the world white. Nels stumbled for his bearings, only finding the bunkhouse by the lamplight showing through the cracks around the door. He undressed and crawled into bed beside Ten-Day.

"You made it back," Ten-Day said.

"Shut up, dammit," Pokey growled from beneath them. "Next man who talks gets a red-hot poker up his ass."

Icy crystals sifted through the cracks in the wall. Nels covered his head and slipped into blackness.

The next morning, the Gabriel blew earlier than usual. The bull of the woods bellowed out a command. "Everyone up and dressed. Storming outside. You men must tramp a path to the cut so the snowplow can do its job."

Bitching and complaining filled the bunkhouse.

"Quit griping," Paulson said. "Ma's got side pork waiting for you."

They formed into rows of ten men across and twelve deep. Nels slipped into the back row between Ten-Day and Yuma, where the walking was easier. Over a foot of snow had fallen overnight and showed no sign of letup. They marched to the cut, stomping through the drifted snow like a bedraggled army on parade, tramping a wide swath behind them.

The push had been right. It did not take long. They turned back to the cookshack. Each man carried fresh snow on hat and shoulders.

The snowplow met them, a wooden vee hitched to a team. Nels pitied that poor bastard. The driver would spend the day clearing trails for skidders and top loaders. Nels would be inside all snug and warm. Not that he enjoyed cutting meat, but he might have a chance to speak to Gertie.

He would change if she gave him a chance. She would be enough to stop his drinking.

Chapter 54
Sister Magdalena

The weight of her sins felt heavy as a load of logs. Things had been going well. Sister Magdalena kept her promise to Mr. Murphy and secured a job for his widow. She sold enough hospital tickets to help the Benedictines expand services. She convinced Rosy to escape from Skunk Hollow. She found a way for Mr. Pettibone to get to Aitkin and carried him on her back the final leg of the journey. She butchered hogs and retrieved Nels's lost money. She was Sister Lumberjack. No one else could have done what she did.

But pride, the sin of Lucifer, stalked and tripped her with its lies. She took the credit for what God had done. She knew better. Without Him, she was nothing. She was only an instrument in His hands, and then, only if she kept out of the way.

Rosy's side of the bed was empty. Gertie and Solveig were already at work. Strange that she had not heard her bedfellows arise.

Sister Magdalena knelt by the bunk. *I confess to Almighty God that I have greatly sinned.*

She shivered and pulled her flannel nightgown over her feet. *In my thoughts, in my words, in what I have done and in what I have failed to do.*

She thought to stay on her knees in penance, but Solveig rattled pans in the kitchen, and the smell of frying meat filled the air. Solveig needed help.

She finished her act of contrition, dressed, and faced facts. Saint Benedict said to begin anew every morning. She would fast until she made amends to both Mr. Pettibone and Nels.

"Good morning," Solveig said when she came out. "I hope you rested well." Solveig chopped the hog's lungs and kidneys, adding the bits to a sizzling frying pan.

Sister Magdalena's mouth watered despite her good intentions. She dove into the most disagreeable tasks she could find, emptying the slops and shoveling the path to the outhouse. The falling snow covered her cape and veil, melting on her cheeks and nose.

Though her stomach growled, Sister Magdalena refused breakfast. She determined to master her prideful selfishness. She had felt put-upon to do Nels's work, and yet Jesus demanded she take up her cross. She had failed as a Christian and as a Benedictine nun. How could she face Nels and Mr. Pettibone after acting like a judge, meting out actual blows in anger? Losing her temper was bad enough, but physical violence was inexcusable. And cursing. Another kneeling pardon when she returned.

Nels tackled the pork barrel as the flunkeys cleared tables and washed the dishes. Solveig saw her chance. She found a meat saw and joined Nels. She sawed through thick layers of fat and bone. Sister Magdalena knew how to make the cuts. She was too embarrassed to look at Nels, not only because he did not know what he was doing, but awkward about the apology she must make. She would wait until they were alone.

Sister Magdalena glanced his way. To her dismay, she saw red stripes across his chin and over his ear, the result of her beating. She was no better than the Romans who scourged Jesus.

"I'll saw the meat if you trim the fat," she said.

Nels avoided eye contact. Together they worked through the morning without a word between them. Nels added chunks of fat to kettles on the stove where it rendered into lard. He lifted the hog's head onto the table.

The vacant stares from the head made her nervous. She turned it around to face the opposite direction until Rosy took it for headcheese. Stutz scrubbed the feet for pickling. Gertie fried the tail. Nothing was wasted.

Around them, the kitchen was a flurry of baking and cooking, a happy whirl of productive work. The melting lard left its greasy stench hanging in the kitchen. Solveig took a sowbelly and hind quarter for immediate use.

Their hands slippery with fat, Sister Magdalena and Nels repacked the cuts of meat into the barrel and tapped down the lid. They rolled it to the corner farthest from the stove. Tomorrow they would tackle another barrel. It would be a daily chore until the end of the season.

Solveig sent them to the root cellar to fetch a sledge of supplies. She handed Sister Lumberjack the key and warned her to lock the door afterwards. "I trust neither two nor four-legged beasts," Solveig said.

When they were alone on the trail, Sister Magdalena mustered her courage.

"Nels, I apologize for my behavior," she said. "I disgraced myself and my habit. I lost my temper. I have no words."

Nels looked at her and, for a moment, Sister Magdalena thought she saw a tear in his eye. It may have been the bitter wind. His blue eyes showed in contrast to his pale skin.

"No need to apologize. I'm the fool," Nels said. "I should have listened to you."

Pious phrases popped into her mind, words of exhortation for him to live a better life. How could she instruct anyone in holiness when she fell short herself?

"Why did I do it, Sister?" Nels said. "How can I face my parents?" A sob clutched his throat. "I lost everything."

She dropped to her knees outside the root cellar as the Gabriel announced the noon meal. *Forgive us our trespasses as we forgive those who trespass against us.*

Nels knelt beside her.

She thought to tell him of his money safe in her keeping, but something prevented her. Overhead the wind roared through the treetops. They gathered supplies and headed back to the cookshack where the others were already eating. She felt weak with hunger. Determined to make amends, she plowed through the drifts to the surveyor shack. Snow almost hid the thin plume of smoke that marked where the swingdingle brought food out to the cut. How the jacks suffered in such cruel weather.

Mr. La'Valley opened the door.

"Sister," he said. "What are you doing here?"

Across the cabin, she glimpsed Jacob Pettibone sprawled across his bunk.

"May I come in?" she said. "I'd like a word with Mr. Pettibone."

"No skin off my hinder," Mr. La'Valley said with a shrug. "I'm not his boss."

Sister Magdalena stood waiting, hoping the surveyor would take the hint, and leave them alone. After an awkward silence, he mumbled an excuse, and left the cabin. Mr. Pettibone sat up, struggling to find balance. Red marks crossed his face and neck. Dear Lord, she could have taken out his eye.

Best get it over with.

"Mr. Pettibone," Sister Magdalena said. "I've come to apologize for my abominable behavior." She took a deep breath. "Please forgive me. I am without excuse."

Jacob Pettibone shook his head. "I was at fault, not you. I caused trouble—and after what you did for me. I am ashamed to look you in the face."

The room smelled of tobacco and dust. The wind rattled the stovepipe. A tray with dirty dishes perched on the end of his bed alongside the prayer book she had given to him. A dismal fate for a man used to his own way, and now at the mercy of other people's charity.

"I am ashamed of myself, too," Sister Magdalena said. "Can we start again?"

She shifted her feet and twisted a frayed thread on her cloak. Something broiled in her mind, a possible remedy for his situation.

"I'm up shit creek without a paddle," he said. "What can I do? Sell apples on the street corner?"

"You have your mind," she said. "You can do many things. Tally ledgers or run a store. Stinky does woodworking with only one leg. God spared you for a reason."

"Never learned figures," he said. "Mr. Starkweather made promises." Pettibone shrugged. "Tried to talk to him this morning, but the scamp had already left camp."

Her heart flip-flopped in her chest. It could not be.

"Sully says he won't be back until payout," Pettibone said. "Claims the weather is not conducive for gentlemen."

"He was supposed to leave a bank draft for me," Sister Magdalena said.

Mr. Pettibone snorted. "I doubt that Mr. Starkweather is concerned about satisfying his debts," he said. "It's against his nature."

Sister Magdalena swallowed hard. Staying until the end of the season felt like a prison sentence. Pettibone was not the only one with disappointments.

"And what are you going to do until then, Mr. Pettibone?" Sister Magdalena said. "You can't lie abed forever." She gathered the dirty dishes and handed Mr. Pettibone his crutches. "I'll teach you numbers, if you are willing." She straightened up. "I would advise you to speak to Barrister for advice. He offers good counsel. But for right now, there is plenty of work in the cookshack. Come with me."

"I don't know nothing bout slinging hash," he said.

"There are hogs to cut. You must earn your keep."

The horn blew. The men headed back to work.

"Come, Mr. Pettibone. Idle hands are the devil's workshop."

"On one condition," Mr. Pettibone said. "That you quit calling me Mister. My name is Jacob."

"Well, Jacob," Sister Magdalena said. She was taking a risk. Pettibone was not known for his discretion, but she had to trust him. "I have a condition for you. A friend hides in the cookshack from a bad man. No one knows except the kitchen help," Sister Magdalena said. "Can I trust you with her secret?"

Chapter 55
Solveig

Solveig sprinkled a handful of flour over the lump of dough and rolled it into a thick layer. With a twist of the wrist, she sliced long strips and eased them into sizzling fat. They dropped down and bobbed to the surface. Gertie stood with a fork, turning the doughnuts to brown on both sides. It was a relief having lard again.

"Rosy, stir up another batch," Solveig said.

Rosy gaped like an idiot. It was as if she did not have a brain in her head. Rosy fumbled with the bowl, cracked an egg, and mixed it with a spoon. Bits of shell floated in the foam.

Solveig sighed. "Pick out the shells." One more batch ought to be enough. How pleased the jacks would be to see bear sign, as they called doughnuts. They would not leave a crumb.

She glanced up from her work as Sister Magdalena guided Pettibone into the kitchen. She held him steady as he lunged forward on his crutches.

Good Lord. Now what.

"Jacob will do chores for you," Sister Magdalena said. "He is willing. He needs something to do."

Nels scowled from the meat cutting table. Gertie stood with fork suspended over the kettle. Rosy scurried to the back room leaving a trail of flour.

"Rosy can come out. Jacob knows about her," Sister Magdalena said. "He won't say anything."

Solveig slammed the rolling pin down onto the table hard enough to rattle the crockery. She was not doing missionary work. Sister Magdalena had no business bringing yet another stray dog into her kitchen and expecting Solveig to take care of it. Nels and Pettibone would kill each other. How would she explain that to Mr. Starkweather?

"Rosy, get your butt out here," Solveig yelled. "There's work to do."

Rosy came dragging back with a face as red as Gumbri's comb. She returned to her mixing bowl with downcast eyes.

How peaceful her prairie home had been. These people vexed her to the point of homicide. Even Sister Magdalena had grown intolerable.

To hell with them. To hell with all of them.

"Here," Sister Magdalena handed Pettibone a knife. "Fat scraps in the kettle, cuts of meat back in the barrel."

Nels glared. Pettibone trimmed meat without comment.

Solveig ruled the kitchen. Irish would have chased them all out with a cleaver. Pettibone was able-bodied enough for some chores. Maybe the sister was right to bring him in, but she should have asked Solveig first.

Sister Magdalena sat between the men who hated each other and brandished knives.

"What's wrong with Sister Magdalena?" Gertie whispered when Solveig returned to the doughnuts. Sister Magdalena did more than her share of chores without the usual joking and bantering.

Gertie's protruding belly forced her to lean over the sizzling grease. Several red spots on her face showed where the lard had splattered. "She acts lonesome."

Solveig snorted. Everyone was lonesome for somewhere or something. Some days Halvor's face crowded her mind until she thought she would go mad. No use talking about it. He made his choice. He was, no doubt, having the time of his life with his new family, playing cards, and learning to polka. She imagined him holding her letter and reading the words of the old song his father had loved.

Foolishness. She was no better than flutterbudget-Rosy, rattled by a missing child. Solveig had not known how happy she had been before her husband and son were gone. How could she not have realized her happiness?

The thought flustered Solveig, and made her relinquish the doughnut-making to Gertie and Rosy. Solveig grabbed her shawl and stomped outside. She would check on her girls. She had to get away from the lunatic asylum for at least a moment of solitude.

Overhead a weak sun filtered through a thin layer of clouds. The snow had finally stopped and great mounds heaped everywhere. The top-loader added more logs to the growing pile on the lake.

She rested her eyes on the expanse of the lake and recalled the Breckenridge Flats. It would not be long. They were well past the midpoint of the season. She would make it.

Three hogs a week for a full crew was not over-abundant, but possible. The hens would lay more as the days grew longer again. Already morning light came sooner and supper was later. Everything would work out.

Nels would not like it, but she decided. Mr. Starkweather was not around to ask permission. She would do it on her own. She could not take it another day.

One stray dog under her table was enough.

She stepped into the cookshack where the smell of rendering lard and fried doughnuts hung in the air. Sister Magdalena was nowhere in sight, maybe praying in the back room. Gertie sliced bread. Rosy and Stutz busied at the dishpan. Queenie rubbed around Pettibone's good leg, the beggar. From time to time, Pettibone tossed a bit of gristle to the cat.

Maybe Pettibone was not so bad, after all. Queenie was a good judge of character.

"Stutz," Solveig said. "Tell Paulson I need to talk to him."

Solveig covered platters of doughnuts with clean dishtowels. Paulson would back up her decision, she was pretty sure about that.

Yuma burst into the cookshack with a clatter. He had thrown off his jacket and his shirt tails twisted around his galluses. He acted like a man possessed, a berserker.

Rosy disappeared into the back room.

Yuma's face turned purple as a rutabaga and his hands clenched into fists. "You're a dead man, Jensen, you lying snake."

Nels stood to his feet, still holding the knife. "What are you talking about?" Nels said. All color had left his cheeks beneath his scruffy beard. "I didn't do nothing."

"Liar!" Yuma said. "You killed my brother."

Sister Magdalena hurried from the back room, still clutching her beads. Solveig grabbed a cleaver, emulating Irish's actions when Pettibone tried to pick a fight with Ten-Day. It seemed like a long time ago.

"Leave at once," Solveig said. Her voice trembled despite her best efforts to speak with authority. "Now. You do not belong here." A mad man. She was no match for him, even with cleaver in hand. She glanced out the window, hoping to see Paulson. No sign of him.

"You did it," Yuma said, ignoring Solveig and yelling into Nels's face as the spittle flew. "Filthy scum." He pointed a long finger toward Nels, his hand trembling. "You killed Elias and lied to my face."

"You're mistaken," Nels said. "I don't know your brother."

"That's not what the Injun said," Yuma said. "Said you traded this for game."

Yuma held out the leather thong holding the blue stone, the one Nels had traded to Gilbert. "Explain this." Then he reached inside his shirt and pulled out an identical stone on the same type of rawhide string. "Our initials are engraved on the setting. We bought them from a Mexican in Yuma. Elias would never sell it. You took it off his dead body."

Solveig did not believe Nels capable of murder, but a drunk was capable of anything. Blood pounded in her temples. She wanted to squeeze her eyes shut and run screaming out of the cookshack.

Solveig looked at Sister Magdalena and mouthed one word.

"Help."

Chapter 56
Nels

Nels exhaled and replaced the butcher knife on the table. He raised both hands with palms forward, as if to hold Yuma back.

"I can explain." Good Lord, how could he make Yuma understand? "Hear me out. I didn't know it was your brother."

Yuma's face twisted as he lunged toward Nels. Nels stepped back and tripped over Pettibone's crutches, landing with a clatter in a tangle of legs and sticks. The cat streaked under the stove.

"Wait." Sister Lumberjack stepped between the two men. She shoved Yuma backwards and helped Nels to his feet. "Let's sit down and discuss this like Christians."

Nels kept an eye on Yuma, lest he attack again. Everyone stared at him, no doubt, believing the worst. His rotten luck. Even Gertie stared in horror, just when she was starting to warm up to him.

"Be quick about it." Ma twisted her mouth with disgust and cast a withering look toward Nels. "Five minutes and no more. This ain't no Grange Hall."

Ma returned to her work. Gertie stared with wide eyes until Ma barked for her to get busy.

"Now, then." Sister Lumberjack paused for breath. "Nels, where did you get the necklace? You have explaining to do."

In America a man was supposed to be innocent until proven guilty. It seemed he was judged already.

"I took a job with an undertaker in Brainerd last fall," Nels said. "A young man was killed by a lumber dray." The story poured out about the lack of identification, the unmarked grave on the hillside, and the blue stone given to him by the undertaker in return for his help.

"I traded it for meat," Nels said. He glanced Ma's way. "I'm a terrible shot. Can't hit the broad side of the outhouse. You know that, Yuma."

Yuma's face turned ashen. "He's dead?"

Nels dared to breathe. "I dug his grave and buried him myself."

"When?" Yuma said. "My mother will want dates."

Nels called out. "Ma, when did we meet up in Brainerd?"

Ma knew the date, as Nels expected. Ma faced the world with an orderly mind, unlike his own whirlwind of confused thoughts and impulsive actions. Ma's coldness radiated like a palpable thing. He had lost her as a friend. Maybe she had been lost to him for a long time.

"Elias dead." Yuma held his head and rocked. "I can't believe it. We had plans. We were going to homestead in the Dakotas after we got a grubstake logging." He groaned and rocked, back and forth, not exactly a wail, but an agonizing keen from somewhere deep inside.

Nels felt like wailing, too. Gertie kept her eyes on her work. She did not care for him and never would. He would end up like Pokey, old and stove up, broke and thirsty.

Sister Lumberjack knelt by the bench next to Nels. The papists sure knew how to put on a show. Gertie crossed herself. Nels looked away in embarrassment. Even Ma paused by the work table, as if she did not know whether to keep working or stop out of respect.

Sister Lumberjack fingered the beads, mouthing the words in silence. Nels counted the beads as sweat gathered under his armpits. They would be in the cookshack all day. Ma cleared her throat and Sister Lumberjack looked up. Then she prayed aloud for the repose of the young man's soul and for heavenly comfort for the bereaved family. After the amen, she pulled herself to her feet and straightened her veil.

"Yuma, your people will rest easier knowing what happened," Sister Lumberjack said.

"Didn't he have any money on him?" Yuma said to Nels. "He had just pulled wages from the bonanza farm. There should have been money."

"Undertaker said there wasn't enough for embalming," Nels said. "That's all I know."

"He must have started a bank account," Yuma said. "He wasn't a drinker."

"Time's up," Ma said. "Everyone back to work." She wrapped a few doughnuts in a clean cloth and brought them to Yuma. "Sorry for your loss."

Then she turned to Nels. "I want a minute with you in private."

Had Sister Lumberjack tattled about his drinking? Ma scowled at him and grabbed her shawl. He felt guilty as hell, and did not even know what she was mad about.

"Walk with me," Ma said. "We've business to tend."

Yuma dragged himself back to the cut. Nels did not have a brother and could not imagine the pain of losing one. The sky had opened and the temperature was dropping. Ma jerked her shawl tighter and walked with determined steps toward the barn. Barrister looked up from mucking the pens, but did not greet them. A Minnesota winter soured everyone.

"Trading with Injuns?" Ma's tongue cut sharp as a razor. "Mooning around the cookshack when you should be out hunting. We almost starved with the game you brought in. I have had enough." Ma snapped her shawl even tighter. "We have supplies through the end of the season. Don't need you anymore."

"Wait a minute," Nels's chance of winning Gertie drifted away like a melting snowflake. "Mr. Starkweather hired me."

"In case you haven't noticed, Mr. Starkweather isn't around," Ma said. "Tell the bull of the woods that you're free to return to the cut."

"Tell him yourself," Nels said as Paulson walked into the barn. The bull of the woods wore a distinct expression of annoyance.

"What's going on?" Paulson said. "I've got work to do."

Ma tattled about Nels's poor marksmanship and that she no longer would tolerate him loitering around the cookshack. Ma had forgotten how he nearly ruptured himself toting her trunk to the barge back in October.

"I need help shoeing the oxen," Barrister said. "Can't do it alone."

"All right with me," Paulson said.

Chapter 57
Sister Magdalena

Funny how things fell into place. To think that Nels, in all his misery, would be an instrument of God to bring closure to a grieving family. Of course, God used an ass to speak to Balaam. Sister Magdalena chuckled.

Sister Lucy once said that life was like a painting with every moment a different dab of the brush. "The colors don't make sense until the artist finishes the work," she had said.

It was easier to see someone else's picture emerge than her own. What had she accomplished in her life? Washed clothes and tended vegetable gardens. And now the fiasco with selling hospital tickets and waiting to collect the money owed to her.

Nels must feel the same way. His face sagged like an old hound dog since losing his hunting job. Solveig gave a noncommittal reply when Sister Lumberjack asked about it.

"Pettibone can cut the meat by his lonesome." Solveig bristled around the kitchen like a broody hen. "Enough men underfoot without Nels."

Sister Magdalena returned to scrubbing, laying tables, and washing dishes. She did not mind. She marked time until Mr. Starkweather returned.

One night Sister Magdalena dreamed her brothers were tumbling down slippery haystacks. Clarence grinned into her face and was about to say something important when Rosy shook her awake.

"Sister," Rosy whispered. "I need to tell you something."

It was dark and cold. Sister Magdalena pulled the quilt around her neck. "What's the matter?"

"I lied." Rosy sniffled back tears. "I told you Jimmy's dad left when he found out I was with child." Hiccups and choking.

Solveig stirred in her bunk. Then her snoring resumed.

"Heck, he never knew. Barely talked to me. But I remember him." Rosy wiped her nose on her nightgown sleeve. "You never forget your first one."

Sister Magdalena snapped awake. She both wanted to hear Rosy's story and have nothing to do with it. Some things were not suitable for discussion.

"Why are you telling me?" Starkweather Timber was a sure path to holiness with all its opportunities to practice forbearance.

"He's here," Rosy said. "Jimmy looks just like him. There is no doubt in my mind."

"One of the jacks?" Sister Magdalena said.

"Pettibone," Rosy said. "Jacob Pettibone is Jimmy's father. Should I tell him? I can't think straight."

"Where did this happen?" Sister Magdalena said. If it were true, why didn't Jacob recognize her? He saw her every day. Flighty Rosy was not above a fabrication of facts to suit her purpose.

"The cribs on the waterfront," Rosy whispered. "I was only fifteen and scared out of my mind. Needed money to pay the boarding house and a friend hooked me up with someone she knew who gave girls work."

Sister Magdalena reached for her hand. It felt small as a bird in her big mitt.

"A man came in, drunker than a lord," Rosy said. "Sweet, in his own way. No introductions, if you know what I mean." Her voice trailed off. "I was scared and crying. He gave me an extra dollar because I was...you know, new." She took a deep breath. "I took the dollar and ran."

A stirring below them. Then quiet.

"So, what did you do next?" Sister Magdalena said. She might as well hear all of it, even if it meant a kneeling pardon. At the rate she was going, she would be on her knees for a week.

"I went back to charring. But then I found out about Jimmy, and I got fired because I wasn't wed. Ended up back in the cribs. Couldn't raise him on my own."

The poor girl must have been terrified.

"I'm not a bad person, Sister. You must believe me."

Sister Magdalena sent a desperate plea for the Holy Family to intercede on Rosy's behalf. She had been alone, scared, and with a baby. What could the poor girl have done differently?

"Should I tell Jacob?"

"Let me think about it," Sister Magdalena said. "We'll talk later."

Rosy rolled over and fell asleep, leaving Sister Magdalena awake. A crippled man without a wife had a son. A desperate woman had a son and no husband. An innocent child had both a mother and father, but languished in an orphanage. *Terror of demons, pray for us.*

It seemed Sister Magdalena had just fallen asleep when Solveig got up and went to the kitchen. Another day to practice holiness. Sister Magdalena denied herself extra sleep, pulled herself out of bed, and knelt for prayer. *Oh Lord, let me take my cross willingly, not compelled as Simon the Cyrene.* She squared her shoulders, and found Solveig cooking coffee in the kitchen.

Solveig answered Sister Magdalena's morning greeting with a grunt. The silence felt like a welcome relief since Rosy's dilemma still clamored in Sister Magdalena's head. Jimmy's life was at stake. A whole family lay in the balance.

Sister Magdalena sliced strips of side pork until her hands and fingers cramped. She stretched her hands and sighed. Holiness proved a long journey.

Gertie waddled to the stove and poured a cup of coffee. Rosy followed with puffy eyes. Stutz brought an armload of wood for the wood box.

"Watch your feet, Stutz," Solveig said. "You're tracking snow across the floor."

Stutz shrugged and left with empty buckets. Pokey came in holding Pettibone's arm to steady him. They tracked wet footsteps to Pettibone's worktable. His sticks clattered to the floor.

"Here you go." Pokey hefted half a hog onto the table.

"Morning," Jacob said. He was not exactly cheerful, but Sister Magdalena saw his greeting as a good thing. He was trying to adapt to his situation. That meant something.

"Good morning, Jacob," Sister Magdalena said. She imagined him as a family man. Impossible things were possible with God.

Frying pork sizzled. Cooking pots scraped across the iron stovetop. Solveig began flipping monkey blankets. Stutz whistled a tuneless song. Rosy skirted behind the stove and cast anxious glances toward Jacob Pettibone. Gertie turned the strips of meat, holding a fork in one hand and her lower back with the other. Jacob cast admiring glances her way. It seemed he took notice only of Gertie.

"Tarnation, Pokey," Solveig said. She slammed a pan against the stovetop until the lids rattled. "The reservoirs are empty and the day hardly started." Pokey muttered under his breath and left with empty buckets.

"Stutz, quit that confounded whistling and wipe the floor," Solveig said. "Someone will slip and break his neck." She looked and sounded as cross and tired as Sister Magdalena felt.

Another day at Starkweather Timber.

Chapter 58
Solveig

The flunkeys were more bother than they were worth. Solveig sighed. Not exactly true. She could not manage the work alone, but she hated bossing people around. They did not work without her nagging them. At Starkweather Timber she was paid to be a bitch.

Rosy lurked in the corners, avoiding work.

"Get busy," Solveig gave the young woman a hard look. Rosy did not belong in camp.

Rosy scurried back to slicing bread. It seemed both Sister Magdalena and Gertie cast disapproving glances toward Solveig. Even Stutz glared at her as he dragged a rag across the wet floor. Everyone was as unhappy with Solveig as she was with them.

It was unheard of for a cook to leave the cookshack at breakfast time, but Solveig had no choice. It was leave or kill someone. Besides, everything was ready. Solveig wrapped her shawl over her head and slammed the door behind her. Morning was only a sliver of light on the horizon. Overhead the sky reminded her of crushed blackberries. She glanced toward the lake, but it was too dark to see the open expanse that often cheered her. Lantern light glimmered in the cookshack windows and spilled weak shadows in the snow.

She met Pokey returning with water buckets. She did not speak, and neither did he. A soft light shown through the open barn door. Barrister led a pair of oxen outside and fitted the yoke. The animals mooed a mild protest. Clouds bloomed by their noses.

Solveig avoided Nels at the feed trough, going straight to the hens perched on an empty pen. She despised a shirker and conniver. What must Nels's parents think? At least Halvor was a good man, a law-abiding citizen, a person of integrity. Halvor was not a drunkard. Her throat choked. But Halvor had broken his word to his dying father and abandoned his mother. Maybe that was worse than intemperance with alcohol. She held Gumbri close, despite flapping feathers and scratching claws.

The Gabriel sounded. Nels and Barrister hurried to the cook-shack. She exhaled a long breath. She willed her anxiety to leave with the stale air from her lungs.

Gumbri clucked a low murmur, almost like a purr. A pang of grief clutched her chest and made her gasp for air. If only Rasmuss were alive. Together they could overcome anything. Alone, she was drowning.

Rasmuss was dead. She could not change that. Halvor was married and gone. She could not change that. She could not farm alone. She could not change that. She would pay off the banknote and figure out her next step.

She might rent out the land and subsist on her garden and hens. She did not need much. With the bank note paid off, she could live on the farm until she died. The years stretched ahead, a lonely life without family or purpose, a life with a grandchild far away.

She absently placed Gumbri on the floor and searched under the other hens. She pulled out an egg, warm to the touch and comforting in her hand. The hen balked and squawked, pecking at Solveig's fingers.

"Now, now," Solveig said. "Be glad you didn't end up in the stew pot."

She would go into the cookshack after the men finished eating, and fry herself an egg. She would not share. She would eat the egg in full view of everyone without apology. They were her hens, after all. Then she would boss the kitchen help within an inch of their lives, and lie down for a bit of rest while they did the work. She was sick and tired of helping everyone else and getting nothing back in return.

Starkweather was not around, and she would get by with a few lapses of industry.

But what would she do after logging season ended? Wait out her days until death sneaked upon her? She thought of Sister Magdalena's advice. Easy for her to say. Foxhome was her very life. How could she move away and start over somewhere else?

Solveig sighed. That was a problem to worry about after the banknote was satisfied. Until then, she would do her duty. And for now, her duty lay in the cookshack.

The men shuffled toward the cut. She clutched the egg and went back inside. *Dumme tosks,* dumb fools. Rosy simpering and gaping, Stutz dawdling over his work, Pettibone grumping in his chair, Gertie too big to do much, the nun distracted by prayers and do-gooding. Let them call her names behind her back.

They could all go to hell and shovel coal.

Chapter 59
Nels

At breakfast, Nels watched Gertie flip flapjacks at the stove, her cheeks flushed from the heat. Tight curls peeked out from her kerchief, framing her face in small, dark blossoms. When she bent to pick up a spoon, the lamplight profiled her upturned nose and arch of neck.

As one voice, a sigh issued from every jack at table. Every eye feasted on the lovely widow. Any of the single men would gladly claim Gertie as bride, even with the baby apparent to all but a blind man. Nels would need sons to help with the farm someday. Marrying Gertie would be a leg-up in that department.

Stutz stumbled over a jack's outstretched foot and almost dropped a platter of monkey blankets. Everyone tittered, but no one dared break the no-talking rule, even with Ma out of sight. Sister Lumberjack pointed the boy toward the dishpan, and took over serving the food herself. Gertie wore a pained expressions as she fried flapjacks. Even Sister Lumberjack looked like she was in a bad mood.

Blame it on Starkweather Timber. It soured everyone.

After breakfast, Nels left at the same time as Yuma and Ten-Day. The dark was changing to morning twilight. Time for the jacks to go to the woods, and Nels to get back to the barn. Nels was leery of the Arizonan since his accusations about his brother. They had parted on friendly terms, mostly, but Nels was still unsure of himself around his former friend.

Instead of speaking to Nels, Yuma grabbed Stutz returning with water buckets. Stutz stared wide-eyed at the burly man, with breath like wispy clouds before his lips.

"You didn't give it to her, did you?" Yuma said. "You little rat."

Stutz stuttered a reply. "I gave it to her just like you said." He pulled away, sloshing water down his legs and onto his shoes. "Look what you made me do."

"What did Gertie do with it, then?" Yuma said. "Did she say anything?"

"Stuck it in her apron pocket," Stutz said with a shiver. "She don't answer none of them. She is always getting notes from one jack or the other." He scurried into the cookshack, out of reach of the angry man.

"Maybe she had no schooling," Ten-Day said beside them. "Send another letter asking if she knows how to read."

"Stupid fool," Yuma said in obvious exasperation. "If she doesn't know how to read, how in the hell will she read a note asking about it?"

"Just trying to help," Ten-Day said. "Maybe she don't read American, only the Old Country lingo where she was raised."

The others passed them on the way to the cut. It was time to get to work.

"I saw her walking to the privy once," Ten-Day said. "Didn't get a chance to talk to her." He added that he might find an excuse to linger near the backhouse. "I heard tell that women in the family way use the privy often. It would not take long to snag a visit."

Nels's hopes dwindled. He was not the only man in love with her. Men left love notes under their dirty plates or tucked in the swingdingle after nooning. Gertie's name was whispered throughout the bunkhouse along with expressions of eternal devotion. The previous night the men had talked of Gertie around the amen corner until Pokey told them to shut up. He pulled out his accordion and drowned out the wistful tales of love and love lost. The men plied Stutz with questions every night, bribing him to be matchmaker.

"I'd give anything to be around her every day," Yuma said.

Gertie would be better off with Yuma. That man had prospects in this life. He was not hampered with bad luck or bottle fever. Nels's chances of winning the beautiful widow melted away like frost on the stovepipe, thanks to Ma and her meddling ways. He suspected that Ma had cautioned Gertie to stay away from him because of his drinking, and purposely separated him from seeing her.

He should be cutting meat, not Jacob Pettibone. God, that man was a vexation. Jacob always got his way. It was Nels's bad luck that Pettibone survived the accident. A decent man would have died and got out of Nels's way.

"My God, it's cold," Ten-Day said. "You're living the high life inside the barn all day."

Poor bastards. Nels did not know how long working with the barn boss might last, but he was in no hurry to go back to the woods.

Barrister had the slings set up for a team of oxen kept back from the cut. "Have you shoed oxen before?" Barrister said. "Takes two men. Need slings. An ox tips over if you try to raise one leg."

Nels shook his head. "I've helped with horses a time or two." His experience was watching someone shoe a horse. He saw no need to tell the whole truth.

"Blacksmith won't shoe oxen anymore," Barrister said in disgust. "Says he is too busy. Of course, he did a poor job on that one that broke its leg." He spat in the gutter. "Better off we do it ourselves."

Nels trotted over to the blacksmith shop to fetch the shoes, still warm from the forge. The blacksmith muttered a curse instead of a greeting. Nels trotted back to the barn, trying to glimpse Gertie through the window. He saw only Pettibone slumped over his cutting knife. It was not fair. It was not fair at all.

Together he and Barrister fitted the slings under the ox's belly, and secured them to a wooden frame built for that purpose. They began the painstaking task of tapping the shoes to each cloven hoof, using eight shoes to outfit a single ox.

"Need spikes when the year is dry," Barrister said through a mouth lined with tacks. "For icy roads. Dangerous if someone gets kicked. Glad for plenty of snow this year."

The ox mooed and struggled. Nels petted between its horns, crooning soothing words to the anxious beast.

"You're good with animals," Barrister said. "A gift."

Nels puffed his chest. At last, someone noticed. He loved animals and wanted nothing more than a small place with his own livestock. And Gertie by his side.

"You have choices to make," Barrister said. "Difficult choices."

Nels looked up in surprise. "What do you mean?"

"The bottle or betterment," Barrister said. "The sooner you choose, the better."

He went on to say that he had not been into town for three years. "I can stay away from temptation, or drink everything away again."

Ten-Day had told him that Barrister camped out in the woods all summer, hunting, and fishing and reading his books. "He's a regular hermit," Ten-Day had said.

The ox lowed. Nels held a handful of grain before its mouth.

"The bottle costs everything a man has." Barrister knelt and tapped nails into the hoof. "Course, you know what it has cost you."

Nels choked on something, maybe pride, or maybe embarrassment. It was as if the man looked right through him. Nels had never talked about his problem with anyone else before. Men never did. They drank together, lost everything together and then suffered together until the next payday. But they did not talk about it.

"I lost my law practice, my bank account, and my health," Barrister said. "Lost it and will lose everything again if I let down my guard. The bottle is always calling me. Best and worst friend I ever had."

Yes, the man understood his predicament. Nels did not want to talk about his lack of success, getting hoodwinked by confidence men, or blowing his wages in a single spree.

"It's bad luck, I have," Nels said. "Rotten luck."

Barrister reached for another shoe. Nels hefted the ox's leg allowing Barrister to tap the tacks into the pads of the cloven hoof. He used a tin snip to snap off the protruding nails on top of the hoof. Then he used a rasp to file down the nail heads lest they catch on something and the shoe pull away.

"Luck has nothing to do with it," he said. "I've learned that much."

Tap. Tap. Another shoe. Snip. Snip. Rasp. Rasp.

"What do you mean?" Nels's curiosity was stronger than his reluctance.

"Simple arithmetic." Barrister moved to the final hoof. "One drink is too many. A thousand is not enough."

The words burned into Nels's brain. He knew it was never enough.

They finished the job and released the ox from the sling. They eased it away from the frame and toward the feed troughs.

"You can't stay in the woods forever," Nels said as they led another ox into the frame.

"Maybe not," Barrister said. "But I do not trust myself in town. Maybe someday."

They shoed another animal, Barrister allowed Nels to do the nails and trimming. A useful skill to learn, one that he might need when Nels had his own place.

"What you doing with your money?" Nels said. "Must count up."

"Starting a business." Barrister predicted settlers would start pouring into northern Minnesota now that the land was cleared. "I've enough for a sawmill, but need a parcel of land for it. All the bolts and wasted wood lying around are free for the taking."

Nels gaped. He had noticed the wasted timber but had not the brains to take it a step further as Barrister did. The value of education. His bad luck not to have one.

Chapter 60
Sister Magdalena

January rolled into February. Near the end of the month, Sister Magdalena awakened to the sound of someone crying. She judged it to be the middle of the night. It was too cold to get up, but then she heard it again. The sound of wood thrown into the kitchen stove and a choking sob.

She inched out of bed and shivered into her habit. She found Pokey pouring coffee with shaking hands, dripping nose, and strangled sobs.

She joined him at a table near the warmth of the fire.

"Cold night," Sister Magdalena said. She opened the oven door and stuck her feet in the oven. "I'll bet Yuma wishes he had stayed in Arizona."

Pokey slurped his coffee. His hands shook so that most of it spilled over his shirt.

"What's wrong?" Sister Magdalena said. "Maybe I can help."

"No one can help me," Pokey said. "I'm done for."

"Tell me," Sister Magdalena said.

The story came out in fits and starts. "I'm not proud of it," Pokey said. "But it's what I did, and now it's blown up in my face."

He told her how he had helped Mr. Starkweather purchase the jobber camp. "He says he won it in a card game, but he didn't," Pokey said. "Gave me ten dollars and a half-dozen bottles of whiskey. Got a half-breed drunk and traded it for this land." Pokey groaned. "It was not right, and I knew it. Starkweather is making a killing at the expense of a poor Indian."

"Why did you do it?"

"Starkweather promised I could be his bull cook as long as I live." Pokey sobbed again. "My old age taken care of, even though I'm no good for nuthin' no more."

"Why did Mr. Starkweather have you make the trade?" Sister Magdalena's mind whirled. "Why didn't he do it himself?"

"Illegal for timber companies to buy land from Indians, but an ordinary person can do it."

The injustice of it stuck in her throat. Stealing from Indians, getting wealthy while ordinary people did the work. It was terrible, a situation that needed remedy.

"I am too old to work and no place to go. No kin to help me."

"But Mr. Starkweather promised employment," Sister Magdalena said.

"That's what I'm talking about." His voice rose and Sister Magdalena made a shushing sound, pointing to the back room where the others slept. "Mr. Starkweather is going out of the timber business."

Sister Magdalena blinked. "When did he get back?"

"Last night," Pokey said. "I would collect your money right away, if I were you. Suspect he'll take off without making payroll." He explained the scheme to fire the men before the company had to pay them. "He and Pettibone planned the whole thing. Elliot was in on it, and some shyster in Duluth."

Sister Magdalena's strength drained from her. She removed her feet and closed the oven door. The sheriff needed to know about these robbers.

"The accident interrupted his plans," Pokey said. "And Yuma was too smart to be bamboozled, but you mark my words. Starkweather will slip away as sure as God made the little green apples."

Sister Magdalena watched the old man leave the cookshack, bent over and broken. Pokey had done wrong, but Mr. Starkweather's behavior was criminal. And Elliot's and Jacob Pettibone's, too.

She did not return to bed, but knelt by the stove and prayed for everyone at Starkweather Timber. Unless God intervened, they were all in trouble.

Sister Magdalena hurried to the office after serving breakfast. Mr. Starkweather poured over ledgers. Sully tallied rows of figures beside him. The boy glanced up with a worried expression on his face, an extra pencil tucked above his ear. Pencil shavings mounded next to a penknife on the table.

"Mr. Starkweather," Sister Magdalena said. "We have business to discuss."

"Ah," Mr. Starkweather said. A twitching eye betrayed his nervousness. He cleared newspapers from a nearby chair. "Have a seat."

A newspaper bore a bold headline. "Panic Deepens with Start of 1894."

"There is the matter of hospital tickets." Sister Magdalena straightened her shoulders. He was not to be trusted. "I have instructions to collect the money owed."

"No doubt you are unaware of the news. Banks are folding. Businesses going under."

"That's terrible," Sister Magdalena sharpened her gaze. "It does not change our agreement."

"I must clarify my situation," Mr. Starkweather said. "I have a contract for the logs, thank God, but payment will arrive later than expected." He cleared his throat and looked toward Sully who bowed over his figures. "Everyone must wait until my invoice is satisfied." He lit a pipe from his waist pocket. The comforting fragrance of tobacco filled the room. "I have decided to liquidate my assets and pursue a new venture." He told of mining opportunities in Montana.

She saw for herself that Pokey was right. Starkweather had no intention of keeping his end of the contract.

Solveig would lose her farm. Pokey would be homeless and helpless. Gertie could not return to her mother. The jacks would be desperate and furious. The hospital ticket program would be scrapped for lack of payment. Everything she had worked for would be gone.

"Of course, the sisters will receive payment," Mr. Starkweather said in a voice that oozed charm. "My highest priority once I sell the timber, I assure you." He puffed again as sweet smoke tickled her nostrils.

She felt her face flush. It was not right. He had promised.

"I am under vows of obedience to wait for your draft," Sister Magdalena said. "The Sisters of Saint Benedict demand immediate payment."

"One cannot squeeze blood out of a rutabaga," Mr. Starkweather said. "You must appreciate my position."

"I understand more than you know. You made promises to Pokey concerning irregular matters," Sister Magdalena said. Her anger boiled up, righteous anger, she hoped.

"Mr. Kokott spoke out of turn," Mr. Starkweather said. "That is a confidential matter."

"It would be wise to satisfy your debts before you leave for Montana." Sister Magdalena felt her temper rising. "Lest your misdeeds become newspaper headlines."

She had done it again. Sister Lucy would have dealt with the man in a dignified manner. Sister Magdalena restrained herself from socking the miscreant on the nose.

Mr. Starkweather eyed her as if measuring her hang rope. He puffed his pipe with a cold look, and bellowed an order. "Prepare a draft for Sister Magdalena at once."

It felt like a hollow victory. She was under obedience to return to the convent, after all, and had no obligation to fight for the others, but the Gospel of Christ demanded love of neighbor and work for the common good.

"How about Solveig and the men?" she said. "Mrs. Murphy?"

Mr. Starkweather's eye twitched. "They will be paid when I am paid. Not a minute sooner. I must wait. They must wait." His eye twitched harder. "Sully, hurry with the draft."

Mr. Starkweather wanted her out of the way. The carpetbagger. More colorful descriptions came to mind, but Sister Magdalena fought them back. Justice was not achieved by name-calling.

The man was afraid for his reputation, no doubt the reason she would receive her money. He did not care about the others who had no voice, the ones who fattened his bank account, the ones who had no recourse to law or justice.

Come Holy Spirit and enlighten our darkness.

"Sister," Mr. Starkweather said. "I would appreciate if you did not repeat anything we discussed today. I will address the men soon enough. Rumors only stir up trouble."

She pocketed the bank draft, and left the office with a million ideas swirling in her brain.

Chapter 61
Solveig

News of Mr. Starkweather's return rippled through the camp. Solveig heard it from Stutz who knew from his brother. A relief to have the old dodger back in charge. Without him, no one knew what to do. In all fairness, Mr. Elliot would have managed things had he lived. Sully might tally figures, but the boy could not be held responsible for anything.

Pokey came into the cookshack with bowed head and sagging shoulders. He handed Solveig a letter. Her hands trembled as she shoved it into her apron pocket and hurried into the back room.

The letter from Gunnar Jacobson included a bank draft for the team. Young Bob and Buck were going to a good home. The money would help pay the note, but, oh. the sorrow of it.

Widowhood proved meaner than a snake. One door after another slammed until she was left alone with nothing. Not exactly nothing. She had her house and land. Gunnar's letter promised another payment for the team's wages at the end of the season. With their wages, her pay, and the money from selling the team, Solveig would carry a small purse into her future.

There would be other horses, but never another Young Bob and Buck. She would never own a horse trained by her husband. Young Bob and Buck fulfilled Rasmuss's dream. Her breath caught. She was glad he had known the joy of his team. Rasmuss deserved all the happiness there was. Living without him was like having half of herself cut away. Without him, she had no dreams left.

She tucked the draft into her trunk and hurried back to the kitchen. Pokey and Pettibone were deep in conversation at the meat cutting table. They whispered too low for Solveig to hear. Not that she cared. She had her own ax to grind. But soon their voices rose.

"God, no." Pettibone's voice sounded alarmed. "You are shitting me. Breaking his word after all we've done?"

Pokey nodded. "Says we didn't keep our end of the bargain."

"Like hell we didn't." Pettibone lifted his stump. "See this? Elliot died keeping our end."

"We danced with the devil." Pokey slammed out of the cookshack with empty water buckets.

Pettibone jammed the cutting knife deep into the table, cursing the day Starkweather was born. He overturned the work table with a crash, sending meat skidding across the floor.

"Stop." Solveig said. "Enough of this nonsense." Solveig fetched the cleaver and stood next to Pettibone. A quiver put a tremble in her voice. "Go berserk on your own time and away from my kitchen."

Rosy scurried behind the stove like a frightened mouse. Sister Magdalena looked grim as a hangman. It was time to fill the swingdingle. No time for foolery.

Pettibone leaned over to gather the fat scraps but was unable to reach them.

"Stutz," he called. "Come give a hand."

"Do it yourself," Solveig said. "Stutz is busy." She resisted the urge to shove the cripple onto the floor and beat him with his crutch. "You should have thought of that before you had your tantrum. We're not your slaves."

Sister Magdalena righted the table. She gathered the scraps and haunch of pork.

"We'll rinse off the meat," Solveig said with a growl. "But one more outburst like that and you'll be out in the snowbank."

She tackled her kneading bowl like an attacking Viking. She punched the dough as if it were Jacob Pettibone's face. She punched hard.

"What's his problem?" Gertie whispered as she loaded the swingdingle.

"It is Starkweather. He is going out of business," Stutz said at Solveig's elbow. "Sully worries he'll sneak away without paying us, but we're not supposed to tell anyone."

Solveig paused her kneading. It could not be true. Mr. Starkweather returned to close camp and pay the men. Even if he were going out of business, he had to finish what he started. There were contracts to fulfill. But Mr. Starkweather might wiggle out of it.

She would lose everything. The payment for the team was not quite enough. Without her wages she was doomed. The thought almost dropped her to the ground. It could not be. She had worked so hard.

Pokey stumbled into the cookshack with water for the reservoir, which should have been filled hours before. There would be no hot water for dinner dishes at this rate. The man looked white as his whiskers. He tottered, then collapsed into a heap. His head thumped on a bucket. Water flooded everywhere.

Rosy shrieked. Sister Magdalena hurried to assist the old man. Solveig stared in disbelief. Good Lord, what else could go wrong?

Pokey groaned. Drops of blood dripped from a cut on his temple. It was time for the swingdingle to go out.

"Stutz," she said. "Take out the swingdingle. Rosy, shut up and fetch a wet rag."

Pokey turned toward her with rheumy eyes. Snot dripped down onto his filthy shirt. A musky smell emanated from him. "Thank you, Missus," he said. "I'm on my last legs."

Pettibone called from the side table. "Leastways you've got legs, you old buzzard."

"Everyone be quiet," Solveig said. To work all winter and lose everything. She was ruined. This could not be happening. "Rest yourself, Pokey," she said at last. "Gertie, fetch a cup of tea with plenty of sugar."

Sister Magdalena lifted the old man to a bench. He staunched the bleeding with one hand and pressed the other to his chest.

"Are you hurt?" Solveig said.

"My heart, Missus," he whispered. "It acts up sometimes."

He sipped his tea as the color came back into his cheeks. Sister Magdalena and Gertie filled plates for the kitchen help. They ate in silence. Gertie wiped tears on her apron. Pettibone scowled. Only Rosy, working for room and board, had nothing to lose.

Soon the warbling sound of the Gabriel sounded through the trees.

"Stutz has much to learn about blowing the horn," Pokey said with a chuckle. "His horn sounds more like a confused crow than an angry moose." He chuckled and grabbed his chest again. "If I live, I'll give him lessons."

Solveig sat apart from the others, and forced herself to chew and swallow. Whatever happened, she needed her strength. They were down in the mouth and gloomy. "Are you sure?" Solveig asked Pokey. "About Starkweather, I mean."

"I'm sure," Pokey said. "And it gives me no joy in telling. He as much as told me that he'd leave."

What would happen to her? Maybe the banker's wife in Brainerd still needed a housekeeper.

"Mr. Starkweather is obliged to pay his debts," Gertie said. She wiped more tears. She leaned over a belly large enough to rest on her lap. "Can't the law make him pay up?"

"Barrister knows the law," Pettibone said.

"Of course, Starkweather should pay, but maybe he can't," Sister Magdalena said.

"Him?" Pettibone said with a snort. "Sly dog has money all over the country. Let it loose once when he had too much to drink."

Pokey's color improved, but his eye swelled and bruised. "Don't tell the jacks how I got this shiner," he said. "A man has his dignity."

Pettibone snorted.

Whether or not they were paid, the men had to eat. "Everyone back to work," Solveig said. Her bunions shrieked a weather report. Bad weather would keep Starkweather stranded in camp. She had a little time before the man could cut and run. She had to find a way to talk to him. Her future depended on getting paid. Without it, she was like Pokey—on her last legs and done for.

Chapter 62
Nels

Ten-Day cornered Nels in the barn. His face showed agitation. Nels looked forward to eating and going to bed. He did not want to hear whatever Ten-Day had to say.

"Did you hear the news about Starkweather?" Ten-Day said. "He's looking to sneak off without paying us."

"You're crazy," Nels said. "He has to honor our contracts."

"No, Pokey told me," Ten-Day said. "Starkweather is up to no good."

The Gabriel blew and they headed into supper. Nels sat between Barrister and Ten-Day near the door. To his surprise, Mr. Starkweather stood at the front of the room.

"I'd like to speak to you men before you eat," Starkweather said. He tugged his swallow tails and cleared his throat. Not a sound in the room. "You may have heard about the panic."

He told how banks were failing and businesses going under. "I am lucky to have a contract for these logs. They are being shipped to Upstate New York, thanks to your diligence." He fiddled with his watch chain and cleared his throat again. "Unfortunately, the payment for the logs will be delayed until late summer, maybe into autumn."

A low rumble went through the room, not exactly words, but a rustling from men leaning forward to hear better.

"You will be paid, but payment will be delayed due to these unforeseen circumstances."

Yuma stood to his feet. "We won't put up with no double dealings."

"You'll be paid," Mr. Starkweather said. "Later than planned, but payment will come. Leave your forwarding addresses with Sully. We will send drafts as soon as possible."

"You'll never get another crew if you cut and run," Yuma said. "We'll see to that."

"I am liquidating my assets and going out of the logging business," Mr. Starkweather said. "This is my final year timbering."

"We'd better get paid," Yuma said. "We will come and find you if we don't. Tar and feathers, make you ride the rail through Duluth. Won't we boys?"

"Mrs. Rognaldson," Mr. Starkweather said. "Begin serving the meal. It smells delicious."

With that, he walked out of the cookshack, with Sully following like a little lap dog.

Back in the bunkhouse, several men started packing up their gear. They said that if Starkweather wasn't paying, they might as well leave early and find other work.

"I'm thinking to sign on with Captain Ben," Ten-Day said. "But he will not be upriver until ice-out. Might as well stay here and keep my feet under Ma's table as long as I can."

Nels felt as if he had been socked in the stomach. Not getting paid was worse than losing it all on a spree. At least for a few days he binged on all the whiskey he wanted. Pure arithmetic. One drink was too many and a thousand not enough.

The next morning, he was surprised to hear Barrister whistling.

"What are you so happy about?" Nels said. "Didn't you hear? We're not getting paid until fall. Maybe not even then."

"You didn't listen," Barrister said. "Mr. Starkweather is liquidating his assets. His equipment, this land, the buildings. This is a chance to make a go of it."

Nels leaned in and concentrated on what Barrister was saying.

"The man is cash-starved and ripe for a bargain." Barrister grinned. "This is our chance."

Nels grinned, too. His luck finally turned.

Nels followed Barrister to the office. The wet snow made every step a slog. Logging season could not last much longer. They found Mr. Starkweather at his desk with Sully tallying sums at his side.

"Mr. Starkweather," Barrister said. "We've a proposition for you."

Mr. Starkweather listened to their appeal to receive the land and a few tools instead of their combined wages. He looked at them for a long moment, and sucked on his cigar, releasing a black cloud of smoke in front of him.

"What do you plan to do with the land?" Mr. Starkweather said.

Nels had a sudden inspiration. They had to convince the old coot that he was getting a deal. "Farming," Nels said before Barrister could speak up. "We are going into farming. We want your single ox and traces, a few building tools and food supplies to get started."

Barrister looked at Nels before nodding. "Yes, farming. We are going to be partners."

"It's poor soil," Nels said. He had to make the old fart believe there was nothing to gain by letting go of the land. "Doubt it will do much for crops, but we'll hunt and trap, and get by somehow."

Mr. Starkweather pulled the ledger from Sully and added up a few numbers on a scrap of paper. "This is your wages," Mr. Starkweather said. "I've two hundred acres of valuable land cleared and ready for tillage."

Nels almost choked. Cleared land? The land was sandy and littered with stumps and brush. Much of it was tamarack and cedar swamp. He started to protest, but Barrister interrupted.

"With the panic on, there's little hope of selling either the land or that lone ox to anyone else," Barrister said.

"The land, maybe," Mr. Starkweather said. "Your wages will cover only the going rate for farmland."

Disappointment rose in Nels's throat. Another setback. Without an ox or a few tools, they would be hard-put to turn a profit.

"Most of its swamp," Barrister said. "Worthless for farming. Throw in the ox and harness, a chain and two axes, and a two-man saw. Then we have a deal."

"Impossible." Mr. Starkweather scowled over the ledger. "I can't give it away."

Nels had a sudden thought. "My wages increased after I took Pettibone's job," he said. "It's in the ledger."

Mr. Starkweather jerked the book away from Sully, and turned a page. He glared at his young clerk, who began sharpening a pencil as if his life depended on it.

"See?" Nels held back a cackle. He had fooled the old Billy goat, yes, he had.

In the end, they walked away with the land, the ox, harness, a chain, two axes and a saw. It was a step forward in every way.

Chapter 63
Sister Magdalena

Her plan was in direct disobedience to Mother's Superior's wishes. She had her money and should return to the convent at once. How could she leave her friends in such a predicament? It was not fair that she should receive payment and they go without.

To disobey was a serious violation and carried consequences. She might be expelled from the convent. The entire community would be affected by her action. Justice demanded she do something.

Her prayers fell flat. She had no one to ask for counsel. Sister Magdalena saw no other path. Everything within her screamed to follow her impulse.

Father, forgive me, I am about to sin.

Sister Magdalena left the cookshack and slipped along the frozen path to the office. She met Nels and Barrister coming out. Nels offered a cheery greeting and made a short bow.

"You're jolly," she said. "Must have good news."

"Maybe and maybe not." Nels appeared giddy. She sniffed. No smell of liquor.

They hurried off at the sound of the Gabriel calling the men to the swingdingle.

What had they to be happy about? Maybe Mr. Starkweather had good news. She opened the door and her eyes adjusted to the dim room. A lantern burned. The south facing windows had yet to catch the sun's zenith. Papers and ledgers spread over the table.

Mr. Starkweather frowned. A foul-smelling cigar tainted the air. Sully glanced toward his employer before answering her greeting.

"Mr. Starkweather." Sister Magdalena placed the bank draft before him. Too late to go back now. "I need a favor."

Mr. Starkweather sighed. "What now? Can't you see I am busy?"

Sully inched away as if afraid the brains of the outfit might strike him.

"Mrs. Rognaldson has a mortgage due," Sister Magdalena said. "She'll lose her farm unless she receives a timely payment from you."

Mr. Starkweather raised an eyebrow and exhaled a cloud of smoke. "I told you before. Everything is tied up in the panic."

"Mrs. Rognaldson cannot wait." Sister Magdalena slowed her ragged breathing and relaxed her clenched fists. Sully was not the only one intimidated by the brains of the outfit. "I'm willing to wait for payment in order for Mrs. Rognaldson to be paid now."

"What?" Mr. Starkweather threw down his pen, splattering ink across a sheaf of papers. "I cannot pay one without paying the whole crew. They each have reasons why they can't wait."

Sully flinched and reached for a blotter. His efforts smudged the ink, making the situation worse. Mr. Starkweather swore at the boy.

"No one will know," Sister Magdalena lowered her gaze. "I'll return this draft with the understanding that you will pay the convent later." Sister Bede Marie would be livid. "Write a draft today for Mrs. Rognaldson, and I will give it to her quietly." She swallowed hard. "Please Mr. Starkweather. She deserves it. She's a widow. Do this act of charity. The Lord will not forget."

He glared for a long minute. "And if I refuse? Will you write letters to the newspaper and besmirch my reputation?" He blew smoke into her face and stubbed the cigar into an ashtray. "I've heard about your undignified behavior at Skunk Hollow and the Aitkin Saloon."

Groveling dealt a hard blow to her pride. "Please, Mr. Starkweather, as an act of charity."

"I once held the sisters in high esteem, but no longer," Mr. Starkweather said. "I've learned that you are a pack of conniving women preying on the troubles of honest businessmen." He fairly spat the words in her face. "The bishop will hear about this. Oh, yes, the bishop will be informed."

"So will you do as I ask?" she said.

"What choice do I have?" he said. He took the draft made out to the sisters and ripped it into shreds. "Sully. Tally the cook's wages through the end of this week."

"The season goes longer," Sister Magdalena said.

"You are not easily satisfied," he said with a sneer. "Take it or leave it."

Sister Magdalena had much to learn about groveling. She should have haggled for more money. She nodded and tucked the draft in her pocket. She thanked Mr. Starkweather and left. The realization of what she had done sank in as she breathed the fresh coldness of winter. Willful disobedience. Reports to the Bishop.

God help her. She was not sorry.

Back in the cookshack, Stutz and Gertie sloshed in dishwater up to their elbows. Jacob set aside the meat cutting and tackled a bushel of potatoes. Rosy joined him with paring knife in hand. Their presence together stood as a jarring reminder of little Jimmy. From time-to-time Rosy glanced Jacob's way. Jacob's eyes were on Gertie.

"Solveig," Sister Magdalena said. "Show me your chickens. I'll be leaving as soon as the weather clears."

Solveig cast a questioning glance her way, but pulled on her wraps. Together they left the cookshack.

"What do you want?" Solveig said as soon as they were outside. "Doubt you want to say goodbye to my hens."

A cold wind blew across the lake, and gray clouds spattered wet flakes. Winter rolling into spring. Even the snowflakes changed to slush.

"I've something for you," Sister Magdalena said. "Let's walk." Sister Magdalena handed the draft to Solveig as soon as they were away from the buildings.

Solveig stared at the draft, reread it, and then again. "What is this? How did you manage?" Tears traveled the lines in her face and pooled in the wrinkles by her mouth. "A miracle."

"I explained your predicament to Mr. Starkweather," Sister Magdalena said. "It took a little persuasion."

"Wait until I show Gertie," Solveig said. "Maybe he'll pay her, too."

"No," Sister Magdalena said. "You cannot tell anyone. I promised Mr. Starkweather that no one else would know. He said it wasn't fair to pay you and not the others. He paid you out of Christian charity. You must keep it quiet."

Solveig cocked an eyebrow. "What did you give him?"

Sister Magdalena chuckled. "You know him too well," she said. "Never mind. Pay your mortgage and keep quiet."

They walked to the barn and found the hens. Barrister and Nels were not back from the swingdingle. Solveig coaxed Gumbri into her arms.

"Saved the land, but what future do I have?" Solveig said. "Living alone out on the farm until I die? No purpose. Not doing anything."

Sister Magdalena's temper rose. She had sacrificed everything she valued to help her friend pay the mortgage. "Listen to yourself. You are healthy and able-bodied. God has a purpose for you."

"What?" Solveig said. "I'm no good to anyone."

"Look around you," Sister Magdalena said. "People are suffering. God asks that we see those around us in need of our help, and help them as we are able."

"I'm too old to help anyone."

Sister Magdalena took a breath, and tried to speak in a calmer tone. "You have everything. You have a home, land, and a bank draft in your pocket. You are strong and healthy. You know how to work, cook, and manage a kitchen. You are not dead yet."

"My son invites me to Bismarck," Solveig said. The hen murmured a low sound. "But I don't want to burden them."

"Then live in Bismarck without burdening them," Sister Magdalena said. "Find a job and make your own way. Our Benedictine hospital always needs cooks and bakers. They have a dormitory for workers."

Solveig kissed the top of Gumbri's head and returned the hen to its roost.

"Or do something else," Sister Magdalena said. "Be willing, and something will open up to you."

"I plan on renting my fields." Solveig looked off into the distance as if considering her options. "Hard on a house to leave it empty."

"Then rent it out," Sister Magdalena said. Solveig was as stubborn a woman as she had ever known. "Look what you have accomplished here. You proved the naysayers wrong."

Solveig grinned. "I knew I could do it."

Nels and Barrister came back to the barn, and Solveig returned to her kitchen. Sister Magdalena greeted the men with small talk about the weather. Barrister guessed it would be no more than a week until the melting snow would shut down logging.

"Sister," Nels said. He fairly beamed with importance. "We're landowners."

"What?" Sister Magdalena said. "How did this happen?"

Nels explained how he and Barrister convinced Mr. Starkweather to let them have the land in exchange for their wages. "He's cash poor and seemed glad about it," Nels said. "Barrister convinced the old skinflint to add the ox, some tools, and enough grub to get started farming."

Sister Magdalena swallowed her surprise. Her father would have had opinions about anyone farming such poor soil. "Farming?" she said. "Really?"

"Not really. A sawmill, actually," Barrister said with a wink. "But keep it to yourself until the season is over. We are starting a business to salvage the bolts. We will cut cedar poles for the railroad. Not easy money, but money for someone willing to work for it."

"We'll be partners," Nels said. "Starting up costs plenty."

Another loose end. Nels's money rattled in her pocket.

"I had hoped to have enough left over to send for my folks," Nels said. "Starkweather will keep the cookshack and bunkhouse for the logs, but the huts will be left for us."

"We'll earn money before long," Barrister said. "You'll send for your folks."

Nels looked grim. "I sure could use that money I wasted. I am an idiot."

"Does no good to think like that," Barrister said. "We have a future."

Sister Magdalena reached into her pocket. Time to fess up. She had explaining to do.

Chapter 64
Solveig

To move to Bismarck seemed as unreachable as moving to Paris, France. At her age? Impossible. Solveig bundled up and made ready for another trip to the root cellar.

Heavy snow from the night before bowed the pine branches low. From time to time a load of snow plopped to the ground, causing the branches to spring up. Solveig must bend, too, if she wanted to know the child. Halvor was as stubborn as a Swede, as hard-headed as a rock. It was up to her.

A noise came from the woodshed. She paused to listen. She followed the sound, and found Rosy blubbering behind a stack of wood.

"What's wrong?" Difficult to be patient with the foolish girl, but Sister Magdalena had urged compassion. "Why are you out here instead of doing your work?"

Rosy's mish-mash of excuses made no sense. The poor woman could not connect two rational thoughts, let alone explain herself. She burst into sobs, wailing, and burying her face in her apron.

"Tell me slower," Solveig said. "I couldn't understand a word you said."

Rosy blew her nose, took a breath, and started again. "He's my Jimmy's father, but he won't pay me no mind, looks right through me as if I'm not there." She blew her nose again.

"My poor Jimmy stuck in the orphanage when he has two able-bodied parents who should be taking care of him. It's not right."

"Jimmy's father?" Solveig said. "Who would that be?"

"Jacob Pettibone," Rosy said with a loud sniff. "At least he used to be able-bodied."

Jacob Pettibone was the last man Solveig would choose to father her child. "Does he know about Jimmy?"

"No, I tried to tell him, but got too scared." Rosy shook her head and honked her nose into a ragged handkerchief. "I never knew his name. Then he started working in the cookshack." She started to weep again. "Haven't seen him since...it happened."

Solveig felt sick. A casual encounter in exchange for money. Wickedness. Perversion. Utter disregard for decency.

Rosy wailed. "Poor Jimmy. What can I do?"

Solveig released her judgement. Rosy had been alone in a world where women were easy prey. She had been lucky. Bishop Whipple gave employment. Rasmuss, introduced by Evan Jacobson, had been a gift from heaven.

"Have you told him?" Solveig said. She was tired of men getting away with everything.

She marched Rosy into the cookshack to where Pettibone trimmed meat.

"Pettibone," Solveig said. "You're a miserable excuse for a human being, but you have a chance to do something decent."

The color drained out of Rosy's face, leaving freckles big as bedbugs. She wrung her hands.

"Tell him," Solveig said. "Right now. Tell him the truth, and get back to work."

"Tell me what," Pettibone said with a growl. He turned his gaze on Solveig and Rosy, looking from one to the other.

"You have a son," Rosy said. "A little boy named Jimmy in the Duluth orphanage."

Pettibone's eyes bulged and he dropped the knife. He stared at Rosy. Stutz crept nearer to listen. Sister Magdalena appeared at Solveig's elbow.

"Stutz," Solveig said. "Fetch more water."

"The buckets are full," Stutz said.

"Empty them in the reservoir and fill them again," Solveig said. "Now."

Stutz poured the water and left the cookshack. As soon as he was gone, the conversation began again.

"You're wrong," Pettibone said. "Impossible."

"You gave me an extra dollar because it was my first time," Rosy said. "I was crying."

His eyes bulged. His mouth dropped open. Recognition flashed in his eyes. "How old is he?" he said. "Me, a father."

Rosy told Pettibone the boy's age and birthdate.

Through the window, Solveig saw Nels and Barrister hurrying toward the office, heads together as if plotting revenge.

"You didn't know before, but now you do," Solveig said. "It's time you stood up like a man and do right by your boy."

"Not doing too much standing these days," Pettibone said. "He's better off with the nuns."

"I'm sure you want the best for your son," Sister Magdalena said. "A child needs his own folks."

"Enough jabbering," Solveig said. "No time to solve it now." She returned to the stove. "Rosy, help Jacob finish that meat. Gertie, start grinding coffee."

"How can I help?" Sister Magdalena said.

"Come with me to the root cellar," Solveig said. "Bring the sledge."

They plodded through the fresh drifts, the snow clumping on the hems of their skirts. The harps played overhead and snow slid from the pine branches laden with the heavy stuff.

"Do you see the lesson?" Sister Magdalena said. "The branches carry their heavy load. Then the sun melts the snow and the branches release their loads and lift their arms to heaven—like a prayer."

More snow thudded down.

"I should be a preacher," Sister Magdalena said with a chuckle.

"Rosy and Pettibone." Solveig shook her head. "Did you know?"

"The last few days," Sister Magdalena said. "I didn't know what to do with the information."

"What will happen to them?" Solveig said.

"It's in God's hands," Sister Magdalena said. "We can only pray."

They entered the doorway. Supplies filled the formerly empty cellar.

"I didn't do so well in planning what we needed," Solveig said. "I was cautious and considered camp might go longer. Instead, we have an early spring."

"You were prudent to take precautions," Sister Magdalena said. "I'm sure Mr. Starkweather is appreciative of your work."

"Maybe," Solveig said with a shrug.

All afternoon Solveig pondered Sister Magdalena's advice. She stood next to Gertie at the stove while frying doughnuts. Gertie would not be paid. Where could she go? No one would give her work at this stage of her pregnancy.

It was not right. Solveig tallied the amount of money she had. It wasn't enough to pay off the mortgage and buy a ticket to Ireland. She could not stop thinking about it.

At supper, neither Mr. Starkweather nor Paulson were in attendance, which made it easier. She decided to go ahead. She had no fear of being fired with camp almost over.

"Boys," Solveig said after the men had eaten. "You are inconvenienced by the delay in wages." Every face looked her way. "Mrs. Murphy is soon to deliver a child. It was her intent to return home to Ireland, but the delayed payment prevents this from happening."

Gertie fled from the room with a red face. Sister Magdalena beamed.

"She is a widow with no family to help her. I am passing a basket around. Give something if you have it," Solveig said. It felt good to be herself again, thinking about others and reaching out to help. "You're all fond of her. I've read the love notes under your plates. Here's your chance to prove it."

It was rare for a man to pass the basket without adding something. Their earnest and whiskery faces. Their clumsy goodness. An act of charity, even though they needed every cent themselves.

"Thank you," Solveig said. "Mrs. Murphy thanks you."

The jacks filed out of the cookshack, craning their necks for a glimpse of Gertie as they left, leaving the basket heaped with coins. It would not be enough for her to return to Ireland, but it would help Gertie for now.

Chapter 65
Nels

He and Gertie could marry and live in the office. They would be happy. He imagined Gertie frying potatoes, with her cheeks flushed from the heat of the stove. They would spend wintry evenings reading by the fire. He would build a bed for them with a mattress from the rushes growing in the swamp. But no, she wanted to return to Ireland. Nels jabbed his pitchfork into the manure pile and pitched dung into a wheelbarrow with enough force to splatter dirty straw over the floor.

"Forget about her," Barrister said.

"I can't," Nels said.

"It's a serious thing to raise someone else's child," Barrister said. "A noose around your neck that gets tighter with the years. The wife favors him over your children. She cannot help but remember her first love. Your children resent him. The boy hates you for taking his father's place." Barrister spat in the manure pile. "You're better off without the bother."

Barrister was usually right. Still, Nels craned his neck to glimpse Gertie as she dumped dishwater outside the cookshack door. She did not look his way.

"I've got to talk to her while I have the chance." Nels stuck the pitchfork into the straw and wiped his hands on the back of his pants.

"Gertie," he called out. She turned at her name and paused to see what he wanted. She blushed red, but waited for him. My God, she was beautiful with her dark eyelashes and upturned nose.

"What are you going to do?" he said.

"Not sure." The lilt of Irish in her voice melted his knees. "Probably go back with Sister Magdalena. At least until the baby is born."

"Barrister and I bought this land," he said. "You're welcome to stay on and cook for us, until you get your wages."

"That would hardly be proper, Mr. Jensen." Her face flushed crimson.

"It would be proper, if you were my wife," Nels said.

"First a cook, and then a wife," she said. "Which do you want?"

"A wife, of course," he said. "I'm not that kind of man."

Gertie sighed. "You're not, I know that, but Ma says you're a drinker." She hesitated. "I know you are trying to change your ways. You told me once that you were sending for your parents." "Yes, I'll send for them when we start earning money," Nels said. "Barrister and I are in business together." He told her about cutting poles and sawing bolts. "Everything has changed. My luck has turned."

"Send for your folks," she said. "I'll believe you've changed when that happens."

Nels swallowed hard. No doubt, Sister Lumberjack had blabbered about his episode in Aitkin, the nosey-Nellie. But it was true. Sending for his parents would prove that he had turned his life around. He would do it. He would show Gertie, and Ma and Sister Lumberjack and everyone else. He would prove to himself that he was a better man.

"Can I write to you in Duluth?"

"Nothing can stop you," Gertie said. One side of her mouth lifted into a smile. "Send mail in care of Sister Magdalena. She will know where I am."

Yuma interrupted them, and Gertie returned to her duties with apron strings fluttering in the breeze. She looked back over her shoulder and smiled before climbing the stairs into the cookshack.

Writing letters was something. Not what he wanted, but something. He would pour out his heart on paper. Barrister would help him find the words to express his love for her. Maybe there were poems that he could copy out. He knew he would convince her. He knew it.

"I'm leaving while I can cross the Mississippi on foot," Yuma said. "I'm heading to Brainerd to see that undertaker."

"Mr. Bean," Nels said. "Tell him hello."

"If I know my brother," Yuma said, "he put his wages into a bank. Maybe in Brainerd. Would be nice to send something home to Ma."

Nels reached out to shake his hand. "I wish you luck."

"Sorry about the misunderstanding," Yuma said. He pulled the thong with the blue stone from around his neck. "You can have it back. Suppose it belongs to that Indian."

They laughed. "I'll see that he gets it," Nels said. Gilbert had not shown his face in camp since Yuma had accused him of murder, but Nels knew where he lived. From now on, they were neighbors.

Yuma wished them luck and hefted his turkey. Melting snow plopped like raindrops from the trees near the barn. It was warmer than early March was supposed to be.

"By the way," Yuma said. "Do not tell anyone I'm leaving. I would sooner hang myself than have Ten-Day tag along."

"I've been thinking about the money from Sister Lumberjack," Barrister said when Nels returned to the barn. "We might bargain with Starkweather for more tools. There's money in shoeing oxen and horses."

"How long do you think it will take to save enough to send for my folks?" Nels said. Everything depended on having them with him.

"I'd think by spring," Barrister said. "Especially if you get another payment from the Dirty Dog."

"Let's do it." The money from Sister Lumberjack astounded Nels. To think she had gone into the saloon and demanded it back. He would have liked to have seen it, but he was blacked out with drink, sot that he was. No, he corrected himself, sot that he used to be.

The deed was in both their names. Barrister had added a statement saying that the land could not be divided or sold without the assent of the other, and then, only after a time period of one month.

"I'm making it impossible for one of us to weaken and turn our venture into ready cash," Barrister said. Sister Lumberjack and Ten-Day witnessed the document.

His parents could live in the filer's hut. He and Gertie and the boy would take the office. He hoped Mr. Starkweather would leave the bed behind. It was a big bed with a featherbed. If not, Nels would build a bed himself. His father would help him in the long winter evenings. He would build Gertie a nice table and a cupboard for her crockery. He would come home from a long day in the woods to a hot meal. He and Gertie and their son would build a life together.

Sister Lumberjack had promised that his drinking days were numbered. She had been right. Nels laughed out loud. She had known all along.

Chapter 66
Sister Magdalena

Sister Magdalena dabbed holy water, made the sign of the cross and headed toward Mr. Starkweather's office. The warm weather melted the heavy snow, making the walk difficult.

Starkweather Timber would close the following day. No one was surprised. It was impossible to move the heavy logs in the soft snow.

Come Holy Spirit. Fill the hearts of your faithful.

She carried a wild inspiration. Of course, it was far-fetched, but she had to try. She stepped inside where Mr. Starkweather labored over bookwork.

"Mr. Starkweather," Sister Magdalena said. "I have a proposition for you."

He shook his head and groaned. "Not you again." He tapped a pencil against the table. "Will you please quit bothering me?"

"Mr. Starkweather," she said. "It's come to my attention that you have extra food stuffs due to camp ending sooner than expected."

"So what?" he said with a growl. "None of your business."

"I'd like to suggest that you fulfill your debt to the convent by giving us the leftover supplies." She explained that feeding the orphans, hospital patients, and convent was a continual struggle. "You will help us and meet your obligation."

He leaned back in his chair as if calculating dollars and cents. "How would you get it to Duluth?"

"The horses and wagons must return to civilization somehow," Sister Magdalena said. "I could ride out with the teamster. Once in Aitkin, I can ship by train to Duluth."

In the end, it was arranged. Mr. Starkweather was almost cordial in his solicitation. He promised transport to the railroad line in Aitkin. The rest was up to her.

When Sister Magdalena left the office, she knelt behind a tree and gave thanks. Tears leaked out of her eyes. Only the all-knowing God could have provided for the unpaid debt, despite her disobedience to Mother Superior. Yes, she would still answer for herself, but no one could be angry for long since she returned with goods worth more than the debt.

None of it made sense. Her failings counted too many to mention, and yet somehow, things had worked out. Sister Magdalena had bumbled through every situation, usually doing the wrong thing. Pride and ego almost defeated her.

She made the sign of the cross. Others succeeded through gifts or talents, but Sister Magdalena had nothing except the kindness of Almighty God, a strong back and a stubborn determination. She leaned hard into His mercy.

One foot in front of the other. Solveig would be relieved the supplies would not be held against her. Sister Magdalena returned to the cookshack where the staff were eating their noon meal. She announced her agreement with Mr. Starkweather and that she would leave with the teamsters the day after tomorrow.

"Day after tomorrow!" Rosy said with a squeal. "I'll get to see my Jimmy."

The day came all too soon. Sister Magdalena and Solveig had stayed up most of the night, packing supplies and emptying the kitchen. Solveig insisted on scrubbing the floors.

"They're tearing down the cookshack," Pokey said. "No sense in cleaning."

"I was raised to leave things orderly," Solveig said as she swept the floor.

Pokey looked at Sister Magdalena and rolled his eyes. Sister Magdalena grinned. The kitchen crew were all leaving camp, riding in the giant wagons as far as Aitkin. Sister Magdalena had begged help to load the supplies from the root cellar the night before. The supplies took up only a corner of the wagon, leaving room for anyone who needed a ride. Ma's hens were crated and Queenie snugged in her basket. Pokey sat on Ma's heavy trunk.

Sister Magdalena tucked her snowshoes between sacks of flour for safe keeping. With any luck, she would be using them again the following year.

Jacob Pettibone hobbled over on his sticks, and Sister Magdalena and Rosy pulled him up on the wagon bed.

"Sister," Jacob said. "Do you know of a school I could go to? I'm thinking to take up bookkeeping, like you said."

"Sister Bede Marie will know," Sister Magdalena said. Just speaking the name of one of her sisters brought a stab of homesickness. "We'll ask her when we get there."

Sister Magdalena would petition the sisters to provide work and lodging for Rosy and Gertie. Begging and groveling might be required, but Sister Magdalena would do so without hesitation. She was Sister Lumberjack, after all, and had learned how to haggle. Perhaps Gertie could help Sister Hildegard in the hospital kitchen in exchange for room and board, at least until the baby came. Rosy must work in the orphanage. Jimmy needed to know his mother. Even Sister Lucy would not argue with that.

"How will you get all this stuff to Duluth?" Gertie said.

"Pray, my friend," Sister Magdalena said. "Ask the Blessed Mother to intercede for us."

She had no money to ship the supplies. She needed a miracle. All of them needed miracles.

Solveig looked back at the cookshack where several jacks were already starting to dismantle the building.

"It's sad to see it torn down," Solveig said. "It wasn't so bad, after all."

"We learned a lot," Sister Magdalena said. "And there's more to learn."

Big Mike himself mounted the wagon box and took up the lines. He looked back to make sure they were all in place. "Hang on," he said as the horses jerked forward. "We've got to cross the Mississippi before ice out."

"Ice is probably gone already," Pettibone said. "Then what do we do?"

"Dunno," Big Mike said. "We'll worry about that when we get there."

Sister Magdalena crossed herself and took her mother's rosary out of her pocket. Behind them lay the ruins of the once-magnificent forest. The jagged stumps and slash showed stark against the morning sky. Nels walked in the tamarack swamp with an ax over his shoulder. He saw them and called out a farewell.

"Look," Rosy said. "It's Nels."

"Goodbye, Gertie. Answer my letters." He raised both hands and waved.

Gertie turned pink, but waved back to him.

"Hate to see the trees gone," Solveig said.

"Trees grow back," Sister Magdalena said. "It is progress. This forest will bless many with new houses and barns. It will be doors and chicken coops and stores. This forest will build America."

Gertie was still looking back at Nels. Only time would tell if Gertie and Nels got together, if Rosy and her son reunited, if Solveig made a new start, and if Nels stayed sober. God alone knew if Pettibone would turn his life around. She would pray for all of them. She had seen many miracles this past year, and needed a few more before she returned to the convent.

Gratitude flooded her heart, and a burst of joy sprouted up like a wellspring. It turned into a giggle, and then a chortle and then a full-out guffaw. She was Sister Lumberjack, the six-foot penguin on snowshoes.

"What's so funny?" Solveig said.

"Nothing," Sister Magdalena said, wiping tears from her face with the corner of her veil. "Nothing at all." She picked up her mother's rosary. The morning sun glinted off the pink coral beads. A perfect day to meditate on the Glorious Mysteries.

Chapter 67
Solveig

Solveig's emotions choked any words she might have said as she climbed off the dray.

Home. Always before it held warmth and welcome. Today the place looked lonesome and dilapidated from being empty all winter. Slushy snow blocked the door to the house. Tar paper flapped in the north window. Dirty drifts against the foundation. No family to welcome her. She gripped Queenie until the cat yowled, then let her down in the yard.

Tomorrow she would pay the bank note. She would never go into debt again. She would arrange for Mr. Olson to rent her fields on shares. She would find an excuse to visit Tildie, her old cow. Solveig missed Rasmuss. Missed her team. Missed her son.

She hefted the crate down onto the ground. Pokey and the drayman unloaded the trunks and supplies that Pokey had purchased in Fergus Falls. Pokey paid the man, as was the agreement.

"So, this is it," Pokey said. He stood a bit, gawking around at the buildings and fences. It lay flat as a sourdough pancake. "I've had my fill of trees."

She carried the crate to the barn and let the hens loose. Gumbri scratched and clucked as if she were glad to be home. Solveig fitted her hand into Rasmuss's print by the door. Her longing for him gouged her innards like a knife, like a blow to the stomach that snatched her wind.

"Ma," Pokey called. "I'm going inside."

She called out for him to go ahead. She dreaded entering the empty house. She had let him get the fire going. Gumbri squawked in triumph and left an egg in the straw. Solveig warmed her hands on this freshest of gifts and cradled it in her pocket. Supper.

She would take the cars to Bismarck as soon as her business was finished. A letter of reference from Sister Lumberjack tucked in her reticule.

Solveig would find another job. Her wages plus the rent on the fields would be enough to keep her independent and out of the poor farm. Pokey would keep watch over her property. Sister Lumberjack vouched for him. Of course, the nun would vouch for anyone, always seeing the good in people, their potential. She had stood up for Rosy, of all people, and Nels Jensen in all his monkey business. Everyone should have a friend like Sister Lumberjack.

Solveig would not tell Halvor of her plans until she settled in a place of her own. That would eliminate any awkward request for her to move in with them and be a bother. She would find a room at a boarding house where she need not cook at all. She would put her bunions up at night instead of washing dishes. She would live like a city person. No responsibility for anyone but herself.

Solveig considered working with the Bismarck nuns. If only they were like Sister Lumberjack. She chuckled. Of course, they would not be like her. There could only be one Sister Lumberjack.

Pokey described Bismarck as a wind-swept hollow on the Missouri River. Where there was a river there were trees. Beyond the trees would be the flat, open prairies that she had learned to love.

Solveig could not think beyond trees and prairie. Britta, Britta's parents, the new baby and Halvor jumbled her mind and left her dizzy. No plan of action clicked into place concerning them. Sister Lumberjack said that God was in the messy of life. He must be very much present in Solveig's life. She had expected to live out her days on this farm. Instead, a new path stretched into her future. As the ax made way for farmers, so cruel blows had swept away her old life.

Rasmuss sang encouragement from beyond the grave. *God strengthen thee wherever in the world you go.*

Bismarck was not what she wanted. None of it was.

"Let God worry about it. He's going to be up all night, anyway," Sister Lumberjack had said. Solveig chuckled. Of course, Sister Lumberjack would say that. She had a practical faith in God that almost made sense, despite her being a slave of the Pope. God had a sense of humor to send a Catholic to be her new friend.

Solveig stepped out of the barn and was greeted by the prairie wind. "I hate this," she said.

Her friend caught her words and carried them away.

A curl of smoke spiraled out of the chimney. A flock of geese flew overhead, a sharp vee heading north, riding the chinook, carrying spring to the flatlands. The skies sparkled as blue as Stink Lake before freeze up, the clear color of Rosy's eyes pleading for refuge at Starkweather Timber, the perfect turquoise of the stone linking Yuma to Nels Jensen.

She carried in her reticule the money that both saved her farm and allowed another adventure. She was older, but not too old.

Gumbri scratched in the weeds, lifting delicate feet over pools of melting snow. Solveig would miss the hens, but knew better than haul them to Bismarck. She could not manage both trunk and crates. She had learned that much.

Queenie would go with her. Any boarding house would welcome a good mouser. Queenie scampered in the weeds and came up with a squirming mouse. Queenie laid the tribute at Solveig's feet and waited for praise.

A bubble of joy crowded a small corner of her heart. When Rasmuss died, she had thought laughter died with him. She wanted to laugh again. She wanted to laugh like Sister Lumberjack, until the tears flowed, laugh until she was undone.

Solveig was not Sister Lumberjack. It was enough that joy dwelt in that quiet corner of her inner self. She was Solveig Olasdotter Rognaldson, a widow who knew how to cook, how to stand up for herself, how to earn her own living, and make her own decisions.

She had traveled across the ocean and made a new life on the prairie. She raised a son and had been a wife. When her husband died, she satisfied the debt that threatened her land. Only shadows lay before her. The path led to either contentment or defeat.

She was terrified, but she would do it anyway. What choice did she have?

Solveig stepped behind the barn, out of sight of the house. She lifted her face, and her friend, the prairie wind, kissed her cheeks and twirled her skirts. Memories transfigured into prayers as sure as Sister Lumberjack counted beads. Grandmother pressing the recipes into her hands as she left her homeland. Kind Bishop Whipple. Friendship with Inga. Evan Jacobson introducing her to Rasmuss. Halvor bereft and crying for his mother. The horror of the Indian war. The despair of the grasshopper plagues. Rasmuss's melodies and too-soon death. Halvor's marriage and betrayal. Sister Lumberjack, Nels Jensen, Gertie, Rosy and Jimmy, Jacob Pettibone and even Tightwad Starkweather.

She would never forget. Nor would she dismiss Sister Lumberjack's wise counsel. Though she was a stubborn Norwegian and slow to learn, the lessons stayed with her when she did learn them. She would carry their wisdom wherever in the world she went.

Solveig glanced over her shoulder to make sure that she was alone. She raised on tiptoe and stretched her fingers wide. She closed her eyes, raised both hands to the heavens and shouted into the face of the wind.

"Here I am, Lord. Take the whole mess."

The wind caught her words and carried them across the melting snow of the Breckenridge Flats, over the empty fields and pastures and into the expanse of sky beyond her prairie home.

A vee of geese called overhead, birds in the back flying forward to take their turn at leading the flock. Solveig watched them for a long minute as their haunting calls faded into the distance. She had followed her father as a child, her husband in her youth, and her son in her widowhood. Now it was time to make her own way.

She squared her shoulders and turned toward the house. She had much to do.

The End

Author's Note

Solveig Rognaldson first appeared as a young, Norwegian immigrant in *Abercrombie Trail*. She became my favorite character because of her strong personality and down-to-earth practicality. I always hoped to write more about her, and *Sister Lumberjack* allowed Solveig to take center stage. Writing her story was like visiting an old friend.

Nels Jensen is loosely based on my Danish grandfather who arrived in 1890 with only ten cents in his pocket. He worked as a lumberjack in Minnesota during the winters, and on a bonanza farm in the Red River Valley of North Dakota in the summers, as did many immigrants of the 19th Century. The white pines of Minnesota built homes and businesses across the Midwest. Everyone thought there was no end to the forest. They were wrong.

The Benedictine Sisters built hospitals across Northern Minnesota to care for injured lumberjacks and miners. Their hospital ticket program, an early form of health insurance, funded these endeavors. Sister Amata sold the chits to lumberjacks working in logging camps across Norther Minnesota, traveling sometimes by snowshoes in the harsh Minnesota winters. She was the inspiration for my fictional character, Sister Magdalena. The hospitals stand today as a monument to the Benedictine's loving service and sacrifice.

I am a grateful recipient of Five Wings Regional Arts Grants funded by the Minnesota Arts and Heritage Funds, and the McKnight Foundation. I am indebted to Nancy Plain, Jeanne Cooney, Niomi Phillips, Angela Foster, and Martha Burns who offered invaluable advice. My writing partners, Beverly Abear and Charmaine Donovan, kept me going when it would have been easier to quit. Krista Soukup of Blue Cottage Agency and North Star Press helped me bring the dream of *Sister Lumberjack* into reality. Thank you.